PRAISE FOR ANTARKTOS

"Apocalypse comes to Antarctica. Jeremy R[...] tion upon a dagger-edge of suspense and adv[...] [...]ing , Robinson opens a new dark continent of terror [...] own risk."
-- **James Rollins**

"Jeremy Robinson is an original and exciting voice. Antarktos Rising has just the right blend of menace and normality---a tale full of intrigue, treachery, and a wealth of secrets. A good old-fashioned suspense story set in one of the most desolate places of earth. It fires on all cylinders in a smart, taut thrill."
-- **Steve Berry**

"An awesome journey into the beating heart of a legend. Jules Verne would be proud."
-- **Stel Pavlou**

A fast-paced chiller that delves into new possibilities about our future...and past."
-- **Steve Alten**

"How do you find an original story idea in the crowded action-thriller genre? Two words: Jeremy Robinson. Antartkos combines history, science and myth about Antarctica to create a jaw-dropping concept so real it will have you Googling like mad to learn more after the story is finished."
-- **Scott Sigler**

PRAISE FOR JEREMY ROBINSON

"Rocket-boosted action, brilliant speculation, and the recreation of a horror out of the mythologic past, all seamlessly blend into a rollercoaster ride of suspense and adventure."
-- **James Rollins**

"With THRESHOLD Jeremy Robinson goes pedal to the metal into very dark territory. Fast-paced, action-packed and wonderfully creepy! Highly recommended!"
-- **Jonathan Maberry**

"Jeremy Robinson is the next James Rollins"
-- **Chris Kuzneski**

"If you like thrillers original, unpredictable and chock-full of action, you are going to love Jeremy Robinson..."
-- **Stephen Coonts**

"There's nothing timid about Robinson as he drops his readers off the cliff without a parachute and somehow manages to catch us an inch or two from doom."
-- **Jeff Long**

"Jeremy Robinson's THRESHOLD is one hell of a thriller, wildly imaginative and diabolical, which combines ancient legends and modern science into a non-stop action ride that will keep you turning the pages until the wee hours. Relentlessly gripping from start to finish, don't turn your back on this book!"
-- **Douglas Preston**

"In Robinson's latest action fest, Jack Sigler, King of the Chess Team--a Delta Forces unit whose gonzo members take the names of chess pieces--tackles his most harrowing mission yet. Threshold elevates Robinson to the highest tier of over-the-top action authors and it delivers beyond the expectations even of his fans. The next Chess Team adventure cannot come fast enough."
-- **Booklist - Starred Review**

"In Robinson's wildly inventive third Chess Team adventure (after Instinct), the U.S. president, Tom Duncan, joins the team in mortal combat against an unlikely but irresistible gang of enemies, including "regenerating capybara, Hydras, Neanderthals, [and] giant rock monsters." ...Video game on a page? Absolutely. Fast, furious unabashed fun? You bet."
-- **Publishers Weekly**

"Jeremy Robinson's Threshold sets a blistering pace from the very first page and never lets up. This globe-trotting thrill ride challenges its well-crafted heroes with ancient mysteries, fantastic creatures, and epic action sequences. "
-- **Boyd Morrison**

ANTARKTOS
RISING
JEREMY ROBINSON

ORIGINS

Book IV

Dear Reader,

My career as an author began in a very different way from most authors. I didn't submit my books to agents or publishers; I self-published them under the umbrella of a small press I created, Breakneck Books. With each book release, I got feedback from readers, both good and bad, and used the critiques to improve my writing. So while most authors take their licks in private in the form of off-the-record advice from industry pros, I was flogged in the public square for all to see. My growth as an author has been a very public affair.

But it worked. Not only did my writing improve with each book, but so did my sales. And by the third book release, ANTARKTOS RISING, I had captured the attention of Scott Miller, my superb agent at Trident Media Group, and Peter Wolverton, editor supreme at Thomas Dunne Books, an imprint of St. Martin's Press, who has signed me on for five novels—PULSE, INSTINCT, THRESHOLD, SECONDWORLD and ISLAND 731, the first three of which are now (4-27-2011) in print.

ANTARKTOS RISING is the fourth novel I wrote (it was published third), but it is the first of my books not based on a previously written screenplay. In some ways, this made the writing of ANTARKTOS more "challenging" because I didn't have a 120-page outline from which to build. However, I didn't have that same outline binding me to a set plot, either. As a result, the story took on a life of its own and went in directions I hadn't planned. Because of that, there are more surprises in ANTARKTOS than in the previous books.

ANTARKTOS RISING was first published in 2007 under my Breakneck Books imprint and quickly became my bestselling novel. Its success directly led to my publishing deal with Thomas Dunne Books. It's still my bestselling book to date and was nearly made into a feature length animated film before the economy tanked. It also spawned a new five book series titled THE LAST HUNTER. The first two books in the "Antarktos Saga" are prequels to ANTARKTOS RISING, book three parallels it, and books four and five finish the stories in both series. Book 1, DESCENT is available now. Book 2, PURSUIT will be out in June 2011.

I hope you enjoy this third chapter of the five books that comprise the origins of my career. Let the flogging continue!

-- Jeremy Robinson

To experience my growth as an author, check out the Origins books in chronological order:

• THE DIDYMUS CONTINGENCY
• RAISING THE PAST
• BENEATH
• ANTARKTOS RISING
• KRONOS

For Dad

ACKNOWLEDGEMENTS

Special thanks go out to everyone who has read Antarktos Rising, enjoyed it and spread the word. Without you, this new and improved Origins edition (not to mention all of the other books) wouldn't have been possible. Thank you!

ANTARKTOS
RISING

"The more rapidly a civilization progresses, the sooner it dies for another to rise in its place." -- *The Dance of Life by Havelock Ellis*

"If Antarctica were music it would be Mozart. Art, and it would be Michelangelo. Literature, and it would be Shakespeare. And yet it is something even greater; the only place on earth that is still as it should be. May we never tame it." -- *Andrew Denton*

"Antarctica represents the last great unknown of modern civilization. She abounds in secrets yet to be discovered and prizes yet to be claimed. She is a shrewd mistress who keeps her most private treasures hidden beneath a skirt of ice that I for one, would like a peek beneath." -- *Antarktos by Dr. Merrill Clark*

"Great God, this is an awful place." -- *R.F. Scott on Antarctica*

"They are dead, they shall not live; Rephiam*, they shall not rise." -- *Isaiah 26:14*

*Rephiam is typically, incorrectly, translated as "deceased."

 # PROLOGUE

"The only thing more dangerous than freezing to death out here is your jack-ass stubborn streak."

"Aimee, do you know what your name means?"

"Of course. Love."

"And do you know who else shares your name's meaning?"

"No, Merrill, I don't."

"Freya. She was the Norse goddess of love and fertility."

"If you're thinking I'm feeling in any way fertile right now, you can go straight to hell. I bore you one child. I'm not going through that again."

"The birth or the conception process?"

"Both, if you don't clamp it."

"You're misinterpreting my remarks. I simply meant that Freya, love goddess of the Norse, lived in a very cold land. And despite the cold, she was loving . . . and fertile—ouch!"

"All your accumulated knowledge of the ancient world won't change the fact that I am freezing cold, hungry, and five miles from camp."

"Don't hit me again. I could have chipped the fossil."

"Merrill, the limb has been preserved on this giant ice cube for millions of years. I think it will—"

"You know, it might not be that old. And you must have this confused with the Arctic. Antarctica is a continent . . . with land."

"I swear, I will . . ."

"What?"

"The sky."

"My . . . Where'd that come from?"

"Merrill?"

"Wrap up the fossil! I'll get the other side. Fasten it tight!"

"There isn't time! Merrill!"

"Aimee?"

"I can't see you through the snow!"

"I'm here!"

"I can't see anything!"

"Leave the fossil! Follow my voice!"

"What's that noise?"

"Ignore it! We need to find each other!"

"Merrill, I—*hmph*!"

"Aimee? Keep talking so I can find you! Aimee? *Aimee*!"

SHIFT

 CHAPTER 1

Anguta grew more terrified as each paddle stroke carried his bone-and-sealskin kayak across the unusually placid Arctic Ocean and closer to the whale. His knotted muscles shuddered in spasms, not from the cold but from the realization that his lifelong goal might finally come to fruition. At age fifty-seven, the idea of single-handedly killing a sixty-foot humpback and towing its carcass back to the village seemed a ridiculous task. And while this rite of passage had been a long time coming, his aging body didn't feel up to the job.

Grasping a bone-tipped spear in his gloved hand, Anguta did his best to ignore the throb of arthritis attacking his knuckles and waited . . . patiently . . . for the leviathan to return to the surface. Three days of tracking and sustaining himself on cured salmon had taken him this far. If he didn't take the beast this year, he would return to the arctic waters off the coast of Alaska to try again—and he refused to consider that option. This was the year. He knew it.

"Come to me, whale," Anguta mumbled through his thickly scarfed mouth. "Come to me and I will honor you with a quick death." Anguta knew the death would only be quick if he were lucky enough to pierce the whale's eye and penetrate its brain on the first blow. Otherwise, his first strike would tether his kayak to the whale's body and a day-long struggle between man and beast would begin. The tradition belonged to his tribe alone, and Anguta was the only man who had yet to achieve the task. He had tried every year since he was nineteen.

Anguta cursed himself for finding the largest humpback in the entire ocean. He had hoped to find a young calf, newly weaned from its protective mother, but instead he had encountered a large bull, perhaps close in age to Anguta himself.

The old man's only consolation was that he was not cold. After years of fruitless arctic hunting trips, he had learned that technology could be useful. His outer layers were traditional Inuit—furs of caribou, bear, and seal hide. This covered him from head to toe, leaving only his eyes exposed. Underneath the furs was a combination of moisture-wicking fabrics and a military-grade thermal bodysuit. His eyes were sealed behind a face mask that not only warmed his skin, but by virtue of its tinted surface also dulled the harsh glow of bright sun on white ice.

Anguta let his eyes wander across the mirrored water which perfectly reflected the cloud-specked sky. He looked for any distortion that would reveal the presence of a rising whale, but saw only sky. His thoughts drifted with the clouds. He pictured his wife, Elizabeth, a French Canadian originally out of Quebec, feeding the dog team. Their marriage had been extremely unconventional at the time but was more common these days. Though shunned at first for his choice of wife, Anguta and Elizabeth's marriage had produced five children and seven grandchildren, all of whom he now missed greatly and wished were there beside him, hunting the whale. His marriage and half-breed children had already broken so many of his people's customs. Why not one more?

# CHAPTER 2

Looking down at the canteen in his hand, Dmitriy Rostov wished that it was full of vodka instead of water. But his lust for the clean spirit's warmth on his tongue lasted only a moment, a much shorter duration than it had only a year ago. Dmitriy, at the age of thirty-seven, had learned he was an alcoholic, a plague that claimed 45 percent of his Russian compatriots. It was said that two-thirds of Russian men die with a bottle in their hands, a fate Dmitriy had resigned himself to . . .

"Dima, come see this."

. . . until he'd met her.

Viktoriya Petrova.

"Coming, Vika," Dmitriy called as he picked his way across the stone-strewn shoreline of Vadim Bay. The bay was part of the Kara Sea, a remote region off the northern coast of Siberia which could only be navigated during mid-summer. The bay was a large U-shaped inlet with cliff walls on either side. Behind the rocky shore grew a forest of strong pines that creaked and swayed in the salty sea breeze.

Rounding a boulder, Dmitriy came face-to-face with Viktoriya; it was the closest their faces had ever come to touching, though still not quite close enough for Dmitriy. She was bundled in a red parka and thick snow pants. Even in the summer, the temperature at Vadim Bay, located hundreds of miles north of the Arctic Circle, was cold enough to chap the skin.

Surprised by Dmitriy's sudden appearance, Viktoriya stumbled back and tripped over a loose rock. She yelped as she plummeted down.

"Vika!" Dmitriy's strong and steady hand had sprung out before he could think about what to do and snagged the arm of her parka. Her descent stopped. Dmitriy thanked God he was sober. A year ago, she would have fallen to the rocks and he would have laughed drunkenly. He realized now that he would never have come this far without her encouragement. He had been headed for a very early retirement from the Ministry of Emergency Situations, but when Viktoriya had been assigned as his new partner, she had seen something worth saving in him. She had an iron will and whipped him into shape; when the reviews came in, his report showed a marked productivity increase. Now only ten days away from his fortieth birthday, he was a new man. His job was saved.

No. More than his job. He not only began to care for himself while on the job but also at home. Showering daily, brushing his teeth, wearing deodorant—all the good habits that Dmitriy had abandoned during his days as a drunk returned. The pale, oily-skinned, puffy-faced waste of a man had, under Viktoriya's influence, changed to the core. He'd shed pounds, smelled clean, and when he finally began shaving again, displayed the handsome face of which his mother had once been so proud. It wasn't that Viktoriya had changed his mind—she'd infected his heart. Like his person, he kept his apartment neat and nicely decorated. Just in case she came to visit. Just in case the day came that he would tell her everything he felt. He'd always imagined being at home, in the city, on that day. But here, alone, in the wild, he felt brave. Today would be the day.

He pulled her up until her cushioned body rested against his. They were closer still than ever before—close enough for Dmitriy to smell the subtle fragrance of her perfume. Rose.

"Vika, are you all right? I didn't mean to startle you."

"Fine. I'm fine." Viktoriya looked into his eyes and paused for a moment. Unspoken words flashed between them, stripped away his bravery, and transformed his mind into that of a nervous fourteen-year-old boy on his first date.

# CHAPTER 3

From her perch high above the city of Portsmouth, New Hampshire, Mirabelle Whitney could see that the trip into town for an ice cream wouldn't be
worth it. Not for another few hours, anyway. Her royal red, nineteenth-
century Victorian house sat atop Prospect Hill, the tallest hill in the seacoast
region at two hundred feet. From her second-floor bedroom deck, she had
clear views of downtown Portsmouth and the ocean beyond. To her left, she
could see Kittery, Maine, across the Piscataqua River, and to her right she
could see the thick tree lines of Greenland and Rye.

This was the view that kept her anchored. There wasn't a single time of
the year when the scenery dulled. Her eyes lingered on the downtown again.
The congestion that clogged the streets and spilled onto routes 95, 1, and 16
was due to the combination of summertime revelers and rush hour traffic.

Tonight, she thought. I'll get ice cream tonight.

Whitney stretched her lean body, allowing her midriff to peek out from
between her white tank top and khaki shorts, absorbing every ounce of
warmth she could. She wasn't a huge fan of the moist New England sum-
mers, but she knew warm summer air would soon be a thing of the past.

Sweet ocean air passed through her nostrils as she breathed deeply, took
half of her long blond hair, and rolled it into a bun on the side of her head. A
quick jab with a decorative chopstick she'd saved from a trip to Tokyo held
the bun in place. As she rolled up the other side, a frigid breeze tickled the
hairs on her forearms. She shivered.

Ocean breeze is cold today, she thought.

After finishing the second bun, she looked at her reflection in the window glass. She looked like an anime version of Princess Leia . . . a dark-skinned, nappy-blond-haired version. Whitney smiled. For the first time in a long time, she thought she looked good. Maybe it was the reflection of Portsmouth and the ocean in the background that caused her to cast a fairer gaze at herself. She wasn't sure. But her brown skin and darker brown eyes hadn't looked this vibrant in a year.

Whitney knew that while her outward appearances were improving, her heart was still healing. No amount of exercise or sleep could erase the torment she had endured the past year.

Cindy Bekoff, her friend and psychologist, believed Whitney's upcoming trip to Antarctica was an excuse to flee from the pain. "There aren't many places on earth more remote," she had said. "You need to deal with your pain before moving on."

What Whitney hadn't, and wouldn't, tell her, was that it was where *he* was . . . it was where he had been hiding all this time. She wasn't running from pain; she was accelerating straight toward it.

The wind reversed direction, flowing up and over the red Victorian home's shingled roof and heading for the ocean. As the gust spilled across Whitney's body, she took note of its sudden warmth. The temperature shift struck her as odd—a cold front and heat wave battling for supremacy. New England was known for its drastic weather changes, but this variation in temperature during a mid-summer day seemed downright freakish.

 CHAPTER 4

Longing for home and family, Anguta failed to notice the first ripples in the water's surface. Something was rising. Bubbles expressed from the emerging creature churned the surface and snapped Anguta's attention back to the task at hand. Raising the spear over his head, Anguta waited for the right time to strike.

The water parted to expose the dark gray flesh of the humpback's hide. Still Anguta waited. An early strike might connect with the beast's tail, causing the man to be thrashed about with every pulse of its mighty fluke. As the whale's head breached the surface, Anguta focused, waiting for the moment when the whale would exhale a spray of mist and expose its eyes.

Anguta felt his heart stop when he made eye contact with the whale, but there was no exhalation from its blowhole to trigger his throwing arm. He stood solidly, gripping his spear, muscles taut, but did not throw. He stared into the eye of the creature, which appeared to be blinded by cataracts. With a heavy heart, he realized that he and the whale weren't so dissimilar. They'd sired families. Traveled the Arctic. Fought the elements. And they'd grown old. Then he remembered their crucial difference. He was a hunter. Years of failed hunts flashed through Anguta's mind, and all the mercy he felt for the blind whale evaporated quickly as the spear sailed from his hand.

As soon as he released his hold on the spear, he knew his aim was true; it was a killer shot into the humpback's eye. The tow line unfurled at Anguta's feet as the spear covered the twenty-foot distance to the whale. The tip of the spear struck home, dead center in the whited eyeball—and glanced off.

The sound and physical reaction of the spear would have been no different if Anguta had flung it at a stone.

He followed the ricocheted spear with his eyes in disbelief at what had happened and annoyance that he'd have to retrieve the spear. But when the weapon struck the ocean, it bounced again. The surface was frozen.

There's no ice here, Anguta thought. Perhaps an iceberg?

The old man scanned the world around him. It was white and frozen. His eyes turned back to the whale. Its skin sparkled with frost—it was frozen solid. It was only then that he noticed the biting cold nibbling at his skin. He had never felt such a degree of cold through his arctic gear. The sensation was similar to rolling stark naked in the snow.

As his muscles involuntarily twitched, working to warm his body temperature, he tried to get his bearings. He had to find shelter. But as he searched the newly frozen ocean for a glimmer of hope, his goggles fogged and he became as blind as the now-petrified whale.

Frustrated and panicked, Anguta removed his goggles and immediately regretted the decision. His eyeballs froze. A jolt of savage pain threw Anguta off his feet and ripped through his body. Images sailed through his mind: Elizabeth, the kids, their little ones . . . would this cold front reach them as well?

Anguta's body hit the kayak with a thud, solid as stone.

 CHAPTER 5

Dmitriy stared, willing his mouth to form words to express his love, but he remained silent. He swallowed audibly and felt a sick feeling in his stomach. He glanced to the side, avoiding her penetrating eyes as his silent embarrassment grew, and noticed she was holding her Geiger counter. He remembered why they were there and wondered if she had found something important. He didn't really care at the moment, but it gave him something to say. "You wanted to show me something?"

She seemed startled by the question. "I, uh . . . " She noticed Dmitriy's eyes on the Geiger counter. "Oh, yes, I . . . Look at this."

Viktoriya pulled herself away from Dmitriy's arms and stepped out toward the waterline where small, frigid waves lapped against the shore. She stopped and held out the Geiger counter. Sweeping left to right, the counter clicked slowly at first, then rapidly, then slowly again. She repeated the sweep two more times.

Dmitriy stood next to her and studied the shoreline beneath her feet. It looked as harmless as the rest of the beach, but he suspected something was buried there. He looked at the Geiger counter's gauge as she swept it over again. The radiation levels read slightly above normal, but not high enough to kill them. Enough to shorten their lives by a few hours, perhaps, but otherwise safe.

They had been sent to the far away place to investigate mishandling of environmental pollutants during the Cold War. Siberia, at that time, had been used primarily for dumping toxic waste and exiled criminals. Now, after all these years, it was finally being recognized as a natural wonder. But severe damage had been done, and Dmitriy believed they were about to uncover more evidence of his country's environmental neglect.

He bent down and scraped several small stones aside. As he set his eyes on a larger stone, he felt sweat gather on his forehead. He was hot. He wrote it off as exertion—he still wasn't in very good shape— picked up the large stone, and tossed it to the side. Beneath it were more stones. This was going to take a while.

"Dima?"

Dmitriy turned and saw Viktoriya removing her parka.

"Are you hot?" she asked.

"Da, but I think I haven't worked this hard in . . ." He noticed she was sweating, too.

Something was wrong. The temperature had risen. Removing his parka, Dmitriy let the heat soak in as he attempted to remember a time in his life when, if ever, he'd felt the air so hot. He couldn't. The temperature seemed to be rising exponentially.

"Dima . . . the radiation?"

Dmitriy looked into Vika's eyes and recognized fear. Had the radiation sprung a leak when he removed the stones? Were they being poisoned? He took the Geiger counter from her hand and swept the area. He shook his head. "No, something else."

Still the heat rose.

His throat began to sting. He took a swig of water and offered the canteen to Viktoriya. She gulped it greedily.

The trees behind them groaned as they bent under a burst of pummeling wind. The wind was dry and hot, like bending over an open oven. Dmitriy blinked his eyes as the moisture was wicked from them. Something was very wrong.

"We have to leave!" he said. He glanced up the shoreline where they had landed the helicopter, a football field away. "Get to the helicopter!"

He took Vika's hand and helped her across the loose rocks. The rising heat made his heart beat wildly in his chest, urged him to sprint at full speed. But he couldn't leave Vika behind. She had saved his life. She was his life. He would not let her die now.

Viktoriya slipped on a stone and fell forward, but Dima was there to catch her. He swept her into his arms and stumbled toward the copter.

The heat continued to rise. Dmitriy struggled to keep his eyes open. The heat was so intense that it felt as though his eyes were peeled grapes. He looked at Viktoriya. Her eyes were clenched shut.

They were halfway to the copter now, and Dmitriy was wheezing. His body was dry. Every bead of sweat that his body produced evaporated. A loud *crack* drew his eyes back to the forest. He saw a tree falling to the ground, pushed over by the punishing winds, but what shocked him was the state of the trees. The needles, moments ago vibrant green, were now tinged brown, dried out. Dead.

A rising cloak of darkness, like an evil apparition, caught Dmitriy's attention as it plumed into the sky above the forest. It assaulted his nose first: acrid smoke laced with sulfur. The trees were burning, and while he couldn't see it, he suspected a volcano had erupted. The blackness poured out from the tree line and rolled over the beach. Dmitriy found it impossible to breathe.

He struck out for the helicopter again, Viktoriya now a dead weight in his arms. He glanced down to check her condition, but found his eyes blinded by the heat and smoke. A jagged boulder caught his shin and he fell forward, dropping Viktoriya and landing on top of her.

The intensity of the heat blistered Dmitriy's skin. His scream was cut short from lack of breath. Through parched eyes, he looked back at the forest in time to see the trees explode into flame. Their heat washed over his body, blinding, searing, and suffocating. He hoped that Vika might survive the inferno protected by his body, but he sensed that she had already passed. So close, he thought. So close.

With a seismic boom, the gas tank of the helicopter exploded. It was the last thing Dmitriy heard before his parched body burst into flame.

 CHAPTER 6

Mirabelle Whitney glanced past her shoulder and out at the town. Everything looked normal. Traffic was still congested. The red brick buildings still glowed in the sun. But something was off. She leaned out her bedroom window to look further.

Strawberry Banke was a well-maintained park, complete with historic buildings and a flower garden. It was often used for functions during the summer months: clambakes, lobster fests, and chili cook-offs. Whitney searched the sea of people for a sign of today's event. She found the answer in the gleaming white glow of a veil caught by the seaward wind: a wedding.

Whitney looked away quickly, avoiding her own memories, and moved her eyes out to sea.

What she saw next made her forget the pain from the emotional scab that had just been picked open. The ocean seemed more distant. In its place was a very long beach where there had been no beach before. This was a port town. If you wanted a beach, she thought, you go south to Hampton or north to Ogunquit. Not to Portsmouth.

Whitney noticed the wedding party and park patrons clambering onto the docks along the river. They saw it, too. She followed the waterline up the Piscataqua River and saw that its shores had shrunk inward. The water that remained was quickly rushing out to sea.

When she looked back, all that was left of the coastline was a small river flowing out of the Piscataqua and a sliver of blue, far on the horizon. The ocean was gone. All that remained was a sandy expanse speckled with grounded boats and flickering reflections of light that Mirabelle realized were struggling fish drowning in the open air.

As the hordes of vacationers began running in droves, fleeing Strawberry Banke and flooding into the downtown streets, Whitney realized what must be happening.

Tsunami.

Remembering a lesson learned from the killer waves that had recently struck Indonesia, India, and so many other countries, people headed for high ground. Whitney watched as rooftops began to fill with people in a panic. The top level of the five-story parking garage was full in minutes, and people on the lower levels struggled to get higher, but room was running out.

Whitney tore her eyes away from the impending train wreck to wonder if there was something she should do. She couldn't get any higher without heading up Route 16 into the mountains, but she should do something.

Whitney turned from her deck and entered the house. She walked into her bedroom, which had once been a decorative masterpiece but was now a laundry disaster area. She took the hallway stairs two at a time, moving swiftly. One by one she swept through the downstairs rooms, closing windows and locking doors. She paused at the front door and looked out at the green grass of the estate that had once belonged to her parents.

She missed them now.

A hiss of leaves drew her attention to the green maple trees bordering the yard. The wind had picked up, but was still headed out to sea.

Whitney slammed the door shut and headed for the basement. Two years ago, she had converted the basement into a base of operations for her photography work. She spent six months of every year on location in one remote part of the world or another, shooting landscapes and animals that most people avoided for fear of life and limb. It was dangerous work, but exciting and rewarding. She worked in the field, but this was her home base for expedition prep, film development, and camera maintenance. For the past year, the room had served as the staging area for her upcoming Antarctic venture. The dim basement was now stacked with food supplies. Gear for surviving the frozen wasteland filled the main room, and electronic gizmos lined the workbenches. Leaning over the GPS satellite phones, she picked up a pair of binoculars and charged back up the stairs.

As she passed through the bedroom, she noted the time: noon. It had taken her five minutes to lock up the window and doors and return to her bedroom. She burst onto the deck and squinted against the sun, which shone down directly above her. She put the binoculars to her eyes and colorful blurs filled her vision. She adjusted the focus and settled on the parking garage. Like penguins huddling from the cold, a mass of humanity crammed itself onto the top floor of the garage, some dangerously close to spilling off the edge. She lowered her view. The next two floors were also full, and everyone was moving in one direction—up.

Whitney removed the binoculars and shook her head. Looking through the field glasses again, she turned her gaze toward the ocean . . . or what used to be the ocean. It had not returned. In fact, she could no longer see any water, save the trickle of the Piscataqua, all the way out to the horizon.

She wracked her brain for an answer. A sinkhole. Something must have opened up in the ocean and sucked the water down . . . something huge. It was the only answer.

Keeping her vigil, she scanned all of Portsmouth. Word of the phenomenon must have reached every nook of the seacoast town by now. The only cars she could see were driving away from town. Even the emergency vehicles were clearing out. They weren't fools—all the sirens, flashing lights, and ladders in the world wouldn't stop whatever was coming. Downtown was deserted, except for the rooftops. Whitney felt the anticipation of every soul on whom she gazed . . . all waiting for something to happen.

She paced about the house unsure of what to do or think. She frantically cleaned her counters and shined her sink; ridiculous, given the situation. When she could no longer stand staring at her warped reflection in the perfectly polished sink, she looked at the clock. It had been an hour.

She looked again at the parking garage; it looked less congested. People were lowering their guard, moving down to the lower levels, some even out onto the street. Whitney wanted to shout at them to run, to leave town, but they seemed slow, almost dazed by the surreal events.

Whitney looked up, forehead furrowed. It was past one o'clock, but the sun still appeared to be directly overhead. In the past hour, the sun had not moved.

"What . . .?"

Everything changed in that instant.

The sun began moving.

The wind shifted directions, billowing southwest from the barren ocean bed.

The temperature dropped and continued to fall with every gust.

Biting her lower lip, Whitney raised the binoculars to her eyes.

She saw an illusion. It had to be. A wall of blue and white churning water surged back into view, spilling from the northeast straight for shore. As the wall grew closer, she knew it was real. A tsunami, more massive than she'd ever imagined the phenomenon to be, was headed straight for her home town.

The people atop the parking structure were the first to see it. They were also the first to realize they weren't high enough to avoid it. Whitney shuddered as a collective wail of panic and despair rose from the city below. Tears brimmed and spilled over onto her face. They were all going to die. And she could only watch.

She'd seen death before and knew she lacked the stomach to witness what was coming. Turning away from the city of her childhood, from the home she had made, from all the places and people she loved, Whitney ran to her bedroom and closed the deck doors behind her. The distant voices were silenced. She leaned against the wall and slid down to the floor, hoping the water wouldn't reach her as well.

The next minute was spent in silence as she waited. In her mind's eye she saw the citizens of Portsmouth clambering over each other, trampling the weak. She knew it was human nature to step on the next guy if it meant saving one's own life. She felt certain a number of people were already dead, long before the wave struck. A sob escaped her as she remembered Cindy's office was downtown. The tears flowed freely now.

Then the voices returned. Grew louder.

Closer.

Whitney stood, opened the door, and stepped out onto the porch. Her timing couldn't have been worse. A seventy-foot wave of water slid through Portsmouth and consumed it all. The people still on rooftops ceased to exist. Those on the streets were swept up and churned in the grinding waters as easily as the brick, concrete, wood, and mortar that held the city together.

The voices returned: "Open the goddamn gates!"

A small group of perhaps fifteen people had flocked to her front gate, probably neighbors who knew her home stood on the tallest peak of the hill. She cursed her father for building the eight-foot stone wall and metal gate that sealed off the estate from the rest of the world, protecting her from unknown predators.

Whitney glanced toward the downtown. The rising waters had consumed the city and were now racing toward her, pounding up the steady incline. Whitney dashed back into the bedroom, calculating how long it would take her to reach and unlock the front door, sprint the hundred feet to the gate, unlock and open it by hand, sprint back to the house with fifteen people, and shut the door behind her.

Too long.

If only she'd fixed the gate's remote! That kind of thing hadn't been her concern lately, and she'd let it go for six months.

A slight vibration in the floorboards at the base of the stairs reinforced the idea that she wouldn't have time. Still, she had to try.

She reached the front door, unlocked the deadbolt, and flung it open. Vaulting down the five front stairs in one leap, Whitney hit the driveway at a sprint. She heard roaring water, breaking glass, and the horrid wrench of metal as the unseen torrent pounded relentlessly forward.

Not waiting for the gate to be opened, the fleeing group began climbing over it. To the left, a little girl struggled with the smooth metal bars. The others were leaving her behind. Whitney leapt at the gate and clung to it like a monkey. She yanked herself to the top, feeling the muscles in her arms tear. At the top, she reached over and thrust her hand out to the girl. "Take my hand!"

The little girl's fingers intertwined with Whitney's, and the girl was pulled steadily up. A bearded man next to the girl saw that she'd clear the gate first and took hold of Whitney's arm to hoist himself.

"Let go!" Whitney shouted as the gate dug into her arm.

"Amber!" another man shouted with shock in his eyes. He lunged at the bearded man pushing the girl back down, and Whitney knew the girl's rescuer was her father. Amber's father wrapped one arm around the aggressor's neck and pushed off the gate with his feet. The action added an unbearable amount of weight to Whitney's arm, but both men fell to the ground. The father seemed willing to die for his child, and as the two men rolled away from the gate pummeling each other, she realized he would.

The water was upon them.

Whitney pulled with all her might, but her muscles had little strength left. The water hit her like an explosion. Whitney was flung back ten feet, her grip on Amber's arm lost. She sat up quickly and looked to the gate. The people were gone, replaced by a churning wall of water that roared like a wounded Kodiak bear.

Whitney shouted as she pushed herself up and ran back to the house. Ten feet from the front stairs, her feet began splashing through ocean water. A surge of water hit her knees and threatened to knock her down, but she lunged up the stairs, freeing herself from the water's grasp.

She entered the house, closed the door, slammed the deadbolt home, and careened for the stairs, hoping another ten feet would be enough to save her life. She reached the top stair in four leaps. As she stepped into the hallway, a force struck the house so hard that she was shaken from her feet. She fell forward and heard a loud crack, but it wasn't the house; it was her head. A stab of pain shot through her skull. As she fell, she saw the wooden chest she'd struck as she'd fallen.

It was the last thing she saw. Her vision blurred and turned black.

As her consciousness faded, the sound of rushing water and groaning wood surrounded the house.

Whitney awoke with a start and clasped a hand to her throbbing head. She struggled past the pain, attempting to gather her thoughts. As the pulsing headache in her left temple eased in intensity, she remembered: the wave. The people. The death. Despair, rage, and confusion attacked her all at once, an emotional lion pride, circling with hackles raised and talons extended. They wanted to devour her alive. But they were old enemies she'd faced before. Using willpower built over the past year's suffering, she pushed the emotions away and faced her grim new reality.

She forced herself to calm and became more aware of her surroundings. She was still on the hallway floor of her house, but she was freezing. Wondering if she was wet, she checked herself and found her clothing to be dry. She looked down the stairs. Even the downstairs floor was dry.

From her position on the floor, she could see her alarm clock, but the power was out. She had no way of knowing how long she'd been unconscious, but it couldn't have been long. It was still daylight, though the previously blue sky was now thick with ashen clouds . . . and something else.

Standing came only after a concerted effort. Her head pounded with every step, and she found herself walking through the bedroom and toward the deck door with her eyes closed. Hands outstretched, she stopped when she reached the wall. She slid her fingers from the wall to the glass of the sliding door.

When the flesh of her finger made contact with the glass, Whitney yelped and pulled her hand away. The pain was like searing heat, but she knew from experience that it was cold. Freezing cold. Whitney's eyes flew open and blinked at the brightness. Despite the overcast sky, something outside was abnormally bright.

Through squinted eyes, Whitney took in her new view.

Extending out from ten feet below her home's foundation all the way to the horizon was a sheet of ice. Thick flakes of snow fell from the sky. She seemed to have been transported to the North Pole. She didn't dare go outside dressed for summer as she was, but from her view behind the glass she could see that everything, from Maine to Massachusetts, was buried under hundreds of feet of snow and ice.

And now she was alone, completely, and she feared that the most. More than the wave. More than the cold. Being alone with her thoughts, with her demons, was just about the worst way she could imagine to die.

 CHAPTER 7

Kneeling in prayer had become a nightly ritual for Dr. Merrill Clark. The topics of his prayers typically centered on what little family remained to him, his safety, his work, and his sanity. He knew prayer was supposed to be equal parts praise to God, personal requests, and asking for forgiveness, but by the time he finished his list of personal requests, he was usually sound asleep. He'd thought about rearranging the order of his prayers but found his sins painful to express, and praise for God, after what had happened to Aimee, was in short supply.

He was a believer still, to be sure, and knew that upon his death he would see Aimee again, but he was certainly not pleased with his creator's timing or methods. The day she disappeared in a sudden snowstorm had been the worst of his life. The wash of white, the bite of frigid air, and the sounds, the howling, had haunted his nightmares for ten years.

The storm had almost claimed his life as well. After reaching base camp, his body had thawed out, but his heart remained cold. He abandoned his Antarctic research and fled home to the States, returning only once to have pictures taken for his book. The bones, after all, had been there for millions of years. And any remnants of human civilization—what he was really after—the existence of which was hinted at on ancient maps dating back to Alexander the Great, would remain buried and untouched.

Aimee was right.

He should have listened.

His stubbornness had cost him his wife's life. It was his greatest sin, one for which he could never forgive himself. And he could not confess it.

Five years after losing Aimee, Merrill was living a lonely life in a tiny, unkempt apartment in Cambridge, teaching paleontology and anthropology at Harvard. He was qualified to teach archeology as well but lacked the energy. He found the Harvard campus and surrounding sprawl of Boston to be overwhelming, and if he wasn't in the classroom he was studying in his home office.

Except for the presence of his noble, black-coated Newfoundland named Vesuvius, Merrill sat alone at home, every day. He had even stopped going to church. Vesuvius was his single comfort in life. The big dog would sprawl out on his bed at night, providing primal companionship for Merrill. Each morning consisted of a ten-minute celebration and face-licking session, as though Merrill and Vesuvius had been reunited after years of separation. But even with Vesuvius, Merrill still longed for human contact.

He did not want to marry again but had moved in with Mirabelle, who had accepted him for who he was and adored the dog. They had lived in the Portsmouth home for three years, and he'd taken up teaching at the University of New Hampshire in Durham. The pace was slower, the air less toxic. And Mirabelle . . . spending his days with her helped dull the pain of Aimee's loss. She was a godsend. An angel. He smiled as he pictured her thick-lipped, squinty-eyed grin and remembered the warmth of her embrace. He missed her now.

She had been a source of strength during his worst days, and leaving her was his second greatest sin. After so many years of neglecting his true calling, the bug had returned: he traveled to Antarctica a second time, this time for good, bringing only fresh gear and Vesuvius. Upon returning, he found everything at the base camp just as he left it. The digs, tents, and gear all appeared untouched.

Base camp consisted of five red tents which had been bolted into the stone floor of one of Antarctica's driest valleys. The crevasse was carved into the Transantarctic Mountains four hundred miles north of the pole, where snow rarely fell; if it did, it was swept away by the fierce katabolic winds. The tents were bordered by crates of supplies placed on the southern side to buffer the freezing wind which rolled down from the center of the domed continent. The valley floor looked like the surface of some alien planet; smooth brown stone slabs were layered in sheets that eventually rose up into steep cliffs. At the top of the cliffs juts of stone separated the valley from the glacier above and kept the slowly flowing ice from entering the valley. The three-mile-long, half-mile-wide valley and everything in it had been freeze-dried for the last twelve thousand years.

Returning had been a painful jolt to Merrill's memories. Photos of him and Aimee rested on trunks. Her clothes were still neatly folded on her cot. Even her scent seemed to linger. It was only after a week of sifting through the past that Merrill was able to stop crying and start working.

He threw himself into his work, uncovering three new species of dinosaur: two small predators, and one herbivore. His most exciting discovery came in the form of a four-foot man-made wall that he dated at ten- to twelve-thousand years old. He knew his finds would be ridiculed on the mainland, so he kept them to himself. The dinosaurs weren't the issue. Since 1994, when the first dinosaur remains—a predator named *Crylophosaurus*—were found on the seventh continent amid fragments of several prey animals, the idea of life flourishing on Antarctica in millennia past was no longer debated. But the subject that had captured Merrill's attention so closely since switching the focus of his profession from paleontology to anthropology was debated with fervor: Antarctic civilization. Some believed that a civilization had once thrived on the mainland of the southernmost continent before it froze over. Most evidence supporting the theory was circumstantial, and promoters of the theory were often Atlantis fanatics who did more harm to the science than good. But to Merrill the smooth stone wall, with its almost seamless joints, proved that someone had lived there.

Yet he wanted more. A wall was not definitive. Hell, it could be argued that he had made it. His evidence had to be irrefutable. He worked in the cold without pause. He was obsessed and kept little track of the days or his health. Supplies were brought via a Dash-7 Turboprop from Punta Arenas on the southernmost tip of Chile and flown over the continent where it stopped at McMurdo Station. The cargo was then flown by helicopter to Merrill's valley where it was unceremoniously kicked out the door. Everything survived the fall, most of the time. Supplies arrived once a month, but he let them sit unopened for weeks at a time, until the first pangs of starvation and the whines of Vesuvius told him sustenance was necessary to continue.

He would have continued in this pattern of work, starvation, and prayer until his dying day, but again God disturbed his plans. When he knelt to pray on the night of July 21, just over a year since his return, the ground began to shake. His red pyramidal tent vibrated and equipment rattled violently. His first thought was that the ancient wall might crumble but as the shaking grew worse, and louder, he feared the valley walls would come down.

The shaking grew so fierce that Merrill found it impossible to stand, let alone kneel. And the sound, like an angry grumble pumped through loudspeakers, was enough to cause his ears incredible pain. He bundled his head inside earmuffs and his hooded down jacket, then wrapped a pillow around his head in an effort to dull the noise. Lying on the floor of his tent, he curled up with Vesuvius. He kept his hands clamped over Vesuvius's ears, knowing that the 120-pound dog's hearing was even more sensitive than his own.

The two remained on the floor all night. Hours into the ordeal, the pair grew accustomed to the shaking and noise. Exhaustion eventually claimed them, plunging them into a deep sleep where Merrill faced his worst fears—his unconfessed sins—the past.

AFTERSHOCK

CHAPTER 8

Though still numb from the shock of seeing the seacoast of New Hampshire deluged and frozen over, Whitney had recovered sufficiently to check the phones. Nothing. The electricity was out, too. She was cut off from the world. If she'd been anyone else in Portsmouth, she'd already be dead.

The arctic chill had invaded the old Victorian, causing Whitney to retreat into the basement. It was only the generous supply of arctic gear and a diesel-powered generator, which she rigged to run off of the full tank of home heating oil in the basement that kept her alive. It took several hours to work a hose from the fuel tank to the generator so that it didn't leak. Thankfully, the generator was inside and already set to vent directly outside, or the fumes would have done her in as quickly as the cold. She only used the generator to operate the single electric heater, which she set on low, just enough to keep the temperature above freezing. She had no idea how long she'd be trapped in her basement and wanted to stretch the fuel. There was food for a month; three, if rationed. By day the room was lit only by a single half-window that allowed the gleaming brightness of sun on snow to shine through. At night she lit a single candle. The flickering flame was her only company.

She dressed in her arctic gear, wearing her cherry-red down jacket twenty-four hours a day. Feeling foolish, at times she removed the jacket. But the cold always won out and she'd retreat to the warmth of her fleece-lined coat. Nights were spent bundled in her -40°C-rated sleeping bag. Food was eaten cold, from the can. And worst of all, a bucket, which she kept covered in the corner, had become her bathroom. The single bright side was that the hum of the generator helped her sleep, which she did often.

Days passed as she organized and reorganized her equipment several times, attempting to occupy her mind. She knew that if she weren't busy she'd turn introspective, and that would be the beginning of the end. But as she organized the five pairs of moisture-wicking socks for the tenth time, her thoughts slipped past her carefully erected mental barriers. Memories that came first were pleasant enough: childhood memories of herself and her parents visiting the Museum of Science in Boston, attending Red Sox games at Fenway, and exploring America's Stonehenge in Salem, New Hampshire. Childhood held the only untainted memories, and they were enough to keep her mind occupied for a time.

Then they ran out.

She was left with her recent past. And it stabbed at her. *He* stabbed at her.

Struggling with the painful memories became overbearing. When thoughts of suicide snuck into her mind, she attempted to distract herself. She sang "Amazing Grace" over and over. It had been her father's favorite song.

"Where are you, Dad?" Whitney said aloud.

With each consecutive day, her situation grew worse. Food was low. The smell from the bucket was rancid. Several times she considered venturing outside to empty the bucket, but the thought of losing what precious little heat she had to soothe her nose kept her firmly rooted in the basement. She knew the generator would run out of fuel soon enough, and then smell would be the least of her problems. Had she thought to bring down a calendar and mark off the days with the rising and setting of the sun, Whitney would have known that an entire month had passed thus.

It was on her thirty-second day in solitary confinement that her emotions broke down. She wept like a child, face buried into the folds of her sleeping bag. She cried about nothing in particular, but the tears flowed for hours. Then she slept.

Whitney woke slowly.

Then her eyes snapped open. Something was wrong. Something had changed.

Whitney searched the basement without moving as the bright moonlight glowed through the window. The dark shapes of her supplies looked the same as they had every night. Nothing had moved.

She listened. Wind swept across the home, which cracked and groaned. She could hear every pop and creak of the old house like never before. In fact, she hadn't even noticed them before.

What changed?

Whitney hugged the sleeping bag to her body. She was cold.

Stretching to the side, Whitney looked at the electric heater. The power light was off. She reached out and touched it. Cold.

Whitney gasped as she realized the source of the quietude. The hum of the generator had stopped. She had no power. No heat.

Hopelessness crept into her sleeping bag like an unwanted lover, smothering her body. She slid deeper inside the bag, hiding from the decreasing temperature, and sealed it over her head. She knew that remaining in the house with no heat was not an option. She'd have to brave the elements. She figured that either path led to death, but she preferred to die trying. Sleep came quickly. She dreamt of snow.

 CHAPTER 9

Scrambling to the entrance of the ruby-colored tent took a concerted effort as the vibrations that had been shaking the valley continued. Merrill leaned out of the tent and dry-heaved above a puddle of old vomit. He'd had trouble keeping food down, and now there wasn't anything left in his stomach to expel. The shaking had continued now for what he believed had been at least a month. Some days the trembling, which fluctuated in intensity, was tolerable, but days like today made him ill. He leaned back into the tent, scurried across the floor on all fours, and lay down next to Vesuvius.

They had both attempted venturing outside in the past few days, but the geological undulations made walking impossible. Merrill had fallen more than once. His fresh-scabbed knees were a constant reminder to only attempt walking when the shaking was less violent. The few times Merrill had hazarded going outside were to procure food and water. They had both grown accustomed to the sound by now, and whenever Merrill spoke to the dog, which was often, he had to shout. He knew Vesuvius couldn't understand him, but it felt rude not to speak up.

Merrill rested his head on a pillow and looked into Vesuvius's brown eyes. The dog returned his gaze, holding an almost thoughtful expression.

"I was thinking," Merrill said, "that this quake, if that's what it is, must be affecting the entire continent."

Vesuvius raised an eyebrow and blinked.

"You see, the shaking is somewhere in the order of six on the Richter scale."

Vesuvius sighed.

"You don't believe me? I spent time in San Francisco, you know. I've felt my share of earthquakes. And this is the mother of all earthquakes. What boggles my mind is where the epicenter might be. If we're close to it, then the quake, other than its unceasing duration, isn't that bad."

Merrill made sure Vesuvius was still listening. The dog continued to stare.

"However, the *cause* of the quake is what has me concerned. As you know, the temperature has been rising."

Merrill looked down at his body, clothed in a T-shirt and a pair of shorts which he created by cutting a pair of pants. "This indicates to me that we might be experiencing some volcanic activity. I know. I know. I'm not a volcanologist, either, but how else can you explain the temperature change? You can't. We must be near a rising chamber of magma . . ."

The ground shuddered worse than usual for a moment. Vesuvius picked up his head and listened. Merrill held his breath.

Vesuvius lay back down and returned his gaze to his master's eyes.

"I suddenly feel very foolish remaining in the valley," Merrill said. "If there *is* volcanic activity in the area and lava was to flow, I'm not sure the walls of our little valley would protect us."

Merrill crawled to the tent's entrance. Placing one foot over the vomit, he slowly stepped outside and stood. Vesuvius was by his side in an instant. Using the tall dog as a balance, Merrill took a step forward . . . and fell. The ground came up fast and he landed hard. Vesuvius plopped down next to Merrill and licked his face.

"Not as spry as I used to be, eh, boy?" Merrill sighed and looked at the distant valley walls where, somewhere, a narrow switchback trail led to the top. "Don't suppose we'll be climbing out any time soon, either."

The two clambered their way back inside the tent, where the blankets and pillows absorbed at least some of the shock from the vibrating earth.

Merrill's thoughts turned to the possibility of dying in the valley. After some deliberation, Merrill concluded that dying in the valley would be fitting. Aimee had died there because of him. Justice would be served if he died there as well. If he wasn't so positive that the vengeful God of the Old Testament had transformed himself into the more forgiving God of the New Testament, Merrill would have thought it was God himself smiting him for his unconfessed sins.

"It's an awful big show for just one guy," Merrill said to God, looking up. Vesuvius was staring at Merrill when he looked back down.

"Just talking to God," Merrill explained.

Vesuvius put his head down.

Merrill was a man of habit and praying at night was his routine, but if there were ever a time to break that routine, it was now. He rolled through his list of usual requests: good health, his work, and end of the quake, which was a recent addition. But unlike other nights, when his prayers were consumed by sleep, Merrill was still wide awake when he finished his requests.

He paused for a moment, unsure of what to say next. "Lord . . . I have sinned. You know that. Of course You know that. You don't need me to tell You. But I guess that's not the point, is it?"

Merrill looked at Vesuvius. The dog's eyes were closed.

"And I know what You want to hear from me, but I'm not ready for that. I'm not deserving. I realize now that I have sinned again . . . not that, I've only sinned twice—sorry, I don't know why I feel I need to explain the nature of my sins to You—You know what I've done, what I think . . . You see the sins of which I didn't even know I was guilty. But this time I recognize it, too."

Merrill listened to the shaking. It seemed to be decreasing in violence and noise. Pauses like these came every so often. He used them to relieve himself and get food, but now he remained in the tent, determined to finish his prayer, to seek forgiveness.

"Forgive me, Lord, for leaving Mira." Merrill's voice broke as he said her name. "I know now that the past, the relics, the discoveries, are meaningless compared to her. Please, if you have any mercy left for me, let me . . . and Vesuvius . . . survive this so we can go home. Forgive me."

Merrill wiped his nose across his arm, leaving a patch of slick hair. Then he stopped, arm against nose. The shaking continued, more quietly than ever. Quickly saying an "Amen," Merrill rushed outside. Vesuvius followed.

As the shaking continued to slowly dissipate, Merrill found it easier to stand. Unsure how long the respite would last, Merrill charged across base camp, heading for the last supply crate that had remained unopened since the quake began. He reached the crate and tugged on its slats with his hands. Desperation strengthened every sinew in his body and the wood began to give way. He considered running back to the tent to retrieve his crowbar but realized he might not return before the shaking resumed.

Merrill stabbed his fingers through a slot in the wood and grabbed hold of the loosest plank. He gave it three quick yanks. On the fourth, he threw his weight into it. The board popped loose and sent Merrill sprawling across the smooth stone valley floor. He threw the plank aside and stood to his feet.

Then he froze. Slowly he turned his head from side to side.

He could see.

The entire valley was in focus. He trained his perceptions on his hearing. The rumbling was still there, but fading. And the vibrations which had blurred his vision for so long were almost impossible to discern.

"It's moving away!" Merrill shouted then realized he was speaking too loudly to compensate for the rumble, which was now fading into the distance.

Another noise recaptured his attention: trickling water.

At the base of the crate was a pool of water that emptied into the smallest of streams, trickling across the valley floor. For a moment, Merrill thought he might have inadvertently opened a water container inside the crate. But there was too much water. Vesuvius saw the water, too, and began lapping it up with enthusiasm.

Merrill rounded the crate and found water again. He followed the small stream with his eyes. Its path wound past his ancient wall, past the dinosaur skeletons, and finally up the valley wall. The water was coming from outside the valley.

"Impossible," Merrill said. "Everything is frozen."

Or was it? He looked at himself again, dressed in summer clothes. Free from the distraction of the constant shaking, he realized how truly warm— and humid—the air really was. It felt like an August afternoon in Miami.

Scanning the valley walls, Merrill located the switchback. He ran for it as fast as he could, Vesuvius bounding around him playfully the entire way. When Merrill began climbing the path, Vesuvius charged up ahead of him, as he liked to do. Mirabelle had told him it was a sign of the dog asserting his dominance.

On his way up, Merrill vowed that he would signal the next supply copter to land. He had never kept a radio at the site. He'd never wanted to be bothered. But now it was time to leave. I'll see you soon, Mira, Merrill thought.

Merrill reached the top of the path and fell prostrate before what he saw. Vesuvius was there, playing in a pool of water and barking joyously. The landscape filled Merrill's vision. A month ago, the world around him had been white, the only variations being the sky and the exposed portions of the Transantarctic range. But now the land was brown and gray. The landscape was barren as ever except for the occasional pool of water, but otherwise, as far as he could see, Antarctica was free of ice and there wasn't a volcano in sight.

The continent had thawed.

 CHAPTER 10

A deep chill gnawed at Whitney's red and yellow full-body snowsuit, but thankfully failed to penetrate it. The Gore-Tex outer shell and down interior were doing what they were designed to do—keep her alive. Behind her, a trail of snow-shoed footprints disappeared over the horizon. Before her was a flat white expanse.

Leaving the house was easier than she'd imagined. She had thought of selling the estate earlier in the year but feared severing the last tie to her past might be more than she could withstand. Now that it had become a freezing cold deathtrap, leaving was easy enough. She'd been trudging through snow for five hours now and had seen nothing to indicate that she was headed in the right direction, let alone still in New Hampshire. When she struck out from the house she aimed south, lining herself up with the front of the house, which faced out to sea. She had a compass, but it didn't seem to be working. It was pointing dutifully north, but the direction wasn't really north at all, but west, away from the ocean. Now, with the ocean and land frozen over and looking identical, she could be walking over the ocean and not even known it.

Before heading out, Whitney carefully packed her bag. Rations for a week went first. Her most prized possession, a Canon EOS 1D Mark II digital camera with a 200mm zoom lens and image stabilization system, went next. With a megapixel rating of 20, a frames per second speed of 8.5, and the ability to save thousands of images, her camera was top of the line. And with no film to worry about, it served her much better in the field. The camera was followed by a small tent, sleeping bag, extra layers of clothing, crampons, an ice axe, binoculars, and a first aid kit. Last was her 9mm Taurus Millennium handgun. She packed the weapon, as she always did, just in case. Typically the gun was kept concealed in a zippered compartment of her handbag, alongside two extra clips. She knew the ammunition was excessive but didn't feel safe without it. Even now, when there was no one left alive to shoot, it gave her a certain amount of comfort knowing that at least she could defend herself if the need arose. She regretted not owning a pair of cross-country skis, but considering what she had survived . . . well, snowshoes would do.

Being physically trained for her Antarctic trip helped as well. She was making good time.

I'll be in Boston by next week, she thought cynically to herself.

And that was the best she hoped for. If there was any place that might have weathered the storm, it would be Boston. Granted, being built on the edge of the ocean put it at ground zero for the wave, but the skyscrapers, the John Hancock Tower, Prudential Tower, and the Federal Reserve Bank should all be poking out of the ice. Survivors might still be inside. She hoped to hole up in a building and scrounge for more food. Then she would head south again.

Five hours later, Whitney's pace slowed. Her legs were weary and her breath was short. She looked at her watch: 6:30 PM. The summer sun wouldn't set for another two hours, but the sun dawdled in the sky. It was a sight she had seen before, the first time off the coast of Alaska, on a cruise with her parents as a child. The sun came and went, but night only lasted a few hours and the sun seemed to linger in the sky.

This was an arctic sun.

Something glinted in the distance.

Whitney fell to her knees, shrugged off her backpack and rummaged for the binoculars. She placed them to her eyes and zeroed in on the shiny object.

A cross.

A gleaming, gold cross. Whitney stared at the cross and details beneath began to emerge. The top of a church steeple was poking out of the snow like a beacon. The structure was almost impossible to see—white paint against white snow—but it was there.

A stiff wind kicked up and made her body shudder. She looked up. The sun had moved. It appeared night might come after all. She left the binoculars slung around her neck, repacked the backpack, and made a beeline for the steeple. For her refuge.

 CHAPTER 11

With burning muscles, Merrill hiked up a thirty-degree slope at the base of
Mount Blood, which became almost vertical a mile up. Though he kept his
eyes on the ground, choosing his steps carefully on the slope, he pictured
the familiar surroundings in his mind's eye. Below him, a half mile away,
his valley split the slope in two. To the left was the Liv Glacier, which slid
inexorably into the Ross Ice Shelf, a floating sheet of ice four hundred miles
long that ended in the sea. It was normally a world of white so bright that it
could damage the naked eye.

Vesuvius barked at Merrill from the top of the slope.

"I'm in good shape, but I'm no dog!"

The dog barked again.

Merrill paused at the apex of the slope and caught his breath. For a moment, he felt afraid to turn around. He knew that whatever had happened
had changed the landscape with which he had grown so familiar. In fact, with
the number of hours he'd spent exploring Antarctica, it could be argued that
no one alive had spent more time on the continent than Dr. Merrill Clark.
He'd lost so much in his life, and now the continent he'd made his home was
becoming a stranger.

Vesuvius nudged Merrill's hand from his hip, demanding a pat. Merrill
stroked the dog's head as he turned around.

Vesuvius let out a yelp. Merrill flinched. He'd inadvertently clenched his
fist in the dog's thick hair upon seeing the landscape. He removed his sunglasses and took in the new world. The scrap of barren land he had seen from
his low vantage point at the edge of the valley was only the beginning. The

typically snow-covered peaks of Wishbone Ridge, Morris Peak, and The Tusk were as exposed as two-thousand-year-old bones at a dig site. The slow-moving expanse of the Liv Glacier did not exist. In its place was a deep valley full of house-sized boulders and a blue, crystal-clear river that flowed out of a more distant fissure that had previously housed the Zotikov Glacier. The river disappeared behind a mountain, Mercik Peak, whose stony walls had also been freed from snow and ice. The familiar freeze-dried white world had been transformed into wet shades of gray etched by several small streams and a thick river. The Liv River, Merrill realized.

Merrill sat down on a large rock, opened his canteen, and took a swig. Looking straight out over the newly formed Liv River valley, Merrill gazed down on what surely could not be real. He could see the ocean just as easily as he could from the Portsmouth house's bedroom balcony. The only remnants of the Ross Ice Shelf were hundreds of icebergs pocking the water's surface.

It occurred to Merrill that not only had the air temperature risen, but the water temperature must have as well. In only a month, from what Merrill could see, the ice cap that had kept Antarctica a prisoner had melted away.

"God . . ." Merrill stood again. "Mira."

His mind became a tornado of information and images. He sifted through the torrent, seeking information he'd heard at countless symposiums but to which he'd never given much thought.

"One hundred and seventy feet." Merrill looked at Vesuvius. "That's how much they said the ocean levels would rise if the entire southern ice cap melted. But her old house, the hill is two hundred feet tall. If she had warning, she could have survived in the house . . . but maybe she was out shopping? Or at the beach. Or . . . .or . . . "

Had there been time to evacuate? Did anyone have warning that the water was coming? It could have swept across the planet before anyone knew what was happening, or how to react. Merrill felt certain that millions of lives had been lost and that the world must have been devastated. But he didn't care about the world. His thoughts were with one person.

"Mirabelle."

Merrill charged back down the slope. He had to make contact with the outside world. Without a radio, his only recourse was to activate his emergency GPS transmitter and hope that someone was there to receive the signal, that someone could come get him. The Ross Sea held no interest. The ancient wall, now fully exposed and stretching hundreds of feet, was inconsequential.

The bones and freeze-dried creatures churned up by the retreating ice flow were no longer worth noticing.

Vesuvius gingerly hopped down the rocky slope, knowing already where Merrill was headed. But the dog ventured further ahead than usual, invigorated by the warm air and sweet, alien breeze. The distance made Merrill uncomfortable. He took his eyes off the craggy ground and cupped his hands around his mouth, preparing to shout to the dog.

But the only sound that escaped his lungs was a shrill cry as his foot snagged on an outcrop of rock. Merrill fell forward and landed on a smooth slab of stone. He slid ten feet and crashed into something much softer.

Merrill grunted as he rolled to his knees. Ignoring the sting that came with his scratched-up hands and the dull pain from the newly opened scabs on his knees, Merrill put his hands on the ground. They sunk in.

"*Soil?*"

The only exposed earth on Antarctica he had ever seen was solid stone, stripped clean by the high winds. He'd never seen anything like this: dark brown, almost black, earth rich and soft to the touch. Merrill rubbed his hands across the topsoil, feeling the sun-dried surface. It reminded him of gardening with Aimee in the spring. The un-worked soil was dry, almost powdery, but it served as a barrier, retaining the life-giving water within. Perfect for growing tomatoes. Aimee had loved their tomatoes. Merrill dug through the dry dirt to the wet and took a pinch in his fingers. He smelled it, allowing the scent to further infect his mind with memories of the past.

Before he was swept away in reverie, something caught his eye that overrode all his senses and erased his thoughts. He leaned down close to the soil and looked at the tiny anomaly. He hadn't seen the color in a year, not including the supplies he had brought with him. Green.

Merrill ran his finger across the tiny sprout's inch-long curved form. He was infinitely gentle with the plant, as though it were an exposed fetus. Its existence on Antarctica was no less amazing.

"I wish you were here to see this, Aimee," he said. His thoughts of Aimee led to a remembrance of Mira. Merrill left the plant to grow on its own, making a mental note to return to the spot first thing in the morning, to check on the little plant's progress. He promised himself that if Mirabelle was still alive, he'd come back with her here and name the new plant species after her. She would like that.

 CHAPTER 12

The scene reminded Whitney of the ending of *Planet of the Apes*, where the Statue of Liberty stood crooked and half-buried in sand, except that this was a church steeple, and the sand was snow . . . and there were no apes, maybe anywhere. Looking for any other signs of the town that no doubt stood frozen beneath her feet, Whitney saw nothing but a flat expanse of white in all directions. As in many New England towns, the church steeple was the tallest structure, and for the first time in Whitney's life it symbolized the same hope it had for others: salvation.

Whitney looked up to see the glimmering yellow cross that had alerted her to the church's presence. It shone brightly even though the sky above had become a churning caldron of storm clouds. She knew the storm would soon descend, and she had no intention of being outside when it did. She approached the church.

The steeple looked intact; this was good because it gave her hope that the church buried below had survived as well, but bad because she could not see a way inside. The spire was constructed of wood. It was hard and stiff to the touch—no rot, no soft spots. Two sides were flat, while the other two had horizontal vents built from angled slats of wood. She grabbed one of the slats and pushed. No give. It was the only weak spot in the steeple she could find.

The wind picked up and pushed the arctic air through her clothing. The atmosphere was changing. Whitney again looked high above to the sky and saw a swirling mass of clouds. She followed their motion and jumped back from the sight snaking toward her.

Whitney had heard of arctic hurricanes before, otherwise known as "polar lows," but she'd never seen one. They were reported by Nordic mariners as fierce freak storms that created havoc with their vessels. The storm's one-hundred-fifty-mile-per-hour winds churned sea and ice into a volatile stew and launched hail like bullets. They were cyclones of pure, frigid pain . . . and this one was headed straight for her. Nature, having missed her during the first pass, was coming to finish the job.

To hell with that, Whitney thought.

Stepping back, Whitney prepared to ram the vent with her body. She didn't know what was on the other side: a floor, or a ten-foot drop. She had to risk it. A broken bone was better than freezing to death. After taking three vaults forward, she stopped and rubbed her aching shoulder. The first thick flakes of snow from the hurricane fell from the sky like shots from cannons. Windswept arctic air found chinks in her winter gear armor, stinging her skin.

"I'm being stupid," she said out loud.

Dropping her backpack on the ice, she opened it and reached inside, fishing through the tightly packed gear. When her hand reemerged, she was holding an ice axe. While not an axe in the traditional sense, it was solidly constructed and very sharp. She began hacking at the vent slats, concentrating her blows on the outer edges. After five minutes, the muscles in her right arm burned and her hand stung from the effect of repeated impacts. Worse, her whole body shook from the cold. She had worn the wood down where vent met wall but had not broken through.

It may be weak enough, though, she thought. It had to be.

The thick flakes of snow had been replaced by an endless white static of tiny white flakes that flew horizontally at great speed. She looked back to the approaching storm, and through the wash of white flakes, saw a towering cyclone . . . a tornado at the center of a hurricane. Its approach was preceded by a loud hiss and wash of snow that caused her visibility to dwindle down to a few feet.

Whitney grabbed her backpack, took a step back, and braced her left boot into the snow. She kicked desperately with her right foot, putting the weight of her body behind the blow. With a crisp snap, the wood shattered. She kicked again, widening the hole, and wasted no time being careful as she leaped inside.

Inside, the steeple was dark and she felt claustrophobic. Whitney took out her small Maglite flashlight and switched it on. Panning the interior revealed a small space, not bigger than a common closet except that it was ten feet tall and tapered to a point at the top. Other than a few cobwebs, the space was empty.

The wind and snow, kept partially at bay by the steeple, howled and pursued her through the hole she'd created. Her reprieve was momentary; if the tornado struck this steeple, she doubted it would be sturdy enough to save her life.

Whitney stomped on the floor, her fury growing with each passing second. It was solid, but more important, sounded hollow. Kneeling to the floor, she scoured the flat surface for any anomaly signifying a hatch or doorway. She was certain that she couldn't hack through the floor. She shifted around and spied a small loop of metal bolted to the boards. She hooked her fingers around it, stepped to the side, and yanked. The wooden panel creaked as it became dislodged from its place in the floor. It wasn't a hinged hatch, simply a block of wood set into the floor.

Placing the hatch to the side, Whitney peered into the opening. Under the light of her flashlight, she could see a long ladder leading down. Whitney snatched up her pack and descended the ladder, pulling the block of wood back into place. The sounds of the wind and storm were replaced by an unqualified silence.

Her backpack scraped against the back wall of the enclosed space, but she made good time down the ladder. At the bottom, some thirty feet down, was a large square chamber. The only feature here, aside from the ladder, was a square, three-foot door with no handle.

She crouched and pushed on the door. It swung open easily and noiselessly. Slightly warmer air rushed across her face, carrying with it an odor that brought Whitney back to her childhood days. Most Sundays had been spent at church. The smell of pews, old Bibles, and crayons invaded her nose. Stepping out into the room, she played the flashlight across a short, round table covered in pencils, paper, and frozen, half-filled juice cups. Sunday school, Whitney thought. The juice stood out in Whitney's mind. Most Sunday schools she'd been to had been very tidy places. Cups left on the table were nearly a crime.

After exiting the room, Whitney headed down a hallway, opening doors as she went. Two more Sunday school rooms, both the same as the first: projects dropped, juice not drunk. The last door was a deep closet full of typical church supplies: an old podium, microphones, a stack of ruined hymnals, several trays of old communion glasses, and a box full of white sticks.

Not sticks, Whitney thought. Candles!

Whitney shuffled past the closet clutter and inspected the box. It was full of previously used Christmas Eve candles, hundreds of them. She reached into the box and pulled out one of the candles. Her elbow struck the communion glass tray on the way past, drawing her attention. She glanced at the glasses and saw a solution to a problem she'd only just discovered. The candles would come in handy for light and heat, but on Christmas Eve, churchgoers singing "Silent Night" held the candles in their hands. There were no candlesticks. Whitney quickly snatched up a communion glass and inserted the candle. It was a perfect fit.

Whitney smiled. "Thank God for pack rat churches."

She stuffed her pockets with candles and glasses then left, intending to come back for more. Her inspection of the rest of the church was brief as she headed down the stairs to the first level. A pair of solid oak doors led to the side of the sanctuary. Following the dim light of the flashlight, she made her way to the podium at the front of the room. She knew that the room wouldn't hold heat well, but had planned on camping out there since she'd seen the steeple. Perhaps it was the familiarity of the place, she wasn't sure, but she felt safest there.

She lined up twenty communion glasses on the podium. Each *clack* echoed through the vaulted room. After jamming a candle into each glass, she pulled a lighter from her backpack and touched it to one of them. Then, as she had on countless Christmas Eves, she lit each candle, one by one, with the first.

It wasn't until she was done lighting the candles that she looked up and saw them. An entire congregation of people, sitting in the pews, bent over in prayer . . . and frozen solid.

 CHAPTER 13

Sleep descended on Merrill. After returning to base camp, he activated the GPS emergency transmitter. It was his intention to do some more exploring: investigate the exposed wall, the churned-up bones, and the amazing new growth. But upon entering his tent, he felt an irresistible urge to lie down and rest. Before his thoughts could wander, he was asleep.

The rest of the day and the following night passed without a twitch from Merrill. He was in a deep REM sleep, brought on by the month-long shake and the day's excitement. He dreamt a dream that had been repeated since childhood. He was in the back seat of his parents' pea-soup-green Chevy Bel Air, being chased by an irate *Dilophosaurus*. The car would speed down a back road, trees crowding on both sides and the dinosaur close behind. A DJ squawked over the radio, reporting on the beast being sighted. The news report always ended with the details of his family's death at the hands of the rogue *Dilophosaurus*.

He woke from the dream calmly. It no longer held the fear it had as a child. He knew it was only a dream. Ironically, it had been that repeating dream that had fueled his interest in dinosaurs and led him to become a paleontologist. His fascination with dinosaurs had waned as he came to believe that, while interesting, digging up ancient animal bones wouldn't ultimately enrich his life. It was only from a study of humanity that he might glean some understanding of human nature. He earned PhDs in both anthropology and archeology, but rather than give up his paleontological skills completely, he focused on excavating sights where extinct creatures and human remains might be found together. His first dig had been uncovering the remains of a saber-toothed cat, which had died amid the bones of several humans. The giant predator had been a man-eater. Eventually, his dual interests led him to Antarctica. When he'd first announced his focus on Antarctic civilizations and dinosaurs, he became the brunt of his peers' jokes. It wasn't until the discovery of *Crylophosaurus* that the critics were silenced.

Ten years later he was still here, and all the evidence for an Antarctic civilization had been unearthed for him. Merrill frowned as he sat up in the cot, rubbing his temples. He wondered if anyone would even be interested in his discoveries after whatever global disaster had occurred.

No matter, he thought. *I* still think it's interesting.

For an instant, Merrill's thoughts returned to Mirabelle. The emotional jolt caused a pain in his chest. He squelched the images of her face with visions of exploring the uncovered wall. Wondering and worrying about Mirabelle's fate caused him too much angst to entertain. Until someone arrived to pick him up, there was nothing he could do about it, anyway. He'd rather stay productive and sane than wring his fingers raw with anxiety.

A sharp bark pierced the air.

Merrill looked around the tent. Vesuvius wasn't in his usual spot. He stood up from the cot, still fully dressed from the day before, and pushed through the tent's exit.

As his eyes adjusted to the bright sun, he became keenly aware of an unfamiliar scent. The air smelled sweet, almost like a bouquet of flowers. He reached into his pocket and donned his sunglasses. The now-polarized landscape came into brilliant focus. Speckles of blue, orange, yellow, and red coated the landscape, dotting a solid patch of green grass. Overnight, the valley had been transformed from desolate, dry wasteland into a botanist's dream come true.

Vesuvius let out another bark. Merrill searched for the dog but could not see him. A third bark revealed Vesuvius behind the supply crate. Merrill crept around the side, wanting to see what the dog was getting into without being noticed. Merrill leaned around the side of the crate and saw Vesuvius lying down in the middle of the newly formed stream, his head buried under the crate. Water flowed around the dog's large body, carrying bits of grass and flowers downstream.

At first, Merrill feared the dog had somehow become stuck under the crate. He knew it was too heavy for him to lift on his own. Merrill stepped forward, making no attempt to mask his approach. Vesuvius pulled his head from under the crate, saw Merrill, and barked again. Merrill could have sworn the dog was smiling.

What was he into?

Vesuvius uncharacteristically ignored his master and dove back under the crate. He was acting like he did when he lost a tennis ball under a couch.

"Vesuvius."

The dog continued to ignore him.

Merrill stepped closer, bending down to look under the crate. From his vantage point, he couldn't see more than a few inches beneath the wooden pallet that supported the crate. He sighed.

"Vesuvius, I swear, if you've become attached to a rock . . ."

Merrill placed his hand gently on the dog's side and Vesuvius reacted as Merrill knew he would. The dog backed away and barked again, allowing Merrill to take a look, but his lowered head and tapping paws revealed he was eager to return to his wet post.

With his hands under three inches of chilled water, Merrill leaned down so that his head was almost in the stream. It was dark under the crate and he couldn't see more than a few dark humps, which he took for rocks, and a slight glisten from the flowing water. Suddenly, one of the rocks moved from its position and launched at his face.

Merrill jumped up with a shout and fell onto a newly grown parcel of grass. He looked back at the crate in time to see a small creature bolt from under the crate and dive through a small hole in the ground. Vesuvius sprang into action, pounding his paws at the small creature, then digging furiously at the hole. Merrill hadn't seen much, just a gray blob of color . . . but it was a living, breathing creature.

His thoughts became analytical. It could have been a mouse, hiding within the crate. No, he thought. It would have been frozen solid until the great thaw began. Merrill pictured a mouse freezing, then thawing and returning to life. He knew some species of frogs could freeze solid during the winter and return to life when thawed. But this was no frog. This moved like a mammal, and he could have sworn he'd seen hair. Merrill had never heard of a mammal surviving being frozen solid . . . unless . . .

Merrill caught his breath. There was another explanation.

Anhydrobiosis. Literally, "life without water." Some organisms on earth had mastered the technique, during which the cells contain only minimal amounts of water. Metabolic activity was completely suspended. Several species of plants, insects, and nematodes were all capable of anhydrobiosis. Most famous were the brine shrimp known as Sea Monkeys. They were the kings of the anhydrobiotic universe, staking a claim in children's rooms around the globe. Merrill smiled. The Sea Monkeys had just been overthrown.

Antarctica was the perfect environment for a species to have evolved anhydrobiotic capabilities. It was so cold that everything not well protected was literally freeze dried. Antarctica, contrary to most people's assumptions, was the driest environment on earth. Merrill was fond of reminding people who questioned this point: ice is not wet. Merrill was among a group who believed that Antarctica shifted between freezing and thawing every five thousand years, give or take a thousand. Now that the ice had returned to its liquid state, the dormant seeds—and creatures—would spring back to life as though they had had a long night's sleep.

Merrill laughed as he watched Vesuvius fruitlessly dig at the dirt around the hole and considered what else might be awakening after five thousand years of dehydrated suspended animation.

# CHAPTER 14

The crystallized skin of the frozen congregation glistened in the candlelight. For five minutes Whitney had stood as still as a frightened mouse, letting her eyes take in each horrific face. Men, women, and children sat in the pews, heads bowed, hands clenched. The church had weathered the tsunami—the dry interior was a testament to that—but the cold killed the people before they could react.

She let her eyes linger on the faces. Two old women sat together, eyes clenched shut. A father cradled his daughter, who couldn't have been more than six, his tight grasp on her never wavering, not even in death. A family huddled together, hands interlocked, faces screwed in pain. A single mother held her infant to her breast, connected as one, forever. A sob escaped Whitney's mouth and echoed in the tall sanctuary. It was the most heartbreaking scene she'd ever experienced.

The strangest thing was that she envied them. No one in the room had died alone; whether with friends, family, or simply their congregation of fellow believers, not one of them had died alone. Even if Whitney survived the storm and escaped to greener pastures, it seemed she was destined to spend the rest of her life alone and without family.

As Whitney lingered on the families, her thoughts turned to her own. Growing up, her parents had seemed inseparable, immortal, and infallible. Now she knew not one of those three adjectives was true. And after what happened, it seemed that even the relationships she'd built on her own couldn't last. And now . . . now, everyone she knew—her friends and extended family living in Maine, New Hampshire, and Massachusetts—might all be gone, too; frozen like the congregation.

Whitney removed her hand from her mouth, where it had been since seeing the group, and took a seat behind the podium. The chair was ornately carved, made of dark-stained wood with crimson upholstery. Like a throne, Whitney thought. As a teenager, Whitney began refusing to go to church, seeing its stringent rules as oppressive and overbearing. She viewed the pastor and any other church authority as power mongers who saw her as nothing more than a peasant. She glanced to her right and came face-to-face with another body. The man was well-dressed and manicured, sitting on another throne-like chair. He was bald and long dead, but seemed to have passed peacefully, his face free of worried creases. A Bible was clenched between his frozen digits.

After recovering from being startled by the man, Whitney realized he was the pastor. He had probably sat there, behind the podium, telling the congregation that God would save them. Seeing the water rush out to sea probably brought people in to the church seeking answers from a higher power, or perhaps just safety on higher ground. When the water rushed in, he would have realized death was imminent and probably talked about heaven, about how death was not the end for them. She pictured him sitting on his chair, watching the people die, one by one, as the cold seized their bodies and hearts. Tears came to Whitney's eyes and she found a new respect for the pastor. He'd maintained his post until the end. She wondered if now, even after death, he would watch her die in the church turned mass tomb. She lit more candles.

"Don't worry"—Whitney leaned over and read the nametag scrawled with black ink—"Pastor Jeff, I won't be dying. Not today. Not here."

Warmed by the heat from the candles, Whitney unpacked her sleeping bag to spend the night on the floor, hiding behind the podium between the pastor and his flock. It felt surreal to be surrounded by all that death, but Pastor Jeff's peaceful face made her feel comforted, less isolated. She loathed being alone even more than being surrounded by dead bodies. She set up three more stations of candles, adding more light and heat to the room.

Ready to settle in for the night and maybe longer, Whitney sat in the chair next to the pastor and sighed. She looked over at him and took note of the Bible again. She hadn't read the Bible since she was a child and thought that now might be a good time. Nothing else to read here, anyway, she thought. Taking hold of the Bible, Whitney gave it a tug. It slipped easily out of the pastor's hands. She flipped through the pages and became over-whelmed by the sheer volume of the book.

Looking over at the placid face of the pastor, his cheeks and bald head re-flecting the light, she said, "So, Pastor Jeff, where do you recommend I start?"

A voice from the past answered her. "Start at the beginning," her father had said when she had asked him the same question twenty years ago.

She scanned the pages and found Genesis 1:1. She began reading. With-out realizing how much time had passed, Whitney read the biblical accounts of creation, the flood, Cain and Abel, and the tower of Babel; all stories she had learned about as a child but which had become dulled in her memory over time. Reading them now, as an adult, she found them much more inter-esting and full of strange details. As she read through the life of Abraham and into the first pages of the Exodus account, she fell asleep.

Unknown hours later, Whitney opened her eyes. She didn't move, breathe, or blink. Then the sound that woke her repeated: *Clunk clunk clunk.* Someone was inside the church, on the floor above. At first she wondered if one of the churchgoers had survived the freeze but knew it wasn't possible. She'd searched every nook of the church and knew there was no one there; no one alive, anyway. Whoever was walking around had come through the steeple. The dull thud of footsteps grew louder then expanded in all direc-tions. There was more than one person.

Listening to the footsteps, Whitney could hear three distinct patterns. They were searching—quickly. When Whitney had checked the upstairs rooms, her search had been thorough, seeking out useful supplies. But these people seemed rushed, as though they were looking for something specific. She felt a twinge of fear as she realized they might be looking for her. She had no idea how anyone would know she was there, but it was the only answer.

Not knowing the intentions of the people searching the church allowed her imagination to run wild. A year ago, Whitney had learned not to trust in people's good nature. It had since become her practice to assume the worst of people and let them prove her wrong. This was no different. She assumed the worst case scenario was real—three men were coming to rape and kill her.

If that turned out to be true, they were in for a surprise. Whitney looked back at the pastor, his frozen expression unchanged. "Any good hiding places?" she whispered. She followed his dull frosted eyes back out to the pews where the congregation still sat in silent prayer. She swallowed in horror at the thought of it . . . but there weren't any other options. "Thanks."

Whitney snatched her 9mm and blew out the candles. She worked her way through the dark, to the third pew back. She shuffled into the pew, slid past a frosty pair of elderly women, their hands clasped tightly together, took a seat and bowed her head in prayer.

 CHAPTER 15

The interior of the science tent had gone from an ascetic space that held Merrill's notebooks to a cluttered mass of hastily organized specimen samples. Merrill cataloged every new species of plant and flower he came across. He even found two very small insects crawling about beneath some loose stones by the stream. He had yet to catch or even see one of the small creatures Vesuvius had trapped, but he was confident they would return.

He counted seventeen varieties of flowers, three grasses, and four larger plants that were sprouting fast. He had no idea what these plants would become, but the outer skin was firm and he could literally watch them grow. He'd sat and watched one for a half hour. During that time, it grew six inches and sprouted three leaves. Life was expanding on the thawed Antarctic continent like a sponge toy in a bowl of water.

It had been three days since Merrill had activated the GPS distress beacon, and he hadn't even seen so much as a helicopter in the distance. He had intended to explore the exposed wall earlier but was afraid he might miss his rescue. He was beginning to think help might be a long time coming. There were more pressing matters in the world than plucking an old man from his self-inflicted exile. He was sure of that.

That morning, after collecting several new species of plants and placing them in the science tent, Merrill and Vesuvius climbed the valley switchback trail, now slippery with moss. At the top, Merrill could just make out the top of the wall. If the newly uncovered wall was designed similarly to the crumbling one within his valley, he guessed it was only a mile away.

Merrill took a swig from his canteen, which was filled with the glacial water trickling through the valley. It was cold and refreshing, unlike the now-tropical Antarctic air, which had laid down a thick blanket of humidity. Wiping his brow clean of sweat and condensation, Merrill whistled for Vesuvius to follow and headed for the wall.

The stone wall ran across the horizon, from the mountains to the Ross Sea. Merrill figured that its placement alone had helped it survive the great thaw. Had it been built along the coast, it would have been peeled away and strewn about as the glacier melted. As Merrill passed the one-mile mark, he began to rethink his distance to the wall and its overall size.

Rather than spend time contemplating the matter, he increased his pace. An hour and three miles later, Merrill began to see the details of the stones. He was almost there. He could tell even from a distance that the wall was massively tall. He looked down, noting the new species of flowers and grasses as he crossed an open field, and began jogging.

It had been a while since Merrill had gone for a run. He was happy that his body hadn't fallen too badly out of shape and that the exertion wasn't too taxing on his heart or lungs. As Merrill ran, he found himself speeding up with every step, allowing the sweet-smelling air to invigorate him. Vesuvius kept pace the entire time, his tongue flapping wetly to the side. If not for the sudden cool darkness of the wall's shadow, he would have careened straight into it.

Merrill stopped ten feet from the wall and looked up.

"Oh, my . . ."

The wall stood twenty-five feet tall and was constructed using carved blocks of stone the size of station wagons, all fit perfectly, almost seamlessly, together. Merrill's first thought was that no man or group of men could have made the wall without the use of modern technology. Then he remembered that many people said the same thing about the pyramids and the Great Wall of China. No, he thought, this is man made . . . but by whom?

Merrill guessed that the wall would have taken a massive slave force to build, and that there should be evidence of such a mass of humanity. He felt a pang of nervousness as he realized it was very probable that the ice flow had carried all of those priceless artifacts out to sea. His life's work may have just been scoured off the continent.

There must be something, Merrill thought. There has to be.

He turned to Vesuvius, who had kept a wary distance from the wall. Merrill's eyes lit up upon seeing the dog. "Vesuvius! Get the bone!"

Vesuvius had a penchant for burying bones, tennis balls, and sticks. If given the command to unearth one of his previous treasures, the dog sniffed around until he discovered something worth digging at, even if it was a location he'd never been to before. He assumed something fun was buried somewhere. The dog didn't disappoint. With his nose to the ground, Vesuvius began sniffing in a zigzag pattern that brought him close to the wall, then away and back again. If anything, the dog was thorough.

Five minutes later, Vesuvius barked happily and began digging. Mounds of dirt and new vegetation flew out from between the dog's hind legs. His hole was a foot deep by the time Merrill arrived on the scene. Vesuvius paused to look at Merrill, barked, and continued digging. After another minute of fervent unearthing, the dog's paws scratched at something solid.

"Vesuvius, heel."

The dog obeyed instantly, knowing that his master would finish the job and reward him by tossing the object for him to fetch. Vesuvius watched from the edge of the hole, ears perked, as Merrill climbed in. Something was buried beneath the dirt. A small bit of something white had been exposed. Merrill started there, brushing the soil away. After clearing a long strip of the hard surface, Merrill paused and scratched his head. He had no idea what it was.

Placing his fingertips on the object's cool surface, he ran them forward into the dirt he had yet to clear. He pushed through the dirt with his fingernails until he felt a rise in the object. It ended abruptly. Merrill locked his fingers around the end of the artifact and pulled. The ground still had a firm grasp, but Merrill felt it give a little. He bent his knees, gripped with his other hand, and pulled gently.

The object suddenly gave way and Merrill spilled backwards into the hole. When he righted himself, he saw something that boggled his mind. Vesuvius had a large five-foot-long bone clenched in his teeth and was dragging it out of the pit, growling as he did so. It was large enough to belong to any one of several dinosaur species, including *Crylophosaurus*, but the bone did not belong to any species of dinosaur. It was human.

A human femur, five feet long.

 # CHAPTER 16

Having read her share of adventure novels while waiting to capture a rare photo of some near-extinct creature, Whitney knew that most heroes felt a sense of reassurance when gripping their favorite weapon. Somehow the cold steel and weight of the thing gave them supernatural confidence. Wielding his single gun, the hero could do just about anything, often with only one shot remaining. She had twelve but was so nervous she doubted she could wound a water buffalo ten feet away. She was used to aiming a camera, not a gun, and the thought of shooting a bullet into something alive made her sick to her stomach.

But someone was coming for her. The three distinct sets of footsteps echoed through the sanctuary. Two were moving slowly; one was heading for the stairs.

Whitney opened her eyes wide and looked around the sanctuary. The room was pitch black. Windows were covered in snow that she knew rose up above the church's roof and part way up the steeple. The snow formed a perfect barrier, blocking all light and sealing Whitney inside. The only way out was through the steeple, past her three hunters.

She squeezed the 9mm in her hands, longing for that heroic rush of confidence to sweep over her. The doors to the sanctuary squeaked open and slammed flat against the walls.

Though every sinew of her body told her to jump, to flee, to fire the gun, she sat as still as possible, willing her heart to stop pounding and her short quick breaths to remain silent. She took the chance to glance toward the doors. A tall figure wielding a flashlight stood in the doorway. From the broad shoulders and stance, she could tell it was a man. But he wasn't moving, wasn't searching the room with the light.

Whitney listened. Barely audible, even though the room was silent, was the sound of sniffing. The man was smelling the air. *Damn it!* Whitney thought. The candle smoke. He knew she was there.

The man stepped into the room, his booted foot clunking on the polished wooden floor. He stopped again and played the flashlight across the room, sweeping back and forth in slow, wide arcs. He did not react to the pitiful frozen congregation but kept searching, insistent.

Keeping her head bowed, Whitney did her best to appear as rock solid as everyone else. She knew if the man lingered on her face with the flashlight, he might notice her skin wasn't glistening like those around her. If not, he might assume she'd left already.

The light crossed over her twice before settling at the front of the room, where it remained for several moments. He'd seen the pastor . . . the candles. But that proved nothing more than he already knew. Someone had been burning candles. For all he knew, it was the pastor's last ditch effort to save himself. The man kept his light on the podium and clomped towards it, his boots heavy on the floor.

Whitney chanced another glance. The light seemed unbelievably bright and she felt naked, exposed to the world. Before returning her eyes to the floor, she noted what the man was carrying in his other hand—an assault rifle. It was large and foreboding. Suddenly her 9mm seemed impotent. If the man had been carrying a knife or bat, she and her twelve shots might have been able to escape, but she was out of her league. The man was most likely some New Hampshire hick survivalist, she thought. What he wanted was a mystery, but the gun in his hand led her to believe his intentions were less than noble.

She heard the man step up onto the stage. The clunk of metal on wood told her he'd put down the weapon. She contemplated shooting him. She'd been to the range a few times and was a decent shot. Though she was by no means a sharpshooter, she figured one of the twelve shots would hit the man . . . if she could keep her hands from shaking. No, she thought, I'd never make it past the other two people with him. Sitting tight, hoping she wasn't discovered, was her best bet.

The man chuckled. "I know you're here, *chica*." The man had a thick Latino accent that was tinged with an air of bravado.

Great, Whitney thought, *my Latin lover has arrived just in time.* She stayed silent and kept her prayerful pose.

"The wax is still warm," he said.

The man scanned the room with his flashlight, pausing on each body. When the light set on her, she felt pain throughout her body as every muscle clenched. Then the light moved on.

After a minute of searching, the man sighed, picked up his weapon, and moved to the front pew. He moved from left to right, tapping the cheeks of each frozen body with the butt of his metal flashlight. *Clink, clink.* He moved on. *Clink, clink.* After searching the front row of twenty-two people, the man moved more quickly. He started on the second row, tapping the faces of each victim, sometimes tapping only once.

The second row was finished in forty seconds. He started on the third row, her row, moving faster. *Probably hoping to flush me out,* Whitney thought. And it almost worked. Her legs longed to jump up and carry her like a cheetah toward the door, but her plan wouldn't allow it. She remained rooted to the pew.

The man shuffled past the extended kneecaps of the frozen churchgoers like he had to pee before the sermon started. He was two bodies away from her. *Clink, clink. Clink, clink. Thud, thud.* The softness of the flashlight's hard handle on her thawed flesh felt like a painful blow.

Then, with suddenness Whitney had never experienced, a feeling surged into her body. Confidence, strength, and ferocity coursed through her, carried by waves of adrenaline. Just as the man turned, she sprang from her place on the pew. One hand grasped the man's weapon and pushed it away. Her other hand, the one gripping the 9mm, swung up. She placed the barrel of the gun under the man's chin and thrust upward.

"Drop the gun or I pull the trigger," she said.

The man relaxed his grip on the weapon without saying a word. It fell between the pews with a loud *clack.*

"Now the flashlight." She knew a heavy flashlight in the right hands could make a deadly weapon.

The flashlight fell into the lap of the woman seated next to Whitney. It landed at an upward angle, casting light on to both their faces. For the first time she could see the face of the man hunting her. His skin was dark and his wavy hair was slightly askew, probably from wearing winter gear outside. His eyes were dark brown and glowing. What bothered her most about his eyes was that they revealed no fear and reflected the smile that spread across his lips.

She couldn't fathom what kind of man would smile while being one false move from getting a bullet in the head. He must be insane, Whitney thought. Better pull the trigger now, before he fights. She tightened her grip on the trigger.

"I wouldn't do that if I were you," the man said. "You could really hurt somebody with that thing."

Whitney pushed the 9mm harder against the man's throat. He gagged slightly.

"Give me one good reason not to," Whitney said.

The man raised an eyebrow and his smile shot up on one side of his face. "If our date ends badly, you might not get lucky, eh?"

Whitney squeezed the trigger but her finger was stopped halfway by a booming voice. "Stand down and drop your weapon."

Another man. Not Latino. Whitney looked toward the door without moving the 9mm away from the man's neck. Standing in the doorway were two more people, a man and a woman, both aiming their weapons at Whitney. She might kill the Latino, but the other two would shred her before the man hit the floor. She was trapped.

"We don't want to hurt you," the big man said.

"Bullshit."

The man lowered his weapon and walked around the pews, calmly striding down the aisle toward her.

"Stop. I don't want to kill him."

The new man laughed lightly. "Easier said than done."

"What—"

A blur of motion and a sharp pain in her wrist was all Whitney's mind had time to register before the Latino had her gun in his hand, pointed at her face. "Like the man says, *chica*, easier said than done."

"Who the hell are you people? What do you want with me?"

The big man placed his weapon on a nearby pew, set his flashlight down so his face could be seen, and extended his right hand. "Captain Stephen Wright, U.S. Special Forces."

She looked into Wright's gray eyes and saw no ill will in them. He was telling the truth. "Are you a rescue team?"

"No, Ms. Whitney, we're here for you alone."

The Latino removed the 9mm from Whitney's face, turned it around, and handed it back to her. His smile faltered. "Besides, *chica*, there is no one else left to rescue."

 CHAPTER 17

The daylight hours stretched longer and longer since the great quake shook Antarctica and melted the ice. Merrill had grown accustomed to working in the constant twilight that glowed on the continent's horizon during this time of year, but now the days were as long as summer days in New Hampshire.

Still the vegetation grew, sprouting faster than anything Merrill had ever seen or read about. The fastest growing trees he'd ever heard of were the Asian paulownia trees which grew about twenty feet per year. By the looks of it, some of the vegetation growing up here could outdo the paulownia without breaking a sweat . . . or a branch. It was almost as though the land were enchanted. An enchanted forest. Merrill smiled at the thought and shook his head.

Several of the short tree species were now flowering, blooming crimson petals as vibrant as any rose. The sky was bright azure, dotted with cotton ball clouds. He'd been transported to paradise. If not for the many new species of biting and bloodsucking insects, the new Antarctica would soon become a tourist attraction, bringing the world's resorts and theme parks in droves. The new trees would be cleared, the unique species displaced, and the shorelines coated in fresh sand, all for what? Antarctic Disney? A roller coaster? Phony thrills did nothing to further humanity.

All the more reason to keep working, Merrill told himself.

He'd returned to the wall, which had been grown over by thick purple moss, several times. At every return trip he sent Vesuvius searching for more bones. He never had to travel far. It seemed the poor oversized-man's body hadn't been too disturbed by the ice flow. They had found a humerus, a few metacarpals, and a radius, all belonging to the man's left arm. There was evidence of a fracture halfway up the radius, but it had been set so well and healed so firmly that it was almost impossible to tell. It was only after scrutinizing the bone under a magnifying glass that he saw the distinct fracture line. His most profound and telling find had been the man's lower mandible. Five teeth were still intact on the right side. The back two were jagged molars, but the next three were sharp, as though filed to a point. But there was no scoring, no evidence that they'd been filed. They had grown that way. This man, with his size and teeth, could have rent flesh from bone as easily as a lion.

Unfortunately, Merrill and Vesuvius had yet to uncover another skeleton. Merrill would liked to have known if the man was a natural aberration or if there were others like him. He was a giant to be sure, like Goliath in the Bible. Based on the size of the femur, he would have stood at least twelve feet tall. That was several feet taller than history's tallest recorded man, who didn't quite top nine feet. For people that tall, physical activity was a challenge. Their unnatural size and weight contributed to early arthritis and other joint ailments, especially in the knees. Walking was sometimes difficult, to say nothing of the physical labor that must have gone into building the wall.

It occurred to Merrill that the skeleton he'd uncovered might have been a king of sorts. If the man was an aberration and as immobile as Merrill believed he would be, people may have worshiped him as a god. He may very well have been carried everywhere. Why then would he have been left to die? A disaster? Merrill wondered if the man had been overseeing the construction of the wall when the continent flash froze so many thousand years ago.

Merrill rubbed his temples. He was getting a headache. He stood up, looked away from the bones laid out on the desk, and stretched. Headaches weren't normally a problem for Merrill, unless he forgot his reading glasses. But he was wearing them now. He removed the glasses, placed them on the desk, and walked out of the tent.

His eyes fell to where Vesuvius lay. The dog's position looked uncomfortable and his tongue hung out. "Vesuvius!" The dog didn't move.

Merrill knelt down next to Vesuvius and placed his hand on the dog's chest. His breathing was slow and shallow. The tightness in Merrill's own chest took his attention away from the dog, and he noticed that the scenery had changed again. The flowers which had sprouted from the tall branchless tree trunks that filled the valley had opened up wide. Thousands of them pumped out small plumes of yellow dust that filled the air.

Pollen, Merrill thought. Vesuvius must be having a reaction. Merrill reached under the dog's bulk and hoisted him up, intending to drag him back into the tent where he hoped the pollen wouldn't find them. But the tightness in his chest spread up through his throat. Merrill felt his own airways becoming constricted.

Merrill heaved himself and the dog back toward the tent in a panic. Every pull brought fresh pinpoints of light that danced in Merrill's vision. As he approached the tent's entrance, he felt consciousness slipping away. With one final effort, he pushed his wobbly legs to the limit and threw himself and Vesuvius into the tent. They landed in a heap, limbs entwined, both unconscious.

When Merrill awoke he was unsure of the time, but given the failing light, he knew it was evening. He looked down at Vesuvius. "Hey, boy," he said.

The dog's eyes opened, and he made eye contact with Merrill. Loud thumping filled the tent as the dog wagged his tail, smacking it on the floor. Merrill sat up. His head was still spinning, but the grip on his lungs had relaxed and he could breathe freely.

Vesuvius sat upright like a bolt of lightning had struck him. His ears were raised, his eyebrows high.

"What is it, Vesuvius?"

The dog snarled then looked up at Merrill with a concerned expression. Merrill furrowed his brow. Only vacuum cleaners spooked him so.

Merrill opened the tent and stepped outside. The world had gone and changed again. The trees had doubled in size, and from their tops sprouted several branches loaded with oval-shaped leaves. The canopy above was near impregnable. Only a few stabs of sunlight made it through. Had all this grown in one day, or had Merrill been unconscious overnight? He had no way of knowing, but the bubbling in his stomach told him the latter was more likely.

The red flowers had fallen away, coating the newly formed forest floor. It was a red carpet fit for Hollywood's finest. Vesuvius stepped next to Merrill, sniffing the ground and sneezing. He was still unsettled. The air was thick with smells of earth and vegetation. He could hear the nearby stream but could no longer see it. And the walls of the valley had disappeared, covered by the thick growth that showed no sign of slowing.

Merrill noticed the hair on Vesuvius's back rise. He'd never seen that before. The dog sensed something. Whatever primal instincts he retained from his wolf lineage were warning him of danger. But from what? Merrill scanned the surrounding area. He heard nothing, saw nothing, and smelled nothing new.

A sound like a deep-voiced clucking chicken reverberated through the jungle. It was unlike anything Merrill had heard before, like a large mammal mimicking a birdcall. Then Merrill sensed it, too. The thing lurked in a patch of brush, not twenty yards away. Merrill could feel its eyes on him, appraising. It couldn't be too large, concealed as it was by the bushes, but Merrill knew that some of the world's most savage predators were its smallest.

It occurred to Merrill that given the circumstances, every living creature that had recently emerged from dehydrated hibernation would be voraciously hungry. The most dangerous time to approach a grizzly bear was just after it emerged from its long winter sleep. The creatures in Antarctica had been sleeping for thousands of years. He imagined that every predator, perhaps even otherwise vegetarian creatures, would eat everything in sight. That put him and Vesuvius, two large, well-fed mammals, squarely on the menu.

Merrill felt his muscles tighten as Vesuvius let out a series of savage barks. Then the creature exploded through the brush, clucking loudly. But the charge was not directed toward Merrill. It was running away, seemingly scared off by Vesuvius's violent bark.

Merrill sighed with relief and petted the dog. "I knew I brought you for a reason."

 CHAPTER 18

The newcomers had come blessedly equipped. They were traveling on snow-mobiles, each pulling a trailer mounted on skis and full of survival gear. They'd unloaded several battery-powered lanterns which illuminated the sanctuary in a dull yellow glow and gave the frozen congregation a warm, life-like aura. Next came a propane gas stove big enough for two pots. Both were filled with dehydrated soup mixes, the kind which typically made Whitney's nose cringe; but a warm meal was a warm meal, and she was in dire need of nourishment. Lastly—Whitney let out a joyful laugh upon seeing Wright pull them from a backpack—were four portable propane heaters and enough re-placement tanks to last for days.

After initial introductions, the four set to work preparing a comfortable place to settle for the night before the long journey south. The Latino man's name was Victor Cruz. He was a demolitions expert with the United States Marines—a handsome man who knew he was handsome—with sharply de-fined cheekbones, suave black hair, and electric brown eyes. The man exuded confidence. Like the heroes in novels, Whitney thought. He had been check-ing and rechecking their supplies, making sure they had enough to get home. Where home was, they had yet to reveal.

The three had been painfully quiet about what was happening in the world. Whitney realized they were sizing her up, deciding whether revealing what they knew would freak her out and make their mission that much more difficult. She'd had plenty of tearful nights already and was no longer likely to be shocked. She knew millions of lives had been lost. She knew her home had been destroyed, along with all her friends. Whatever they had to say couldn't be any worse than that.

Whitney looked at the woman, who was cleaning her sniper rifle for the second time. Her name was Katherine Ferrell, but she corrected Wright's introduction with a quick "Just call me 'Ferrell.'" Since then, Ferrell hadn't said a word. She seemed able to interpret everyone's body language, constantly one step ahead. Whitney watched as Wright approached Ferrell. Without a word, she picked up a propane tank and handed it to him.

"Thanks," he said.

Ferrell nodded and he turned away, affixing the tank to the last of the portable heaters. Whitney thought the woman must have ESP. She decided to test her theory. She stared at Ferrell, thinking about how the woman would be perfect for one of those B-movie babes-in-jail skin flicks: she'd be the tough one that beat up newcomers. Quicker than Whitney could move her eyes, Ferrell glanced up and held Whitney's gaze. "You wanna knock that off?"

Whitney swallowed. The woman was psychic!

"Only my lovers can look at me like that," Ferrell said.

Cruz plopped himself down next to Whitney, a smile already on his face. "That's why I always look at her like that. Eh, Ferrell?"

Ferrell smiled with her eyes, squinting at Cruz. "I can hit a mouse from nine hundred meters. You want to find out how I do at close range?"

"You're a sniper?" Whitney asked.

"Kind of obvious," Cruz said. "You think that pig shooter is for show?"

"This pig shooter," Ferrell said, growing truly agitated for the first time, "is a Parker Hale M85. At six hundred meters, I could take off both your arms in two shots. Before you even felt the pain, I could bury a third in your head."

"I heard the British L96A1 was better," Cruz said.

Ferrell raised the rifle and aimed it at Cruz's forehead. The woman had reassembled the rifle in seconds without Whitney even noticing. Whitney's heart thumped in her chest. Ferrell wasn't psychic; she was a cold-blooded killer.

Not that Cruz noticed. The man actually had the gall to blow Ferrell a kiss and wink. "Be a shame if you pulled that trigger, Kitty Kat. I might flinch." He motioned to the side with his head. Down next to his knee he held Whitney's 9mm, pointed at Ferrell's chest.

Ferrell smiled. "Nicely done." She lowered her rifle.

"I try," Cruz said. He spun the gun on his finger and grabbed the barrel. He handed it to Whitney. "Thanks for letting me borrow it."

Whitney was confused. With the exception of Wright, these people didn't act the way she pictured disciplined military people would. They were like a couple of cutthroat pirates. "So what branch of the military are you with?" she asked Ferrell.

Kat smiled. "I'm not military."

Cruz leaned back and crossed his legs. "She's a mercenary."

Wright stepped over and sat down, handing Whitney a piping hot cup of soup. "Kat has worked with me and our Special Forces on . . . lesser-known missions."

Whitney sipped her soup. Too hot. "What are they called? Black ops?"

Wright nodded.

"Doesn't the Army or Marines or whatever have their own snipers?" Whitney asked.

That elicited a laugh from Ferrell. "None as good as me, honey."

"I still don't see why—"

"I'm not shackled by treaties or laws. I shoot whomever they want me to and don't leave a trail."

Whitney's eyes grew wide. "You're an assassin?"

Ferrell nodded. "The best."

Whitney grew nervous. She needed to know who these people were and what they really wanted. She looked at Cruz. "And you? Are you really just a demolitions expert?"

Wright peered over his mug after taking a sip. "Whitney, all you need to know is that we're the best, and we're on your side."

Whitney raised her eyebrows and glared at Wright.

"She's a tough *chica*, Cap. I better answer her question before she gets rowdy," Cruz said.

Wright shrugged and returned to his soup.

"United States Marines. Demo expert. Like Ferrell, I'm the best."

"But?"

"Accidents happen. When Ferrell misses—"

"That only happened once," Ferrell said sharply.

"Whatever. When she misses, she takes a second shot and finishes the job. If I screw up, there is no second shot. Everybody dies."

"How many times have you screwed up?" Whitney asked.

"Once."

"How many people died?"

Cruz looked at the sanctuary floor, studying the red rug's weave. "Three hundred plus—men, women and children. It was a cave in Afghanistan some Taliban had holed up in. We didn't know they'd taken an entire village hostage."

"Doesn't sound like it was your fault."

"When three hundred people die, someone takes the fall. It was my op. I should have sent recon first." Cruz shook his head. "I was in Leavenworth for the past four years."

"Strange," Whitney said.

"What?"

"I didn't hear anything about it on the news."

"When three hundred innocents die in the middle of nowhere," Ferrell said, "no one hears about it."

"Oh . . ." Whitney looked at Wright. His scruffy face and steely eyes seemed to absorb the light, hiding his facial expressions. "And you?" she asked him.

Cruz laughed. "You got a bona fide Boy Scout there, *chica*."

"Started out in the Marines and moved up to the SEALs," Wright said. "From there I started running special ops, working strategy, and commanding a task force."

"Like I said: Boy Scout."

Whitney felt slightly relieved that at least one of them had a clean slate. She couldn't help but wonder why, and by whom, the three had been tasked to save *her*, of all people. She had no military training. She had no knowledge of anything important. She was a wildlife photographer. "Why you three?"

This question got Wright's attention. "We're the best," he said.

"Bullshit. I'm sure you're not the only military left on the planet, because if that were true, you wouldn't be risking your asses to save my life. There are two things I can't figure out. First: why you three? Anyone could have come to get me. It doesn't take the 'very best' to pull someone out of the snow. I can't find anything you have in common, but I know it exists. What is it?" Whitney glanced from one set of eyes to the next.

"You're a runner, *si?*"

"Answer my question," Whitney demanded.

"We're all runners, too," Cruz said. "I run away from things that blow up. Kat runs after things she needs to kill. And Wright just runs in circles." Cruz laughed. "The point is, *chica*, we can all handle a marathon and more."

Whitney bit her lip for a moment, trying to find a point. Nothing came to mind. "Why?"

"Because where we're going next, we're going to be running for our lives."

Not good, Whitney thought. "Why me?"

Wright put his empty mug on the floor and cracked his knuckles. "We need your help finding someone."

"Who?"

"Dr. Merrill Clark."

Whitney found it impossible to mask her surprise. "What? Why? I don't understand."

"Given your relationship—"

"*Previous* relationship."

"Right. Given that, we believe you are our best bet for finding Dr. Clark."

"Why do you need him so badly?"

"He has information vital to the success of our mission."

"What mission?"

"Ensuring the existence of the United States."

Cruz slapped her on the back like they were old pals. "We gotta save the country, *chica*. What's left of it, I mean."

Whitney glared at him. She didn't like digging for information she deserved to know. She didn't like talking about Clark. She didn't like being smacked. And she didn't like Cruz. "You call me '*chica*' one more time and I'll pay Ferrell to give me a demonstration of her sniper rifle."

Ferrell laughed but it sounded more like a growl. "I'd do it for free . . . *chica*."

 CHAPTER 19

Whitney shivered from the cold that had assaulted her since the group left the warm church five days previous. She clutched Wright's waist as they sped across a plain of packed snow. Her muscles were tense, not from holding onto Wright but from a tension created by learning more about the state of the country. Washington D.C.—the Pentagon, the White House, and the Capitol Building—had all vanished, buried beneath hundreds of feet of ice and snow. Whitney had learned that the president and most top officials were off the ground when the wave and chilling air struck, but everyone else—the entire population except for a few lucky prepared souls—had perished. Further inland there were more survivors.

The water had reached a few hundred miles in, further where there were large rivers, scouring the land of life before freezing over. But beyond the range of the killer waves, millions either suffered a slow, freezing death inside their homes or fled south. The livable portion of the country now consisted of Florida, Georgia, Alabama, Mississippi, Louisiana, Texas, New Mexico, Arizona, and Southern California. No one had heard from Hawaii; it was presumed destroyed. Alaska had taken a beating, with sweeping waves of water and a sudden and violent drop in temperature killing most living creatures in the area. A few surviving military units, stationed in underground bases, reported their status when the situation settled down. The ice had melted and the temperature had warmed considerably. Alaska was habitable, but only a few hundred Americans had survived.

The situation was worse than Whitney had expected. When Wright had finally told her the details of the devastation, she'd wept until falling asleep.

When she awoke, the tears continued for hours. While most numbers were estimates, they might be off by thousands and still be chilling. Canada had no survivors. Like most of the United States, it had suffered a deluge followed by the sudden freeze. Japan held perhaps five hundred thousand survivors. The Philippines were gone. Indonesia was totally devastated, with survivors ranging in the hundreds of thousands. Cuba and the Dominican Republic no longer existed, having been swept away by the raging seas. Australia was nearly frozen over—only the northern territories remained thawed. Mexico and much of South America had fared well but weren't unscathed. The climate had dropped by twenty degrees in Central America and the northern half of South America. The southern half of South America had warmed considerably and was suffering a drought which incited immense wildfires.

Russia and much of Europe had become an arid wasteland. Fires and hellish hot dust storms spurred by newly formed active volcanoes ripped across the lands, stripping trees of bark and flesh from people. The northern hemisphere around the globe had become uninhabitable, although countries like China, the entire Middle East, and North Africa had become lush paradises.

The coastline of every nation across the globe had been devastated. Whitney nearly vomited as she recalled the number of dead: 1.5 billion. That was, as Wright had put it, a conservative estimate. Of some nations there were no reports at all, and no one had the resources to investigate. It was believed that total casualties probably ranged from 2 to 2.5 billion, nearly halving the human population of the world. More died every day from disease, starvation, dehydration, or extreme cold.

On the six populated continents, countries were absorbing another billion displaced refugees. Even with the drastic reduction in population, there wasn't enough habitable space for all the people. Disease ran rampant, food supplies were low, and with governments collapsing, much of the world was descending into chaos. Of the surviving nations, eleven were struggling to maintain order and run the world. The United States, the newly reunified Soviet Union, China, India, the newly formed Arab Alliance, the struggling and recently formed European Kingdom, South Africa—which had expanded to include several other African countries as far north as Congo—and the South American nations of Peru, Chile, Argentina, and Brazil had discussed the fate of the planet and had come to a solution that seemed fair: immediate action had to take place. What that might be, Whitney had no idea, and Wright said he couldn't explain. Not until the final word was given.

Whitney's survival defied the odds on a grand scale; it was, according to Wright, the first good news they'd had in a long time. She failed to see how her life was of any consequence. The world certainly wouldn't miss a wildlife photographer.

When Whitney had asked for the status of Antarctica and those stationed there, including Dr. Clark, Wright had simply said the state of Antarctica was "in flux." Whitney struggled with that now. "In flux" could mean so many things.

"Hanging in there?" Wright yelled from up front.

Whitney's thoughts returned to the rushing wind, biting cold, and stark scenery. She wished he hadn't asked. "Fine," she said.

"Only two more days of this," Wright said. "Then it should warm up some. We've got an HH-60G Pave Hawk waiting for us at Fort Benning in Georgia. They'll fly us the rest of the way to Dallas."

Whitney struggled to speak through the wind that whipped about the snowmobile. "What's in Dallas?"

"New capitol. President, vice president, and what's left of the country's elected officials are all there."

"Why do we need to go there? I thought we were going to Antarctica."

"Like I said," Wright shouted against the wind, "Antarctica is in flux. When we came to get you, no one knew if there was an Antarctica left to go to. If the global plan is executed, our orders will come straight from the president's mouth to our ears."

"We're meeting the president?" Whitney couldn't fathom, not for all her life, what knowledge Clark was privy to that made him so important. The world was falling apart around them, billions were dead, and now they needed *him*, of all people? For what?

Whitney saw the back of Wright's head nod. "This will all make sense in a few days."

Finished with the conversation, Whitney let her eyes drift. To their left she saw Cruz, hunched down on his snowmobile. The man had softened over the last few days, as they shared stories of how each had survived the wave, freezing weather, and riots. He had even stopped calling her "chica."

Ferrell rode to their right and behind a little. She sat straight up, as though daring the wind to pull her out of her seat. She had remained aloof, keeping to herself. If they weren't riding, sleeping, or eating, she was polishing that damn sniper rifle. Like there was anyone left to shoot.

"Until I'm the last bitch left on earth," Ferrell had said one night, "there'll always be someone left to shoot. Don't think because the world took a hit that everyone's going to play nice now."

"It's the only way we'll survive this," Whitney had said defensively.

Ferrell had smirked, saying, "You don't think human civilization's gone through the wringer before? Floods, wars, famine; all those things do is make us stronger in the end. The weak starve. The less intelligent are slaughtered. The slow drown. What's left is the best of the bunch. This disaster is just the next test for mankind. The strong will survive, the weak will die. With no natural predators aside from ourselves, it's nature's way of applying natural selection to humanity. Maybe a billion more will die when this is all through. Maybe more. What's left will be the strongest, smartest, and quickest." She lovingly tapped her sniper rifle. "And this is what ensures me a place in the future."

Ferrell's words echoed in Whitney's mind. Humanity had suffered its worst eradication since the biblical flood, but if Ferrell was right, this was just the beginning. Life on earth would get much worse. Beyond the starvation. Beyond the disease. Whitney feared that man's most vicious killer would soon be upon them.

War.

# CHAPTER 20

The sensation of looming danger had hovered around Whitney for the past hour. They'd been traveling through downtown Dallas on foot. The first and only time she'd been to Dallas, the temperature had been 103 degrees and the streets had smelled of asphalt and exhaust. Now it was 45 degrees and the air reeked of refuse and human waste. The streets were packed with refugees. Some had set up shop, claiming sidewalks and street corners as their new front yards. The chaos was enough to make Whitney actually miss the freezing cold. The frozen congregation was more calming than the hysterical swarm of people, buzzing like angry, dislocated bees. Many were just passing through, hurrying for the Mexican border, which was rumored to be closing.

It seemed all the illegal immigrants in the United States suddenly wanted to head home . . . along with millions of legal U.S. residents. According to whispers on the street, the unceasing river of humanity heading south would be stopped at gunpoint upon reaching the Mexican border. A few million people had already amassed and were getting ready to storm across the border. The bloodbath would last until the Mexican defenders ran out of ammunition, but the worst would come after that. Mexicans and Americans would fight and kill each other for any land to the south. Millions would die if a solution wasn't announced soon.

What Dr. Clark had to do with that solution, Whitney could not conceive. The biggest thing he'd ever done was write that book. *Antarktos*. She'd taken the photos for it; he'd written the text. Subjects ranged from ancient Antarctic civilizations to long-extinct Antarctic dinosaurs. They'd traveled the continent together, putting the pieces in place. Ultimately, after it was ill-received by Clark's peers, the book drove a wedge between them. Even so, there were people more knowledgeable about the seventh continent than Clark; some were members of the military. Why did they need him so badly?

A solid blow to the shoulder sent Whitney spinning onto the pavement and out of her mental reverie. Her hands scraped against the ground, forcing small pebbles beneath her skin, burning like hot coals. "Watch where you're going, asshole!" she shouted. Looking back she saw that it was a woman holding a limp child, yelling for help.

A strong hand reached down and pulled Whitney up, but she couldn't take her eyes off the woman. "There is nothing we can do for her?"

Whitney looked at Wright, who had just removed his hand from hers. His eyes held compassion for the woman, but his expression was resolute. They could not help her, and her child was beyond help. Whitney dusted herself off. After so much time in winter gear, it felt strange to wear jeans again. At Fort Benning, they had exchanged their winter and military gear for civilian clothes. Anyone perceived as authority was presumed to have answers. Every living soul on the streets would mob them with questions, for some clue to their fate. But there were no answers to give.

All four wore blue jeans and some variety of jacket, which had been scuffed up and dirtied to make them appear as though they'd been camping like everyone else. The helicopter had dropped them outside the city limits, and they'd been walking ever since. Conversation was nil. Tension ran high. Everyone in their group carried handguns, just in case, but the threat of being suffocated by the weight of so many pushing and shoving people never subsided.

After a half hour of walking, they reached an alley where a group of fifteen rather large men had set up camp. It was like the Dallas Cowboys had hunkered down together. Behind them the alley was empty. Strange, Whitney thought. Every alley they'd passed thus far had been cramped, full of refugees. Wright approached the large men while Ferrell and Cruz stayed back. Cruz took Whitney's arm. "Don't get too close. These guys are real twitchy."

Whitney strained to hear Wright's words. After a full minute of quiet discussion, the group of large men quietly parted just enough for the four to walk through. As Whitney passed through the group, a malnourished passerby saw what was happening and shouted, "Hey! They're getting in!"

Apparently the sealed alleyway hadn't gone unnoticed by the hundreds of nearby campers.

The starving man rushed for the opening. A large man from the blockade stepped out, took the smaller man by the throat, and squeezed. There was a crack, and the man fell to the ground, unmoving. Whitney put a hand to her mouth and was yanked through the line, which closed behind her.

They hurried down the alleyway toward a single door at a dead end. Whitney realized who must be behind that door. The poor starving man had been killed so quickly, and without any question from Wright, who was pulling her down the alley. They were about to meet the president.

"Hands up, palms open," Wright said as they stopped at the metal door. He knocked twice. A hatch slid open and a pair of eyes peered out at them, scanning them from head to toe.

Whitney suddenly felt like a member of the underworld. What they were doing felt wrong. A man had been killed. They were dressed to dispel attention. And now they were standing at a door, being inspected by a stranger with beady light blue eyes.

The door unlocked and swung open. Wright shook the man's hand. Whitney recognized him immediately. "Mr. Vice President," Wright said.

"No formalities here," the vice president said. "Call me Kyle."

"Right. Kyle," Wright said. "Good to see you again."

"If only the circumstances were better, Stephen."

The vice president gave Wright a pat on the shoulder. "Maybe next time, eh?"

"I'll do my best to arrange it."

"I know you will." The vice president's eyes zeroed in on Whitney and she felt naked under his gaze. "Is this . . .?"

Wright nodded.

The vice president smiled. "Then our odds just got better."

"From a million to one to a million to two," Wright said.

This got a small laugh out of the vice president. He ushered them through the door. "Come, come. He's waiting for you."

Whitney passed through the doorway last as the vice president held the door open. She wasn't sure if she should wave, curtsy, or shake his hand. Her eyes met his and he smiled. His hand was already extended. "A pleasure to meet you, Miss Whitney. Hope all this isn't too much pressure on you. I know it's a lot to ask of someone."

A knot tightened in Whitney's stomach. "I haven't been told what we're doing."

The vice president's face fell. "Oh. Well then. Follow me."

The vice president slammed the metal door shut and locked it. A guard took up position next to the door, and they trotted down a long dim hallway that seemed to grow smaller with every step. Whitney realized the hallway wasn't shrinking; rather, her vision became distorted as her frayed nerves and exhausted body wanted nothing more than for her to pass out. For the first time since her home had frozen, she was truly terrified. She knew they were going to ask her to do something dangerous. She knew she'd most likely be going to Antarctica, which was fine; she'd been preparing for that anyway. But she also knew it had something to do with Clark; that scared her more than anything.

Seeing him, after all this time . . . she wasn't even sure what she would say. Even with the fate of the world mysteriously in his hands, shooting him, after what he had done, would still give Whitney some sense of justice. She shook her head and fought against the weariness. This wasn't a meeting she could coast through with half a brain, like she had in school. If she missed a detail now, the result wouldn't be marked with red ink, it would be her blood.

 CHAPTER 21

Whitney squirmed in her seat. She hadn't voted for the man sitting across from her. In fact, she hadn't voted at all. She couldn't shake the feeling that it was going to come up, like the man didn't have a world of problems to deal with already.

The president—or "James," as she'd been instructed to address him—was taller than she'd imagined and had a handshake grip that defied his age. His eyes were bright, reflecting sharp intellect and unfaltering confidence, but the flesh around them was sunken and dark. She imagined he didn't sleep much. His gray hair was combed back and he wore blue jeans and a T-shirt . . . a Budweiser T-shirt she assumed wasn't actually his.

He stared at her without saying a word for almost a full minute. She let her eyes drift around the room, feigning indifference to the man's scrutinizing gaze. There were two doors with two guards at each. The casual clothes they wore stood in stark contrast to the automatic weapons slung over their shoulders. The room was large, perhaps two thousand square feet, and lit by rows of recessed lighting. The area in which she sat was laid out like an office, similar to photos she'd seen of the Oval Office, but not enclosed. It was open to the other areas. One corner looked like a communications center, holding four computer consoles, a large screen, and maps of the world. Next to that was a long table surrounded by plush chairs that looked like a corporate board room. Closest to them was a kitchenette, which appeared well-stocked. Along the far wall was a single-lane bowling alley, candlepins standing in place and balls ready to roll.

Completing her mental journey around the room, Whitney noticed that James was still observing her. She looked at Cruz, Ferrell, and Wright, still seated, all waiting patiently, indifferent to the long delay. Whitney had never been on hold longer than a minute in her life. She couldn't stand waiting when she knew someone was just being slow. President or not, James was wasting time.

Whitney stood up, eliciting a sharp glance from Wright, but she ignored him and strode across the room. She felt the eyes of the four guards following her. In fact, all eyes in the room watched her, burrowing in to her skull. She ignored the urge to return to her seat and approached the bowling alley. She picked up one of the balls and felt its weight in her palm. Not too heavy. Stepping back, she raised the ball to her chin just like her father had shown her. After two quick paces forward, she let the ball fly. Her right leg slid out sideways and her left bore the weight of her leaning body. She held the position as the ball roared down the alley. Pins exploded into the air as the ball made contact, clearing the left side and leaving the outer four pins along the right.

"The four horsemen," Whitney said, repeating the name her father had given the four-pin arrangement that could run from center to the left corner or center to the right.

Whitney picked up a second ball and, forgetting the watching eyes, took aim and sent it rolling toward the pins. The three pins to the right of center spun into the air with a crackle of wood. "Damn it," she muttered.

Quickly taking aim with a third ball, Whitney flung it down the alley, letting her arm fall directly over the center arrows. The ball spun forward and struck the center pin, sending it spinning through the air. A perfect ten.

Whitney turned around and came face to face with James. He was smiling. "Not bad," he said. He leaned over and pushed the reset button. The remaining pins were swept away and set back in place.

James picked up a recently returned ball, stepped back, and let his hands hang next to his hips. He rolled the ball down the alley. It struck the pins and cleared eight. The ninth and tenth pins wobbled for a moment but settled into an upright position. The remaining pins were the front center pin and the back left—two of the four horsemen. A hard shot.

Without pause, the president took his second roll and clipped the right side of the center pin, sending it tumultuously back and to the left. The pin swiped the other and both disappeared into the collection bin.

James turned to Whitney and raised his eyebrows in triumph.

"Show-off," Whitney said.

"I don't like to lose," James replied.

Whitney stepped past the president and pushed the reset button. Ball in hand, she took the president's position while he sat down behind her. She felt the ball in her hands, the smoothness, the weight, and spun it around. She felt a tiny notch, which she positioned beneath the tip of her middle finger. Placing the ball to her chin, she took aim, stepped forward, and flung the ball forward. At first the ball appeared to be severely off course, but it curved back in. Striking the center pin at a slight angle caused the pins to burst into the air with amazing energy. When the pins were done rolling and clacking about, not one remained standing.

Whitney turned to the president. "Neither do I."

James clapped his hands. "Well done, young lady!"

Whitney took a seat next to the president on the seventies-era bench that gave the area a traditional bowling alley air. "Mind telling me what all this is about?"

James ran his hand through his hair. "I've found that prolonged silences can reveal people's weaknesses . . . or, as with you, their greatest strengths. I now know you are determined, resourceful, strong-willed . . ."

"And?"

"Impatient." He smiled. "Miss Whitney, I'm the President of the United States. The longest anyone has ever gone without saying a word was five minutes. You just bowled a nineteen in under four." The man laughed loudly.

"With all due respect, sir, I think four minutes spent in silence, even bowling, is a monumental waste of time right now."

"Too true, Miss Whitney. Unfortunately, your departure from here is set in stone. We have some time to kill, I'm afraid. And if I'm putting the fate of our country in your hands, I need to get to know you a smidge." Whitney sensed the seriousness that lingered just beneath the man's pleasant expression.

"Yes, sir," she said, remembering that this man was the president. She met his eyes again. The edge was gone. "Sir, I would be grateful, to say the least, if you would tell me what you need with Dr. Clark, and why you need my help to find him."

The president stood and headed for the kitchenette. "Of course, of course. You must be as confused as a fly in a spider's web." He opened the fridge, took out a bottle of water and tossed it to Whitney. "I don't mean that metaphorically, of course. Take a seat back with your friends."

Whitney looked back to the office area where Wright, Cruz, and Ferrell were all still seated and waiting.

". . . and I'll fill you in on the details," he continued. "Then we can finally get you folks out to the starting line."

# CHAPTER 22

The president sat across from Whitney with his fingers pressed so tightly together that she could see the color draining. The playful tone in his voice had disappeared. His stature seemed somehow diminished. And his strength seemed to dwindle as he sat in his plush chair.

Whitney wondered how the burden of what had happened could be affecting the most powerful man in the world. If anyone could be held responsible for predicting and preventing whatever had happened, it was he. It seemed that the destruction of forty out of fifty states had stolen just as much of his inner strength.

The president's voice cracked as he finished recounting the global destruction that had already been explained to Whitney by Wright. Hearing it all again brought the direness of their situation to the forefront of her mind. The world was screwed.

"And I'm afraid that with Canada, Japan, and most of Europe out of the picture, we're left to deal with more foes than friends." The president shook his head.

"But how?" Whitney asked. "I understand the end results, but I can't understand how this happened. Meteorite? Volcano? What?"

"From what I understand"— the president looked at Wright—"and correct me if I'm wrong…"

Wright nodded.

". . . the earth's crust is an average of twenty miles thick on the continents; an average of six miles thick under the ocean. Forget what you know about tectonic plates, we're talking about the earth's crust as a whole. It's not several separate slabs; they're all connected and floating on the earth's mantle, which is composed of molten layers all the way down to the core. The crust literally floats on the mantle. We are all adrift on a sea of lava, Ms. Whitney. And sometimes it shifts. This theory was first proposed by Dr. Charles Hapgood in 1958. He suggested that the earth's crust had survived several displacements. That's what he called them 'earth crust displacements.' Some of his evidence included a frozen mammoth in Siberia that crystallized so quickly it still had a mouthful of vegetation."

"I saw that happen to my hometown," Whitney said, remembering Portsmouth and her now-frozen friend Cindy. Morbidly, she wondered if, five thousand years from now, some archeologist would dig them up and discover what they had been eating.

"Other evidence includes coral found in Newfoundland and evidence that swamp cypress once flourished within five hundred miles of the North Pole. Further evidence, of which you're well aware, has been found on Antarctica itself. Fossils of ferns, tree stumps, even dinosaurs remains have been found. This all indicates the world was a much different place at one time, more different than tectonic shift can account for. And more than all that, there is something else . . ."

Whitney found herself on the edge of her seat. She'd heard all this before, but heard it now with fresh ears. This was real. Not theory.

"We have a map," the president said. "The original is not complete right now. We have yet to retrieve the missing portion, but for all intents and purposes, it fits our needs. It shows the coastline and much of the interior of Antarctica in great detail, but—"

"You have the Piri Reis map?" Whitney's eyes were wide. She had heard of only a small piece of the original having ever been found. The map was created in 1513 by Piri Reis, an admiral in the Turkish fleet who had access to ancient documents kept in the Imperial Library of Constantinople. Some of the original documents, now lost, dated back to the fourth century BC, and even earlier. It depicted the Antarctic at a time when there was no ice on the continent's surface. Its detail was greater than even modern maps had achieved.

The president smiled. "You've heard of it?"

"Anyone who has set foot on Antarctica has heard of it. The map is legendary!"

The president nodded and rubbed his nose. "And your Dr. Clark based an entire chapter of his book on the map. I reckon he'd like to get his hands on it."

Whitney felt compelled to ask about Clark, to discover what he had to do with all this, but kept silent.

"What we've done," the president said, "is combine our map with high resolution images of the Piri Reis fragment. We now have a complete, accurate map of the continent. I imagine poor Dr. Hapgood would have killed for the entire map. It would have done wonders to support his earth crust displacement theory." The president shifted his weight. "Most scientists have shunned the notion since Hapgood first theorized it, but the doctor has been proven correct. Of course, the recent devastation wasn't as bad as Hapgood predicted."

"It could have been worse?" Whitney was stunned.

"Much worse," Wright said, nodding. "By all rights, every volcano on earth could have blown. Earthquakes could have been so violent that every structure on the planet would have been destroyed. And vast underground stores of water, combined with the melt from the poles, could have swept over every continent on earth."

"A global flood. The promise was kept," Whitney murmured.

"What was that?" the president asked.

Whitney felt embarrassed. She didn't buy into that stuff, but she answered anyway, "Noah. The flood. God promised not to completely deluge the earth again. I'd always believed the flood was a regional event, but based on what you're saying, it could have been global."

"Here I am a churchgoer, and that never crossed my mind," the president said. "Tell me, when was Noah's flood supposed to have happened?"

"Some say five to six thousand years ago; some as much as twelve thousand years ago. I'd say closer to twelve, but that's just an opinion."

The president slapped his knee. "Mystery solved!"

Whitney looked at him quizzically.

"Hapgood hypothesized that crust displacement events took place every twelve thousand years or so. The biblical record could very well be accurate."

Whitney shook her head. For so long she'd written off the Genesis accounts as ancient fiction. The events described were so fantastic they defied logic. But here she sat, a survivor of the very same event that caused the biblical flood. Science was proving the Bible correct. "Why wasn't the effect the same? Why weren't we completely destroyed?"

"You mean other than God sparing us?" Wright said.

"I don't believe in God," Whitney said. "Why did the earth spare us?"

"The shift was relatively smooth," Wright said. "The whole crust came loose and shifted in tandem. Only a few volcanoes erupted. Earthquakes were severe in some locations, but only near larger fault lines. It was the dramatic temperature shift that got most people: freezing instantly or burnt alive by the severe heat. The floodwaters came in only because as the earth moved, the water wanted to stay still. It was swept away to the south in this hemisphere and to the north on the other side of the planet. Later, after it began moving as well, the water caught up with the continents and swept over them. The melt from the north and south poles refroze at the new poles, and the water level never rose too high; it is currently almost back to normal."

"But how does the crust displacement happen in the first place? How can the crust come loose?"

"According to Hapgood, as the earth rotates in orbit, there is a slight wobble to its movement caused by accumulation of ice on the poles."

Whitney caught on quickly. "Especially in the south, where ice covers Antarctica, making it heavier than the ice over the north pole. It would throw the balance off."

The president stabbed a finger at Whitney. "Precisely. But this wobble has remained constant, only fluctuating slightly every once in a while."

"Until now?"

"Picture the earth's crust and core as a large tangerine. Detach the skin from the fruit without peeling it, and you have an approximation of what earth's crust is like. Now attach off-centered weights to the top and bottom, more on the bottom, and spin it. What do you think will happen?"

"It will slip." As the words escaped her lips, Whitney understood what had happened.

"Mm," the president agreed.

"Where are the new poles? How far did we shift?"

The president looked at Wright. "Stephen, would you mind . . .?"

Wright stood, walked across the long room, picked up a map from the communications area, and returned it to the president's desk. He unrolled it and held it open for them all to see.

Whitney recognized the continents, though the shapes of many had changed, and some smaller island nations were missing altogether. But this map was odd. It was as though the cartographer had drawn it from the southern pole looking up. Antarctica was just below the equator. "Oh . . ."

"'Oh' is right," the president said. "The crust shifted by forty degrees, making the new north pole somewhere around North Dakota. This is most likely the largest shift in history, we assume, because it was so smooth. Other shifts were more violent and probably stopped moving sooner."

"Then the United States is—"

"Gone," the president said. "Unless the crust shifts us south again, the northern states will be forever frozen over—a northern version of Antarctica."

Whitney began to suspect what the president was getting at. "But not anymore. Antarctica must be thawed."

The president looked at Wright. "You did good by saving this one. She's quick as a whip." He looked back to Whitney. "It was a full month before we even thought of looking at Antarctica. It was another two days before one of the few remaining satellites with which we still have communication got a good shot." The president reached inside the center desk drawer and pulled out five 8x10 photos. He threw them on top of the new world map.

What Whitney saw caused her to hold her breath. The overall shape was similar to the Antarctica she knew so well, but it was different. For one, it wasn't white; it was green, save several blue splotches that looked like enormous lakes.

"Seems the seventh continent didn't just thaw," the president said. "It bloomed."

"The shape is different, too."

"To our eyes, yes," Wright said, taking out another map. He opened it and placed it down next to the photos. Whitney knew she was looking at the Piri Reis map. The continent's outline matched those in the photos perfectly. "With all the ice sheared from its surface, the continent actually rose, perhaps twenty more feet above sea level. It's a new world over there."

"What did McMurdo report?"

"They didn't."

"Vostok?"

The president shook his head. "As near as we can tell, they're all gone. Swept away with the ice."

"There are more than five thousand people on Antarctica at any given time," Whitney said. "They can't all be dead."

"Two and a half billion people are dead around the world, Miss Whitney. Another five thousand isn't a lot to add."

Whitney's head hung low. "Then why the interest . . ."

"In Dr. Clark?" The president interrupted. "Clark is one of the foremost authorities on Antarctica, followed closely by you. No one has spent more time on the continent than Dr. Clark. And while you're a photographer by trade, you've spent more hours trekking across that continent than anyone else at my disposal. Clark is our best bet at leading the team to its goal. You are our backup."

"Who will he lead?" Whitney asked.

The president swept his arm from left to right, motioning at Whitney, Wright, Cruz, and Ferrell. "The four of you."

Whitney was becoming annoyed. "For what purpose?"

"A race," Wright said. "Try to understand the state of the world: entire continents have become unlivable. A billion people have been displaced, and there is no room in what's left of the inhabitable world for them. The majority of the previously northern hemisphere, whether by severe heat or freezing cold, has become a wasteland. Antarctica has become the opposite. A continent the size of North America is now lush and available."

"Then what's the problem?" Whitney asked. "Why aren't we setting up the displaced people?"

"Not everyone wants to share," Wright said. "New nations and alliances have formed, and they see this as a chance to gain control of the world."

"Then it's war."

"Not quite," the president added. "We were able to avoid war by proposing a new, less bloody solution."

Whitney scrunched her face. "Are you saying we couldn't win a war?"

The president leaned back in his chair and chewed on the question for a moment before answering. "We have several Navy fleets still functional. We have a limited Air Force, but our ground forces have been greatly diminished. We still have the technologic advantage, but in sheer numbers, we lose every time. It would only be a matter of time before China or the Arab Alliance took us out of the picture. If we didn't still have enough nukes to kill the remaining four billion people left living, they'd probably already be here. Of course, if we used our nukes preemptively, you can bet every other nation on the planet with nukes would start launching. Basically, the world has reached a stalemate."

"And this race," Whitney asked, "how does it work?"

"After a week of international talks via satellite communications and various embassies, all overseen by the remaining members of the United Nations, an agreement was found. The only peaceful solution we could all agree on was a good old-fashioned land claim like they used to do in the old west," the president said. "The first three nations or leagues of nations to reach the geographic center of Antarctica split the continent into three equal parts. There are eleven parties involved, several of which we simply cannot allow to win. That the Arab Alliance even agreed to this means they feel very confi- dent, and that scares the bejeezus out of me. Imagine trying to share a physi- cal border with the Alliance . . . or even the new Soviet Union, for that matter. There is so much bad blood in our shared histories. War would be inevitable. And we don't expect they'll all play nice, given the current, des- perate situation.

"This is a race, plain and simple," the president continued. "But it is the longest, most dangerous race in human history. Starting points for various nations will be on the shores of now-missing ice shelves; Ross—where you'll be starting—Ronne, Amery, Filchner . . . you know them?"

Whitney nodded slowly, as though she'd just been asked if she understood where she was about to be hanged.

The president continued. "You'll not only have to cross nearly one thou- sand miles of uncharted land on foot, but you'll have to deal with the other teams who are also starting along the Ross Sea—the Chinese, the Arab Al- liance, and the European Kingdom. Now you'll be rendezvousing with the European team five hundred miles in and going together from there, so they won't be a problem. The Chinese have been hard to read, but the Arab Al- liance will certainly be hostile. We have some concerns about the Soviets as well, but they're starting from the Amery Sea side with Brazil and South Af- rica. There are no laws on Antarctica, and there are no rules to the race ex- cept: get there first."

Whitney bit her lip, realizing for the first time just how dangerous the mission was going to be. "What are the chances of open conflict with the Chinese or the Arab Alliance?"

"Good, I'm afraid," Wright said. "We're opting for speed, stealth, and better intel—that's where you and Dr. Clark come in. The Chinese are mobi- lizing a force of two hundred, perhaps in ten squads. If we cross paths with them, we're going to run like hell."

Whitney was aghast. "Then why aren't we sending more people?"

"Two hundred turtles still can't beat the hare," Wright said.

"But they can eat it," Cruz piped up for the first time with a wide smile. No one returned his smile and he sat back.

Whitney leaned forward. "I understand the race. I understand the state of the world. I understand why you need me to go. But if everyone on Antarctica was killed during the shift, why are you so interested in Clark?"

"Six weeks after the shift, we detected a GPS distress beacon from Antarctica. After tracking the signal to its source and doing some serious digging to find out who was there, we discovered it belonged to Dr. Clark."

Whitney had been wondering about his fate from the outset but had been afraid to ask. Now that she knew the truth, she wasn't sure if she was relieved or disappointed.

"From here you'll fly to Brazil, stop over in Chile for your final outfitting, then set sail for Antarctica. If Dr. Clark is still alive, you will collect him, tend to his health concerns, and be airlifted to your start position."

"And when does the race start?"

"Two days."

 # CHAPTER 23

The whirlwind of activity that surrounded Whitney after her surreal meeting with the president left her mind feeling scoured. After stealing out of Dallas, they were taken via helicopter to Sheppard Air Force Base in Texas. They transferred to a massive C-5 Galaxy cargo plane and all of their gear was crated up and loaded on to the plane with them, along with eleven three-person teams. Wright explained that witnesses from each country were required to be present at every starting location to ensure that everyone started at the designated time. The teams of three looked like science types and civilians, but Wright had added that all were actually Special Forces. If things went sour, they could fight their way free . . . or at least die trying.

Whitney spent the flight sleeping as best she could, letting the hum of the C-5's four massive turbines drown out her anxiety. She found no comfort until her thoughts turned to Sam. What would he think of all this? She pictured his charming smile, goofy laugh, and chalk-white skin of a computer programmer who spent most of his time in front of a computer screen. When it came to adventure, his extremes peaked at computer games and paintball. He'd gone to Africa with her once but had spent the last week over a hole dug in the earth. Montezuma had crossed the ocean to dole out his revenge. Whitney smiled, remembering the month's worth of jokes he told at his own expense after they returned home. Each joke, while outwardly designed to make her laugh, was also his way of reminding her to never ask again. And she hadn't.

Would you come with me now, Sam? Whitney wondered. Before she could answer her own question, she drifted off to sleep.

She awoke as they landed at Brasilia Air Base in central Brazil, where the plane was refueled and checked over. With the fate of the United States contained in the C-5, no one wanted to take the chance of a malfunction over Argentina. Whitney learned that though the base was Brazilian, America had been allowed access due to the fact that the Brazilians didn't want China, the Arab Alliance, or the Soviets in Antarctica, either. Brazil had fared better than most countries during the shift, and was in a good position to help.

Back in the air, Whitney caught some more sleep. She didn't mean to be antisocial, but she had a feeling that sleep would soon be hard to come by. Turbulence over Uruguay stirred her from sleep again. She wiped the drool from her mouth and noticed Wright staring at her from his chair across the aisle.

"I'm surprised you can sleep with all this noise," Wright said with a smile.

Whitney gave a tired smirk, stretched, and took in a deep breath that smelled of metal and machinery. "In the field you learn to sleep while you can."

"Nature photography, right?"

Whitney nodded.

"Any close calls?"

"What, with animals?"

"Nature in general. Animals included."

Whitney laughed. "You mean aside from the giant arctic cyclone that chased me into a frozen church after the entire crust of the earth shifted and killed a third of the planet's population?"

Wright smiled. "Point taken. Just animals, then."

Whitney sat up straight. "I was stung by a scorpion in the Mojave, but the worst was when a mountain lion in California had a go at me."

Wright looked surprised. "I've heard some amazing things about those cats. I'm surprised you survived."

"Yeah, me, too. I got lucky. It tackled me and pinned me to the ground. It was going for my neck, and I swung at it blindly with my pocketknife. Tagged it right in the nose. Even drew some blood. It disappeared as fast as it had shown up."

"God. Were you in a national park?"

Whitney laughed again, stirring Cruz, who had been sound asleep one seat in front of Wright. "I was visiting some friends and went for an early morning jog. Typical southern California neighborhood. The cat jumped out from behind a line of flowers . . . birds of paradise, I think they're called."

"You carry a knife while jogging?" Wright asked with a smile.

Whitney reached into her pocket and snapped open her small jackknife. "Never leave home without it."

"You know those aren't allowed on planes anymore," Wright said.

Whitney looked back over her shoulder, peering past the rows of seats and out into the main cargo hold which contained Humvees with mounted machine guns, crates labeled "live munitions," and lines of weapons mounted against the walls. "Please," she said, "I think the contents of this plane would be enough to overthrow a small country."

"Hey," Cruz said, rubbing his waking eyes, "where in So Cal were you?"

"La Crescenta, just outside Los Angeles."

Cruz perked up. "Shit, man, I grew up in Glendale."

"They have the best downtown," Whitney said, and Cruz nodded in agreement. "Though I preferred Pasadena."

Cruz waved his hand in the air like he was swatting a fly. "*Pffft.* Pasadena's for tourists."

The conversation went on for hours, delving into the lives and experiences of Wright, Cruz, and Whitney. Only Ferrell remained sleeping. Cruz explained that Ferrell could sleep through anything. He called her snoozes "Kat Naps." There was no lag time between when she woke up and when she took action. "It's like someone snaps a rubber band under her ass," Cruz explained. "She bounces up and is good to go."

Time passed quickly as the conversation grew more in depth. Sooner than Whitney believed possible, they were landing in Chile. The scene on the ground was chaotic. Crews were dispersed to a fleet of waiting helicopters, which flew away one at a time. Weapons were stowed. Gear was removed from crates and repacked. Everyone stripped and redressed in jungle gear, from hiking boots to fully packed backpacks. In half an hour, they were ready to hack and slash their way through any jungle on earth.

Before boarding their copter, Wright pulled Whitney aside and offered her a weapon. It was unlike anything she'd ever seen. "This is an XM29 assault rifle. It's an integrated dual munitions bursting weapon."

Whitney's confused expression said all that needed to be said.

"Glad you asked," Wright said. "The top barrel fires bursting munitions using a fire control that programs the round. A ballistic computer with range-finding capability allows it to program each and every round to within one meter of its target. The rounds know where to blow up."

"And where is that? Er, typically?"

"Inside the target."

Whitney hid her grimace. "Right."

"The bottom barrel is a standard 5.56mm assault rifle that can cut down just about anything with one to four legs."

"One leg?"

"Gotta watch out for those peg leg villains." Wright smiled, and when Whitney didn't return the smile, he continued. "Just think of it as a machine gun with an insurance policy. If you can't hit the target, pop a few of the exploding rounds in the target's general area and the shrapnel should take care of things for you."

Wright picked up a second XM29 and held them both up.

"And why are you telling me this?" Whitney suspected why but hoped it wasn't true. She had grown comfortable with her 9mm, which she had already strapped to her side, but this *thing* was another creature entirely.

Wright handed her one of the weapons. "This one's yours." He handed her the other. "And this is for Dr. Clark. You can deliver it when we get there. I know you've spent some time at the range. Think you can handle this?"

"Think I'll have to?"

"Better to be prepared."

Whitney laughed. "You *are* a Boy Scout."

Ten minutes later, Whitney held two of the world's most sophisticated assault rifles in her arms and was seated between Cruz and Wright on an XM1 Nighthawk, one of the president's official helicopters. The flight plan took them out over the ocean where they would refuel several times on aircraft carriers strung out along the way. Ferrell took another Kat Nap, sleeping soundly despite the rattling chop of the rotor blades.

Whitney absorbed her surroundings. The smell of the copter's leather interior and the fresh odor of their new gear mingled in her nose. The feel of the plush presidential seat stood in contrast to the hard, heavy metal of the XM29s resting against her hands. She was surrounded by soldiers trained to kill, about to enter a world unknown to mankind for thousands of years. She couldn't imagine a more chaotic and confusing environment

Whitney looked at her watch. Two more hours, she thought. Two more hours and she'd be confronted with her oldest fear and newest fear. She would face *him* again, then she'd start a race that would determine the fate of the world. There wasn't a word for fear in the English dictionary that could accurately describe the level of trepidation Whitney felt. She was about to undergo the most mentally, physically, and emotionally charged challenge of her life. And she knew she wasn't up to the task.

# CHAPTER 24

The elastic that held Whitney's blond hair in a tight ponytail did little to keep the humidity from making her head look like a kid had scribbled her hair in with a yellow crayon. Her striking features, dark skin and light-colored locks, combined with the survival gear and weapons strapped to her back, made her look like a modern Amazon warrior.

At least, Whitney thought, I've still got both breasts. She'd been terrorized as a child when her father related stories of Amazonian women lopping off their left breasts so that they could more easily shoot a bow and arrow. She'd been even more shocked after she saw her first archery contest. The women competing appeared to have either very small breasts or no breasts at all. Later in life she learned the truth: sports bras were constricting bastards.

She squirmed as her newly acquired, military-grade sports bra dug into the sensitive flesh beneath her breasts. She fought the urge to adjust the bra; if Cruz noticed a comment would be forthcoming. Not to mention that adjusting a bra should be a secondary concern when preparing to jump out of a helicopter.

The group hovered above a canopy of foliage that looked more like Madagascar than Antarctica. Whitney had been stunned since the coastline first came into view: green and blue where lakes had formed. It was hard to imagine all that growth had taken place in under two months, but here it was. What had been a frozen wasteland for thousands of years had become a tropical paradise ripe for the hotel industry to move into.

Standing beside her, dressed in the same olive green camouflage fatigues, were Cruz, Ferrell, and Wright. They looked confident, even excited. She took a deep breath. These people were professionals. They were the best. Killers. Heroes. She looked at them and saw qualities she'd never achieve.

Just as Whitney considered backing out, Cruz and Ferrell leapt from the copter's open door where two jump-lines descended into the forest. The lines attached to their harnesses snapped tight as they plummeted down through the canopy and disappeared. Twenty seconds later, Cruz's voice sounded clearly in her micro headset. "Cerberus to Phoenix. Over."

"I got you, Cerberus," Wright said. "How's our LZ? Over."

"A few branches on the way down," Cruz replied. "But the ground is clear. Over."

"Copy that. Stand back, you have incoming." Wright looked over at Whitney. Her apprehension must have been obvious. He put his hand on her shoulder and smiled. "Keep a loose grip on the line and the harness will do the rest."

Whitney gave a weak smile and nodded.

"Just don't let go." Wright smiled wide. "On three."

Whitney mouthed the numbers as Wright said them aloud. On three, both jumped over the edge and descended into the jungle.

She landed more softly than she imagined possible from the end of a rope slung out the side of a helicopter. Cruz helped her undo the harness. Once she and Wright were free, Wright signaled the copter and the ropes flew back up through the trees. They stood motionless for several minutes, waiting for the chop of the helicopter to fade completely.

The jungle was silent. Upon seeing the vast spread of vegetation, Whitney had automatically pictured the trees full of monkeys and the ground swarming with insects. It was an environment with which she was familiar, having shot pictures in most of the world's rainforests. But here, she couldn't see anything but tall, straight tree trunks leading up to large leaf-covered branches that spread out like the limbs of an umbrella. The ground had a slim covering of vegetation; little sunlight filtered in between the large leaves to promote floor growth.

"It's quiet," she commented.

"A little too quiet," Cruz said then laughed. "C'mon, that was funny." He took a step, and the jungle floor came to life beneath his foot. A serpent wrapped around his ankle and pulled him off the ground, yanking him upside down and ten feet off the ground.

"What the hell?" Cruz was more pissed off than frightened. Whitney noticed a nearby tree limb bouncing. A line ran from a branch, over the limb of another tree and down to Cruz's ankle.

Wright took out his blade and stepped toward Cruz, who struggled to keep his gear and weapons attached to his body.

"Don't move!" Whitney shouted. She recognized the trap and knew there were more. But it was too late. Both of Wright's ankles were snagged. His feet were pulled out from under him and he was dragged through the ground brush before being launched into the air. He bounced up and down next to Cruz.

Whitney looked at Ferrell with serious eyes. "Don't move." But she saw by the look in Ferrell's eyes that staying put was the last thing on her mind.

"Screw that," Ferrell said. "We're sitting ducks."

With a speed and agility Whitney had never witnessed, Ferrell had a grappling hook and rope in her hands, which she slung over the nearest tree. She pulled herself off the ground, swung to the tree, and began climbing it. Whitney could see her logic. Both ropes were looped over a branch at the top of the tree. Ferrell could cut both men down without stepping on the ground. What Ferrell didn't understand was the logic of the man who'd set the traps. A slight click froze the shuffle of Ferrell's boots on the tree.

"Oh, shi—"

A branch from the other side of the tree came free from its binding, swung around the tree, and slapped Ferrell from its side. She fell to the earth and a second trap was sprung. A homemade net, weighted down by rocks, fell from the canopy above, where it had been concealed by the large leaves.

Ferrell didn't bother to struggle. She grunted as she sat up beneath the net, her eyes displaying her rage. She looked at Whitney. "Okay, smartass. Who set the traps and why the hell do you know about them?"

Whitney didn't respond. A noise in the brush behind her caught her attention. Something short but large was headed toward her. Then it stopped.

Whitney hefted her XM-29 into the firing position Wright had shown her and waited for the danger to present itself.

"*Chica*!" Cruz whispered from above.

"I told you not to call me that," Whitney said, not moving her eyes from the brush.

"Whatever, man! Take the freakin' safety off!"

Whitney looked down at the weapon. The safety was on. As she moved her fingers to flip the switch, the creature charged from the bushes. Whitney saw a blur of black and brown fur as the large animal jumped up and tackled her to the ground.

She could have sworn she heard Cruz swearing in Spanish, but in the confusion of the moment it was impossible to tell. Besides, she was about to be eaten by some never-before-seen predator. But the searing pain of being eaten alive never came. A wet sensation coursed across her face and over her clenched eyes. Again and again, she was being licked.

She opened her eyes and saw a very happy face looking back at her. "*Vesuvius!*" She grabbed the dog's head and shook him around. He licked her and barked with excitement.

A rustle of foliage behind her took her attention away from the dog. She turned around and saw the man she knew so well but who looked very different than she remembered. His beard was long and scraggly. His clothes were enmeshed with a litter of leaves and twigs—a camouflage technique she'd learned to use herself, just like the traps, clustering them in a tight group to maximize effectiveness. He looked like a wild man, but his eyes betrayed him to be the same man she had loved for so long and who had left her so suddenly.

"M . . . Mira?"

Whitney pulled herself to her feet, fending off Vesuvius who still bounded around her in ecstasy. She let her weapons and gear fall to the ground.

"Hi, Dad."

RACE

 CHAPTER 25

As blade drew across skin, Ian Jacobson did his best not to flinch. He'd never been fond of shaving his own head, but in the field he had no choice. They'd arrived on the Antarctic coast the previous day, and the race to the continent's interior was due to start shortly, as soon as all the competitors were in place at their respective starting locations along the coast. The razor in his hand was dull compared to that of Jonus, his barber back in London, and his small pocket mirror distorted his image so much that he appeared to be shaving a cone head. He pulled the razor from front to back one last time and rinsed it off with water from his canteen. He'd never been fond of his hair. At a quarter-inch in length, it began to swirl moronically, taking away any sense of his being a lethal killer. Being a member of the British Special Forces required as much.

Of course, he wasn't a member of the British military anymore; they had merged with what was left of the other European nations to become the European Kingdom . . . only there wasn't much of a habitable kingdom left, making it imperative that his team be one of the first three to reach the goal.

His team consisted of nine other men—three French, two more Brits, two Spaniards, one German, and one Italian. The common language, thankfully, was English. Jacobson couldn't speak a lick of anything else.

Jacobson put the razor back in his backpack and closed it up. He leaned over, checked that his boots were tight, and picked up his weapon. He walked through the clearing, which had been created the day before by a destroyer off the coast. It had leveled the overgrown area with its cannons, providing a starting location for the team and the delegates from the other competing nations who were there to make sure everyone started on time.

He looked at his watch. Fifteen more hours of waiting. He hated waiting.

Jacobson approached the Chinese delegates—serious men dressed in business suits. They stood by a large rock in a field of green grass that ran all the way to the ocean, three hundred feet away. All three of them wore thick black glasses and striped ties. He figured the Chinese were going for a neutral look, but they really just looked bloody awkward. Jacobson stood before them wearing a smile that said he wasn't going to cause trouble. "Good day, gentleman. Do any of you speak English?"

One of the men nodded. "A little."

"Are all the teams at the starting positions?" Jacobson asked.

"Ah, no," the delegate replied. "The Americans have yet to arrive."

"Damn Yankees," Jacobson said. "We should have never let the colonies go. Then they might be punctual."

The delegate looked confused. "Forget it," Jacobson said. "Thank you for your help." Jacobson realized the man didn't speak English well enough to be pumped for information. He really didn't care that the Americans were late. He knew they would be. He knew what they were up to. In fact, he was counting on it. His team and the Americans had a rendezvous point about five hundred miles into the race. The plan was to reach the goal together, along with the Brazilian team, and hold out there against the Chinese and Soviets, the front runner communist nations, and against the Arab Alliance. Antarctica would be a democracy.

The Arab Alliance didn't pose as much of a threat. With only limited forces on the continent and self-destructive tactics, they'd kill themselves before doing in the rest of the teams. That, combined with the fact that no other team wanted them to win, sealed the AA's fate. Their part of the world had been in chaos since the dawn of time, and no one wanted to be their new neighbor.

As Jacobson walked back to his team's encampment, he looked out at the Antarctic jungle and imagined what the trek was going to be like. The vegetation that had grown up so quickly was unlike anything else on the planet. They had no idea what was edible or what was poisonous. Brushing up against the wrong leaf could mean serious infection or death. They'd all heard reports of small creatures being sighted at the camp's periphery. Life of all varieties was springing up around the continent. Going into the most inhospitable jungles on earth would have been safer, because they'd know what to expect, what to avoid, what to shoot. Here they were blind. The canopy blocked out all satellite imagery. The terrain had shifted when the ice melted, and the entire continent had risen twenty more feet above sea level. Where he now stood had only two months ago been underwater.

Jacobson paused and rubbed his hand across his smooth head. Even with the dull razor and plastic mirror, he'd done an acceptable job. There were only a few rough spots. He just hoped he'd survive this whole mess so that Jonus could finish the job right . . . that was, if Jonus was still alive. What a mess the world had become. Jacobson sighed, knowing the next few weeks would be even messier.

 CHAPTER 26

Dr. Merrill Clark absorbed everything he was told with mouth clenched shut, eyes wide open. Only the occasional headshake of disbelief gave evidence that he was still listening. Wright laid it all out for him minutes after Merrill had freed them from the traps and disarmed the others yet to be triggered. The world was in chaos, but ultimately, humanity had survived. What could have been an extinction event might still allow the human race to continue its dominance of the planet.

It was the most horrifying story he had ever heard, but even so it failed to capture his full attention. Merrill's thoughts were with his daughter Mirabelle, whom he hadn't seen in two years. She stood ten feet away, arms crossed, face set like stone. The distance he felt between them now was worse than when she had been on the other side of the planet. It broke his heart.

Wright finished his explanation of the race: "The first team to reach Antarctica's geographic center splits the continent with two other nations." Merrill felt Wright's eyes upon him, waiting for an acknowledgement of his statement. "Dr. Clark?"

"I'm not convinced," Merrill said, "that even with my help we will be able to find where you want to go. This is a large continent. Getting lost won't be difficult."

"We have maps," Wright said.

Merrill chuckled. "Antarctica has been coated under a crust of ice, a mile thick in some places, for the past 12,000 years. You don't have a map."

Wright produced some large photographs, satellite images of Antarctica from space. Merrill inspected the photos, feeling a wash of emotions as he saw that the entire continent had truly been transformed. The photos were spectacular, but they wouldn't keep them from getting lost. "All we can see from these are mountain ranges, some large lakes, and lots of green. These are no good."

"And what if you combined them with a map of the interior?" Wright asked.

"Like I said, unless it's a twelve-thousand-year-old map, it's useless."

Wright pulled a small cardboard tube from his pack, popped it open, and unrolled a large map. "We have one for everyone."

Merrill held his breath. "What . . . what is that?"

"You've heard of Piri Reis?" Wright asked.

"You have the complete Piri Reis map?" Merrill's eyes were wide, his jaw slack. "Let me see it! Give it here!"

Merrill snatched the map from Wright and inspected it. After a moment, he found the portion of the map he knew so intimately, where the southern coast of Africa came down to the coast of Antarctica. It matched. It was a complete map of Antarctica, interior and exterior, that dated back more than twelve thousand years. The original sources were said to have been created by a pre-Sumerian culture, the first culture that had developed language, writing, and, obviously, nautical expertise. Never in his life had he imagined holding the entire map in his hands . . . even if it was a copy. "I'll do whatever you want," Merrill said, "but I have a condition."

"Name it."

"I want to go for a walk with my daughter."

"I'm not sure that's a good idea." Wright glanced at Whitney. She was staring at the dirt, pursing her lips. "She seems . . . upset with you."

Merrill nodded. "Very much so. And it's for that reason we need to hash things out now. You certainly don't want us stopping to have a father-daughter spat in the middle of a race, do you?"

Wright rolled his neck, feeling the vertebrae pop one by one. "How much time do you want?"

"Two hours."

"Two—" Merrill's expression reflected his resolution. He wouldn't be going without this talk. "Two and that's it. If you're not back in that time, we'll leave you both here."

"Fair enough," Merrill said. He started to stand but paused. "Captain Wright, tell me: why didn't Sam come with Mirabelle?"

Wright looked puzzled. "Who?"

"Samuel Whitney. Mira's husband."

Wright's face reflected a moment of clarity which was quickly replaced by a glumness that told Merrill all he needed to know.

"Oh, no." Merrill felt as though he would vomit.

"She was widowed about a year ago, Dr. Clark. You didn't know?"

Tears welled up in Merrill's eyes so quickly there was nothing he could do to keep them from rolling down his cheeks. He stood and walked away, plunging himself into the shade of the jungle.

Ten minutes later Merrill was back at camp. The tears had slowed, but his face was wet with salty moisture. I'm a damn fool! Merrill thought. He'd left her alone. All this time, he'd been out searching for ancient relics, while the living, breathing person he cared about most in the world was suffering. He'd abandoned her to face the worst days of her life by herself. He knew what losing a spouse could do, how it could change a person. How it could destroy a person.

Merrill kicked a nearby crate. He looked up and saw the sky through several spaces where trees had failed to grow because of his equipment. "God, what have I done?"

"Dad?" The voice was distant. Mirabelle. "Dad, are you there?"

Merrill's voice cracked as he spoke. "Here."

Mirabelle entered the camp from the forest. She saw his tears and her own welled up. He reached her, embraced her, and held her closely, sobbing like a child. They both were. "I'm sorry, baby. I'm so sorry."

"He's gone, Dad. Sam is gone." Whitney let a year's worth of pent-up sorrow flow from her soul all at once. Her breath came in sudden spurts between sobs. "He was shot. We—we were out late . . . robbed . . ." Whitney was overcome by tears again.

Merrill pulled her closer. He had no idea what to say. He knew the pain of loss, yet couldn't conceive of how to comfort her. In ten years, he'd been unable to find comfort for himself. After holding her for five minutes, rubbing her back, rocking her gently, letting her tears soak into his shirt, he said the only thing he could think of to say. "I love you."

Merrill pulled back and looked his daughter in the eyes. His throat constricted. Her brown eyes, coffee-colored skin, and blond hair brought a flood of memories to his mind. She looked so much like her mother, with the exception of the blond hair. Aimee was from South Africa, an archeologist studying ancient African tribes. They'd met at a symposium and struck up a friendship that quickly blossomed into a romance. Whitney was born two years later. And here she was now, old enough to have married and lost a husband.

Smiling weakly, Mirabelle said, "I love you, too."

Merrill smiled wide and hugged her again. When he pulled away, he said, "I was worried that I would never see you again."

She wiped her nose. "So was I."

"I'm sorry," Merrill said with a sniff. He cleared his throat and spoke again. "Was it bad? The . . . event? What's left of Portsmouth?"

"Nothing. It's gone."

"Oh. How many survived?

"Just one, that I know of."

Merrill's eyes widened. "Oh—oh my. You're the only one?"

Mirabelle nodded. "Just like you."

"What do you mean?"

"You're the only survivor."

"In the region? McMurdo didn't make it?"

"On the continent," she said. "You're the only one left."

Merrill shook his head then seemed to arrive at an understanding. "He's watching out for us."

"I'm not in the mood to talk about God," Mira said.

Merrill wasn't surprised; at the moment, he wasn't in the mood to talk about God, either. Something else was on his mind. Something only his daughter would appreciate. Not those military stiffs. "Good," he said, catching her off guard. Merrill looked at his watch. "An hour and forty-five minutes left. Plenty of time, but we'll have to hurry."

Merrill took Mirabelle by the hand and led her to a path on the opposite side of the camp. It disappeared into the shadowy jungle.

"Where are we going?"

"I have something to show you. Something unbelievable."

# CHAPTER 27

General Zhou Kuan-Yin surveyed his troops. They were lined up in perfect formation. Two hundred soldiers had been put under his command for this most important of missions. Zhou had been honored when he was requested to lead the mission. Every soldier standing before him had been handpicked, including his second-in-command, Captain Zhou Lei. His son.

Lei walked the lines, inspecting the soldiers' uniforms, stature, and weapons. If anything was out of place, the soldier would be removed from the ranks and sent home in shame. But Zhou was under no illusions. The professionalism and perfect appearance of his troops would disintegrate as soon as they entered the jungle and began their trek toward Antarctica's center. The current show of perfection was to intimidate the competition. He saw the delegates from the other nations watching the spectacle with wide eyes. No doubt they had never seen such a display of discipline and would nervously report the situation back to their superiors. Intimidation worked wonders in battle.

And it was a battle. His men weren't armed to defend against trees. He knew the Americans and Europeans wouldn't want to share a border with the Chinese and would do all they could to stop them. No matter, Zhou thought, they cannot stop all of us. Thanks to some timely intel, he also knew the American ranks would be thinned by the Soviets long before they reached the goal . . . if they made it that far at all.

With the Soviets distracting the smaller competitors, China would stake its claim unchallenged. Communism would govern Antarctica. They would see to that. Communisim had sustained his country for so long and made the

Soviets a superpower. The world had seen what happened when a nation lost its communist roots: poverty and despair. For that reason, they hoped to share the continent with the Soviets. Not only did they share views on Communism, but being neighbors already would make the transition smooth. As for the third nation to share Antarctic soil, South Africa was the choice. Not only were they in a geographic location that was extremely beneficial—it would be a six hour flight from old South Africa to the new South African Antarctic—but they also wouldn't be able to defend against invasion, if the threat of it failed to influence them. It was a flawless plan.

Lei finished his inspection and found everything and everyone in readiness; Zhou felt a brimming pride. Not in his son's performance but in his troops. They too were flawless.

"General," Lei said as he approached, snapped his legs together, and saluted.

"Report," Zhou said.

"All men are accounted for and prepared to enter the jungle."

Zhou nodded. "Instruct them to hold their position until the race has started."

Lei paused. Zhou looked him in the eyes. "Captain?"

"Sir, forgive me," Lei said, "but it is ninety-six degrees and very humid. The troops are in full uniform and will become rapidly dehydrated. Sir, there are six hours left before the race begins."

Zhou's eyes burned with anger. Insolence from his own son could not be tolerated. He slapped the young man across the face. Lei was shaken but remained resolute. "Father—"

Zhou slapped Lei again, hard enough to draw blood. Zhou leaned in close and said with a growl, "Tell the men they will remain standing in formation until the race begins. Anyone caught so much as slouching will be shot on sight. By you. Do you understand me, Captain?"

Lei's lip quivered for a moment before he pulled himself together, straightened his legs, and gave a rigid salute. "Yes, sir!"

Lei turned to leave, spinning in a quick pivot.

"Captain," Zhou said, causing his son to pause. "If you call me 'father' again while in uniform, I will shoot you myself and send your corpse home to your mother."

Lei gave a slight nod.

"Go," Zhou said. Lei strode away, his stature perfect, legs rigid, arms taut.

The boy was still young, confused. Zhou knew he'd make an excellent leader some day, but his priorities had to be clarified. With the world in chaos, there was no time to pursue the trite longings of youth. Lei wanted to be a photographer, of all things, not a soldier. He chased after girls and wrote them poems. His head was in the clouds. On this mission, Lei would be taught the importance of respecting and serving his country. He would learn that drawing the blood of China's enemies was an art in itself, and the sounds of death were poetry so beautiful it could only be expressed once in a lifetime. His curious will would be broken and he would carry China into the future.

And if Lei didn't measure up, Zhou would leave him behind. He had no use for cowards. They were on the brink of installing a new world order where chaos and immorality would be wiped away, replaced by order and discipline. After Antarctica was secured, built up and populated under a communist banner, stability and prosperity would return to the world...and a new super power would shape it.

 CHAPTER 28

Whitney saw her father glance down at her 9mm which was holstered on her hip. He had never liked weapons and was staunchly opposed to war and killing. He even opposed the death penalty. He used to say, "We're all sinners, Mira. We all deserve a chance at forgiveness. Murder in response to murder is still murder. A man strapped to an electric chair poses no threat. A murderer locked in a jail cell is no danger to society."

She would argue that society shouldn't have to pay for the food murderers ate, or even the water they used flushing the toilet. If they were dead, society as a whole could forget them and move on. This argument never worked with Merrill; she always got a response akin to, "Killing someone to take money or save money . . . both are murder. It is not our place to judge whose life is forfeit and whose is not. It is not our place to condemn a soul to hell. A murderer can still find salvation, Mira."

She wondered if he'd say the same thing now, knowing Sam had been murdered over a watch. His killer, a twenty-year-old kid, got life in prison. It was a sentence he didn't deserve. How could someone who so quickly took a life be left alive, even if his remaining life was spent rotting in a jail cell?

"Nice gun," her father said.

Whitney tripped over a root. She wasn't expecting a comment like that. It didn't even sound sarcastic.

"Did the military give you that?" Merrill asked as he pushed some brush to the side, leading Whitney down a long, dark path through the woods. "Be careful up ahead. There are traps on either side of the path."

"The gun is mine," Whitney said.

"Can you shoot it?"

"I can hit a Coke can from fifty yards . . . standing still."

"Good enough," Merrill said.

Whitney was confused. The anti-Charlton Heston gun control promoter was glad she had a gun?

Merrill climbed a large rock that led up an incline. "Did the military give you a weapon?" He turned and offered his hand to Whitney.

Whitney took her father's hand and was pulled to the top of a moss-covered rise that led to a new path. "It's an XM-29 assault rifle. It's got to be the scariest weapon I've ever seen. Dual barrel: an assault rifle combined with a secondary weapon that has smart, explosive rounds."

"You can shoot that?" Merrill looked surprised.

"Not yet," Whitney said. "And I hope I don't have to."

"Don't get your hopes up," Merrill said.

"Dad . . ." Whitney's voice stopped Merrill in his tracks. "What's going on? You hate guns."

Merrill rubbed a bandana across his forehead. "Still do," he said. "But I recognize their worth in certain situations."

"How is this different?"

"To start with: your gun. I understand why you have it. I imagine you take it everywhere. God knows if your mother had been killed by human hands, I probably would have changed my opinion on capital punishment." Merrill took a deep breath and let it out slowly. The heat and humidity took their toll on him. While he was used to trekking this route every day, he wasn't accustomed to holding a conversation at the same time. Vesuvius wasn't much of a conversationalist.

Merrill's eyes widened. "Where's Vesuvius?"

"I left him with Wright. They were hitting it off."

"We should have brought him," Merrill said.

Whitney could that see her father was truly nervous. Vesuvius had been all he had for years. Losing the dog would be like losing a family member. "He'll be fine," she said.

"I'm not worried about him," Merrill said. "Vesuvius has become quite good at warning of danger."

"Danger?" Whitney said. "There is no one around for hundreds of miles. The race doesn't start for another six hours."

"Mira, I set the traps long before I knew about the state of the world and this foolish race."

Whitney held her breath. That hadn't occurred to her. She'd assumed they were for trapping food, but there were more than a few, and they had been designed to lift heavy weights. "What have you seen?"

"Nothing. Not yet," Merrill said. "But I can sense it. The hair on my arms rises. My blood pulses behind my ears. It's like a primal sense warning me of danger. Vesuvius usually picks up on it at the same time. I don't know what's out there," Merrill said, looking into the jungle depths, "but I know it's been watching me."

Whitney scanned the area. Her father had never been prone to fits of imagination, aside from his belief in God and ancient mythology. He was cut and dried, black and white. But she had no idea what he'd been through on Antarctica, alone for so long. "Do you have any idea what it could be?"

"Follow me," Merrill said as he hurried down the path. "We're not far now."

Ten minutes of rushing through the jungle brought them to a large tree that blocked the view beyond. Merrill turned to Whitney. "Beyond this tree are things I have searched my whole life to find . . . and now I wish I hadn't. If what I fear is true, then I'll want one of your XM-29s as well."

Whitney couldn't help but smile. Her father was always dramatic before unveiling a find. "Good, because I'm tired of carrying yours."

Merrill was shaken from his dramatic presentation. "They're giving me a gun?"

Whitney nodded. "But it's meant for shooting people."

"People are the least of our worries," Merrill said and stepped around the tree.

Whitney followed and gasped as the jungle gave way to a massive wall. The structure had been created from gigantic, intricately cut stones. It was unbelievable craftsmanship. Whitney quickly shed her backpack, unzipped it, and took out her camera. The lens was attached in seconds and she was snapping pictures from a variety of angles and zooms. She lost track of her father and didn't notice him waiting thirty feet to her right and closer to the wall. It wasn't until she saw him in the frame, waving her over, that she realized he wasn't interested in the wall at all. He was standing over an excavated area, just below the wall.

She was there in seconds. When the excavation came into view, Whitney gasped and came up short. The bones of a man, a very large man, were intertwined with those of . . . a *dinosaur*. The creature's jaws were locked over the top of the man's head. His neck looked broken. And in the man's hand was a long blade that still looked polished, buried in the chest cavity of the dinosaur. They had died in battle, killing each other simultaneously. A dinosaur and a man. Whitney's eyes wandered back to the dinosaur's head and she recognized the boney, ornate crest above the creature's eyes. "*Crylophosaurus.*"

"Very good!" Merrill said. "This man isn't as large as the other specimen—"

"He's got to be ten feet tall!"

"Ten feet, three inches." Merrill pointed to a distant excavation. "You should have seen the one I pulled out of there."

Whitney then noticed there were test holes approximately every ten feet and full excavations at about a third of them. Her father had been busy.

"Fourteen feet, five inches," Merrill said proudly.

"Impossible."

"The crust of the earth shifted forty degrees, killing 2.5 billion people, thawing Antarctica, which has become a tropical rain forest the size of the United States, and you're telling me a fourteen-foot-tall man is impossible?"

Whitney saw his point. Everything that had happened during the past two months was impossible. "A race of giants, then?"

"Indeed."

"Any idea who they are?"

"Nothing substantiated, but I have a few ideas."

"You'll explain them to me?"

Whitney could see that her father understood her invitation was more about rekindling their relationship than an interest in ancient giants. "Of course," he said.

Whitney looked back at the horrific scene of violence and death frozen in time. "And this is what you're afraid of? Giants?"

"Not the giants. They may be big, but they're still human. They wouldn't have survived the freeze-dried conditions. Obviously, the rest of the continent had been designed to survive cycles of freezing and thawing, but these people were most likely not indigenous. Crylo, however, was designed to utilize the process of anhydrobiosis—to survive the drying, freezing, and thawing."

"Designed or evolved?"

"It doesn't matter which you believe," Merrill said. "All that matters is that, like the rest of this continent's ancient denizens, *Crylophosaurus* has returned."

Whitney couldn't help but raise a doubtful eyebrow. "What makes you so sure?"

Merrill pointed to the side of the dig. A trail of footprints had been pressed into the dirt excavated around the two bodies. "That appeared the day after I dug this up."

Whitney bent down and inspected the three-toed impression. In addition to the three clawed digits, a fourth was at the back. It dug in deep. She turned her camera on the footprint and excavation and began shooting pictures. "This is amazing, Dad. Really."

The clicking of photo snapping was all Whitney could hear. Her father, however, seemed to have better ears. He took hold of her arm and squeezed. She paused to look at him and noticed his eyes locked on the jungle.

"What is it?"

Merrill bent down to the excavation and pried the dead giant's fingers away from the prehistoric blade. "Get your gun ready," he said. "Something's coming."

CHAPTER 29

These dogs were afraid of him; Ahmed al-Aziz could see it in the eyes of the delegates. And not just the Americans. The Chinese, Europeans, Soviets, Brazilians, and the rest. All were afraid of him. They stood only thirty feet away, glancing in his direction but quickly looking away when he met their eyes. Perhaps they knew Allah was on his side. They'd experienced God's wrath firsthand, and now they knew the truth. God loved the Middle East.

The Americans had been frozen, suffering millions of deaths and losing the majority of their land. A fate they deserved. The Soviets had burned for their transgressions against Allah's land. The Europeans and their craving for all things American had been equally decimated. All this occurred while the Middle East had been moved to a prime location. The desolate sands were quickly becoming lush, fertile land, and Allah's people were thriving.

It was true that the Israelis had benefited as well, but they were too busy to compete in the race. A jihad had been declared by the new Arab Alliance. Israel still held a technological advantage, but with sheer numbers and countless martyrs the Arab Alliance would soon reclaim the land that rightfully belonged to Allah's people.

Yes, Allah had blessed the Middle East and cursed the infidels. And He would continue to pour out his blessings with a victory in this race. It did not matter who shared the continent with them. Jihad would be proclaimed and the infidels would be erased from the new land Allah had given them.

Al-Aziz moved his cold stare from the delegates to the thirteen pairs of men—fellow servants of Allah and soldiers of the Arab Alliance—waiting rather impatiently for the race to start. They had gone with the strategy they knew best and with which they had the most experience: while a core group of twnety men ran for the goal, fifteen cells of two, each with enough explosives to wipe out the other teams entirely had missions of their own. One at a time they would destroy themselves, securing their reward in the next life and keeping every other team from reaching the goal. Ideally, the AA would be the sole winner. With only one winner, the other nations involved would fight over the other two spots, giving the AA time to set up defenses around the entire continent and eventually claim all of Antarctica for Allah.

Al-Aziz let his hands linger by his waist. He reached inside his black vest and felt the squares of C4 strapped to his body. The same explosives were strapped to both men in every cell. The explosives weren't armed currently and wouldn't be until minutes before they were needed. They also carried RPGs, mortars, and AK-47s. They would tear into the enemy with everything in their arsenal, and when the enemy was off-balance and confused, they would run through the ranks and become Allah's martyrs.

"Ahmed," a voice called. It was Abdul, his partner. He walked closer and whispered into his ear. "Why don't we kill these infidels now and get started? Just one of us could disintegrate them into dust. Let the birds pick at their bones."

Al-Aziz knew Abdul's hatred for the outside world ran deep. His family had been killed by a bomb meant for Saddam Hussein. Al-Aziz had no love for that dictator, either, but Hussein wouldn't have taken his entire family in one shot. It was a crime Abdul had been eager to avenge for many years. But it made him reckless. His eagerness to kill made him less effective.

"No," Al-Aziz said. "Would you have us kill the serpent or these worms?" He looked Abdul in the eyes. "They are nothing. If the other nations hear we have killed their people and left early, they will send teams just to stop us. And that is a delay we cannot have. We must abide by this one rule so that we can best do Allah's work."

Abdul considered this, searching his thoughts for an opinion. His eyes landed on the delegates. The Chinese were stoic. The Brazilians chatted loudly. And the Americans pretended to act casual, but any fool could see the vigilance in their eyes. One of the Americans caught Abdul's eyes . . . and smiled!

"*No!*" Abdul whispered with vehemence. "They are all infidels and jihad has been proclaimed on them all. To let them leave alive is to sin against God. They must die."

Al-Aziz sighed. Abdul, of course, was right. But it would not be easy, and it had to be done right. He took Abdul by the shoulders. "We will wait until the race has begun. Let them contact their superiors and report our timely start. When they believe we have left, you and you alone will return to finish them. I will carry the weight of our mission alone."

Abdul grinned. "Thank you, Ahmed. I will be waiting for you with virgins to spare."

Al-Aziz smiled. "And I will join you soon enough. Now tell the others so that no one else returns." It was uncommon for cells to communicate, but proximity and the importance of this mission allowed for a break in protocol. He was sure that others like Abdul had entertained the idea of returning, and he couldn't risk more than one cell, his cell, being handicapped.

Running the race alone was of no concern to al-Aziz. Allah would bless his efforts. "Allah be praised," al-Aziz whispered. "I will not fail You. Fill me with the spirit of your servant Mohammed, may your blessings and grace be upon him, so that I might slaughter the dogs and fulfill your will."

 CHAPTER 30

Brandishing the curved blade like an ancient warrior, one feature of Merrill's stance revealed that he'd never faced violent conflict—he was shaking. Whitney had never seen her father so afraid. The print in the mud looked so real, but she found it hard to believe that it had been created by a living, breathing dinosaur.

Eyes on the jungle, Whitney unclipped her 9mm and slowly brought it up, listening intently for any sign of approach. Somehow her father had been able to hear, even sense, the approach of something through the jungle. She had still seen no evidence of an intruder. "Dad," she said. "I don't see anything."

He shushed her and took a step forward, his ear cocked toward the foliage. "I've become accustomed to the sounds this jungle makes," Merrill said. "I'm telling you: something is out there."

Then Whitney heard something, like the rubbing of sandpaper on wood. It seemed to come from a distance, but if her father was right, taking chances was not an option. "What should we do?"

Merrill shrugged. "I usually wait it out with Vesuvius. I think whatever is out there doesn't know what to make of him. The original denizens of this continent have seen humans before." Merrill glanced at the excavation, eyeing the giant man and dinosaur, entwined in death. "We are not strangers here, but Vesuvius is like nothing that has ever lived here."

"And now that Vesuvius isn't with you . . .?"

"I don't know."

Whitney searched the area for hope of escape and found none. Their backs were against the twenty-five-foot wall. The jungles stretched for hundreds of yards in either direction before enveloping the wall. They were trapped.

The coarse rubbing sound filled the air again. Closer.

"We should make a run for it," Whitney said. If they left now, before it got any closer, they might make it back to the others.

Merrill shook his head. "Too many traps."

"We'll follow the path."

"We can't."

"Why not?"

Merrill pointed to the area of jungle where the path entered the clearing. A grove of ferns shook. "We have company."

Whitney caught sight of something in the ferns. Glossy deep green skin sporting a red stripe briefly rose and fell over the ferns. Whitney's breath became short and fast. Her heart hammered away, trying to break through her chest. "Shit."

Merrill glanced at her.

"Sorry," she said, finding it almost humorous that her father was still concerned with her language when they were about to be eaten. She noticed his expression darken.

"This is unacceptable," Merrill said.

Whitney couldn't hide her sarcasm. "Really," she said. "Being eaten alive isn't how you pictured our reunion?"

"I wasn't talking to you."

Whitney feared that her father had become schizophrenic during his days alone in the jungle. Then she remembered he was prone to talking out loud to God. She glanced at him and saw his lips moving. He was praying. "I don't think that's going to help," she said.

"Have a better idea?" Merrill said. Small saplings at the border of the clearing some twenty feet down from the path swayed open for a moment; further down, the foliage quivered. There was more than one. They were being surrounded.

Whitney took Merrill's sword and felt its considerable weight in her hands. She couldn't picture her father even getting a swing in with the thing. In the giant's hand it appeared small, but in her own it was massive, like a curved broad sword—it could be swung but was unwieldy. "Hey, what are you—"

Whitney thrust her 9mm into Merrill's hands. "Shoot anything that comes out of the jungle. I do have a better idea." She slung off her backpack, pulled out a bundle of rope, and quickly tied one end to the sword. She stood, holding the sword in her hand. "Stand back."

The sword flew up through the air and arced over the top of the wall. Whitney saw the rope land across the eroded seam in the rock for which she had been aiming. When the clang of sword on rock rang out, she pulled on the line until it snapped tight. She put her weight on the rope and it held.

Taking the 9mm from her father, Whitney said, "You first."

Merrill opened his mouth, but Whitney cut him off. "We don't have time to argue, Dad, now move your ass!"

Merrill took hold of the rope and pulled himself up, hand over hand, using the wall to brace his feet. He was moving, but not quickly. Whitney trained her gun on the moving section of ferns. She'd been terrified of the XM-29 when Wright had first shown it to her, but she longed for it now. She would be lucky to take down even one of the crylos with the limited number of rounds in her 9mm; if that was in fact what they were up against.

Whitney noticed brush shaking and heard sandpaper scratches all around the clearing now. There was no escape. She looked up. Merrill neared the top.

A clatter arose from the jungle like a flock of giant birds, calling, squeaking in waves of sound. The brush shook violently. Whitney knew her only chance was to reach the top of the wall. Without firing she holstered her gun and lunged up the rope. As she climbed, she heard an explosion of vegetation—breaking branches, shredding leaves, and bending tree trunks.

They were charging.

Seconds later she heard shrieks that could only be interpreted as surprise. The *whoosh* of tree limbs through the air told her several of her father's traps had been sprung. Whitney reached the top in fifteen seconds. She'd always been the first up the rope in gym class. Teachers had always told her math could save her life; she now knew that phys. ed. was the lifesaver.

Whitney shouted as something from the top of the wall gripped her arm. She looked up and saw her father, scraggly-bearded and dirty, looking like some pro wrestler and straining to pull her up. She rolled on top of the wall and for a moment felt safe. After taking three deep drags of air, she looked to the side and noticed that the rope on which she lay was still taut. It had weight on it.

Whitney drew her weapon and shouted, "Cover your ears!" She fired three shots in rapid succession until the rope snapped. A thud and shriek arose from below.

"Good thinking," Merrill said as he pulled up the rope from the other side and retrieved the sword. He held it and surveyed the top of the wall warily. "Now what?"

Whitney listened. She heard the scratching of claw on stone as the creatures below strained to climb. She could hear the sandpaper scratches and the screech of primal communication. Above all that was a sound that gave her hope: the chopping of an approaching helicopter.

Whitney searched the sky. A helicopter flew across the sky in the distance, but the team wasn't coming for them. They didn't know where they were. Whitney remembered her headset. She positioned it over her head and turned it on. "Wright, this is Mirabelle, do you copy?"

"Whitney, where the hell are you?" Wright sounded angry. "The race starts in four hours!"

"We're under attack," Whitney said.

"Where are you?" Wright replied.

Whitney took the sword from her father and held it up, letting the bright sun glint off its surface. "Look out your left side window."

Whitney saw the helicopter bank left and head straight for them. "Are you still under fire? Should we come in hot?"

Whitney listened and heard only the sound of the helicopter. The creatures had fled, most likely frightened by the unusual sound from above. "Negative," Whitney said. "They're gone."

"Who was it?" Wright asked. "Did you see their uniforms?"

Whitney couldn't help but chuckle nervously. "You wouldn't believe me if I told you."

A minute later, father and daughter were lifted into the air, secured by harnesses and pulled up by a winch. Whitney was surprised to see Wright, Cruz, Ferrell, and Vesuvius already on board and ready to go. The pilot gave them time to strap in and then they were off, cruising low over the canopy, toward the starting line and the beginning of the most daunting challenge any one of them had ever faced.

# CHAPTER 31

The jungle closed in on Duscha Popova in a way she had not anticipated but could easily handle. She'd worked in jungles before, but the dim light filtering through the leaves still bothered her. She preferred darkness. What made this experience different from the rest was its complete unfamiliarity. The trees, the terrain, even the air smelled different, bitter.

Stepping over a large rock, Popova felt her foot sink into the mud. She lifted her foot and cursed. Her clean boots were soiled. She knew it wouldn't be long before she was covered in dirt but preferred keeping herself clean as long as possible. It helped her move more quickly. Popova lingered above the muddy depression and saw gobs of rotten vegetation mixed in with the earth. It occurred to her that the smell in the air was caused by rapid decomposition. Whatever had been frozen in the mud for so long was now being steeped in humidity.

Popova continued, slashing at ground growth and hanging vines with her machete. Travel was slow, but she was alone and had a day's head start. Technically, she had nothing to do with this race. If she was killed or captured, the Soviets would deny any knowledge of her presence; such a claim would hold up because she wasn't part of any military. Her mission was simple: get ahead of the other teams and kill them one by one. Destroy morale. Impede by injury. Wipe them out. The official Russian team was composed of ten military men, all good and worthy combatants, but none could match Popova's brutal aptitude for killing.

Only the American, Katherine Ferrell, posed a threat. Both had been trained by the same man. Assassins by trade for the highest bidder, both were now loyal servants of their homelands. Assassins turned patriots. That was why the Americans were her first target and chief among them, Ferrell. With her out of the picture, Popova could function without fear of reprisal.

She'd been trudging through the jungle for ten hours and had covered perhaps twenty miles. It would be another forty before she reached the American team, and she would not rest until then. The Americans would be tired from their first day of travel and wouldn't expect an attack so soon into the race. Surprise was on her side.

Popova came to a sudden stop upon smelling the air again. The smell of decomposition was still tangy in her nose, but it had changed. She realized with some consternation that she smelled rotting flesh. Popova held her machete at the ready in her left hand and drew her side arm with the right.

She smelled the air again.

The gentle breeze tickled the blond hairs on her neck. The smell came from straight ahead. The twang of metal on wood sounded as Popova hacked through the wall of saplings blocking her path. As they fell to the ground, she took aim at the large forms standing before her and fired. She hit the foremost body with two slugs. Both ricocheted off the massive form that had little to fear from bullets.

"Damn it," she muttered. It wasn't like her to get spooked, and certainly not to shoot statues. A waste of ammunition.

As Popova approached the nearest statue, she found herself in a small clearing that was encircled with similar creations. Each had been fashioned from single stones and reminded her vaguely of the ancient busts discovered on Easter Island. But these were more than busts; they were full bodies from head to toe, standing like warriors frozen in time, forgotten in the jungle. Then she took note of their weapons—swords, spears, axes, and giant hammers. They were like gods and stood just as tall, perhaps twenty feet.

She was curious how the tall sculptures had survived the thawing of Antarctica as the ice and snow from across the continent slid into the ocean. She knelt down at the feet of the nearest stature and saw that the base was buried in the ground. How far the base descended she would never know, but for the statues to remain standing so straight after thousands of years, she imagined their roots descended as far down as the statues stood tall.

As interesting as the sight was, she had little time to waste in admiration of a long-dead civilization's artistry. She started to pass through the circle when she noticed the eyes of the statues watching her. She spun around and found twelve pairs of gigantic eyes staring down at her.

No. Not at her. At where she stood, in the middle of the clearing. It was odd, she thought, that no plants grew in the clearing. Taking note of the earth beneath her feet, she noticed that the land inside the clearing was lumpy, unlike the rest of the smooth jungle floor. It was as though the thin layer of topsoil covered a field of stones.

Unable to resist, she knelt, dug into the dirt with her finger, and pulled up on one of the rocks. The stone came loose and lifted free of the earth . . . only it wasn't a stone at all. It was a skull, minus the mandible. The size of a large dog's head, the skull was not large, but it was imposing. The face was narrow, and the empty eye sockets cast a sinister gaze. The crest on the top of the skull, an unnatural protrusion, gave it the look of something alien. It wasn't until she saw the top jaw lined with sharp, serrated teeth that she realized she held a dinosaur skull.

She looked around the circular clearing again and at the statues surrounding it, guarding it. She realized it was some kind of sacrificial area, perhaps once a pit. But it was obviously man-made. How could they have been sacrificing dinosaurs? Popova looked at the skull and, perhaps through some long-dormant maternal instinct, realized that these weren't small, full-grown dinosaurs. They were babies, killed by human hands. When Antarctica was claimed, she would tell her superiors about this place. The implications were infinitely interesting, even to an assassin.

Popova dropped the skull and smiled up at the nearest gargantuan icon. She had a newfound respect for their builders. They were hunters, like her. With sword and spear they hunted and killed dinosaurs, predators the likes of which modern man had no equal. As she moved out of the clearing and into the jungle, she made a promise to the stone giants behind her.

"The hunt begins again. I will make you proud."

 CHAPTER 32

"I will not leave it behind!" Merrill shouted. "Leaving the other finds at my camp was bad enough. This sword is priceless and of extreme historic importance."

After they had reached the starting line with a half hour to spare, Wright had confronted Merrill about the sword. "It's too heavy, Dr. Clark. You'll slow us down."

"Then leave me behind."

"Not an option."

"You can't make me go," Merrill said, trying to sound like Wright's elder but as the words left his lips, he knew he sounded more like an emotional fourteen-year-old kid. He had tried explaining the significance of the sword, what it could teach them about the people who made it. But the man didn't care.

Wright drew his side arm and leveled it at Merrill's head. "Leave the sword with the delegates. They will make sure it's kept safe."

Merrill was stunned. He'd never had a gun pointed at him before. He didn't think Wright would use it, but the sensation of staring down a barrel was unnerving. "I will not let this sword out of my sight!" Merrill held his ground.

It was then that he saw a figure moving in his periphery. It was coming quick. He assumed it was Ferrell or Cruz coming to tackle him and physically remove the sword. But he never took his eyes off the gun. And Wright never looked away from Merrill's eyes. His aim never wavered. He never saw Mirabelle coming.

She took to the air, performing some kind of flying kick. Merrill assumed she must have taken some kind of karate class along with shooting lessons. The kick wasn't graceful, but it had the desired effect. Wright was knocked to the side but turned the fall into a roll and readjusted his aim toward Mirabelle.

She drew her weapon just as quickly and the two held their side arms pointed at each other's skulls. Merrill fully expected Wright to take charge, but it was his daughter who made the demands.

"You ever so much as point that thing at my father again and I'll kill you."

Merrill wasn't sure if the anger was an act or not, but he was convinced. Apparently, so was Wright. He lowered his weapon. "Fair enough."

Wright stood and dusted himself off. She did not lower her weapon.

Wright smiled. "I wouldn't have shot him."

Mira didn't move.

"I never took the safety off."

The gun remained leveled.

Merrill could only imagine what Sam's death had done to Mira. Repressed feelings toward his killer could be surfacing. Wright could be in real danger and not even realize it. Merrill stepped forward and placed his hand over Mirabelle's gun. "Honey, put the gun away."

She lowered the 9mm, holstered it, and gave Wright another sour look. "Never again."

He nodded.

Cruz hustled over, his gear packed up on his back. His eyes were wide with anticipation. "Ten minutes, *niños*; pack up and get ready to pound dirt."

Wright snapped his head toward Merrill. "Leave it or you're not coming."

"You need me," Merrill said.

"Whitney can do your job."

Merrill would be damned before letting them take Mira away from him. He looked at the priceless sword. He pictured the giants who had formed its blade and crafted its hilt. The Stone Age hadn't ended until around 6000 BC, when bronze tools began to appear. But this weapon predated the Bronze Age by at least six thousand years and wasn't bronze at all. Merrill wasn't sure what metal it was, but it was one of a kind. A relic of some advanced civilization.

Merrill looked up and saw Mirabelle sling her equipment onto her back. And in her, he saw all that remained of Aimee, her mother. Merrill looked at the sword again.

I'm insane, he thought, and tossed the sword aside. It clanked loudly against a stone. Merrill flinched. It sounded like it broke. Spinning around, Merrill found that indeed the large blade had become separated from the hilt. But something, some strand of metal, still connected the two. Even Wright became interested as Merrill bent down and picked up the sword. A smooth sound of metal on metal slid through the air as Merrill drew a second sword, perhaps a dagger to the giants, from the original blade. Merrill understood at once. The massive sword was both a weapon and a scabbard. An enemy could be run through and the dagger detached and withdrawn without removing the sword. It was an amazing piece of work.

Merrill inspected the newly freed blade. A design like ancient text had been etched into the blade, which was two feet long and slightly curved. "Have you even seen anything like this?" Merrill said, holding the blade up to Wright.

Wright shook his head. "It's impressive . . . but you still can't bring it."

"The hell I can't." Merrill said, as he snatched his machete from its sheath on his belt and replaced it with the dagger.

Wright sighed. "We need to be at the wood line in five minutes, Dr. Clark. Let me help you get that backpack on."

Merrill smiled. "Thank you."

"Don't mention it," Wright said. "Just protect me from your daughter. She's a firecracker."

Merrill's smile stretched even wider. "You have no idea."

 # CHAPTER 33

Watching from the tree line where he, Abdul, and the twelve other cells had entered the jungle at the start of the race, al-Aziz prayed to Allah that Abdul would find success. The delegates were still standing in the clearing, now just five minutes after the race had begun. Most of the delegates were communicating with their superiors, letting them know that the Arab Alliance had started the race on time and without incident.

The dogs had no idea what Allah had prepared for them. Even now, Abdul was working his way around the clearing toward the coastline where he would sneak up on them from behind. Long before their transports arrived to take them home, they would be just so much blood and guts spread out across the landscape. Abdul would see to that.

Since he was a child, al-Aziz had known that Allah had plans for his life, that he would be used as an instrument of Allah's will on earth. Abdul had discovered his path to martyrdom. Al-Aziz knew his own path would soon reveal itself.

He edged closer to the jungle and raised his binoculars to his eyes. He could see the delegates clearly. The only ones not preoccupied were the Americans: three men, all standing still, arms crossed. Al-Aziz hadn't seen them move once. Only their heads turned, from side to side.

Al-Aziz lowered his binoculars quickly as one of the men looked his way. They were watching! The dogs did not trust them! Typical Americans. Lack of trust was just one of the evil attributes that culture had produced. Lust, greed, envy, lies, deceit, murder, and chaos were all at home in America. Al-Aziz had been taught that order could only be found through culling the chaos, through *jihad*. A holy war against the evil in the world. That was what America represented. Evil.

He hadn't always believed such things. His father had been a peace-loving carpenter and a good Muslim. But during the Americans' "Desert Storm," he'd been shot and killed. "Wrong place at the wrong time," one of the soldiers had told him. It was the closest thing to an apology al-Aziz ever received. He'd been only ten years old at the time and might have taken his father's death as an honest accident. But his mother, indignant and repulsed by the incident, had fled from Iraq to Pakistan, where she began her children's education in the ways of jihad.

He'd resisted the training for years, watching as men were shot, hung, beheaded, and disemboweled before his eyes. But even as he resisted their ideals, he excelled at weapons and explosives training. At times he was little more than a captive among his own people. Those who didn't fully embrace the cause only left the community through death. But as time passed, the killings and teachings that were so different from his father's peaceful ways offended him less and less.

It wasn't until the Americans returned with their "Operation Iraqi Freedom" that he began to see them as the destroyers he'd been taught they were. Iraq was once again inundated with foreign troops and the blood of his people, innocent Iraqis like his father, was again spilled. Still he clung to his father's teachings of love and peace.

The day his mother had walked up to an American roadblock and detonated the bomb strapped to her chest, taking the lives of five soldiers along with her own, al-Aziz truly recognized the glory of jihad. In that moment, his mother ceased to be a living being, but through her act of martyrdom became immortalized in history as a most dedicated servant of Allah—one who would give his or her life. His father's teachings died with his mother and al-Aziz took her place in Ansar al-Sunna, a militant organization dedicated to reclaiming Iraq for Islam. But Allah had other things in mind. The global catastrophe struck six months later, and the Arab world united. Al-Aziz, his closest friend Abdul, and six of his other Ansar al-Sunna brothers volunteered for the Antarctic mission as soon as it was announced.

And now they were here. Ready to serve the will of Allah. He smiled. His mother would be proud.

Al-Aziz whispered a prayer to Allah that Abdul would go undetected, that he would carry his holy mission to fruition. He looked through his binoculars, out into the clearing again, and found that all three Americans had turned away.

He spotted Abdul running, crouched low, behind a large stone that kept him hidden from the delegates. He was very close. Within fifty yards. The distance could be covered in seconds as long as no one saw him.

Al-Aziz saw Abdul taking quick peeks around the stone. He was waiting patiently for the right time to strike. Allah loved a patient man, because impatient men often failed. Al-Aziz saw the Americans turn away. He searched the rest of the delegates. No one looked in Abdul's direction.

Abdul crept from his position and made a mad dash toward the delegates. At the last moment, he would shout praises to Allah and detonate the bomb strapped to his body, taking himself to heaven and sending the rest to hell. Abdul was ten steps into his charge when a violent splash of red erupted from his chest.

Al-Aziz gasped. He'd been shot!

Al-Aziz frantically searched the area. A muzzle flash spat from the jungle not far from where Abdul had exited. The second shot tore through Abdul's right leg. He began to fall, but even in death he did not forget his obligation. He raised his hand toward the sky, thumb on the detonator. He might not kill them all, but at this range many of the delegates would still die.

Binoculars in position, al-Aziz waited for Abdul's thumb to depress the trigger and finish his martyrdom. Just as al-Aziz thought the moment had come, a third flash from the jungle was followed by an explosion of red from Abdul's wrist. The button would not be pushed. Abdul had failed.

For a moment, al-Aziz contemplated making a noble charge himself but realized someone had planted a sniper in the jungle. He would make it no further than Abdul had.

No, al-Aziz thought. Allah has a better path for me.

He turned away from the clearing and tore into the jungle. The race had begun.

# CHAPTER 34

The monotonous sound of metal blades slicing through vegetation filled the jungle. Lined up in formation, fifteen men wide, the Chinese soldiers hacked their way through the jungle, clearing a path wide enough for a future freeway. Creating a wide path was hard work, but a single-file line was not an option. What good was a force of two hundred if they couldn't see or support each other?

That was General Zhou's theory. Tight formation and efficient work would get them safely to the finish line first. Every ten minutes, the fifteen men in front would step to the side and rest, taking up the rear after the other 185 men passed. The next fifteen in line would begin hacking, and the line would continue moving steadily forward without exhausting the men or slowing.

Of course, the men also knew that if they should quit or fall from exhaustion, they'd be shot. Zhou didn't think he was a cruel man; he felt enormous pride in his men and how well they represented the strength of their homeland. He kept them well hydrated after entering the jungle and the breaks provided after ten minutes' cutting ensured that every man got to rest.

Zhou was confident he wouldn't have to shoot anyone.

The men proved him wrong.

Zhou had positioned himself at the center of the large force. He knew that if he were to fall in battle, disorder would consume the men. Lei would be in charge if Zhou was lost, and he wasn't entirely confident the boy could handle a force this size on his own. Not yet.

It was from his view at the center of the force that Zhou first noticed the anomaly working its way toward him. The men were stopping. In under a minute, the entire group had stopped dead in its tracks. Zhou knew that the only person who could have ordered a halt was his son. Lei tracked the ten minute work times and kept the men moving at the front of the formation.

He'd regret having to shoot his son. But if there wasn't a good reason for the delay, Zhou would have no choice. Giving preference to any one man, even a family member, could spark dangerous dissention. A second change in the men surrounding Zhou told him Lei believed there was a good reason to stop. A single clenched fist from the man at the center of each line, moving in a wave from front to back, issued a command to take defensive positions.

A flurry of emotions took hold of Zhou. Attack could be looming. Danger. So soon? He realized that could not be true. Even if the Americans had come straight for them, it would take weeks to traverse the distance! The thought made Zhou fearful: if Lei had indeed called for defensive positions in error, he would certainly have to shoot his son.

The men around him took action. Those on the outer fringe knelt on one knee and took aim at the surrounding jungle. Those behind them took aim and remained standing. Any living thing in the jungle would be cut down by wave after wave of bullets. All the forces involved in this race combined couldn't stand against the fury of his men.

For a full minute the men remained tense, focused. Zhou waited. An attack never came, and he realized it would never come. Stepping through the lines, Zhou made his way forward, gun in hand. He was greeted by a breathless man wielding a machete, a man from the front line.

"Why have we stopped?" he said to the man. "Report."

The man took a deep breath and spoke quickly. "Sir, Commander Lei is gone."

Zhou's eyebrows shot up and his heart skipped a beat. Had his son deserted?

"Explain."

"We were cutting through the jungle. It was very loud." The man paused as though unsure how to continue. He looked at the ground. "There was a noise, like . . . like dogs. Howling. But it was hard to hear."

Zhou nodded, giving no impression of his growing rage. Howling should not have stopped their advance or caused his son to flee!

"Lei ordered a pause so he could hear the noise. He feared an enemy was lurking."

Foolish, Zhou thought. If Lei had any mind, he would have realized that their enemies were still too far off.

The man continued with his tale: Lei had taken five men to investigate. That was when the defensive order was given.

"And?"

"Lei and the men did not return." The man squirmed. He didn't want to report what had happened.

"Soldier," Zhou said, pointing his pistol at the man's chest, "finish your report in the next thirty seconds. China has no time to wait for the fear of men."

The soldier stood straight to regain some of his professional posture. "Sir, there were sounds in the jungle, like fighting."

"I didn't hear any gunfire."

"Not guns, sir." The man looked down at his machete. "Sir, I led a second team of ten into the jungle after them. We found the bodies—"

Concealing his boiling emotions became a challenge. He'd suffered casualties without a shot being fired. It was shameful.

"They had . . . sir, they . . ."

"Take me to them."

The man looked relieved that he didn't have to speak anymore. He bowed, spun around, and hurried back toward the front of the line. Zhou followed him, noticing the whispers filtering through the ranks. He'd have to put an end to this.

Zhou cleared the front line, striding confidently, as though nothing had ruffled his feathers. The men would follow his lead. He barked an order at the two front lines. Thirty men quickly fell in behind him, weapons at the ready. The reporting soldier led them forward into the jungle.

"They're just beyond," the man said, nodding his head toward the brush.

Zhou nodded, ordered the men to fall behind but to stay ready, and stepped beyond the brush. What he found on the other side was unlike anything he'd seen in all his years of military service. He'd seen men shot and stabbed, even blown to bits. But nothing topped the scene he now faced. Four men, stripped of their uniforms, lay on the ground, headless and quartered.

Zhou bent down and inspected the nearest body, taking care not to step in the growing pool of blood. The limbs had not been cut free; they'd been pulled. The wrists and ankles of the body had been crushed where something had taken hold and yanked. The shoulder bone of the arm at Zhou's feet protruded from the torn flesh. The heads, frozen in a twist of agony, lay together several feet away. Some were crushed.

Just as the soldier had reported, Lei was nowhere to be seen. Having seen the carnage, he would not blame his son for fleeing, if that's what had happened. Zhou inspected the surrounding area. He found large patches of crushed terrain where something heavy had walked. Looking up, he noticed several broken tree limbs. The attackers came from above.

Zhou had seen enough.

He pounded back through the brush and shouted a command that snapped all the men's weapons up toward the trees. After returning to the ranks five men short, Zhou turned to the man who had led the second team and reported the event. "What is your name?"

"Jun Shan," the man replied.

"Take Lei's place. Lead the men around then resume on course. No stopping. Keep the men together. We will not be taken off guard again."

Jun nodded. "Yes, sir. And what of Captain Lei, sir?"

"If he returns, welcome him. If you find his body, inform me. If he does not return . . . he is lost to us."

Jun nodded again.

Zhou returned to his position at the center of the group. The idea of leaving his son to an enemy was worse than the idea of shooting him for desertion. A pang of guilt struck Zhou as he realized he'd assumed the worst of his son. The boy's actions had been appropriate and brave. Zhou's thoughts turned to his own father. He remembered the man rushing to his aid as childhood bullies pummeled him for being smaller. He had taught him it was noble to protect the weak, but Zhou listened to the voice in his heart, which cried for revenge. And now, when his son had needed his protection the most, his first thought was to shoot the boy. Lei had most likely been taken as a prisoner to be interrogated and tortured, a fate no soldier deserved.

When the race was over and won, he pledged to find the attacker of his men and son. His father might have been right, but the voice in Zhou's heart shouted louder than ever before: vengeance would be his.

 CHAPTER 35

"So you believe that giants used to live here?" Cruz asked over his shoulder before chopping straight through the base of a small tree and kicking it over. He continued past the fallen tree followed by Merrill, Whitney, and Wright. Vesuvius trotted next to Mirabelle, nuzzling her hand for a pat. Ferrell was somewhere ahead, on point.

Merrill thought for a moment as he stepped over the fallen sapling. "Not on the scale of the jolly green giant, mind you, but to us, yes. They would be considered giants."

Four days previously, the trek had become arduous and conversation moved at a pace quicker than their progress through the jungle. It served as a nice distraction from the burning muscles, sticky sweat, and gnat-like swarms that congested the air with little panicked bodies. The subject had gone from classic cars, to true Mexican food, to favorite books, and finally to the bones Merrill had uncovered back in the valley.

Merrill began to feel the first pangs of frustration. Cruz had vehemently doubted Merrill's assertion from the get-go. Merrill expected such treatment from his scientific colleagues but could hardly tolerate it from a demolitions expert.

Cruz continued hacking at the vines and brush, cutting a wide path for the others to follow. "So how big are we talking here? Eight feet? Nine?"

Merrill sighed. He knew in advance what Cruz's reaction would be. "The specimens I found ranged from ten to fifteen feet."

Cruz laughed loudly. "The Lakers could use some of those guys, eh? Fifteen feet! You find some new plant species to smoke while you were on your own?"

"Hey, *chico*," said Mira, "when you learn to do anything other than blow things up and make tacos, then you can criticize my father's work."

Cruz snorted. "You have some testosterone for breakfast, Whit?"

"You have enough for all of us."

"I can share, if you want."

Hearing Cruz talk to Mira like that quickly wore thin on Merrill. He wanted nothing more than to draw his sword and slap the flat edge against the side of Cruz's head. Instead, he steered the topic back on course. "Mirabelle saw the bones. She will support my claim."

"That's right," she said. "And the *Crylophosaurus*."

"Crylo what?"

"*Crylophosaurus*," Merrill said. "A native predator similar to *Allosaurus*, but smaller. They ranged in size from ten to twenty feet long from tail to snout. They could easily take care of you or me. The first fossils were found on Mount Kirkpatrick, not far from where we're headed. They had a horned crest on the top of their head that looked a little like a crown. It grew just above their eyes and probably served both defensive and offensive roles, but was more likely designed to attract a mate."

"Sorry for butting in," Wright said from behind. He'd remained quiet most of the time, keeping his senses sharp. "But how could you have found a dinosaur and a giant man together? Men didn't appear on earth until long after the dinosaurs died."

"Too true," Merrill said. "It was believed that crylo lived during the Jurassic period, and I'm not saying it didn't, but I believe it adapted to survive the freezing and thawing periods that Antarctica regularly goes through."

"How regularly?" Wright asked.

"Every twelve thousand years, give or take a few thousand. It's not an exact science yet."

"And they went extinct during the last freeze, when men lived on Antarctica?"

"Did I say they went extinct? No, no, I didn't."

"Well, of course, I just assumed—"

Merrill's head swiveled back toward his daughter. "You didn't tell them?"

Mira's eyes were wide. "I thought you did."

Cruz paused mid-swing. He turned around. "This ought to be good."

Merrill faced Wright, whose face reflected the seriousness of his inquiry. "Crylophosaurs . . . did not become extinct, Captain. They are among us now."

Wright's face lost some color. Cruz laughed again and returned to hacking.

"You're sure?" Wright said.

Merrill nodded. "There is no reason to believe they went extinct. The fact that they survived until twelve thousand years ago means they had already adapted to survive the freezing and thawing of Antarctica. If that's true, then they are here now, reclaiming this continent just as the trees have."

Wright sighed. "Is that what attacked you back at the wall?"

"We never saw what attacked us," Mirabelle said.

"There were footprints, though," Merrill added, not wanting to be doubted again.

"Good enough for me," Wright said. "I need to know everything there is to know about these things. Mobility, weaknesses, attack capabilities— everything."

"The crylos are theropods, like *Tyrannosaurus*. They hunt prey and eat it, probably alive. Their teeth are serrated for slicing through flesh, which they would swallow in chunks. Scientists have assumed that based on their size, they were most likely solitary hunters . . . but from experience I can say that is probably false. We didn't see the group that attacked us, but we heard them. It was a large group. Maybe twenty or so."

Merrill rubbed his hands together nervously. He didn't like thinking about the crylos. He'd avoided the topic in his mind because he knew that dwelling on the creatures might cause him to turn tail and run. He pressed on. "Each forearm—which is a functional appendage, unlike those of the T-rex—is armed with three razor-sharp claws. The hind legs have three similar claws and a curved, backward-facing talon, like *Velociraptors*."

"I've seen *Jurassic Park* too, Doc," Cruz shouted back.

"Imagine the agility, intelligence, and ferocity of a raptor in a body half the size of t-rex, and you have *Crylophosaurus*. This predator has the best of both worlds. It's no wonder that it's survived so long. Only the crocodile has been as successful."

Wright looked more wary but held his composure. "Any weaknesses?"

Merrill smiled nervously. "None to speak of. There isn't much else known about them. The skeleton I uncovered is the only complete specimen ever discovered, and I didn't have much time to study it. I don't know much of anything about their habits, territory ranges, or behavior."

"Next time you have intel like that, you tell me," Wright said. "You could have gotten someone killed."

"With all due respect, Captain, if crylophosaurs attack, I doubt there is anything any of us can do but run."

"If they can be blown to bits, we'll be fine," Cruz said. "In fact, I look forward to it. It's not everyday I get to demo someone's imaginary friend."

Merrill ignored the comment, which was obviously designed to incite him. He was about to look away from Cruz when he saw the man freeze. Cruz placed a hand on his communications earpiece. "I think I hear Ferrell," he said.

As though responding to Cruz, Vesuvius growled. The hair on his back rose and he crouched into an attack position. Something had him spooked.

Wright eyed Merrill. It was clear that if something had happened to Ferrell along the lines of a prehistoric attack, Merrill would be held responsible. Merrill was relieved to hear Ferrell's voice return, but didn't like what she had to say.

"Wright, this is Ferrell. You read me?"

"I got you," Wright said. "What's up?"

"We got company."

"How many?"

"Just one."

"Have you made contact?"

"In a sense," Ferrell said, sounding angry. "I was hit."

"Details."

"Sniper round. Took a chunk out of my arm, but I patched it up."

Merrill had no idea what to think. Moments ago he feared a creature straight out of a child's nightmare, and now he faced a very modern fear. A sniper was taking shots at the team. He wondered how long his aging mind and body could handle this kind of excitement.

"Lingering threat?"

"Negative. She left."

"You were that close to the shooter?"

"Negative. I never saw her."

"Her?"

"I recognize the bullet. I use the same. Homemade, just like we were taught."

Under his breath, Wright let loose a string of curses.

"Ferrell knows this person?" Mira asked.

"We both do," Wright said. "Duscha Popova. Ferrell's contemporary and competitor. Both were minor assassins, taking small jobs until they were recruited by an underground network of mercenaries, Armed Response. They needed women operatives, and recognized the innate talent both women had. They were trained together, both becoming master snipers—and for a few years they fought together, though I gather they didn't get along. Armed Response dissolved after a CIA investigation and subsequent raid took the group's leaders out of the picture. Ferrell and Popova became free agents again, though much more deadly. Popova chose to work with the Russians and has been a thorn in our side since. The Cold War may have officially ended in the '80s, but the quiet cold war continued right up until the global shift. In a way, it's still continuing now. We've tried taking her out more than once and failed every time."

"That's because you never sent me," Ferrell said over the com. "And thanks for the trip down memory lane."

Wright seemed to know what Ferrell would do next and spoke very loudly. "Ferrell, do not pursue. You hear me, Kat?"

After a moment of silence, Ferrell said, "Sorry, Wright. I'm the only one who can take her out. Hanging around with you makes me an easy target."

"You?" Cruz said. "What about us?"

"She'll want me out of the picture first. She knows I'm the only real threat."

"What happens if you fail?" Whitney asked.

"You're all dead."

It was the last thing they heard Ferrell say before she switched off her com. Wright's expression soured for a moment, but his look was quickly squelched. Drawing his machete, Wright moved past Whitney and Merrill. "Until we hear from Ferrell, we're double-timing it."

"And if we don't hear from her?" Merrill asked.

"Then we don't stop running."

Merrill had been afraid of that. He was in fairly good shape and could run for some distance, but he feared his aging body couldn't keep up with the rest. The weight of the backpack and the enormous XM-29 he'd been granted made walking a task; running for hours on end was not possible for him. As Wright plunged into the foliage, hacking and slashing as he ran, Merrill looked at his daughter. She looked concerned. "Don't worry about me," he said. "I'll keep up."

But that was a lie. If Ferrell didn't succeed, he would be the first to fall. The weak member of the herd that fell behind was always the first to be killed by the predator. It was a law of nature. Merrill was beginning to realize that nature's laws ruled Antarctica.

He charged ahead with Vesuvius at his heels. Mira came after him, followed by Cruz, who had waited behind. They moved at a marathon pace, dodging in and out of trees and tearing through brambles and thorns without pause. It was as though the jungle itself was trying to impede their progress. Merrill closed the doors to his imagination and focused on running. He knew that to dwell on the forces working against them would labor his breathing and tax his energy.

Merrill recalled President Franklin D. Roosevelt's famous statement: "The only thing we have to fear is fear itself." Merrill now knew that Roosevelt had been wrong. He'd never been to Antarktos.

 CHAPTER 36

Ian Jacobson was glad to see that the others could keep up with his pace. He didn't bother hacking at the brush. He didn't slow when thorns scratched at his legs. Plowing through at near top speed worked well; so well that they were a day ahead of schedule and probably the front runners in this race. Of course, getting to the goal wasn't necessarily going to be the hard part; holding it would be. The only advantage to securing the goal first would be time. Time to prepare.

As Jacobson breathed heavily through his mouth like he'd been taught not to do, he tasted something foul in the air. Like death.

Just as quickly as it came, the taste and smell were gone with the wind. The trees swayed above, creaking in the breeze. The large leaves slapped against each other. The trees made a considerable amount of noise. Jacobson knew that they would have trouble hearing danger because of the noise created by their running, as well as the wind in the trees, but at their pace, running into an enemy force was unlikely.

That and the fact that he enjoyed extreme physical activity—he loved the runner's high. It allowed him to relax and let his thoughts wander. Antarctica had become a mystery for the ages. Not only had it thawed, but it was full of new life. He thought back to his collection of mythology books and wondered if any of the ancients had ever visited these lands before.

He'd been transfixed when, as a boy, his family visited Loch Ness. After a three-day stay at the loch, his family had not seen anything unusual, but the stories told by the locals had him hooked. He returned as a teenager and launched an expedition of his own. Not having any equipment aside from an old 8mm camera with a 2X zoom didn't discourage him. He rented a boat and set out by himself for an entire day. At the end of the day, he had a ten-second clip of a three-humped object cutting through the water. It was enough to get him on the news and propel his hobby forward.

After joining the military, ever seeking out action, he used his leave time to hunt for other mysteries. He journeyed to Canada in search of Sasquatch. Mexico for *la Chupacabra*. The Congo for Mokèlé-mbèmbé. He had traveled the world in search of its greatest living wonders, and now he was running a race in the world's most extraordinary wonder. He felt privileged, awed, and humbled to be there. It was like suddenly being able to travel to Mars.

Lost in thought, Jacobson didn't see the sudden dip before him. He tumbled forward and fell. The ground opened up in front of him and dropped ten feet. As he tumbled, Jacobson stretched out his arms, snagging a low branch and sparing himself a broken bone or two. His upper body swung out over the drop with his feet still on the ground, and was quickly pulled up by one of the Frenchmen.

Before he could thank the man, his senses came alive. A smell like rotted steak struck his noise. A cacophony of noise like shrieking birds rang in his ears. The racket came from below, where he'd almost fallen.

He shared a look with the Frenchman as the rest of the team slowed behind them, instinctively drawing their weapons. Jacobson crouched low and crawled toward the edge. Looking over, he saw the most unusual thing: a flock, if it could be called that, of large birds that stood at least three feet tall. They had the coloration of penguins, black on the back and white on the front. Long, bright orange feathers grew from above their eyes in a crest and spread to each side of their heads. They had feeble wings that couldn't possibly achieve flight but stood on powerful-looking legs and were adorned with sharp, curved beaks. Five of them squawked and picked at a dead body.

The carcass was unidentifiable but had obviously been dead for some time. The Frenchman crawled up next to him, "*Mon Dieu*, what are they?"

Jacobson shook his head. He had no idea. Not even in mythology was something like this recorded. They were like penguins on steroids crossbred with an ostrich. Whatever they were, the team didn't have time to deal with them.

The Frenchman had different ideas. "I wonder," he said, taking aim, "what they taste like."

Jacobson put his hand on the man's gun. He shook his head again.

"Why not?" the Frenchman asked. "We're ahead of schedule and there is no better time for a break."

"We'll break when I say . . ." Jacobson noticed that the birds had fallen silent. He looked back down. Four of the five stared up at him, their dark eyes stabbing into his. The fifth was nowhere in sight.

A flash of orange to his left betrayed the attacking bird as it hopped through the brush and lunged for Jacobson's throat. His rifle was too ungainly and heavy to aim in time, so Jacobson whipped his knife from its sheath and cut out in a wide arc. He felt the blade slice flesh and heard the bird's squawk become a gurgle. Jacobson ducked as he swung and the bird soared over him to land on the Frenchman. The man jumped up shouting. The bird was dead, but a spray of its blood coated the Frenchman from head to chest.

Jacobson turned to the other birds. All four were still there, watching. Sizing him up. They showed no fear of humanity. Jacobson had stared down some of the world's most dangerous predators while searching for myths and had seen the worst of them shrink away from people. These creatures were different. He didn't like it.

He raised his rifle and prepared to cut the gaggle down. But before he fired a shot, something else caught the birds' attention. All four whipped their heads to the right and gazed into the jungle depths. Their feathers fanned up on their heads, an unmistakable warning. Without making a sound, all four birds leapt away, bounding quickly into the forest.

The Frenchman held the dead bird high and said, "Now can I eat it?"

The French were too concerned with food, Jacobson thought. He slapped the bird from the man's hands. "Put that down, you baboon!"

The Frenchman looked offended for a moment then noticed the rest of the team aiming their weapons at the surrounding jungle, in the direction the birds had looked before fleeing. He brought his weapon up and took aim.

"What is it?" the Frenchman whispered.

"Something worse," Jacobson said, nodding to where the birds had been feasting. A tree in the distance swayed, cracked, and fell over. "Something much worse."

 CHAPTER 37

Whitney noticed the chill as their group descended the hillside, but the jungle canopy kept the reason for the temperature drop a secret until they reached the bottom. As the hill became level, the trees thinned and a large swath of blue cut across the spaces between the trees. Another minute of hiking brought them to the shore of an immense lake.

It was so large that the opposite shore could not be seen, and from left to right, the shore continued on into the horizon. The air at the edge of the lake felt about fifteen degrees cooler than the jungle air, and a gentle breeze brought the fresh smell of moist earth and blooming trees to Whitney's nose. It felt like spring in New England and was a welcome change from the sweltering, stuffy forest.

Vesuvius thought so too. He pranced to the water's edge, gulped in several mouthfuls, and waded in. His audible panting and dangling tongue had grown worse with every day of rapid travel, but now his expression returned to its naturally jovial state.

Whitney crouched next to the dog and took some water in her hands. She drank it and felt herself come alive as the cool liquid slid down her throat. She realized she was drinking some of the cleanest water on earth. It had no doubt been a glacier for thousands of years, its bounty of water remaining hidden from the world's pollutants. She took another drink and smiled. Poland Springs has nothing on this, she thought. Then she remembered that Poland Springs was buried beneath a mountain of snow and ice, and the water didn't taste as good.

Wright spoke into his com. "Ferrell, you out there? You copy?" Whitney could hear the loud scratch of static that returned. The cacophony was enough to make Wright tear out his earpiece.

"Not working?" Whitney asked, though she knew it wasn't.

Wright shook his head. "Interference." Wright addressed the group. "Coms are down, so stay within earshot at all times."

Nods all around.

The lake, though its fresh water and cool temperature was a blessing for them all, presented something of a challenge to their goal. Walking around might add a week's travel time, or more. Whitney looked at her father. "Do you know where we are?"

Merrill scanned the surroundings. "Not a clue." He gave Wright a smack on the back. "Looks like you all picked the wrong guy for the job."

"None of this is familiar to you?" Wright asked as he put his backpack down at the water's edge.

"Not one bit." Merrill said. "Keep in mind that this isn't my hometown. This is an entire continent. I could spend a lifetime here and still not be able to recognize this spot. I—oh . . ."

Whitney followed her father's gaze. A distant mountain. "What is it?" she asked.

"The old goose neck," he said, pointing at the mountain's peak where a jut of stone really did look like a goose head, complete with a neck.

"Then you know where we are?" Wright asked.

Merrill smiled and nodded. "Last time I was here it was covered in a half-mile of ice and snow." He looked up and pointed. "I was standing up there. Things look a little different now."

"I've never been here," Whitney said. "When were you here?" She cringed the moment she asked the question. It was a foolish thing to ask, because she knew the answer.

"With your mother," Merrill said, looking out at the azure water. "She would have loved to see this, you know."

"I know," Whitney said. "Maybe she can."

"Nice try, young lady." Merrill gave her a small smile. "But I know you don't believe in God. And I don't believe she can see us. The dead are no longer with us."

Whitney shook her head. What a depressing belief system. "That's not exactly comforting."

"Of course it is," Merrill said. "I'll be seeing your mother again. It's *your* soul I'm worried about."

"Don't worry about me," Whitney said, secretly glad her father still had her well-being in mind. He had always been concerned with eternal things—people's souls—though his obsession with the past held a much stronger hold on his psyche than the present seemed to. She sensed a change in him, though, as if the past was losing its grasp. Thoughts about ancient civilizations, biblical events, and dinosaurs typically filled his conversations, but lately he seemed much more interested in the here and now. In her.

"I pray for you every night," Merrill said. "For your protection. And for your forgiveness."

Whitney looked into her father's eyes. They were wet. "Forget about it, Dad. It's not your fault."

"I should have been there."

"I don't blame you for leaving," she said. "I understand now the void you've always felt since Mom . . . You can't blame yourself. You couldn't have done anything to stop it." Whitney hugged her father. "It's ancient history." She smiled. That had been her father's favorite expression while she was young. He always got such a kick out of it. This was the first time she shared in the humor.

They both laughed. Merrill pulled away. His eyes were still damp, but he was smiling. "Egyptian ancient?"

"Pre-Sumerian," Whitney replied.

Merrill chuckled. "My favorite!"

"Ugh," Cruz's accented voice cut in. "Cut the father-daughter crap, eh? You're giving me a migraine."

"Did you even have a mother, Cruz?" Whitney said, laying on the sarcasm.

Cruz searched for a witty comeback but found nothing. He cursed under his breath in Spanish.

Whitney turned to Wright, who was repacking the contents of his backpack. On the ground next to him was a square of blue material, neatly folded. "Any idea which way around the lake is faster?"

Wright pointed straight out across the water. "That way."

"No kidding," Whitney said. "But I'm not that good a swimmer."

Wright smiled. "Neither am I." He pulled a cord that Whitney had not seen attached to the blue square. A sudden hiss ripped through the air. In seconds, a sturdy inflatable raft floated on the water's edge. "Boy Scout, remember?"

Whitney raised an eyebrow.

"The lake is on the satellite photos," Wright said. "It's generally not a good idea to run a race without knowing what the track looks like." Wright held his hands out to Cruz, who pulled two folded oars from his pack, snapped them together, and handed one to Wright. "All aboard."

Vesuvius cheerfully clambered out of the water and shook a spray of water that covered everyone's legs. He looked up innocently and barked. Whitney looked at the dog and realized they had a problem. "What about him?"

Wright bent down to the dog and got his face licked as he inspected the dog's claws. He glanced at Merrill while dodging more happy licks. "The boat is fairly rugged and should be able to handle his claws, but better not to take chances. Don't suppose you have any dog nail clippers on you?"

Merrill shook his head, looking worried. Whitney was worried, too. Just by looking at the boat, it was easy to tell that Vesuvius's sharp claws would make short work of the inflated pontoons. She was about to demand that something be figured out. She couldn't stand to see her father lose another family member. But Wright was up to something.

Digging in his backpack again, Wright pulled out two pairs of socks. He kneeled back down to Vesuvius. "Paw," he said. Vesuvius lifted a front paw and Wright slipped a sock over his paw. He repeated the process on all four legs until it appeared Vesuvius was wearing dog leg warmers. Wright snapped his finger at Cruz, "Electrical tape."

Cruz shook his head. "All this for a dog." He handed the tape to Wright. "You know, I might need that."

"I won't use much," Wright said as he wrapped the tape snugly around the socks, holding them in place. When he was done, he gave Vesuvius a pat on the head. "Good boy." It was enough to earn him a full-fledged smile from Whitney. He returned it and handed the tape back to Cruz. "Good to go."

Whitney could see herself falling for a guy like Wright. But she suspected there was something between him and Ferrell. They seemed very comfortable around each other, though they did a good job of hiding it. Call it women's intuition, but she had sensed his concern when Ferrell went after Popova. Wright had searched for the source of every sound that echoed from the jungle, but not with the look of a defender. His eyes were hopeful, but when no one appeared, no amount of acting could hide his disappointment. The Boy

Scout and the assassin. Whitney shook her head. Go figure. She knew leaving Ferrell behind must bother him, but she also knew they had no choice. Ferrell could already be dead, and if they didn't keep moving, they might be next.

On the water, Whitney found herself able to relax. Wright and Cruz moved the boat steadily across the lake with the oars. Relieved of her backpack and boots, and with Vesuvius snuggled up against her and her legs dangling in the glacial waters, it was nearly enough to lull Whitney to sleep.

As slumber loomed, Whitney's thoughts ran free. She thought about what her father had said about God. He was so firmly rooted in his beliefs that he was hard to ignore. Her father was a brilliant man, she knew that. Yet he was still her father, and his religious beliefs had always worn thin on her. But now, with the dramatic changes in the world and the disasters that had befallen them both, she longed for that kind of assurance.

Her father was confident he would see her mother again. But she knew she'd never see Sam again. He was gone. That was what she believed. Her father clung to a hope that she could not comprehend. Not just a hope of being reunited with loved ones; something deeper, something more profound, something that had not changed when the rest of the world went to hell. No, the only thing about the world that had not changed was her father's faith, and that spoke volumes. For the first time in her life, she felt . . . interest in what he believed. She knew the standard things that were taught in church, but she didn't know how her father could believe such outrageous things so earnestly, or how he reconciled what he knew about ancient history with what was recorded in the Bible. She made a mental note to ask as her mind slowed and gave in to sleep.

The last thing she heard was the sound of lapping water and the gurgle of rising bubbles from the depths beneath.

 CHAPTER 38

The inward barrage of self-deprecating insults Popova hurled at herself was worse than any physical pain she'd endured. For the first time in her career, she had missed. And of all people to miss . . .!

She had no idea how Ferrell had sensed her presence. She had been so completely concealed that sight was not a possibility. She wore no perfume and was covered in earth and detritus. She was upwind, so Ferrell couldn't have smelled her. She had remained perfectly still, buried in shrubs, looking down from a hilltop, when she'd seen Ferrell creeping through the jungle.

How fortunate she had been to come across Ferrell first. She took aim through her scope, placed her finger gently on the trigger, and squeezed. Through the sight, her aim had appeared true. Ferrell fell backwards. But as she neared the ground, she did not fall limp. Ferrell flung herself back, tucked into a roll, and dove behind a tree.

Popova had sprung to her feet only a second after realizing she'd missed and torn off into the jungle. She knew her position had been exposed and that retaliation would be forthcoming. A violent explosion ripped her hiding place to shreds seconds later, knocking Popova off her feet. She scrambled up and wove haphazardly through the forest so that her trail would be harder to follow. She knew Ferrell would give chase, and it brought a smile to her face.

The game of cat and mouse had begun. The only remaining question was who played the cat and who would be the mouse.

After a mile of running Popova slowed, not because of exhaustion, but because she'd spotted the perfect place for an ambush. A mound of tall stones that looked almost carved rose up thirty feet off the ground, topping out near the green leafy jungle ceiling. As she climbed the rock face higher and higher, more of the jungle came into view. She'd be able to see Ferrell coming with ease.

Reaching the top, Popova assembled her rifle and set it down on the flat stone surface. As she turned to lay down behind the large rifle, she looked for the first time over the back side of the rock mound. What she saw held her gaze steady. A large depression in the ground, perhaps a quarter mile in diameter, had been carved out. More large stones were scattered around the interior, some still imbedded in the earth and others partially-carved statues, blank-faced versions of the ones she'd discovered previously.

It was a quarry. The stones were hewn by men.

While intriguing, the stones could not hold her interest. Not while Ferrell was out there. Popova would deal with her first and when the Americans came looking for her, they would fall next. She slid down to her belly and gripped the rifle. She scanned back and forth, searching for any sign of movement, no matter how obscure. Ferrell would not be an easy target, especially now that she was aware of the danger, but she could not approach Popova's hiding spot without exposing herself.

Ten minutes passed quickly. The following twenty minutes dragged. And the entire following hour became torturous. She wondered if Ferrell had rejoined her team and moved out. She quickly dismissed the thought, remembering how slowly and methodically Ferrell worked. Popova, on the other hand, was a swift killer.

She realized that Ferrell had most likely identified her as the sniper. The bullet, if recovered, would be a dead giveaway. That was why Ferrell moved so slowly. She was trying to wear down Popova's patience.

It won't work, Popova thought. She conceded to waiting all day and night, if need be. Ferrell could move as slowly as she wanted, but the moment of her death would come just as surely either way.

As the day lingered on, Popova's thoughts drifted while her senses remained on guard. She considered how quickly Ferrell had literally dodged the bullet. She couldn't imagine how Ferrell had detected her presence. She'd heard, through mutual acquaintances, that Ferrell, dubbed "The Kat," had a kind of sixth sense that warned her of danger. She'd always assumed that it was propaganda spread by Ferrell herself to intimidate her enemies, but now she wasn't so sure.

She shook the thought from her mind.

A stiff wind picked up and the trees began to sway. The large leaves rustled and the tree trunks groaned. If Ferrell was going to make an advance, it would be now. She watched a hundred trees dance back and forth. Sunlight filtered through the leaves, undulating on the forest floor. Popova remained focused, scanning with her rifle, prepared to shoot.

The light around Popova shifted with the trees, but she suddenly became cast in unmoving shadow. The rest of the forest was still active, alive, but something blocked her light from above. Someone was standing above her.

Popova rolled over like a cat, drew her side arm, and unloaded the semiautomatic clip in seconds. It wasn't until her gun ran out of ammo that she stopped firing. She stared straight ahead in astonished silence. She realized that firing as she had was probably the worst thing she could have done. It only seemed to amuse the monster, which had taken every bullet yet remained standing. Blood oozed from bullet holes pocking the behemoth's chest, but it showed no reaction other than to glare at her the way a magnifying-glass-wielding child does an ant.

Popova screamed like a banshee, just before her life was crushed from her.

Ferrell froze.

She'd heard the shots, the scream. Popova.

High in the swaying treetops, she'd been making her way slowly forward to where she knew Popova would be hiding. She'd been one step ahead all along. She'd watched Popova hide herself in the brush. She'd even allowed Popova to take the first shot. It was only fair. She knew it was the only shot Popova would get. But she hadn't counted on someone else getting the best of Popova before she was able to.

She moved more quickly now, leaping from treetop to treetop with a little less care. Without the fear of a sniper round zipping through the trees, she was free to put her legendary agility to the test. She moved across the trees quickly and when she was over what she believed to be the rock mound, she paused and listened.

She heard nothing. Scanning the area around her, Ferrell noticed a patch of trees in the distance tipping and bouncing as though a strong wind blew through them. All she could see for miles in every direction was the tops of trees, like an emerald blanket. In the distance was a mountain range, the Transantarctic range, she guessed. Other than that, it was blue skies above and not a thing out of place. She looked back to where the trees had been moving. They were once again gently swaying in the wind. Nothing more.

Ferrell lowered her head through the leaves and looked straight down on the rock mound where Popova had been positioned. Her sniper rifle sat on the boulder, bent and broken amid a crimson pool of blood dripping down the rocks.

Ferrell couldn't fathom what had happened to Popova, but one thing was clear: the woman was dead. All that was left of her was a bloody smear.

Snap! The tree she clung to shook and fell as though pushed over from below. As the tree fell forward, careening toward the forest floor, Ferrell leapt off and clung to a nearby tree trunk. She loosened her grip and slipped down to the ground. Without looking back, Ferrell ran.

Somehow, whatever killed Popova had returned without her sensing its approach. Popova had been swatted as easily as a fly. Its skill at stealth—and killing—dwarfed her own. Ferrell knew she didn't stand a chance in hell. Trees snapped behind her and the ground shook. Something very large was giving chase.

And it was howling.

 CHAPTER 39

Even though Wright and Cruz were making good time across the lake, to Merrill it still felt like a lazy day at New Hampshire's Lake Winnipesauke. Of course, Winnipesauke was now frozen over, like the majority of the United States, and he would never again see its shores or visit its quaint, historic towns. Wolfeboro, Meredith, Laconia, Alton Bay . . . all gone. Merrill sighed and looked out at the coastline. The old towns of New Hampshire would soon be replaced by new ones on Antarktos.

Merrill had begun calling Antarctica by its older name: Antarktos. It seemed fitting, though he was sure the continent would eventually be re-named completely, since it was no longer located in the Antarctic at all. Peeling his gaze away from the shoreline, Merrill returned his attention to the large piece of paper spread out in his lap—the Piri Reis map.

He hadn't had the time to study the map since he'd first laid eyes on it and was using the lazy trip across the water to inspect it and commit as much of it to memory as possible.

The detail of the map was amazing, and even though the continent had been covered with ice for thousands of years, the land's topography had changed little. Glacial valleys were larger and deeper, to be sure, but the ice had served as a protective barrier against erosive forces that reshape all conti-nents at will: wind, water, tides, and other natural phenomena. The result was that the Piri Reis map was as accurate that day as the original source doc-uments had been perhaps twelve thousand years ago.

Every nook and cranny of the shoreline was intricately drawn. River sys-tems had been included, and several internal geographic features as well.

Mountain ranges and lakes covered the map's surface. Merrill turned the map and brought his finger to the area in which he believed them to currently be. The lake they were crossing was on the map. Several rivers were shown flowing into the lake, and one large one was shown flowing out to the ocean. If they needed a way back to the ocean, that river would be their best bet.

Looking at the map, Merrill scanned the area around the lake and found several interesting features. Behind them, from the direction they had come, was what appeared to be a large pit, full of rocks. In the water itself several oblong creatures had been drawn. And in front of them were what looked like two men, or apes, dancing. Merrill couldn't help but wonder if, like the geological elements, the other items on the map were accurate. But he had no way to verify such a thing.

Or did he? Tracing his finger straight back toward the ocean, roughly along the path he thought they had taken, Merrill came to his valley. He was delighted to see his wall. The map showed it to be much longer, dipping into the valley, then out along the coast. What he hadn't expected to see on the map was drawn on the other side of the wall, the side he was never able to inspect. A city, large and imposing, lay etched into the side of a mountain, apparently fashioned from the same cut stones. Next to the city was a large, elaborately drawn foot, almost the size of the city itself.

A twinge of excitement shot up Merrill's spine and swirled within his skull. The map confirmed his find. It not only revealed that there was much more to explore, but the large foot hinted that the people who lived there were of unusual size.

Merrill was about to tell Wright and Cruz about his find when Mira awoke with a scream from the front of the boat. She yanked her feet into the boat from where they'd been dangling in the water. Vesuvius leapt to his feet, ears perked, tail tucked down.

"Are you all right?" Merrill asked.

Mirabelle looked around the boat, scanning the blue water, searching for something.

"Must have been one bad dream, eh?" Cruz said. He and Wright had stopped rowing, hands on weapons.

She shook her head. "Wasn't a dream. Something touched my foot."

Wright dropped the oar and raised his XM-29. "Any idea what it was?"

"No," she said. "It was smooth. Almost soft."

Vesuvius began barking at the water; however, he sounded more playful than angry and the scruff of his neck, which normally rose in the face of danger, remained flat. Still, something was out there.

Wright and Cruz aimed their weapons at the water, waiting silently for some sign of danger before they unleashed hell. Merrill looked at the lake, then back to the map where oblong creatures had been drawn in the water. On paper they didn't look imposing, but one never knew. In fact, the overall shape looked familiar. The creatures were shaped like torpedoes, with eyes at one end and tapered bodies. What were they?

As the boat was bumped from below, Merrill realized he'd find out soon enough. Wright and Cruz moved from side to side, searching for something to shoot but seeing nothing. Merrill looked behind the boat and saw a ten-foot-long shadow pass by. He swallowed and said, "Whoa."

"Whoa, what?" Wright asked.

An eerie, high-pitched call reverberated out of the water, rising from below. It was unnervingly loud and inhuman.

Merrill found himself unable to speak for a moment.

"What did you see?"

"It's big," Merrill said. "Maybe ten feet."

"Switch to the exploding rounds," Wright said. "Careful not to shoot the boat."

Cruz nodded, made the change, and took aim again. Wright shot an incredulous look at Merrill, then at Mirabelle, who were both transfixed on the water. "What are you waiting for?" he said.

Merrill picked up his XM-29 and stood unsteadily as the boat floor flexed under the heavier pressure points created by all his weight pushing down at his feet. He had no idea what firing a gun would feel like, let alone a high-powered rifle with exploding rounds. He thought they'd all be safer if he didn't have one at all. The boat was bumped from below again and Merrill was knocked off balance. As he fell, his fingers flinched and pulled the trigger. The round exploded from the XM-29 and sailed across the water, coming into contact with a tree on the approaching shore, splitting it in half. Merrill, already falling, was launched into the air by the weapon's considerable recoil. The XM-29 fell out of Merrill's hands and landed in the boat.

Merrill and the shattered tree hit the water at the same time.

Coughing as he resurfaced, Merrill was struck by two sensations. First, the water was freezing cold. While the air was a tepid steam bath, the water had retained its glacial chill. He realized the lake must be thousands of feet deep. Second, whatever creature roamed those waters was headed straight for him.

Water rose over the creature's dark gray back as it swam toward Merrill.

Vesuvius barked, trying to jump out of the boat. Mira strained to hold him steady. "Shoot it!" she yelled.

"He's too close!" Wright said. "Switch to conventional rounds!"

As Wright and Cruz frantically switched their weapons' modes of firing, the creature closed in and Merrill could make out light and dark spots speckled across its gray hide. He suddenly recognized the creature for what it was. "Hold your fire!" he shouted.

The creature continued forward and struck Merrill in the chest. The impact wasn't hard, but he was dragged under the water, yelping as he plunged under. The creature's features came into view under the water, lit by the sunlight filtering in from above. It looked at him through big black eyes that held no malice. As the creature turned away, Merrill was freed.

Merrill kicked to the surface, where he was yanked out of the water before taking a breath. Wright and Cruz set him down in the boat.

"Are you okay?" Mira asked.

"Fine, fine," he said with a broad smile.

"He's gone *loco*," Cruz said.

"I've always been a little crazy," Merrill said. "But we're in no danger."

"That thing tried to eat you, man!"

"No, it's just curious . . . and there is more than one."

The boat was jostled again. Everyone looked into the water. The large creature swirled around just below them. Cruz took aim.

"No!" Merrill shouted, pushing the man's weapon down. "It's just a seal."

Cruz looked confused. "A seal?"

"They're Weddell seals," Merrill said. "They only eat fish. We're in no danger."

"Seals live in the ocean," Wright said. "How did they get here?"

"There's a river that leads from the lake to the ocean," Merrill explained. "It's on the Piri Reis map. If the seals were indigenous to this lake before Antarctica froze over, they could have migrated to the ocean when the continent froze. When it thawed, their genetics told them to come back. They must be adapted to both fresh and briny water."

As if on cue, the large Weddell seal poked his head out of the water and gave them an appraising look. Wright laughed. "I'll be damned." The seal twitched its long whiskers and gave a snort.

Mira leaned out of the boat and patted the seal on the head. "You're just a curious fella, aren't you?" The seal dipped back beneath the water then called out again, its voice echoing through the water. "Loud, too."

Vesuvius let out a bark and tried again to jump into the water. He seemed eager to play with their new friends. Mirabelle held him tightly and watched the water bubble from below as something massive rose.

A group of maybe twenty seals, ranging in size from six to ten feet long, rose out of the water. They swam in elegant circles around the boat, playing with each other, inspecting the visitors, and nudging the boat. Cruz and Wright resumed rowing while Mira and Merrill kept the seals occupied, talking to them and reaching out for physical contact. They'd made friends.

The seals escorted the boat the rest of the way across the lake and waited thirty feet from shore as the crew unloaded. Whitney said a quick goodbye to Argus, the name she'd given the large bull seal that had first introduced himself. Then they were off again, venturing back into the dark jungle where something much less friendly waited.

 CHAPTER 40

With twitching muscles, Jacobson maintained his aim, though he had no target. From their position just above where the odd penguin-like birds had been spotted, the view of the surrounding jungle was minimal. He could see the team in tight formation behind him, and the Frenchman ready to defend against an attack. But from where?

Through the few breaks in the overgrowth, Jacobson could see only another ten feet. Visibility was nil. He hoped that whatever was out there would have just as hard a time finding them.

A sound like sandpaper rubbing against stone sifted toward them through the trees. "What is that?" the Frenchman whispered.

Jacobson gave the man an angry glance, shrugged, and put his finger to his lips. Too concerned with food and too loud, Jacobson thought. Then the calls rang out. The sound was like a pack of giant angry turkeys, both humorous and terrifying. The men pointed their weapons toward the sound and held their aim. They knew not to fire until they had an actual target.

Realizing too late that they'd made a fatal flaw by leaving their rear unguarded, all Jacobson could do was drive to the side, taking the Frenchman with him as the attack came skillfully from behind. Olive green bodies coated in maroon stripes burst from the forest, spraying a cloud of leaves and brush into the air.

The men got off a few shots. Within ten seconds all were dead. It wasn't until the creatures had begun consuming his teammates that Jacobson got a full view of the creatures. Of the dinosaurs. They ranged from ten to fifteen feet in length. Yellow serpentine eyes darted back and forth as the beasts snapped at each other with serrated dagger-sized teeth, each vying for a body to consume. They pinned the men to the ground with their sharp talons and tore off chunks, clothing and all, swallowing them one bite at a time. There was no squabbling, no rivalry, just a feast.

Jacobson and the Frenchman were inching away from the carnage as inconspicuously as possible when the ground behind them shook. They spun around and faced the largest of the monsters. It was a thirty-foot behemoth and looked capable of eating a man in two bites. Its head was low, body taut. Ready to pounce.

The men froze. The large creature leaned forward, confident its stunned prey wouldn't move a muscle. It sniffed Jacobson first then moved its head to the Frenchman. Upon smelling the Frenchman's blood-stained clothes, the creature reared back, let out a wild turkey call, and lunged forward. Its bite extended over the Frenchman's head and down to his shoulders, picking him up off the ground and shaking him in the air. The Frenchman's cries of anguish were short lived.

Drawn by the clamor, one of the smaller dinosaurs turned its attention to Jacobson. It let out a high-pitched screech and charged. Jacobson's speed came from fear and his action from years of dedication and training. Yanking a grenade from his chest while simultaneously pulling the pin, Jacobson hurled it at the creature's open mouth. The dinosaur's reflexes were like lightning. It snapped with its jaws, capturing the grenade and swallowed it down.

"Now that," Jacobson said, "was a bad idea."

Jacobson dove away from the large dinosaur and fell ten feet into the area where the savage birds had been feasting. Jacobson found it hard to move with the wind knocked out of him, but managed to drag himself close to the ledge. A muffled explosion above shook the air and sent gobs of dinosaur flesh raining around the jungle. A cacophony of shrieks rang through the jungle as some of the dinosaurs fled and others writhed, injured, on the ground. The behemoth called out, angry, savage. Jacobson felt the ground vibrate as the thirty-foot dinosaur searched for him.

Staying low, Jacobson scrambled deep into the jungle until he was sure he was out of eyeshot. Then he ran at a pace that put his original speed to shame. He knew this speed would cause him to stop more often and for longer periods of time, but his main concern was putting as much distance between himself and the dinosaurs as he could muster.

He looked at his sleeves as he ran and saw specks of blood that had fallen from the sky after the explosion. He was covered in the creature's blood. They'd be after him before too long. His best chance at survival was to wash the scent off somehow and continue, not stopping until he reached the rendezvous point with the U.S. team. If they were still alive.

 CHAPTER 41

The going had been relatively smooth after they'd crossed the lake. The air wasn't as humid as before, and the sun found its way more easily through the new species of tree that populated the interior of Antarktos. The trees were tall, as though grown with supernatural fertilizer, perhaps a hundred feet in height and holding needles like those on pine trees. At the end of every needle was a small red berry. The fragrance created by the looming trees held a citrus tang, mixed with the natural odors of wood and dirt.

Ferrell had not been seen in a week, and they had given up hope of being reunited with their missing teammate. Wright grew distant and reserved. He told them that searching for her was not an option: they didn't have the time and had covered a hundred miles since her departure. If she was alive, there was no guarantee she was traveling in the same direction. They could be two hundred miles apart. The decision obviously pained him, perhaps even more than the rest of them, but Merrill knew he was right.

Camp was pitched early that night as the sun fell. They were ahead of schedule and exhausted. A campfire had been built and dinner—a short, furry mammal of some kind—had been caught, skinned, and cooked over the open flame. Merrill felt a tinge of guilt at the prospect of eating a creature that had only just reemerged from a twelve-thousand-year anhydrobiotic hibernation, but he knew his strength would be maintained by eating the meat, and for the first time in weeks, he'd feel satisfied. For that he was thankful, so much so that he led the group in saying grace.

He thanked God for protecting them despite their hardships and asked for Ferrell's safe return, and guidance in the coming weeks. When he was done,

Merrill looked up and was happy to see Wright mouth an "Amen" before opening his eyes. Then he saw his daughter smile at him from across the fire.

"You forgot the food," she said.

Merrill thought back through his prayer. He had, indeed forgotten to mention the food. "He knows were thankful for that," Merrill said defensively while silently thanking God for the food.

Wright carved the animal and served it on the small metal military plates they all carried. He handed them each a plate and they all dug in. Even Vesuvius got a large portion, though his consisted mainly of the parts no one else would eat: heart, liver, and tongue. Vesuvius didn't mind. He ate and lay back down before Merrill had even tasted his meat.

Merrill took a bite and was surprised by the meat's tenderness. Wright might have been a cook before joining the military. It was flavorful and only a little gamey. But after not eating any real meat in weeks, Merrill thought it was the best thing he'd eaten in all his life.

Apparently, so did everyone else. Not a word was spoken for ten minutes as each consumed their portion with relish. When the animal had been reduced to bones, the group lay back and enjoyed the fullness their bellies craved.

Cruz was the first to speak. "So you believe all that Bible-God stuff, huh?" He was looking at Merrill.

"'Bible-God stuff?'"

"Adam and Eve. The flood."

Merrill nodded. "I do."

Cruz sat forward. "Why? I mean, is there any physical evidence for that stuff? If the whole world was flooded, wouldn't there be some—I don't know . . . *something*? I've never seen anything scientific to support a world-wide flood."

"Well, then, you're in luck."

Merrill caught a glimpse of Mira's growing smile. She knew he loved this topic.

"Why's that?" Cruz asked.

"Because," Merrill said, "I'm a scientist."

Cruz smiled wide, his well-groomed teeth gleaming in the firelight. He seemed to enjoy the topic as well. "Well, if you've got some proof on you, show me, Mr. Scientist."

"*Doctor* Scientist, thank you." Merrill straightened and took a deep breath. He hadn't lectured in some time and found himself eager to test his abilities of remembering the material and addressing skeptical students. "Let's talk about the Flood, then. It's a hotly-debated subject and one that most people either believe or discount."

Cruz nodded. "Sounds good." He pointed at his chin, as if to say, "hit me" and said, "Let me have it."

"Some of the more common arguments against the Flood are what? Anyone know?" Merrill was trying to gauge the knowledge of his audience. He knew where Mirabelle stood, but he wasn't sure about the others.

"Not enough water," Wright said.

"Correct," Merrill said. "But the opinion is wrong. As you know, and now have firsthand experience with, ice caps can certainly melt. This alone raises water levels dramatically. During the last shift, the ice caps could have remained thawed for quite some time. Second, there are vast stores of water under the earth's surface. This water, under the right circumstances—say, a more violent crust displacement—could have been brought to the surface, further deluging the planet. On top of all that are geographic possibilities that are rarely considered. The Mariana Trench in the Pacific Ocean is 11,000 meters deep; that's 36,000 feet below sea level. We assume the trench existed during the time of the flood, but what if it was created *by* the flood?"

"Water pressure and a weakened crust," Wright added.

"Precisely." Merrill wasn't in a classroom anymore, but their current setting was more appropriate, anyway. The others would learn that soon enough as well. "The water levels would have fallen as the ocean's trenches opened up, the ice caps refroze, and the land water eventually filtered back underground."

"What about Gilgamesh?" Whitney said.

Merrill knew she'd pipe up eventually and go straight for the kill. She knew her ancient history as well as some of the best minds on earth, but history had been taught to her by people with little vision and a narrow view of the universe. Science and religion had traded places, in Merrill's opinion. Science was now afraid to really search for the truth, clinging instead to a few comfortable theories. Most of his colleagues believed the Big Bang and evolution removed the need for God. In truth, the mystery of the Big Bang—everything from nothing—supplied enough evidence for God that some were becoming uncomfortable with the theory. As for evolution, it wasn't the idea of humanity emerging from a simpler species that bothered Merrill—he had no desire to claim perfect understanding of God's methods—it was the statistical impossibility of life emerging at random. The initial formation of a single protein, the basic building block of all life, had been proven a mathematical impossibility.

The theories did little to offend him. They had never hindered his faith. It was the misguided belief that the Big Bang and evolution disproved the existence of God that irked him. He was beginning to believe that some of his fellow scientists were conforming to a new religion of their own making; like many recognized religions, it was comfortable because they could always change it to fit their needs.

New age science.

Belief without indisputable evidence proven by scientific method.

Faith.

Science held to fictions conjured by men with multiple degrees who molded their results and theories to fit their personal views. It was a travesty against real science not committed since Copernicus's *De Revolutionibus Orbium Coelestium* was placed on the Index of Forbidden Books by the Roman Catholic Church in 1616. Modern science was becoming the new church, and they could ban unbiased science just as efficiently but with less objection. Real science was being silently strangled by the men and women who claimed to support the institution, but feared investigating every possibility. It was a topic that angered Merrill, but he felt his current audience would be glad if he kept silent on it for now.

Whitney continued, ". . . and how do you account for all the other cultures on earth that have a flood myth? The story of Gilgamesh isn't the only one. You know that. Isn't it likely that the ancient Hebrews simply adapted the mythology of other cultures?"

"The fact that so many other cultures have flood myths supports the biblical account. All over the world there is a universal account of a flood. This could only happen if the story had been passed down orally through the generations, starting with the original flood survivors: Noah and his family."

"That's it?" Whitney said. "That's your answer?"

"You expected more?" Merrill smirked inwardly. He was sure Whitney expected to trip him up, to get him stuck in a corner, but it was a simple question with a simple answer. He decided to expound for the group's benefit. "Ninety-five percent of the world's flood myths state that the whole earth was covered with water. In the ancient world, that was accepted as fact. Seventy percent say that the world's survival depended on a boat. Sixty-seven percent say that animals were saved as well. Eighty-eight percent say that a favored family had been saved. Need I go on?"

Whitney sat back, deflated. "Okay, okay, move on, please."

"That's all interesting," Cruz said, "but where is the physical evidence? You can say that the trenches were created after the flood, but there is no proof. I want physical evidence, man."

"Sediment," Merrill said. "Sedimentary rock is formed underwater when pieces of rock are dissolved and deposited in a new location. The point is this: Seventy percent of the planet's surface is covered by sedimentary rock, which could only have been formed underwater." Merrill raised a finger in the air. "Now before you say anything, the rest of the earth's surface is composed of volcanic, igneous, and metamorphic rock, which is constantly being produced by earth's geologic activity. This means that it is entirely possible that the entire planet was at one time completely covered in water."

Cruz snickered. "No way could water cover mountains."

Now it was Merrill's turn to laugh. "Sedimentary rock has been discovered at the top of Mount Everest."

"Oh."

"That's right, Cruz. Even the world's tallest mountain was at one time covered by water. That is a fact of science. But please understand that, unlike my counterparts, I'm willing to consider other possibilities. It's possible that a body of water, even an ocean, was present at the site of Everest prior to the mountain's formation. I'm not claiming that my beliefs are scientific fact, only that the evidence is compelling; yet because it lends credence to the Bible account, science disregards it completely. It is, however, what I believe to be the truth."

Wright perked up. "I've never been able to figure out how two of every animal on earth could have fit into an ark. Isn't that billions of species?"

"Billions of species today," Merrill said. "But there are key species from which natural selection and breeding create new variations. Dogs are a perfect and extreme example." Vesuvius perked up his head. "Not you, Vesuvius." His head went back down. "Noah wouldn't have had to have every species of dog on the ark; at the time, they did not exist. Two wolves are all that are needed to, eventually, after thousands of years, result in the thousands of dog, wolf, and fox species found throughout the world today. The same holds true for every other animal on the planet. A key pair can create innumerable variations over time. This brings your billions down to eighteen thousand. You can even add a few thousand for species that have gone extinct in the last twelve thousand years. The ark, given the measurements found in the Bible, would have been big enough to hold and support an estimated 137,000 ani-

mals. The actual number of animals on board would have numbered around
seventy-five thousand. And they would have only taken up 60 percent of the
boat. That left 40 percent of a massive boat for living space and storage.
Science, when applied without bias, finds no fault in the flood account."

There was a silence among the group as everyone chewed on the information. Merrill was glad to find that no one was arguing right away. They were
really listening. Even Mirabelle.

"So," said Cruz, "you really believe Noah, his family, and the animals
were the only survivors?"

"Yes," Merrill said, but as soon as the word escaped his mouth he realized
it was an incorrect statement. "I mean, no."

This surprised Mira. She glanced toward her father. "Who else was there?"

Merrill's mind was a flurry of thought. Why hadn't he thought of it earlier? It was so obvious, so apparent before him. "The Nephilim."

Before Merrill could explain or expound, a crash from the woods broke
his train of thought and snapped Wright and Cruz to action. Their weapons
were brought to bear in seconds. Vesuvius, however, simply cocked his ears
and raised his eyebrows. Merrill knew before she appeared that it was Ferrell.

Ferrell barreled through the surrounding brush and crashed to the ground
next to Merrill. He thanked God that Wright and Cruz weren't trigger happy, or Ferrell would most likely be dead. But by her appearance, he guessed
that she was halfway there already. Wright dropped his weapon, leapt across
the camp, and caught Ferrell in his arms before she crashed to the ground.

"The fire," she said, her voice hoarse and strained. "Put out the fire."

 CHAPTER 42

The added weight of the explosives wrapped around al-Aziz's waist made travel slow, but he knew they would eventually be the key to his success, so he suffered their burden and pushed on. Suffering would only make his reward that much more wondrous, and that was what mattered.

For a moment he wondered how the twelve other cells were doing. Had they encountered the enemy? Had they become martyrs yet? Though he'd never admit it, he missed Abdul's company. They were supposed to be in this together, fighting side by side. But Abdul had given his life prematurely. Worse, he had failed to kill a single Zionist. And the result was that al-Aziz was now alone, facing the fear faced by all martyrs—death. He turned his mind from such thoughts, as he'd been trained to do. They lead to doubt, which lead to hesitation and ultimately to failure. He was alone. It was Allah's will. And he would not fail.

Wiping sweat from his eyes, al-Aziz paused to note his surroundings. The jungle was thick with small insects buzzing and swarming, but none seemed attracted to his soft flesh, thank Allah. But the heat had become oppressive and all al-Aziz's prayers for cooling went unanswered. His skin was slick with perspiration and humidity that made his clothes uncomfortably sticky. He no longer noticed the pungent odor of the forest, not because it no longer smelled but because he'd given up breathing through his nose. The odors were often too strong to bear, and the sticky mixture of humidity, dust, pollen, and gnats clung to the inside of his nose. It was best if he focused on moving forward and forgot the annoyances of the world.

He longed for the dry desert. In the midday sun, with temperatures much hotter than these, he could walk comfortably dry. He wondered why his people desired this land. It was putrid in so many ways. Of course the strategic value of the land was undeniable and would keep the Americans from regaining their superpower status in the new world, opening the door for a new Arab Alliance world order. That was the goal. That was Allah's will.

After taking a long swig from his canteen, al-Aziz resumed hacking at the vegetation with his machete and pressed on.

Within minutes, the water he'd drunk had seeped back through his skin. He was quickly becoming dehydrated, and the heaviness in his legs urged him to stop. But he couldn't. His relentless spirit to serve Allah pushed him forward. The ground beneath his feet suddenly dipped. Al-Aziz tumbled forward, arms splayed, and fell. The dip turned into a full-fledged hill. Gravity and momentum pulled him downward.

He stopped with a sudden jolt that made him cringe as he remembered the explosives strapped to his body. Death was not a fear, but failing in his task, his martyrdom, would mean receiving no reward. It would be a terrible fate. After catching his breath he sat up, and even though the tumble had knocked the wind from his lungs, he stopped breathing.

Spread out before him was a kind of carnage he'd never seen. Bodies were strewn about, disassembled, and gnawed upon. He'd seen a man eaten by wild dogs once. This was something worse. These men had been torn apart and consumed by a very large creature, or several. Al-Aziz collected himself and his spilled gear before moving closer to the carnage. He held his AK-47 nervously before him and inched forward, inspecting the bodies.

After discovering a pair of dog tags and noticing the skin color of what remained of the men, al-Aziz concluded that they had been the European team. He hoped for a brief moment that his initial assessment of what had happened was wrong. He searched for signs of an explosion.

His heart soared briefly as he found a blast zone. Flesh and blood were scattered in a familiar pattern. But it was wrong. The amount of explosives each member of every cell carried would have flattened the trees for fifty feet around. This explosion was much too small; a grenade, perhaps.

As al-Aziz searched for other clues, he came to a portion of jungle that had been cleared of brush and trees. A path heading south through the jungle had been carved. It was as though Allah himself had cleared a road for him.

"Allah be praised!" al-Aziz shouted. For he now realized the truth. His mission was so sacred, so supported by Allah, that He had come to the mortal world himself to clear a path and destroy his enemies. Allah had come to earth to aid al-Aziz, to show him the path to salvation.

The adrenaline from such a fantastic revelation had al-Aziz's heart pounding, but the physical weariness from dehydration still lingered. He looked back at the mangled bodies and saw a canteen on the ground next to a severed arm. He rushed to it and picked it up—it was full! He drank from the canteen greedily and when he was finished, clipped it to his belt.

Allah had shown him the path and had provided the sustenance to continue his righteous jihad. Al-Aziz broke into a run, moving faster than ever down the cleared path that he knew would eventually lead him to his enemies. Then home to Allah, where his reward awaited.

# CHAPTER 43

Camp was broken down as soon as the first glint of sunlight pierced the forest. The remainder of the previous night had been spent patching Ferrell's wounds, which ranged from thorn scratches to two broken fingers on her left hand. She looked like she'd gone a few rounds with Mike Tyson during his early years. Her dark eyes, once cool and collected, now moved rapidly, searching for danger like a wounded animal.

In hushed tones Ferrell had told her story. She recalled Popova's sudden and gruesome death. The American assassin had then been chased through the jungle by something she could only describe as very large. She had seen only the results of its attack on Popova and felt its destructive power as it knocked trees over like sticks stuck in the dirt. Visibly shaken by recalling what she'd seen—or, not quite seen—she skipped forward to how she eventually eluded her pursuer. She had jumped from a cliff, one hundred feet down to a deep pool of water, breaking her fingers when she hit the bottom. She swam to shore and tore off into the forest, following their original course. She'd lost her pack and weapons during the chase, ditching them for speed.

As Whitney looked at her now, carrying Merrill's XM-29, she was bruised and beaten but otherwise appeared to have made a remarkable recovery. Though she limped slightly and her wounds must have ached, the killer had returned. It was a quality Whitney thought must have been forged in childhood. She wondered what kind of life the little girl Ferrell had endured to sustain such a scare, such a beating, and be ready to fight again the next day. Only her eyes had changed—less relaxed, more aware.

Whitney wasn't sure she wanted to know what had killed the Russian assassin or chased Ferrell. She was happy in her ignorance. Her father had insisted that the attackers were crylophosaurs, but no one, not even Ferrell, believed that. Whatever had attacked her had given her the intense impression that it was intelligent, thinking, plotting. "No dinosaur, no matter how smart," she had said, "could have followed my trail." Whitney believed her. The woman was a ghost when she wanted to be.

The rest of the day passed swiftly and without incident. No one felt much like talking. It was during that quiet period that Whitney began to pay attention to her other senses. The sounds of the forest were peaceful. Creaking trees and whooshing red-berried needles swayed in the wind. Small animals called from the trees and scurried across the ground. The sensation that became most uncomfortable was her smell. It wasn't the smell of the forest; if Whitney could smell that, she'd be happy. But nothing could overpower the smell of her own stench. Unable to bathe while moving so quickly, the team had taken to slathering on deodorant in liberal portions, which had worked for everyone but her.

Like her mother, Whitney had an ample chest. It was there, with her breasts cinched to her body by the tight military sports bra, that a rancid smell had begun to linger. At first Whitney had been able to ignore her own odor, thinking about other things. But now it was as though someone had cut a fresh onion and hung it around her neck. She could think of nothing else. It would take a monumental distraction to take her attention away from the stench.

When distraction finally arrived in the form of an odd noise, Whitney was momentarily thankful. Then the body odor rising from her chest seemed a pleasant, fading dream. The forest around them filled with a sandpapery noise that reminded Whitney of a carpentry shop. But in the context of Antarktos, she knew that sound came from something infinitely more dangerous than angry carpenters.

"Crylophosaurs," Merrill said, his voice hushed, Whitney's 9mm clutched in his hand.

Vesuvius began a savage barrage of barking and his hair rose on his back.

"Shut him up!" Cruz said. "He'll give our position away."

"They already know where we are," Merrill said. "His barking might be the only thing that keeps them from attacking."

Wright grabbed Merrill by the shoulders and looked him in the eye. "You know these creatures better than anyone, Merrill. What do you suggest?"

Whitney was surprised by her father's sudden change from a weary, old scientist cum theologian to a take-charge warrior. "Fall back slowly. Running will only entice them to attack. Find a defensible position that can only be attacked from one side."

"Why are you listening to him?" Cruz asked. "What are we supposed to do after we've gone and trapped ourselves?"

Merrill smirked. "Let them group and funnel in for the attack." He patted Wright's XM-29. "Then unleash hell."

Cruz couldn't hide his smile. "I like the way you think."

"Get on it," Wright said. "Ferrell, you lead. Merrill, Whitney, you follow. Me and Cruz"—Vesuvius let out a savage bark followed by a low growl—"and Vesuvius, will bring up the rear. Go."

Ferrell led the way, moving swiftly but not running. The rest followed in tight formation. The sound of scratching rang out all around them.

Ferrell located an outcrop of tall stones that formed a basic U-shape. They entered and faced the jungle, aiming their weapons. Vesuvius continued to bark. As though sensing their prey was trapped, their pursuers called out with shrieks and guttural chortling. The din was hellish.

As she held her heavy XM-29 at the ready and prepared to fire, Whitney looked at her shaking hands and realized that she wasn't at all prepared for something else.

Death.

 # CHAPTER 44

It surrounded him now like never before.

Death.

General Kuan-Yin Zhou had seen his fair share of it over the years, but this put all his years of military service to shame. Men dying, screaming for their lives.

For the past five minutes his men had fought bravely, but the ranks were broken. The enemy had charged and horrified his army with their size and ferocity. Some men stopped fighting and simply stood, waiting to be butchered like cows at a slaughterhouse, resigned to their fate. But for Zhou, flight or standing stupefied were not options. He lobbed two grenades at the nearest attacker and, before they exploded, picked up a dead man's weapon and unloaded a clip. The bullets tore into the skin of the first attacker just as the grenades exploded.

The burst of metal and flame mercifully killed the few Chinese soldiers in the area, but the attackers remained unscathed. They continued the assault. Some men were crushed underfoot or smacked against trees. Others were torn limb from limb. And still others, whom Zhou believed suffered the worst fate, were taken alive.

Like Lei.

Ten minutes ago, the world had been a different place. They were making impressive time and ahead of schedule. They were an efficient machine eating its way through the jungle like a caterpillar devouring a leaf.

When the jungle sounds created by the scads of unknown species ceased, Zhou had called for defensive positions. The formation was perfect. The defense was solid. A wall of firepower.

That's when the howling started. It was a sound so deep and constant that Zhou feared his ears would be permanently damaged. It was a battle cry. All around them the jungle stirred with motion as the massive attackers pressed forward. Trees bent and cracked in their wake. The ground shook.

Zhou's first impression was that another team had managed to sneak a tank group onto the continent. It would have been difficult to achieve such a feat undetected, but it would have been a masterful move. It wasn't until he saw the first enemy soldier that he remembered that whoever had taken Lei had come from above.

Zhou's men unleashed a fury, the likes of which had never before been seen on the continent. The sound of a hundred automatic weapons firing was deafening. Then the shoulder-mounted rockets and RPGs thundered with the chorus. The forest for a half mile around was flattened. All that remained standing when the men paused to reload were four large, angry behemoths.

After weapons were reloaded, the men did not resume their attack. Not only had the attackers survived, but they appeared unscathed. It was unimaginable. They were able either to dodge bullets or unnaturally absorb them. It was when one moved that Zhou's latter suspicion was confirmed. The creatures had taken the bullets and explosive rounds without injury, protecting the trees behind them from being felled by the barrage. They were impervious to harm—an undefeatable enemy. One of them opened its mouth and howled.

He knew from that moment that he and his men were doomed, but to lay down arms and surrender was not his way. He ordered the second command to fire, but before a shot was fired, the attackers were on them, shredding men five at a time.

Now the chaos was almost over. Perhaps fifty men had escaped into the jungle. One hundred and fifty were either dead or dying. Zhou was the last man still putting up any kind of resistance.

The four brutes turned their attention to him and stalked forward. He unloaded his pistol, dropped it, and picked up a dead man's assault rifle. He fired every round at one of the titans, hoping that a concentrated burst might do some harm. But every bullet that pierced the skin entered the body and disappeared. The bloody wound left behind quickly healed and faded away. It was as though the ancient Kuan Ti, god of war, had come to earth to finish what the great cataclysm had begun.

The weapon ran out of ammunition and they were upon him. In a last-ditch effort, Zhou dove toward a man carrying a rocket launcher. He gripped the weapon, rolled over, and fired at the closest attacker. Zhou was thrown into the air by the rocket's propulsion and his back was burned by the flames deflected by the ground. But he landed on his knees and watched.

It dodged. The monster simply leaned to the side, letting the rocket pass. But its body had blocked the view of the towering figure behind him. Rocket connected with forehead and exploded, taking the attacker's head with it. The body toppled like a fallen tree and crashed to the forest floor, landing atop several already dead soldiers.

Zhou felt a certain pride in slaying one of the attackers. It seemed an impossible task, but he knew their weakness now. If only his men had remained fighting, they might yet have won the battle. But alone and now unarmed, Zhou knew his life was forfeit.

After glancing angrily at his dead companion, the closest attacker reached out and took hold of Zhou. The general felt his arms snap under the pressure of the giant's grip. Arching in pain, he tried to scream, but the air had been compressed out of his lungs. A moment later he felt a quick, hard slap on the back. The pressure was gone, replaced by a breeze that whipped through his hair.

Zhou opened his eyes and found himself enjoying a most peculiar view. He saw mountains in the distance. And a large lake. Beyond that, the ground rose up sharply. And below, the green canopy of the jungle. As he continued floating higher, he felt for a moment that he was magically flying over the jungle.

When gravity took hold again and he fell back toward the jungle, he realized what had happened. He'd been thrown, tossed into the air like a stone. He suppressed his scream and prepared for death. He'd fought well. He'd led well against insurmountable odds, and he'd killed one of the giant men.

The slap of the leaves was much harder coming down and almost knocked him unconscious. He was awake enough to hear, for a fraction of a second, his spine shatter as he struck a tree trunk.

He was dead before he hit the ground.

 CHAPTER 45

As the crescendo of agonized bird-like calls rose in volume, Whitney recognized the strategy from her first run-in with the crylophosaurs. The scraping sound, which Whitney believed was created by the creatures rubbing their rough skin against tree bark, grew to a fevered pitch. As the chorus turned tumultuous, she sensed an attack was imminent. She knew the only reason they had yet to be assaulted was the brave Vesuvius, standing his ground before certain death.

Vesuvius stood at the front of the group, his hair raised, his teeth bared, and his ears perked. He was ready for action even if none of the others were. Of course, if the crylos were the adept predators her father claimed they were, Vesuvius didn't stand a chance.

"Switch to explosive rounds, if you haven't already." Wright's voice made her jump, but she did as he instructed.

The brush around the U-shaped enclosure shook. It was the final stage of preparation for the crylos before they attacked. They'd done the same thing back at the wall. Whitney could see how it would be useful. If not for the XM-29s in their hands, she was sure they'd all be reduced to cringing, waiting for death.

"On my mark," Wright said, "open up with everything you've got."

Nods all around signified readiness. She saw her father look at the tiny 9mm in his hand and frown. He drew his ancient sword and stood ready, like some old world swashbuckler. He was handling the situation well. Much better than she was.

For all her adult life, Whitney had easily dismissed the idea of life after death. She wasn't necessarily atheist, but she saw no evidence to prove or disprove the validity of any religion. She had been surprised and rather shaken by her father's evidence for the flood, especially given the recent changes the planet had undergone. If he was right, if the flood really did happen, one of the greatest, most unbelievable portions of the Bible was confirmed. And if that was true . . . what about the rest? She had always been so certain that eventually she'd find some way to shake her father's faith, but it was he who had shaken hers. Her belief in nothing was suddenly challenged, and the fate that they now faced seemed that much more perilous.

The shaking brush grew so violent that leaves sprayed into the air. It was all the incentive Wright needed. "Let 'em have it!"

Whitney flinched as Wright, Ferrell, and Cruz opened up with their explosive rounds. One moment the charges burst loudly from the weapons, the next they exploded in the jungle, shattering trees and sending up plumes of dirt . . . and blood. Shrieks rang out and the monsters pounced forward.

Ten of them lunged into the clearing and pounded forward, claws outstretched and jaws wide open. Whitney saw the creatures for the first time; they were, in fact, her father's crylophosaurs. Large teeth for tearing flesh. Sharp claws that seemed much more dangerous when not fossilized. And the crest on the head flaunted their power, their rule over the land. Truly, these were the kings of Antarctica.

"Fire! Damn it, fire!" Wright was shouting at her as he laid a line of explosive rounds in front of the attacking horde. The ground sprayed up in a cloud, hiding prey from predator and vice versa. Five of the creatures burst through the plume and charged forward. Whitney aimed at the one headed her direction and pulled the trigger.

Nothing happened.

The safety! She cursed herself and flipped the safety off. Her father stood by her side as she raised her weapon. He fired a steady stream from the 9mm, but the bullets had little effect. The crylo hissed at him as though to say, "You're next," and continued for Whitney.

Her arms shook as she fired off four rounds in quick succession. The first two missed and exploded in the ground, sending more dirt into the air. The second two struck the crylo in the chest; it reeled back from the impacts, but remained standing. Then the dinosaur ceased to exist. The exploding rounds did as they were designed to do: burst the target from the inside out. The explosion was close enough to knock Whitney and her father off their feet.

Whitney opened her eyes and looked up at the sky. She saw bright blue through the tall pine-like trees and for a fraction of a second, felt peace. Even with the barrage of explosions, the shrieks of death, the wailing attack calls, and rattle of gunfire, Whitney felt like she was floating. As the sensation dissipated, a sharp pain followed by wet, warm moisture on the back of her head told her that she'd banged her skull against something hard, and it was now bleeding.

Unconsciousness loomed. For a moment she thought she saw the Grim Reaper standing high above her, possibly floating in the sky. When her eyes refocused, she realized she was half right. Standing on the top of the rock formation were two more crylos. One was average sized, perhaps fifteen feet long. The other was a monster, pushing thirty feet from tail to snout, with a massive head. The smaller of the two leapt from the outcropping and landed twenty feet from Whitney, a distance she knew it could cover in one hop.

She rolled over and felt her mind spin. Her equilibrium was totally out of whack. She tripped over something solid and fell to her knees. Whitney saw that the object which tripped her was her father, lying unconscious. She picked up the 9mm and squeezed the trigger several times.

Nothing.

In desperation, she took hold of her father's ancient sword and wielded it weakly, waving it at the approaching crylo. She noticed the dinosaur glance at the weapon, which only seemed to incense it more. The crylo's throat shook as it let out a loud gobble and lunged forward. Whitney drew the sword back and prepared to swing at just the right moment. She knew a blade would do little against a predator whose jaws were full of blades, but she had to try.

A shadow leaped from above. At first she thought it was Vesuvius, performing his last act as mighty protector, but then she noticed the head, round and impeccably smooth. It was a man. In one hand, he clutched a bowie knife. With the other hand, he grabbed the crylo's neck and swung around behind it.

With a ferocity she'd never seen in a man, she watched him plunge the knife into the crylo's throat. Its mutant turkey call turned to a gurgle. Then the blade was withdrawn and stabbed straight down through the dinosaur's head, just behind the crest. Whitney winced as the blade audibly pierced through bone and flesh to jut out through the crylo's lower jaw. The crylo fell limply and crashed to the ground.

Everything fell silent. The shrieks of injured dinosaurs faded into the forest. The large crylo was gone from its perch. Whitney struggled to sit up and saw that the group was bloodied and exhausted but that everyone had survived. Even Vesuvius, who was growling and pulling at the flesh of one of the crylos, had survived the attack. A bloody scratch over his left eye would leave a scar, but otherwise the dog had lived up to the power his name represented.

Wright, Cruz, and Ferrell raised their weapons and surrounded Whitney's savior. The man raised his hands and dropped his weapon. She finally got a good look at him. His face was kind, though covered in blood. His clothing was definitely military, but not American.

"Who are you?" Wright asked. His voice and body language indicated that if he didn't get a satisfactory answer, the man's fate would be the same at the crylo's.

"Ian Jacobson. I'm all that's left of the European team."

Weapons lowered immediately.

"You're it?" Cruz asked. "Damn."

"What happened to you?" Wright asked.

Jacobson nodded to one of the dead crylos. "They did. Caught us in the open while we were distracted. Buggers cut through my team in seconds. They've been dogging me since." Jacobson looked around at the carnage. Eight crylos lay dead. "Looks like I signed up with the wrong team, eh?"

Wright knelt and inspected the knife wound on the head of the crylo Jacobson had killed. "You didn't do so bad yourself." Wright picked up Jacobson's knife and handed it to him. He pulled helped Whitney to her feet and moved on to Merrill, still unconscious on the ground. "Hey, Merrill," Wright said, giving him a few gentle smacks on the cheek. He came to with a start, shouting and flailing.

Whitney knelt at his side. "Dad, you're okay." She placed a gentle hand on his shoulder. His wide eyes looked into hers and relief swept across his face. Tears welled up and he squeezed her. "Thought I'd lost you," he said. "Thought I'd lost you."

Whitney watched as the four soldiers conferred. Wright spoke to Ferrell in a quiet voice. "Is that what killed Popova and chased you?" He pointed to the dead crylos. Ferrell shook her head. Whitney couldn't hear her response, but she could read her lips. "They were"—Ferrell looked bewildered—"taller."

 CHAPTER 46

A sense of bewildered joy consumed al-Aziz's body as he ran. The road carved by Allah slowly faded, branching out in several directions before disappearing altogether. But Allah had taken him so far, so fast. He was now ahead of schedule, even with the slow start to watch Abdul's attempt at martyrdom.

The gear and explosives he carried seemed a lighter weight than before. His legs no longer burned from exertion. He'd been given another gift: unending endurance. He would run this race like no other . . . and he would win. Allah had made sure of that.

With a sudden repetitive beep from his wristwatch, Allah called al-Aziz to *salat*, to prayer. It was noon.

Al-Aziz unrolled his prayer mat and checked his compass. After the shift, it had appeared that compasses no longer worked. In truth, they worked fine; it was human interpretation that failed. Magnetic north and south still existed, but the land that had once been north was south. The reverse was also true. It depended on where in the new world one was. Those with keen minds, like al-Aziz, adapted to the change and learned to trust the seemingly false compass readings.

He found north and lay the mat down so it faced, approximately, Ka'aba, the holy house at Mecca. He knelt down and lay prostrate, arms outstretched, saying, *"Allahu Akbar."* He rose to his knees again and clasped his left wrist with his right hand and held them before his chest. He began praying the traditional *fatiha*.

"All praises and thanks be to Allah, the lord of the Alamin. The most gracious, the most merciful. The only owner of the day of recompense. You alone I worship, and You alone we ask for help." Al-Aziz prayed loudly and couldn't help but interject his own thoughts into the rest of the fatiha. "Aid me in my quest, which You have so graciously bestowed upon your servant. Show me where Your will would have me go next. Reveal to me my enemies so that I might smite them with your holy vengeance."

Al-Aziz continued, eager to finish and be on his way. "Guide me to the straight way, the way of those on whom You have bestowed your grace; not the way of those who earned your anger, the Jews; nor those who went astray, the Christians."

In the original prayer, Jews and Christians weren't included by name, but even moderate Muslims knew whom the prayer referred to. Long before the cataclysmic events of three months past, al-Aziz had been shown a Muslim Web site by a colleague who used the Internet for video conferencing with his brother, who was studying to be a doctor in London. It was user-friendly, bright and cheery, very appealing. The site was easy to navigate and well-designed. He followed the links on the website and came across a Flash animation of how prayer was to be performed by a good Muslim. It was educational, and everything was translated into English. Back then, ten or so years ago, it was the belief of many Muslims that conquering America could only be done through peaceful conversation. It was one of the reasons Islam was the fastest-growing religion in the world. But al-Aziz and many others knew that simple outreach wouldn't be enough.

As he'd watched the animation progress forward he read the Arabic version, written out just as it was said. But when he read the English translation, he smiled from ear to ear. There he was, reading the traditional prayer on a Muslim website, created by the same Muslims who might denounce a terror bombing or martyrdom, and the truth was revealed. With parenthesized text added by the website administrator, the translation read: ". . . not the way of those who have earned your anger (the Jews), nor those who went astray (the Christians)." The loathing—some might say "hatred"—for Christianity and the Jews, that was really God's divine will, had filtered into mainstream Islam. It was no wonder that so many eager Muslims joined in jihad when America lost most of its power. It was only fear of the great evil that had kept them silent. Now they were free to act!

This thought inspired the remainder of his prayer and he added, ". . . and the Americans, who have also earned your anger and who will feel your wrath through jihad, destroy them with your might, Allah."

Al-Aziz raised his head to the sky and shouted, "A'meen!" It was traditional that if the prayer was said loudly it should be ended loudly, but the effect was unusual. Before al-Aziz could move on to reciting medium-sized *suras* of the Qur'an, a flock of odd-looking birds displaying blue, purple, and red plumage burst from the jungle and spread into the sky. At first, he thought he'd simply scared them with his emphatic "A'meen," but then it occurred to him it might be a sign.

Allah was responding to his prayer.

For the first time in his life, al-Aziz got up from his mat before finishing his prayers and strode toward the portion of jungle from which the birds had fled. He didn't draw his machete or ready his weapon. He left them next to the mat with the rest of his gear. He had nothing to fear. Allah was protecting him. Perhaps Allah meant for al-Aziz to be his next great prophet? Al-Aziz smiled as he moved through the overgrowth, spreading the green tendrils away from his face as he pushed forward. But he emerged into a ghastly scene a thousand times worse than the remains of the European team he'd discovered.

The stench from blood and bile spilled out on the forest floor in puddles like thick soup. Parchments of flesh hung from exposed muscle and bones. Fillets of red meat lay neatly upon an altar of stone. Rusty metal hooks pierced decaying flesh. The bodies hung limp, their entrails dangling to the ground. The gnawed—

He had to turn his head away.

Everything he knew to be true about the world, about Allah, about good and evil, and about himself changed in that instant. He fell to his knees, lying prostrate again, but instead of uttering a prayer he vomited violently.

CHAPTER 47

Three days passed without further attack or incident. The U.S. team, including Jacobson, made good time and began to hope that the crylos had lost interest. The creatures were probably not used to prey biting back. Merrill just hoped they didn't have brains enough to hold a grudge, or they'd be back with a vengeance.

After climbing at a slight but constant incline for days, Merrill was happy when the ground leveled out. Soon the trees and brush began to thin. Then, as suddenly as the lake had appeared out of the jungle, they entered a field of tall plants. The five-foot stalks resembled wheat but were thicker, taller, and green.

Ferrell took to a tree, climbing to the top in seconds and shouting her report: "No way around. We have to go through."

Wright shook his head and, for once, Merrill knew just what he was thinking. Crossing the field would leave them exposed to their enemies, human or otherwise. There would be no cover, no place to hide, no defensible position. For all intents and purposes, they'd be sitting ducks.

A cool wind stroked the stiff leaves growing from the top of every stalk, rubbing them together. The sound was like loud static. Wright shook his head again. They wouldn't even hear an attack coming.

"This is bloody terrific," Jacobson said. Merrill hadn't had too much time to get to know the new addition to the team, but he seemed like a nice enough man and his accent gave him a pleasant aura, even when he was upset. The only strange part of Jacobson's personality was his compulsion to have a perfectly smooth head. Even when they were hiking, he would take his over-used Bic and scrape it across his head, removing whatever infinitesimal amount of hair had managed to grow since he last took the razor to it.

"I want weapons unslung and safeties off until we clear the field," Wright said. "Stay in a tight line. If something so much as twitches out there, fire a few rounds. If it twitches again, unload until it stops. Understood?"

Nods all around confirmed that it was. Wright entered first, followed by Cruz, Merrill, Mirabelle, Vesuvius, and Jacobson. Ferrell brought up the rear.

Inside the thick field, the air was stale and the breeze failed to penetrate. It was stiflingly hot and very dry. Sweat was absorbed into the air long before it had a chance to cool the skin. Merrill licked his lips and his tongue felt like sandpaper. He twisted the cap off his canteen and took a swig.

His thoughts were not on the discomfort of traveling but on the dangers the group might face during this final week of travel. The others were confident that they'd faced the worst Antarktos had to offer, but Merrill wasn't so sure. *Crylophosaurus* was only one of the many original denizens that had stalked Antarktos twelve thousand years ago. He feared other, perhaps more fearsome predators waited for them. There was no fossil evidence for that assumption, but around the world, where medium-sized theropods like the crylos had lived, larger, more dangerous predators had always existed in tandem. *Tyrannosaurus rex*, *Allosaurus*, *Carcharodontosaurus*, and *Giganotosaurus*—who was two meters longer and two tons heavier than the T-rex—could have Antarctic cousins. Just because no fossils had been found didn't mean they had never existed. Antarktos had proven itself to be a world where prehistory and modern history collided.

He feared that clashes would continue, perhaps even worsen, with the introduction of modern man. They already had. He considered the skeletons of the giant man and *Crylophosaurus* he'd found back in his valley. They appeared to be mortal enemies, clashing soldiers. Perhaps the wall was built to keep the crylos at bay . . . Merrill longed for this race to end so he could return to his work and uncover countless mysteries. It was his hope, of course, that Mira would join him, perhaps make a photo documentary of their work. They could publish his second book together, *Return to Antarktos*.

Of course, Merrill realized that the world might not care so much about history or reading books for some time to come. Not until the displaced billions were resettled and Antarktos had been divvied up, clear-cut, and paved over. He imagined the names of future cities would likely be named after those destroyed. New Boston. New Washington. New New York? No, that wouldn't work.

Merrill tried to picture where the cities would be located. No doubt the expansive coastline would be peppered with city after city. The large lake they crossed would probably sport one or two large cities.

The stalks became even rows, separated by several feet. It reminded Merrill of a cornfield he'd walked through as a child. It had an almost agricultural feel to it. The feeling was unshakable. "This isn't a natural field," Merrill said. "Plants don't naturally grow in lines like this."

Wright paused the forward-marching team. "You're sure?"

Merrill nodded. "This is, without a doubt, a man-made agricultural field."

"You think someone's already living here?" Whitney asked.

"No," Merrill said. "The plant must be native to Antarktos. So when the rest of the anhydrobiotic plants sprang back to life, these did as well. But these were planted by the original settlers."

"The giants?" Whitney asked.

Merrill nodded. "The Nephilim."

"The Nephilim?" Jacobson said, suddenly interested. "The heroes of old, men of renown."

Merrill smiled widely. He knew he liked Jacobson, and now he knew why. He could see the glimmer in his eye, the spark that revealed an excitement for the mysteries of the world. Merrill chimed in. "Genesis 6:4."

Jacobson's eyes grew wide. "They were here?"

"I believe so," Merrill said, eager to launch into a discussion about the ancient giants. But Wright had other ideas.

"Save it," Wright said. "And no more talk until we're clear of the field. I don't want to draw any attention."

Jacobson nodded and a professional guise slid onto his face. Merrill couldn't hide his disappointment. He took his place in line and skulked forward. A pat on his shoulder caught his attention. He turned and saw Jacobson flash a smile. He gave Merrill a thumbs-up sign that said, "We'll talk about it later." Merrill was content to wait, but if he was right, he would seriously reconsider building on this land. It could very well be horribly tainted.

Merrill pushed thoughts of the Nephilim from his mind and returned to the subject of city building and renaming. After unrolling his copy of the Piri Reis map, he held it low so that he could see where he was walking while inspecting the map. He found the lake they had crossed then worked his way inland. Forests and hills were depicted, followed by a large flat area divided into squares. He couldn't be sure, but he thought it might be the fields they currently walked through. He noted that beyond the field was a brief portion of forest, a few tall mountains, then . . . Merrill folded the map so he could hold it steady and scrutinized its contents. Beyond that was a large mountain; carved into the side of the mountain was a fortress of some kind. At the top of the fortress was what looked like a human skull. At the base of the mountain was a river that came from inside the mountain itself, perhaps from an underground spring, one of the many around the world that accessed the vast subterranean reservoirs that had aided in the original deluge.

Merrill became consumed by the image drawn so long ago. The human skull captured his attention. He wasn't sure if it was meant as a warning. This place was either dangerous or was a geologic formation, something like New Hampshire's once-noble Old Man on the Mountain. As he looked at the details surrounding the mountain, he gasped. Intertwined in the drawing of the mountain, so subtle that he hadn't seen them at first, were two large feet. They were similar to those found elsewhere on the map, but these looked stronger, larger. Symbolism was everything in the ancient world. He thought about what it could mean.

Distracted as he was by the images on the Piri Reis map, Merrill failed to notice the wind pick up. A sudden gust tore the map out of his hands and pulled it through a corridor in the stalks. Merrill charged after the map.

"Clark!" hissed Wright. "Get your ass back here!"

Merrill was inches from the floating map and didn't want to lose it. They all had a copy, but he doubted the government would create a new one for him when all this was over. If he lost his copy, he might lose it forever.

The wind gusted again and the map was lifted up higher. Merrill leapt and snagged the corner of the map between his thumb and index finger. Map safely recovered, Merrill didn't concentrate on his landing and spilled over gracelessly.

He heard the rest of the team run toward him and stop. He prepared for whatever verbal barrage Wright might unleash, but nothing came. He looked up to see the entire team looking beyond him. He followed their eyes to discover that he'd stumbled into a perfectly circular clearing in the wheat-like field.

Beyond the trampled stalks that were bent like a perfect crop circle was clothing—uniforms—from pants and socks to helmets and weapons, scattered throughout the field. The team slowly entered the clearing, wary of a trap. Ferrell bent down to inspect a discarded uniform and found an emblem stitched to it—a red rectangle with a large gold star in the upper left corner, and four smaller stars arranged in a vertical crescent to the right of the large star. "Chinese," she said.

Wright picked up one of the assault rifles and handed it to Merrill. "Upgrade," he said. Merrill took the weapon. It was heavier than the 9mm but lighter than the XM-29. In his hands he knew all three were useless, but he'd be more likely to get in a lucky shot with an automatic weapon. He slung it over his shoulder.

"What happened here?" his daughter asked.

"Crop circle," Jacobson said.

"Hogwash," Merrill chimed in. Crop circles were the creations of pranksters and jobless teenagers, and only interested UFO enthusiasts.

"Some theorize that energies from inside the earth create the circles," Jacobson explained. "It's possible that they were, for lack of a better word, vaporized."

"Complete hogwash."

"I'm surprised, Dr. Clark," Jacobson said with a smile, "that with your knowledge of the Nephilim, you fail to see the connection here."

Merrill felt the turning gears in his mind groan to a halt and reverse direction. Jacobson was right. Strange, demonic abilities had long been attributed to the Nephilim. It did, after all, run in their blood.

Wright stepped forward. "Look. You two can confer about all this mumbo jumbo mystical history stuff just as soon as we clear the field. This is the last time I'm going to tell you."

"Agreed," Merrill said, though not for fear of the consequences. He knew Wright would do nothing to harm them. But now, more than ever, he wanted to get out of the field. "But can I make one suggestion?"

Wright raised his eyebrows, declaring his impatience but waiting for Merrill to speak. "Stay off the cleared paths." Merrill shared a look with Jacobson. "They might not be safe."

They ran the rest of the way, plowing through the thick stalks, and didn't clear the field until nightfall. They set up camp after returning to the darkness of the forest, careful not to make too much noise or create any light that could be seen. After settling in, Merrill thought he and Jacobson might be able to rekindle their conversation, but before he had a chance, Mira's voice cut through the darkness.

"Anyone smell that?" she asked.

Merrill took a deep breath and nodded, even though no one could see him. "Smoke."

CHAPTER 48

After much protest, Merrill was forced to stay at camp with Vesuvius while the others searched for the source of the smoke. The dog had proven his worth, but Wright didn't want their position betrayed because of an ill-timed bark.

Plodding through the darkness, Whitney began wondering if she too should have remained behind. Sure, she had fired her XM-29 and successfully killed a crylo, but she knew it was dumb luck. She wasn't a soldier. That same sinking feeling she'd had back in the frozen church came back in spades. She wasn't a hero. She wasn't adept at being stealthy, beyond sneaking up on animals with a camera. The only things she'd shot before the crylo were cardboard cutouts of gangsters at the shooting range and photos of animals.

Whitney frowned as she realized she'd been so preoccupied by their trek that she had completely forgotten to take pictures along the way. If any of her photography friends were left alive, they'd scoff at her. But not having taken pictures left Whitney with an odd sense of peace. This new world was so strange, so wondrous, and so captivating that photos would not do it justice.

A low-hanging branch audibly slapped against her forehead. She paused for a moment and listened, knowing that her misstep might have given them away. She knew she shouldn't have come. But nothing happened. There was no movement.

A voice came in the faintest whisper: "Careful, *chica*."

Cruz knew she couldn't argue or smack him. The jerk.

The group moved slowly and silently with Ferrell leading them toward the place where she believed the smoky odor was originating from. The scent, Whitney noticed, grew stronger and more intense. She stifled the urge to cough and hoped they would soon find the source, turn tail, and get the hell out of there.

A quick climb up a short hill brought them to the crest of a much steeper incline, which led to a clearing. Before looking over the top, Whitney tied a dark green bandana on her head. She was confident her dark skin would conceal her in the shadows, but her bright blond, frizzy hair would be a beacon. Bandana securely in place, she peeked up over the crest. A blazing bonfire raged at the center of the clearing. A single figure sat by the fire, rocking back and forth, muttering to himself. His voice was so soft that the words he spoke were too quiet to hear. Even so, Whitney had the distinct feeling that he was not speaking English.

The team ducked back behind the cover of the hilltop. A thinner tree line allowed moonlight from the full moon above to filter through the trees. Whitney could see the bemused faces of the others, cast in pale blue. The man was stripped of clothing to his underwear and wore a strange, thick belt around his waist that almost reached up to his ribs. It looked like a thick corset. His skin was dark, but that didn't help place his country of origin. Many of the competing counties were comprised of dark-skinned men and women. His hair was also black and curly, cut short. The area around him was full of strange objects, but in the wash of light from the fire Whitney couldn't make out the details.

Wright spoke with amazing clarity even though he was barely audible. "Ferrell, Cruz. Circle around. Move on my mark. No firing unless fired upon."

The two departed quickly and silently, one to the left, one to the right. Wright continued. "Jacobson. Stay on my nine." Jacobson nodded. "Whitney, you're on my three."

Whitney furrowed her brow. "What?"

"My three o'clock."

Whitney knew he was using military lingo for directional positions, but she still wasn't sure how it worked. She shrugged.

Wright sighed. "My right."

Whitney stifled the urge to make a sarcastic comment, as doing so now might get them killed. She took her position at Wright's side and the three inched their way down the hill, sliding on their bellies.

Upon reaching the bottom of the hill, all eyes were on the single sitting man. He was still rocking back and forth as he sat cross-legged on a red mat before the fire. He mumbled incoherently and, Whitney thought, nervously. Wright slowly stood and motioned for the others to join him. He stepped forward into the clearing and suddenly gave a loud whistle. In an instant they were running into the clearing, weapons and flashlights trained on the lone man. As Whitney ran in with weapon aimed, she saw Cruz and Ferrell enter the clearing from the other side.

As they approached him, Wright held out his arm and stopped Whitney in her tracks. The others had stopped as well. She searched the man with her eyes and found the reason for the others' apprehension around the man's waist. It wasn't a belt; it was blocks of explosives, wired together. He appeared to have a detonator in his hand. She could also see that the man was of Middle Eastern descent—part of the Arab Alliance.

Whitney noticed a subtle change in Wright's aim, from the man's head to his hand. Could he really stop the man from blowing them all to bits by shooting his hand? She hoped they wouldn't have to find out.

The man had yet to acknowledge their presence. He seemed delirious, spouting his repetitive mantra which Whitney now recognized as Arabic. She couldn't speak the language beyond "hello," "goodbye," and "thank you," but she'd spent enough time in Egypt shooting photos on the Nile that the language had become familiar.

Ferrell, on the other hand, was fluent. "Take your hand off the detonator," she said in Arabic. "Remove your hand now."

The man's eyes fluttered. For a moment he appeared terrified, so panic-stricken that Whitney was afraid he would detonate the bomb; but when his eyes met Ferrell's, he paused. She was not who he was expecting to see. He searched the faces of the others, one at a time, taking them in. "Who . . . who are you?" he asked Ferrell.

"The United States team," she replied. That much Whitney understood.

The man removed his finger from the detonator and placed it on the ground. He sighed with relief and spoke in English. "Thank you! Thank you for coming!"

"This ain't no dinner party, man," Cruz said, weapon still aimed. "Why the happy reception, eh?"

The man seemed momentarily confused then understanding dawned. "No . . . I thought you were them. The giants."

Whitney's stomach twisted. She stepped forward. "Who?"

"The ones who did this." The man swept his arm out in an arc, motioning to the surrounding clearing.

As Whitney turned she realized that in their haste to secure the man, they had not inspected the surroundings. Her father would be disappointed. With all his trap-setting, he would have thought to look around first. Whitney's initial reaction was relief as she realized there were no traps. The second was horror.

The fire seemed hot enough to sear skin. The odor of the burning wood carried something else, something putrid. She breathed through her mouth, trying to ignore the smell, but the dry, ashen air stung her throat. Her discomfort quickly became overshadowed by intense fear as her eyes took in the rest.

Surrounding them were stone altars and wooden stakes arranged in a circle. Impaled on each stake was a human head, Chinese, by the looks of them. On the altars rested slabs of meat—human flesh, neatly carved into fillets and arranged in an elaborate pattern. Several naked, headless corpses hung from hooks, their intestines spilling out and dangling like vines. There was a large central altar, above which a crylo had been nailed to a tree and, like the human bodies, disembowelled. Its skin had been peeled away and stretched out, nailed to posts on both sides, revealing internal organs, sinewy muscle, and broken, jagged ribs. Its face was frozen in agony. The creature had been mutilated alive. It was the centerpiece of the macabre scene.

Surrounding the fire, etched into the dirt, were symbols both intricate and ancient. Whitney suspected even her father couldn't read them. Her eyes trailed back up to the carved bodies and she fell to one knee, hand over mouth, straining to keep the rising bile from exploding from her mouth. A crime had been committed, not against the Chinese or the Arabs or the Americans. This was a crime against humankind.

As the Middle Eastern man spoke, Whitney knew that he realized this as well. "My name is Ahmed al-Aziz. I would like very much to join your party. Please."

 # CHAPTER 49

A wave of nausea passed through the entire group. Jacobson had his hands on his knees, head down, breathing hard. Cruz had the crook of his arm wrapped around his nose and mouth. Even Ferrell was visibly shaken. Her weapon was lowered, her hand over her mouth, eyes glistening . . . with tears?

Only Wright reacted with something other than disgust and sorrow: rage. He shoved the muzzle of his XM-29 against the temple of al-Aziz. "What did you do?" he hissed. "What did you do to these people?"

Al-Aziz shook with fear. His eyes went wide and glowed in the firelight. "I did nothing!" He shook his head. "They were like this when I arrived."

Wright kicked the man's shoulder, toppling him sideways with no regard to the explosives wrapped around his waist. "Then who set the fire?"

Al-Aziz's eyes showed a flicker of panic. "I—I did."

Wright took aim and stepped back. He had clearly made up his mind and was going to shoot the man. But Whitney wasn't convinced the man was guilty. The scene was too inhuman, too evil. "Stop!" she yelled.

He held his aim but did not fire. "Take your hand off my shoulder, Whitney."

"He didn't do this," Whitney said. Wright didn't respond, but at least he was listening. "Look at the stakes, Wright. Look at the altars. He's just one man. There is no way he could have done this. How many Chinese uniforms did we find in the field? Fifteen? Do you think one man could have captured fifteen soldiers, stripped them bare, carried them all here, and then done this thing?"

Wright took his eyes off al-Aziz and looked at Whitney. "Someone needs to answer for this."

"And someone will. But not him."

She looked at al-Aziz and met his eyes. He looked like a scared animal caught in a bear trap. She couldn't help but feel sorry for him.

Wright lowered his weapon.

"Thank you," al-Aziz said, bowing his head in gratitude, first toward Wright then toward Whitney. "Thank you."

"You can come with us," Wright said to al-Aziz. "But you must agree to forfeit your place at the finish. You must remove yourself from the race."

Al-Aziz nodded. "Agreed, but I would prefer to not finish the race at all . . . leaving this place would be best."

"I don't care what you think is best," Wright said. "You will not carry a weapon. You will not have an opinion."

"Then I am your prisoner?"

Wright considered for a moment. "If you want to leave, by all means, do so. These are my conditions. Whether you did this or not, that bomb around your waist aligns you with terrorists, which in my opinion aren't so different from whoever *did* do this."

Al-Aziz nodded. "I—I understand. Seeing all this . . . this mutilation. It reminds me of things I have seen before. Things I have seen done to men in my country. When I saw this place, I understood what it was we have done, what I have done to others. I turn my back on jihad. And can no longer hold to the true teachings of Islam."

Whitney could scarcely believe what she was hearing. She knew enough about radical Islam to realize that the things he was saying, even if a ruse, would be enough to earn a swift decapitation in much of the Muslim world. He seemed in earnest.

Wright motioned to Cruz. "Remove the bomb."

Cruz stepped toward al-Aziz, but the man scrambled back on his hands and feet. "No! The bomb cannot be removed."

Wright took aim again. "Now is not a good time to argue."

"It is . . . trapped. It will explode," al-Aziz said, his breath quick and nervous. "To remove it is to die."

Wright stared at al-Aziz, apparently sizing him up. He lowered his weapon again. "Stupid terrorists." He shook his head in exasperation. "This was supposed to be a one-way trip for you."

Al-Aziz nodded his confirmation. "Martyrdom cannot be achieved without losing your life."

Wright appeared incensed again, and Whitney suspected he'd dealt with terrorists before. His eyes gleamed more brightly than the glowing embers of the fire. Al-Aziz noticed, too.

"I am not that man anymore," al-Aziz said. "You have nothing to fear from me now."

That brought a faint smile to Wright's face. "I never did."

Jacobson stepped into the circle, laying on his accent, trying to calm everyone down. "Aziz, can you tell us about those who did this? The giants?"

Al-Aziz seemed momentarily terrified by the memories of what he'd seen, then he spoke softly, almost like a child. "I was . . . the path was clear. In the jungle. Then I came to this place. I spread the leaves and I—I . . ." He pointed to the dirt near the edge of the clearing. "I vomited."

Whitney saw that he was telling the truth. Normally vomit made her queasy, but the ghastly scenery surrounding them was far worse. She hoped al-Aziz's story would be brief. She wanted nothing more than to leave.

"I was afraid," al-Aziz continued, "and fled back into the jungle. But I did not go far. They returned an hour later, carrying more men. I watched as they carved the bodies, and . . ." Tears welled up in the former terrorist's eyes. "They ate them."

Nausea didn't describe the sensation rising from Whitney's belly. She felt as though her worst unrealized nightmares had sprung from her mind into her waking life.

"They performed many . . . incantations."

Jacobson nodded, letting al-Aziz know he'd used the right words.

"They stuffed some bodies into large packs and left." Al-Aziz's eyes hardened. "I was waiting for the dogs to return."

Whitney understood. Though he'd given up his belief in Allah and probably in the benefits of martyrdom, he was still willing to give his life to kill a few of the men who'd done this. "How long have you waited?" Whitney asked.

"Three days. I do not think they intend to return."

Whitney could no longer hold back her growing curiosity. "What did they look like?"

"Pray you will never know," al-Aziz said. "They were taller than giraffes, maybe twenty feet tall. They carried whole trees for burning like they weighed as little as a single branch."

"'We saw the Nephilim there,'" Jacobson quoted. "'The descendants of Anak come from the Nephilim. We seemed like grasshoppers in our own eyes, and we looked the same to them.'"

All eyes turned to Jacobson. "What is that from?" al-Aziz asked.

"It's from the Bible. The Book of Numbers, I think."

"Then you know what . . . who they are?"

Jacobson nodded slowly. "The devil's children."

Wright frowned, picked up al-Aziz's discarded clothes, and threw them to him. "Get dressed. We're leaving."

NEPHILIM

# CHAPTER 50

Upon seeing Mira's face, Merrill knew something had gone terribly wrong. Vesuvius had warned of their return with a whine and tail wag, so Merrill wasn't surprised when she emerged from the jungle, but he was nervous about her stricken expression. As she walked back into camp, illuminated by the moonlight, her wide eyes danced anxiously back and forth. Merrill rushed up to her. "Mira, what happened?"

She shook her head and moved past him, allowing the others to enter the campsite. Wright was next, followed by Cruz . . . and the face of a stranger—wrinkled forehead, solid brown, wide eyes, and a strong jaw covered by a thick, black beard that merged with a messy head of wavy hair. As he emerged from the forest, Merrill made a quick assessment of the character and deduced that the man was a Muslim. Then he noted the explosives strapped to the man's waist. Not just a Muslim, a Muslim extremist—complete with a suicide bomb!

He reached for his weapon, but before drawing it he noticed Ferrell and Jacobson bringing up the rear. The man was with them. "What's going on here?" Merrill asked, aghast.

"He's with us, now," Wright said.

That was it? That was his explanation? "He's a terrorist!" Merrill shouted.

"Get over it," Wright said.

Merrill couldn't fathom what had happened in the forest that could make Wright so cold and make them all ignore common sense. His face grew red with rage.

"I have given up jihad." The man looked to the ground, his expression solemn. "I have forsaken Islam."

Merrill glared at al-Aziz. What neither this man nor many other people knew was that Merrill had friends working in Israel digging at an ancient site where evidence of multiple occupations were discovered. Greek, Hebrew, Egyptian, and Babylonian remnants were found in layers that gave a succinct timeline as to who occupied the area and when. It was only by chance that they had gone to the market one Friday evening. It also happened to be the same evening two suicide bombers chose to end their lives and those of four-teen others, including those of Merrill's friends. He'd held a personal grudge since.

Merrill seethed as he spoke. "I don't care how *unaffiliated* you are now. The fact that you were a terrorist is enough. It's people like you who make this world as dark and sinister as it is. The world is in chaos and the only thing you can think of"—Merrill pointed at the bomb around al-Aziz's waist—"is blowing yourself up and killing innocents. Men, women, children . . . you couldn't care less who gets mowed down, as long as you get your fairy tale virgins." Merrill leaned in close. "I have news for you, buddy. There are no virgins waiting for you. Just a special place in hell."

"Dad," Mira's voice cut in. He could tell she wanted to stop his tirade, but the tone of her voice also said she wasn't going to push it. Good, Merrill thought, because I'm not done yet.

"You're evil. You're despicable."

"I know."

"You're . . . What?"

"I know," al-Aziz repeated. "I have seen the truth about what I was and what I believed."

Merrill's enraged mind had trouble assimilating the revelation. Had this man truly come to understand how misguided his extremist beliefs were? He didn't buy it. Merrill prepared to unload another tongue-lashing, but some-thing inside froze the words in his throat.

"Please," al-Aziz said, "I do not deserve it, but if you can: forgive me."

Merrill's body became rigid. His humanity cried for vengeance, for justice against this man who could have very well, in some way, helped commit the murders of hundreds, maybe thousands of people. But the voice that he prayed would influence every choice he made shouted more loudly than his own bitter emotions, and it called for one thing that he did not want to give—forgiveness.

A torrent of emotion swirled inside Merrill. A battle raged in his soul between what he felt was just and what he knew was right. Vengeance. Mercy. Retribution. Compassion. Condemnation. Forgiveness. Merrill couldn't fight what he knew to be the right course of action.

Merrill lowered his head and stared at the ground, unable to look al-Aziz in the eyes. "I forgive you," he said.

Then the strangest thing happened, one that Merrill just moments ago would have shot the man for trying. Al-Aziz stepped forward and embraced Merrill.

"Thank you, friend," al-Aziz said. "Your heart is bigger than mine."

Al-Aziz was crying, which in turn brought tears to Merrill's eyes. It was a reconciliation neither of them had believed would ever happen in their lifetimes. Years of hatred and misunderstanding melted away. But the joy of accord would be short lived.

Merrill felt a gentle hand on his shoulder. He pulled himself away from al-Aziz and looked through wet eyes to see Mira smiling at him, her own eyes damp with tears. He glanced at the somber faces around him. The experience had touched something within them all, yet on the surface was something more, a kind of dread that had nothing to do with al-Aziz.

"What happened in the jungle?" Merrill asked.

"The Nephilim," Mirabelle said. "They're alive."

 CHAPTER 51

The night had become a whirlwind of staggering emotions for Merrill. He sat down on a toppled tree. "What do you mean, alive?"

"Alive and kicking," Wright said. "Like the crylos, they've somehow come back. Or never left."

"The *Nephilim*?" Merrill doubted any of them knew enough about the Nephilim to make such a judgment, except perhaps Jacobson. He looked at the Englishman. "You're sure?"

"Couldn't be anyone else," Jacobson said. "Not if Aziz's description is accurate."

Merrill turned to the new member of the team. "You saw them?"

Al-Aziz nodded, eyes wide with fear, and told his story in detail. That he produced their description without knowing that such a thing as the Nephilim existed made his story even more difficult to refute. That, combined with the fossilized giants Merrill had himself dug up, led him to believe it was true. But how they had survived for thousands of years on Antarctica was beyond him.

"This is not good," Merrill said when al-Aziz had finished. "Not good at all."

Wright sat across from Merrill. "And you thought you weren't going to be useful."

"I'm beginning to wish I wasn't," Merrill said. He knew that, as with the crylos, Wright wanted to know everything he knew about the Nephilim. Merrill accessed his memory, incorporating tidbits from biblical and non-biblical history and searching for a place to start.

He stood and opened his backpack. After reaching deep inside, he pulled out his old black leather Bible.

"You brought a Bible with you?" Cruz said.

"I bring it everywhere," Merrill said before retaking his seat on the fallen tree.

"Take a seat," he said to the others. "This might take some time." As the group huddled in close and sat like kids at a campfire ghost story, Merrill recalled the Nephilim's first mention in the Bible. He turned to Genesis, found the verse and began reading aloud: "'When men began to increase in number on the earth and daughters were born to them, the sons of God saw that the daughters of men were beautiful, and they married any of them they chose. Then the Lord said, "My Spirit will not contend with man forever, for he is corrupt; his days will be a hundred and twenty years."' Wait, there's more."

"'The Nephilim were on the earth in those days—and also afterward—when the sons of God went to the daughters of men and had children by them. They were the heroes of old, men of renown. The Lord saw how great man's wickedness on the earth had become, and that every inclination of the thoughts of his heart was only evil all the time.'"

"Here's the kicker," Merrill said and continued reading. "'The Lord was grieved that He had made man on the earth, and his heart was filled with pain. So the Lord said, "I will wipe mankind, whom I have created, from the face of the earth—men and animals, and creatures that move along the ground, and birds of the air—for I am grieved that I have made them." But Noah found favor in the eyes of the Lord.'" Merrill looked up at the group. "That's Genesis six, verses one through eight."

"That's the beginning of the flood account," Wright said.

"What does it mean, 'sons of God'?" Cruz asked.

No fond memories of lecturing students came to Merrill this time, as the questions came. He wished to talk about this as little as possible now. It had been fascinating as ancient history, but now it was real and he wanted nothing to do with it. He answered only because if he divulged all he knew, they might not ask him any more about it. "The sons of God," he said, "were angels, *bene Elohim* in the original Hebrew."

"'*Were* angels'?"

"Fallen angels," Merrill added. "Demons."

"Oh."

"Angels, like man, were given free will. It would be impossible to love God without it. We'd all be robots, otherwise. And like humans, some angels made the wrong choices. They lusted after human women, married, and fathered children—the Nephilim."

"But . . ." Mirabelle had a confused look on her face. Merrill knew this must all be earth shattering for her. First the flood evidence and now the Nephilim, real and alive. The Bible was coming to life for Whitney, and she was beginning to question things. "How can angels . . . you know . . . have children? They're genetically similar to humans? They reproduce?"

"Angels and humans are totally different," Merrill said. "Angels are immortal, lacking souls because of their immortality. We don't really know what they look like, only that they can pretty much look like whatever they want. In Genesis nineteen, two angels visit Sodom, staying in the house of Lot. They're seen by the men of Sodom who surround Lot's house and demand the visitors be sent outside . . . so they can have sex with them. It reveals the depravity of the time, but also that the angels, in human form, could be, at least from the attackers' point of view, raped."

"That's sick, man," Cruz said.

"Very," Merrill said. "And it resulted in Sodom's destruction."

"Stick to the Nephilim," Wright said. "It's late and we're getting up with the sun."

Merrill nodded. "So we have demons having children with human women. The children are named Nephilim, which literally means 'fallen ones,' from *naphal*: 'to fall.' They were renowned in the ancient world for their size, strength, and wickedness. They are mentioned throughout the Old Testament under several different names given to their various tribes. Rephiam, Emim, Horim, Zamammim, and Avim were all Nephilim. And they populated the pre-flood world until only one truly human family was left."

"Noah . . ." Whitney's eyes were wide. Merrill could see her mind putting things together.

"Exactly," Merrill said. "Most people overlook the Nephilim, seeing them as a side note in the biblical account. But their influence has reshaped the planet. You see, it's possible that even back then, angels knew about Jesus, about how he would give his life to save those who believed in him. They also knew that his bloodline would be pure—not from sin, mind you, but genetically. From Adam, to Noah, to David, and eventually on to Jesus himself, the bloodline, the DNA, remained 100 percent human. If the Nephilim had succeeded in genetically corrupting the entire human bloodline, Jesus would not have been conceived. That is why God wiped out the entire planet except for one family, to preserve the geneology of His son. When the Bible says the world was corrupt, it doesn't just mean morally—it's talking genetics."

"Then why are the Nephilim here," Wright asked, "if God wiped them all out?"

Merrill considered that and found two answers, neither of which he liked at all. "In the verses I read it says, 'The Nephilim were on the earth in those days—*and also afterward.*' That's after the flood. The Nephilim, at least some of them, survived the flood. The ancient Sumerians wrote about the Nephilim as well, describing them as master boat builders and navigators. It's possible that the source documents for our Piri Reis map were drawn by Nephilim, perhaps the very ones living here today."

"You're saying they're immortal?" Wright's face looked skeptical, but also like a man hoping to be wrong.

Merrill nodded. "With such an odd parentage, I wouldn't be surprised. That and the Nephilim don't have souls. Isaiah 26:14 says, 'They are dead, they shall not live; they are Rephiam, they shall not rise.' The Rephiam are one of the well known Nephilim tribes and the verse clearly says that they will not rise from the dead; they have no eternal soul, but unlike their immortal fathers, they can be killed."

"At least that's some good news," Cruz said.

"I wouldn't count on it being easy," Merrill said. "They survived the flood and a second extermination attempt by Joshua, the man who led the Jews into Israel after Moses died. Many people think of Joshua—and God, at the time—as being savage killers, conquerors of the Promised Land. But what they don't consider, again, is that it is possible that the Canaanites of the time were actually a second infusion of Nephilim. Fallen angels again came down and bore children, but on a much smaller scale. Joshua's own troops reported that they were like grasshoppers in their sight."

"The book of Numbers," Ferrell said from her perch above the rest where she'd been silently watching the jungle. Merrill didn't hide his surprise. "Jacobson covered that already."

Merrill nodded to Jacobson. "Very good."

Jacobson returned the nod.

"Did Joshua destroy the Canaanites?" Whitney asked.

This was the issue Merrill was just now beginning to understand. "No," he said. "Some of them escaped and, I expect, are still living among us to this day."

Jacobson suddenly sat upright. "The crop circles!"

Merrill scrunched his forehead, not following.

"Crop circles are seen all over the world. We've always assumed that they were messages from something, someone, but what if they're a by-product of Nephilim . . . spells, or whatever you want to call their powers. We saw the circle in the field here. It was a perfect crop circle. And the clothing on the ground, as though it had just fallen from the men's bodies. That had to be Nephilim." Jacobson grew pale. "There have been thousands of crop circles found to date and hundreds more every year; in fact, there are more and more every year."

The implications made Merrill shudder. It would mean that there had been Nephilim living among, perhaps influencing, humanity since the flood. He didn't want to think about it. "Crop circles or not, the point is that the Nephilim have an extreme hatred for humanity. They envy our immortal souls because ultimately, while we live on eternally, they will one day cease to exist. The future biblical resurrection isn't an option for them. They have powers granted them through their demonic parentage, along with giant stature, inhuman strength, and physical immortality, but no souls."

"And the cannibalism?" Wright asked.

"Not recorded in the Bible, but the Nephilim had populated the whole earth at the time of the flood. There are cave paintings, ancient pictographs that tell stories of men who could carry logs that six modern humans could not move. The math here . . . the lifting power of six men makes the logs heavier than 1800 pounds. Other pictographs and the recently recorded oral traditions of a few tribes describe their bodies as being covered with ritualistic tattoos and their diets including human flesh. Worst of all was their physical appearance. Double rows of teeth, long red hair, six toes, six fingers, and in some cases, horns."

"If that's the case," Wright asked, "how could they hide among us?"

"Teeth can be removed. Hair can be cut. Surgery can remove fingers, toes, and I imagine even horns. And height . . . through selective breeding they could, in theory, reduce their size to that of humans, but if any of the first Nephilim were still alive in the outside world, they would have to be in hiding. I wouldn't have believed it myself two hours ago."

"Give us crylos any day over Nephilim," Cruz said.

Merrill nodded. They were beginning to understand. The Nephilim were mankind's oldest and most dangerous enemy. Merrill briefly posed the idea of calling off the race in order to return home and report on the Nephilim, but it was quickly shot down. He knew it was a futile effort, but didn't feel right not trying. Wright's response to the idea confirmed Merrill's thoughts. They would press forward, and if the Piri Reis map continued to prove accurate, they'd be headed smack dab into the middle of Nephilim territory where the skulled fortress was carved into the base of the mountain.

And if they survived long enough, they would see the skull fortress for themselves.

 CHAPTER 52

Jacobson's respect for the American team grew with every encounter they had. They handled the crylos with a skill his team had lacked. They'd welcomed him to the team without question and had treated him as a professional from their first meeting. And now al-Aziz, a Muslim extremist who had just now turned from his destructive faith and asked for forgiveness, was also welcomed, though with much less trust. The fact that he hadn't simply been shot on the spot spoke volumes about this team.

Merrill stood out to him the most. It was clear that he'd had a history with terrorism, maybe even lost a friend or family member. His rage was understandable. If he'd shot al-Aziz, it would have been within reason. But he hadn't. He had forgiven the man. Jacobson shook his head as he remembered the exchange: the pained look on Merrill's face as al-Aziz asked for forgiveness. And then, just as it seemed Merrill would pounce, he offered the forgiveness, which ended in an embrace. It was a more powerful experience than all of the death and carnage visited upon Jacobson since the race began. It gave him hope. But not hope in terms of Merrill's religious beliefs; hope that the world would put aside old grudges in the face of a greater enemy.

Now they were moving again, heading inexorably toward the goal. Merrill had given a brief protest with which deep down Jacobson agreed, but his own loyalty to queen and country pushed him forward. If there was a chance that Antarktos, as Merrill was now calling it, could be claimed for Europe along with America, then cleansed of the Nephilim, he had to take it.

Of course, the more time spent traveling, the longer he had to pursue Whitney. Not that he'd made a conscious choice to woo the woman, but he found her endlessly fascinating . . . and attractive. The exotic combination of her naturally stark-blond hair and coffee-colored skin, along with those fiery eyes; it was an odd sensation to him, when their eyes met occasionally. It seemed he couldn't pull away, even when awkwardness set in. It wasn't until she smiled, pulling his attention from her eyes to her plump-lipped smile, that he was able to break away. It took all of his effort to resist looking back. When he felt his distraction was becoming unsafe, he requested to guard the rear of the line. Of course, covering the rear of this little trek had its distractions, too. Even now, he had to work hard to keep his mind on enemies potentially lurking in the jungle and off of her ass.

The jungle was thinner now and had been growing steadily thus. Merrill had explained that they were within two days' travel of their goal which was also, he believed, a Nephilim hot spot. The Piri Reis map, which had been accurate so far, depicted a forest, some mountains, and a fortress, a Nephilim fortress. And they were headed straight for it.

The fact that an ancient fortress might still exist after twelve thousand years under the crushing ice seemed unlikely. But so did living dinosaurs and half-man half-demon giants. Jacobson had to admit it was a possibility. And if the Nephilim had taken up residence there once again, they were in for a fight of biblical proportions. When the Israelites had fought the Nephilim, they had God on their side. Jacobson wasn't sure if any of them, except maybe Merrill, had the almighty watching their backs.

As the trees grew shorter and more sparse, Jacobson knew that their elevation was getting high. Soon they would feel lightheaded and increasingly winded with every step as the oxygen continued to thin. They'd been hiking uphill for several hours and now seemed to be climbing a mountain. The going was rough and taxing, but no one slowed or asked for a break. They were like guided missiles that couldn't be called off . . . very slow-moving missiles.

Jacobson put his machete away. There was no longer any brush or vines to hack. Ferrell, at the front of the line, raised her hand in warning. As had been discussed, Merrill, Whitney, Vesuvius, and al-Aziz instantly fell back while Wright, Cruz, Ferrell, and Jacobson took the front line. When Jacobson reached the front, he saw what had given Ferrell pause.

Fifty feet ahead, a portion of the forest had been cleared. At the front of the clearing, which stretched forward up over a crest like a road, was a pillar of stone thirty feet high that looked strikingly like an Egyptian obelisk. Most obelisks found in Egypt were covered in hieroglyphs, but this one appeared to have only one, about ten feet up. From a distance, Jacobson couldn't make out the symbol, but it seemed somehow familiar.

He took a step forward. "Stand your ground," Wright said. "Wait for Ferrell to give the all clear."

Jacobson looked. Ferrell was gone. He hadn't seen or heard her leave.

A birdcall from the direction of the obelisk brought his attention forward. Ferrell was there, giving a thumbs-up sign. "All clear," Wright said then motioned for the others to fall in behind him. They moved forward as a group. Wright ran a tight ship. It wasn't exactly Jacobson's style, but maybe that's why the American team had yet to lose a single member. In fact, they'd grown by two.

Once in the clearing, Vesuvius broke into a run, prancing happily toward Ferrell, who, to Jacobson's surprise, bent down and petted the dog. Jacobson would have doubted the wisdom of allowing a dog to join the team, but it was undeniable that with all the horror they had seen, Vesuvius was a great morale booster.

Standing before the obelisk, Jacobson was struck by its size. It stood in the middle of nowhere, probably carried there by the giants, a testament to their strength. He saw the symbol clearly for the first time and recognized it instantly. There were three rings intertwined. Three lines ran through the middle of each ring then out the other side, ending at different lengths. On the longest line were three more short lines extending at 90 degree angles.

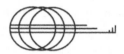

"It's a crop circle," Jacobson said.

"What makes you say that?" Merrill asked.

"I've seen it before."

"Doesn't it have to be in a crop to be a crop circle?" Cruz added.

"It was. I saw it from two thousand feet . . . in a plane over England." He turned and looked at Merrill. "Last year."

Merrill's eyes widened. "What does it mean?"

Jacobson shrugged. "I have no idea. No one does. That's why the circles are so interesting. It could be a mile marker. It could be a tombstone. I don't know."

"Or," Ferrell said, "it could be one of the most common signs found all around the world, in every culture. 'Keep out.'"

Whitney and Vesuvius had moved beyond the obelisk to the crest where the clearing disappeared. Jacobson kept a close eye on her. It was lucky he'd shown up when he had, saving her from the crylo; the next time she needed help, he intended to be there. "It's a road," Whitney called out. "It goes on for miles."

"Looks like we'll be moving a little quicker from here," Merrill said with a slight look of relief.

The old man must be getting tired, Jacobson thought, which wasn't surprising; even Jacobson himself felt exhaustion nagging at his limbs on a daily basis. He was amazed that Merrill had kept up so far. His resolve was indestructible.

"Negative," Wright said, as Jacobson suspected he might. "We'll stick to the cover of the trees for as long as possible."

No one argued. Jacobson thought that even Merrill, who could have used a nice road to walk on, must have understood Wright's motivation behind the decision. Taking the road would be like walking into battle with a strobe light on; the enemy would see them coming . . . and would merely have to wait.

 CHAPTER 53

Throughout the rest of the afternoon, no one spoke for fear of being heard. Whitney could tell that even the trained soldiers were growing weary. And Vesuvius, whose tongue had nearly doubled in size and hung out the side of his mouth, had slowed. It was the kind of exhaustion every runner feels when the end is in sight. Whitney had experienced it herself when she ran the Boston marathon once. She'd pressed on past the point of unbearable pain; then it had subsided. Some people called it a second wind. But as soon as she knew the end was near, her mind said, "slow down," "you don't need to try as hard," "give in to the weariness."

They all heard that voice now, and if there was a gift from God to be granted, they'd already received it several times over. She'd witnessed the horrible fate that had befallen the Chinese team. What had happened to Jacobson's team was no better. And she'd survived her own brush with death, fending off the crylos. She knew if it weren't for Jacobson, she'd be halfdevoured in the pit of that dinosaur's stomach. From a religious standpoint, it would seem that some higher power was watching out for them; to Whitney, it was just dumb luck.

A burn in Whitney's calf muscle pulled her out of her thoughts. She searched the area. The trees were short here, perhaps fifteen feet tall and growing shorter as they climbed higher, but their foliage was thick and the sky difficult to see. The forest floor was moist and mossy, making the going slow and slippery. Whitney's hands were filthy from catching herself, grabbing at the ground as she tripped and fell. Above, the blue sky hung like a curtain. At least the sky was familiar.

An hour into the climb, when the angle grew steep, the team broke their single file formation and climbed in a haphazard group. Jacobson brought up the rear, just behind Whitney, Merrill, and Vesuvius, who stopped every few feet to wait for his master. Wright, Ferrell, and Cruz led the way, trailing al-Aziz, whom they didn't want to get too far away. Whitney eyed the bomb strapped to al-Aziz's waist. It was the one thing that kept her from accepting his reform. She knew his claim, that it couldn't be removed, but it could be a trick. She knew Cruz had the detonator, but still, a bomb that could not be removed seemed counterproductive. What if, after all, al-Aziz decided to escape? Would he have to wear the bomb forever or kill himself anyway?

Whitney was lost in her thoughts when her foot failed to find purchase on a mossy rock. She let out a yelp and slid backward, gaining momentum quickly on the steep decline. Vesuvius let out a bark and Merrill shouted as she plummeted past them.

Whitney's body jolted to a stop. She looked up. Jacobson had a vice grip on her backpack. She smiled. "That's twice you saved me," she said.

Jacobson grinned back. "Maybe you'll get to return the favor someday, eh?"

Their eyes locked as they had over the past few days. She felt the stir of emotions she'd been trying hard to ignore surge through her body. She wasn't just interested in Jacobson. She wanted Jacobson in a primal, sexual way. She'd chalked it up to being in the wild, like kids at summer camp, but it was now too strong to ignore. A wave of guilt waged war with her desire. Was it Sam crying out to be remembered? Jacobson leaned in closer, as though sensing her desire. She closed her eyes and parted her lips to accept him. He's only been gone for a year! Whitney's conscience screamed at her, jolting her eyes open, urging her to resist the kiss. But it was too late; Jacobson's lips found hers. His lips pressed gently against her top lip and she wrapped her lower lip around his. It was gentle yet infused with so much care, she couldn't help but enjoy his embrace.

Jacobson parted from her and stood her up. As they shared a quiet smile, Jacobson winked.

Then he was gone. He flew from the ground as though yanked from above. Shouting, he rose up through the thick canopy and out of view. A battle cry was followed by a barrage of bullets that swept through the forest. Jacobson was fighting for his life.

With no clear enemy to attack, Wright, Ferrell, and Cruz took positions in front of the others. Merrill prepped his assault rifle. Whitney stood unmoving as she listened. The gunfire abruptly stopped, as did Jacobson's screams. A moment later, his bent, broken body fell back through the trees. His body landed at their feet, a twisted corpse that was almost unrecognizable as Jacobson. Only moments ago the man had snuck past her hurt and given her hope. Now he was gone. The pain of losing Sam began to seep through the fresh wound, brimming tears in her eyes. But then she saw something that replaced her anguish with fear.

Whitney saw them, standing only one hundred feet away, among the tree trunks. Two limbs like trees, but with a curve and shape that identified them as very large legs. She pointed at the legs. "There."

Wright saw them. "Exploding rounds," he whispered. "Two bursts on my mark at the kneecaps, then run like hell."

Everyone with an XM-29, including Whitney, took aim. "Fire."

Eight small explosions pierced the air, then four louder blasts echoed down the mountainside as the explosive rounds hit their targets. Flesh exploded from the towering legs and a howl of pain shook the forest floor. Whitney turned with the others as the retreat began, but with a quick glance back, she knew their chances for escape were slim. The legs were healing.

As Whitney scrambled with the others, running away and up in a diagonal line, she felt a firm hand grasp her shoulder. She spun quickly, prepared to fire, and leveled the gun at Merrill's head. She lowered the weapon quickly, relieved that she wasn't being attacked but terrified she'd almost shot her father. However, he didn't seem fazed by the near-death experience. His eyes were wide, horrified, searching for answers. And he was frozen to the ground.

"Dad, what's wrong?" Whitney asked as she tried to pull Merrill up the rise. "We need to keep moving!"

"That sound," he said. "The howl. I've heard it before. When your mother—"

Cruz bumped into them from behind. He shoved Merrill hard. "Move it, pops, or I'll leave your ass behind."

Whitney squeezed her father's hand. He didn't flinch.

"If you don't move, Dad, I'm staying with you. Then I'll die, too. Is that what you want?" Merrill's eyes locked onto hers and he was moving again, running up the grade with the others.

So, too, were their hunters. The ground vibrated beneath them as the giants gave chase. Whitney heard trees snapping and the scent of fresh-cut wood. They were plowing a path through the forest like it was tall grass. And they were gaining.

Vesuvius was at the front of the line, leading the group away from danger while holding to the same basic route. He stopped and stood atop a rock at the peak of a crest and barked loudly. Behind him was nothing but sky. They'd reached the top and pressed on without pausing to take in the amazing view.

Running pell-mell, Whitney stumbled and tripped. Merrill heard her shout as she went down and spun around. She landed rather gracefully, rolling with the fall, but the delay set her twenty feet behind the team as they continued down the other side of the mountain.

As Merrill bent to help her up, Whitney saw his face contort to a mask of dread. She rolled and fired before he screamed, "Mira! Behind you!"

Whitney fired two rounds in midair. Both missed the intended target, a gargantuan silhouette that blocked out the sun above; the recoil thrust her hard against the stone. Her head struck a rock and throbbed with pain, but she managed to take aim again. This time, with her body braced, she was able to fire a full spread. Explosive rounds and bright tracers zipped into the air. Some shot skyward, exploding high in the atmosphere, while others struck the tall body directly.

Whump! Whump! Whump!

Muffled explosions from inside the giant's body tore holes in his sides, and blood burst from each wound for an instant. The towering man fell to his knees, bracing his body on his hands as the explosions continued. He howled as the explosions persisted, past the point when Whitney expected the man to die. But the howl wasn't of pain, it was of ecstasy, as though suffering was a wonderful pleasure. When the explosions ceased, the man began to laugh, a deep guttural noise that was wet with blood.

As he began to right himself, Whitney finally got a glimpse of the man. He had a face like a man, with eyes, nose, and mouth, but as he laughed, Whitney was sure she saw several rows of teeth, all sharp. The man's hair was dark red, not Irish red, but almost as though it had been dyed deep crimson—like blood. Around his head was a golden metal band inscribed with symbols that could have been more crop circle designs. On his body he wore armor, like the ancients, pieced together from metal plates and animal hides. He was like some overgrown Viking. She was reminded of her father's description of the giants recalled in Native American legend and glanced at the man's hands. He had six fingers.

The myths were right.

These were the giants recorded by cultures around the world, who were almost wiped out by a flood that was also recorded worldwide and reported accurately in the Bible. These were the Nephilim.

Gun shots from the distance told Whitney the others were having their own encounter and wouldn't be back to save the day. She was on her own.

A streaking bullet of a man, a dwarf in comparison to the Nephilim, charged from the side, sword drawn. The man shouted and Whitney recognized the voice. "Dad! Don't! Get away with the others!"

But Merrill didn't hear her or didn't listen. "Nephilim corruptors!" he bellowed. He swung the sword down at the Nephilim, but it simply took the blow on its forearm and stood. Merrill continued slashing at the giant, but had no effect. Whitney watched in horror as every wound healed. Even the holes created by the explosive rounds were now fading scars. As Merrill swung again, the giant caught the blade of the sword in its thick hand and pulled it away from Merrill.

As the sword was wrenched from Merrill's grip, he was thrown off-balance and fell to the ground next to Whitney.

They looked up in horror as the giant stood above them, looking at the sword, his yellow eyes probing it from blade tip to hilt. He turned his eyes toward them, leaned down, and asked with a booming voice, "Where did you get this?"

Merrill and Whitney shared a confused glance. They each knew what the other was thinking: They speak English?

The giant seemed to read their thoughts. "We have had many teachers over the years. We know much about your kind."

Whitney felt her father seethe with anger. He recognized these brutes as biblical enemies, foes to humanity that God himself had declared an enemy. "Then you know we have souls, Nephilim. And if you kill us, we will continue while you will cease to exist!"

A crooked grin filled with razor teeth gleamed at them. "And you are the first since our current teacher who has known so much about us."

Then, as though a scent of a nearby barbecue had caught his attention, the giant sniffed at the air. He leaned in closer to Merrill and Whitney, sniffing all the way, his teeth bared, his yellow eyes blazing. The smell led him to Whitney. His watermelon-sized head was only inches from her as he sniffed her up and down, lingering on her bright hair. "The hair is different . . ."

"Get away from her!" Merrill shouted and drew the 9mm handgun. The giant snapped at Merrill with a growl and clamp of his jaws. It was clear that he could have killed Merrill if he so desired; he could have killed them both, but he was sparing them for some reason. Merrill dropped the gun as the giant's teeth snapped together like two clapping coconuts.

The Nephilim leaned back again and raised a clenched fist in front of his face. Whitney feared he would strike her father down, but the man's hand opened, revealing purple dust, which he blew into their faces. It was the last thing Whitney saw. She was unconscious before she realized what the giant had done.

If she'd been conscious, Whitney would have felt her body picked up and slung over a giant shoulder. She would have heard the screams and gunfire in the distance as her friends were attacked. She would have lost all hope.

There, at the center of the world, there was no hope.

REVELATIONS

 CHAPTER 54

"Two more on the left!" Wright shouted then fired a barrage in that direction.

He realized too late that the one giant who'd chased them from behind was not the actual attack. He'd simply flushed them out into the open where the others waited. It was a basic but effective strategy, and Wright cursed himself for not anticipating it. He was better than that.

As they approached the tree line, he realized that they'd become separated from Merrill and Whitney and was about to turn around when two more dark shapes rose out of and above the tree line. They were giants in the truest sense of the word, each standing about fifteen feet in height. They were downhill a bit and stood at eye level with Wright, grinning sickly grins, like rabid dogs about to attack.

Then they did.

The group fled into the forest where the trees obscured the giants' view and slowed them down, though not by much. Others waited in the forest. Wright couldn't count how many. He just saw a line of legs disappearing over the tree line. One of them crouched to all fours and howled before charging after them like an obscenely large rabid bear.

They'd been running since the attack began, using explosive rounds to slow the enemy; but ultimately, they had little effect. The monsters healed as rapidly as they were injured. Wright concluded quickly that Merrill had been right. These were the true, pure Nephilim, whose demon fathers made them immortal but also, it seemed, invincible. Escape was the only choice for the group, now composed of Wright, Ferrell, Cruz, and al-Aziz. Vesuvius once again led the way, though Wright suspected the dog had not seen its master fall behind.

A hand jutted out from behind a tree as Wright ran past. An exploding round shot from behind pierced the palm and exploded, blasting all six fingers into the air. Wright looked back, and Ferrell nodded. The woman never missed.

Wright could see through the trees that they were approaching a tall, solid cliff face that rose up at the base of the slope. They needed to continue down, but the wall gave him an idea. He turned his head to Cruz, who was bringing up the rear with al-Aziz. "Rig something quick," Wright shouted as he pointed to the wall. He knew Cruz would understand what he wanted, though he wondered if the demolitions expert could do it on the fly.

Wright was insane! Cruz was by far the best in the game, especially since many of his competitors had been presumably killed in the crust shift, but what Wright wanted was impossible. "*Esto es una idea realmente mala,*" he muttered under his breath.

"What did you say?" al-Aziz asked as they jumped a fallen tree together.

"This is a really bad idea."

"Tell me what to do," al-Aziz said. "I will help you."

Cruz knew the captain wouldn't approve of giving al-Aziz anything more dangerous than a flyswatter, but the alternative was winding up like the Chinese soldiers. Cruz unclipped his backpack and held it out to al-Aziz. "Take out the black case."

Al-Aziz dug through the backpack while they ran neck and neck. He flinched when Ferrell opened up with a bunch of exploding rounds that zipped past Cruz's head and exploded ten feet back. Cruz looked over his shoulder and saw one of the giants tumble. "*¡Mierda santa!*" How'd he get so close?

"Got it," al-Aziz said as he pulled out the box.

Cruz slung the backpack over his shoulders. The hill became steeper and the team was really picking up speed. Cruz could now see clearly what Wright had seen. The base of the stone cliff rose up before them, towering one hundred feet above. At first he thought they would have to run along its edge and take down a part of the wall so that it buried their pursuers, but now he could see a rift in the wall, maybe four feet across. Wright wanted it sealed behind them. But it would have to be a big seal to stop the giants.

"Give me four blocks of C4, a detonator, and a timer. And be careful."

Al-Aziz did his best to keep the box steady as he opened it, but the terrain was not even and he jostled with every step. The four blocks were handed across. Cruz held them in one arm like a football. "Now the timer and detonator. You'll have to attach them and connect the wires."

Al-Aziz found both items, removed them from the box, and handed the box to Cruz. He attached the two items easily enough; they were designed to clip together. But these things were not meant to be done on the run. Wires were normally spliced together, then secured with wire caps. Al-Aziz worked as best he could, but it was slow going.

Cruz looked forward. The wall was a hundred feet ahead. They'd be there in seconds. "Hurry up!"

Al-Aziz finished the first pair of wires, twisted them quickly, then moved to the second. He got this pair in good time, but while twisting them his finger snagged the first wire and pulled it apart. "There's no time!" al-Aziz shouted.

"Give me the timer. I'll stay behind and blow it myself!" Cruz wasn't keen on the idea of stopping to wire the bomb. He knew that if the Nephilim didn't catch him, the blast most likely would. But he was a soldier first and had some of his own personal demons to destroy along with the Nephilim.

"There's another way," al-Aziz shouted.

They were thirty feet from the wall. The thundering footfalls of the giants pursuing them shook the ground all around. Up ahead, Vesuvius, Wright, and Ferrell were already in the crevasse, running forward without looking back. They were on their own.

"Do you still have my detonator?" al-Aziz shouted, pointing at the bomb around his waist.

The man was still eager to blow himself up! "Yes, but I thought you were done with martyrdom."

"I don't want to kill myself," al-Aziz said, then ripped the explosives from around his waist. Cruz flinched. Nothing happened.

He shot al-Aziz a quizzical glance as he continued to careen toward the wall.

"I lied," al-Aziz said. "You might have killed me otherwise."

Cruz couldn't help but smile. Al-Aziz was a crafty man. "I still might," Cruz said. "Drop it ten feet from the entrance and run like you've got a rocket under your butt."

If either man had looked back, they would have seen a wall of giants descending on them. But neither looked back. They entered the cool cavern and kept their blistering pace. Al-Aziz dropped his suicide bomb.

"It's done!" he shouted.

Cruz tried to estimate the distance. Al-Aziz had enough explosive wrapped around his waist to level a city block, and in the crevasse all that energy would be squeezed tight. The impact would be incredible. Looking forward he could see Wright and Ferrell disappear into the shadows. They were safe.

He looked back and saw the crevasse entrance fall dark as the first Nephilim entered. He had to blow it soon, but he and Aziz were still too close. Then, in a blur, he saw a crack in the side wall as they ran past. He reached out, clutched al-Aziz by the shoulder, and pulled him to a stop. "Here!" Yanking al-Aziz back, he dove into the crack.

As Cruz fell he saw that four Nephilim had entered and were sliding through sideways. They were directly over the bomb. "Regenerate this, *diablos!*"

Cruz depressed the detonator. The explosion that followed was the loudest thing he had ever heard. The force created by the bomb enclosed in such a tight space made its effects that much more violent. Cruz felt the earth shudder beneath him. Pebbles shook from the roof of the large crack into which he and al-Aziz had ducked. And then the heat. A wall of flame roared down the crevasse and licked at Cruz's back.

Al-Aziz was on top of him in an instant. Under other circumstances, Cruz might shoot the man for tackling him like that, but he knew al-Aziz was protecting them. He covered Cruz, who still clutched four blocks of C4 and wore a backpack full of more explosives. Al-Aziz screamed as flames danced across his back, singeing his exposed skin.

Then the shaking grew worse. A rumble like a stampede of elephants shook through the cavern. After al-Aziz stood and allowed Cruz to stand, Cruz stuck his head out and looked back down the crevasse. They'd been successful. The entrance was sealed by a hundred-foot wall of fallen stones, and there at the base a large hand protruded from the avalanche. The hand didn't move.

The rumble persisted. Cruz looked up.

"Get back!" Cruz dove back into the crack and tackled al-Aziz to the ground. Dust and stones spilled into the crack and pelted their bodies. This time, Cruz shouted as stones pummeled his body.

When the rumbling stopped, it was pitch-black and the air was so full of dust neither man could breathe. Realizing they were sealed in stone with little oxygen made Cruz wish he had blown himself up with the Nephilim. Suffocation wasn't a pleasant way to die.

 CHAPTER 55

The blast knocked Ferrell off her feet and the air from her lungs. As she looked back, she understood two things: if she, Wright, and Vesuvius had been any closer to the blast, they would all have been cooked alive. And second, Cruz and al-Aziz were dead.

"What the hell did they use?" Wright shouted. "Damn fools!"

Ferrell thought so, too.

In the last ten minutes, their team had been whittled down from seven and a dog to two and a dog. That was why Ferrell worked alone. All the extra baggage only slowed her down and got people killed. She was glad she hadn't gotten to know any of them better. It was easier that way. Yet she had come to respect them . . . all of them. Even al-Aziz.

Ferrell wasn't the type to hold grudges against people, even terrorists. She was an assassin after all, and their jobs weren't too dissimilar. They were all warriors fighting for what they believed in, right or wrong. All had gone through the gauntlet on this mission, and now only the best survived.

It was a cruel and cold way to think, but Ferrell knew that with the others dead, the chances of success grew. She had found working with a team to be distracting and cumbersome. Someone always needed saving. Choices were questioned. Now, she and Wright, the only one in the bunch she really cared about, could get things done and leave this thawed-out hell.

Wright offered his hand and helped her up. "You all right?" he asked.

"You know I am."

Wright pulled her close and held her in an embrace. "Can't blame a husband for worrying."

Not even the U.S. government knew that she and Wright were married, which they had been for ten years. In fact, Wright often employed her services, and sometimes she'd tag along in the shadows of his ops just to make sure he made it through okay. Occasionally one of his men would notice an enemy drop from a sniper shot, but no one made an issue beyond joking that God had a sniper rifle and was watching Wright's back.

Not God, Ferrell thought. Me.

They had been vacationing together on their yacht when the cataclysm struck. After two chaotic weeks at sea battling the giant waves and new currents, they'd managed to make it back to shore. After Wright was assigned the mission, he made sure she was on the team. It was her first official op for the United States. They knew the mission was going to be extremely dangerous and that there would be no tagging along in the shadows. She had to be on the team; if the end was to come, they'd face it together.

Of course, Ferrell knew it was more likely that they'd defeat it together, and so far, they were proving that right. They had also been doing a phenomenal acting job. No one suspected their love, and no one knew about their late-night rendezvous. They were just that good.

Wright kissed her gently on the lips. He was done acting. "We need to keep moving," he said.

She nodded and they were on their way. Before they'd walked ten feet, Ferrell stopped. "What's wrong?" Wright asked.

"The dog," Ferrell said. "Where's Vesuvius?"

She looked and saw Vesuvius twenty feet back, staring at the wall, padding back and forth nervously. His high-pitched whines could be heard even across the distance. For the first time in a very long time, Ferrell felt compassion for a creature other than Wright. She felt ridiculous that it was for a dog, but he'd proven himself to be loyal and a capable warrior; two things she respected.

"You're worried about the dog?" Wright said. "He'll catch up when he's ready."

"No," Ferrell said. "I'll get him."

She jogged back to the dog, who wagged his tail upon seeing her. It was another secret relationship she had kept on this mission. She and the dog had grown close. She knelt down and looked into his sad eyes. He'd lost his whole family.

She petted his head. "C'mon, boy. We gotta go."

The dog didn't respond. He just stared at the wall of stones.

"Look," Ferrell said, feeling ridiculous for talking to the dog. "There's a chance they might still be alive. If they are, we'll find them."

The dog wasn't responding.

"Mirabelle?"

Vesuvius looked at her, probing her with his big brown eyes. She had his attention.

"Mirabelle and Merrill," she said. Vesuvius wagged his tail. Ferrell stood and walked away slowly. "This way, boy. Mira and Merrill."

Vesuvius gave one last look at the wall and stood. He caught up to Ferrell and stuck to her side, his head just under her hand. He stayed there for the entire mile hike out of the crevasse, all the way through the forest on the other side, and up to the river's edge where they stopped. Across the river was a tall mountain with a sheer, gray cliff face. Cut into the stone was what looked like a fortress, complete with multiple layers, walls, gates, and towers. At the top was a large, crudely sculpted skull. A human skull. It was the fortress Merrill had told them about.

For a moment Ferrell wished the old man was with them again. He might provide some valuable intel on the place and what they could expect inside. But he wasn't there, so they were going to have to do things the old-fashioned way. That didn't bother Ferrell one bit.

"Over the river and through the woods," Wright said.

Ferrell raised an eyebrow. "Your grandmother had two sets of teeth and twelve fingers?"

Wright smiled. "You should have seen her warts."

They skirted the river, sticking to the trees and searching for a way to cross the fifty-foot-wide river without being swept away. Vesuvius stayed with them and remained quiet, as though he sensed their need for stealth. Ferrell did her best not to let her hand touch the dog's head too often, because when it did she would pet him; she would rub his ears and squeeze his neck. She was already more attached than she should be, and she knew the dog wouldn't survive the next leg of the journey. She didn't deal with loss very well. She had a tendency to kill things.

 # CHAPTER 56

Whitney's first sensation upon waking was that she was freezing cold. The second was a hammering headache. The floor beneath her was solid stone and did nothing to comfort her aching body as she levered herself up. Her eyes opened to slits and the sudden light stabbed at them, creating pain that reverberated through her head like rippling water in a bucket. She groaned and rubbed her temples.

Sitting up, she could clearly feel the texture of the floor on her flesh. She looked down and gasped. She was naked and wet. She looked around and found her clothes next to her in a heap. As she struggled to put on her clothes, a creeping fear took root. Had she been molested? She quickly probed between her legs with her fingers and felt no blood or pain, so the fear subsided briefly; but she had been stripped and apparently washed.

Maybe the Nephilim had sensitive noses. She didn't smell like an old onion, though, not anymore. She dressed and scanned her surroundings. The cell was large, perhaps forty feet wide and thirty feet high. Two walls were solid, one had an open glassless window, and the last was a crisscross of metal bars. She was in a jail like any other, but this was a Nephilim-sized jail.

There were two beds attached to opposite walls, a blanket piled on each. At the back of the room was a large hole. The stain around the edge told Whitney what it was used for. She darted her eyes away and noticed a heap at the back corner of the cell. At first it appeared to be a pile of dirty laundry, but she quickly realized it was her father.

She ran to his side and found him naked and shivering, still unconscious. She yanked one of the blankets from the bed, finding it to be amazingly soft, and draped it over her father's body. He stirred and clasped his head.

"It will pass," Whitney said.

"Mira, you're still with me?"

"We're in a Nephilim jail cell."

Merrill winced again. "What did he hit us with?"

"Some kind of powder."

"Feels more like a baseball bat." Merrill reached up a hand. "Help me up." He started to stand. Whitney grabbed his hand and saved him from any embarrassment. "What is it?"

Whitney motioned with her eyes for him to look under the blanket. He glanced down through squinted eyes. "Oh."

Five minutes later, Merrill was dressed and acting much more like himself. "This is amazing," he said, tracing the contours of the wall with his hand. "The craftsmanship is clearly ancient, but it smacks of so many other cultures! It's mind boggling!"

Whitney couldn't have cared less how the jail cell was built. All that mattered was how they were going to get out of it, escape to the coast, and get off this ill-fated continent. "I think we should try to focus on the problems at hand, Dad."

"Right," Merrill said, turning away from the wall. "You're right. Sorry." He walked to the crisscrossed metal bars. The square openings were big enough for his head to fit through, but not his shoulders. He stuck his head through and looked in both directions.

"It's just a hallway in either direction," Whitney said. "Don't bother looking."

"Well, maybe my keen eyes will find something you didn't."

"Dad, there's nothing out there to—"

Merrill yanked his head back in, his eyes were wide. He'd seen it. Across the hallway was another cell, but this was stacked ten feet high with human bodies. They appeared to be of several different nationalities. "They . . . the other teams . . ."

"I told you not to look."

"We're not prisoners," Merrill said with a quiver in his voice. "We're cattle, fresh meat for the slaughter." He sneered. "*Heroes* of old . . .! They're devils just like their fathers."

Whitney knew that the least helpful thing for her father to do was go on a moral tirade. They needed to escape, or they would end up a Nephilim meal. She was about to calm him down when two voices echoed up the hallway. One was clearly a woman. Her voice held a normal pitch. The other, a deep bass, belonged to a Nephilim.

They were arguing. In English.

"Enki, please. They are different than the others," the woman pleaded.

"They are human like you, teacher. If I find them to be useless, I will at least find them to be a filling meal."

"Enki, I can see it in their eyes and among the articles they carried. They would make excellent teachers as well."

A pause. Then, "The conflict between the sons of men and the Rephiam has begun anew. I cannot suffer their presence."

"They carried the book."

"A Bible?"

"Yes, just as I did when you found me. And Enlil said they knew who he was, that the man called him by your first given name."

Another pause.

"Please, master," the woman said. "Spare them for now and judge their wisdom for yourself. I believe you will find them of some use."

"Very well, teacher. But if you are wrong—"

"I know."

The voices faded. They were moving away. Whitney and Merrill stood still, gripping the cell bars with tense hands. Their eyes met.

"Do you understand what you just heard?" Merrill asked.

Whitney nodded. "We have a friend, and that might be our only way out of here."

"No," Merrill blurted. "The names. Enki. Enlil."

"What about them?"

"They're Sumerian gods, worshiped by the first human civilization. The Nephilim are immortal. They have no souls, but they live forever. These Nephilim, the ones that escaped the flood, are the original leaders, the ancient gods worshiped by our ancestors as gods. There has been speculation that the Nephilim were the inspiration for several myths and deities—the Titans, the Pantheon, Olympus, Atlantis, Valhalla. All these myths that we have always believed to be conjured up by the human imagination reside in a foundation of fact."

"You're saying they're gods?"

"To the uneducated, they might seem as much. They can't be killed through any means we know of. They live forever. They're giants with inhuman powers lent to them by their unholy fathers. In a crude sense, they are gods, having been worshiped throughout history. But they are not God.

"Enki was one of the major Sumerian gods. He was the god of water, fertility, and creation. His sacred fortress was called the Mound of Creation . . ." Merrill paused and a smile spread onto his face. "We could be standing in the very same Mound of Creation right now!"

"Dad, I don't—"

"Wait," Merrill said. "There's more."

"I don't see how this is going to help us," Whitney managed to say.

Merrill looked her in the eyes. "Know thy enemy."

Whitney pursed her lips. He had a point.

Merrill continued. "After the biblical Adam, recorded in Sumerian history as Allum, their first king, the world had fallen and the sons of God, the rebel angels, were impregnating human women who then gave birth to Nephilim children. Enki was one of the first." Merrill hopped up and sat on one of the beds. It was so high that his feet dangled two feet above the floor. "Enki was a key figure in the Sumerian flood story. The Sumerians wrote that Enki instructed Ziusudra, long thought to be the Sumerian Noah, on how to construct a ship that would save humanity from the coming flood. But it could have been a second boat. A boat used by the Nephilim to escape the flood. It's right there in the Bible: 'The Nephilim were on the earth in those days— and also afterward.' The Nephilim built their own boat and escaped to Antarctica, where they've been ever since."

"That's all very fascinating," Whitney said. "But it doesn't help."

Merrill grinned at her. "Oh, I think it will."

 # CHAPTER 57

In the pitch darkness that enclosed Cruz and al-Aziz, breathing became distinctly difficult. Not from lack of oxygen, but from the thick plume of dust filling the void. Cruz found a bandana, wet it with water from his canteen, and wrapped it around his head, covering his mouth. After catching a breath, he pulled a second rag from his pocket, did the same, and handed it to al-Aziz.

After a minute, they had calmed down and found breathing easier. Cruz noticed that it wasn't the wet cloth that made the air more breathable; he felt the dust being pulled away. The entrance to the small crevasse had been covered completely, but air was still moving.

Cruz stood and bumped his head on the stone ceiling. The space was about five feet tall and tapered at the top, so for those without cone heads, the actual standing height was closer to four and a half feet. Cruz opted to kneel. He dug through his bag and found two flashlights, his primary and a smaller backup. He clicked on the large light and handed the smaller to al-Aziz.

Al-Aziz was covered in gray dust. He looked like a survivor of a building collapse. His eyes were wide but he wasn't panicked. Cruz was happy about that. Being trapped in a cave with a *loco* Arab was not his idea of a good time. Of course, being trapped in a cave with a sane terrorist didn't rank much higher.

"The air," al-Aziz said, holding out his hand. "It moves."

"I know," Cruz said. "Try to find the source."

The two men set about the task quickly. Cruz searched with his flashlight, which cast a bright circle onto the gray stone and glistened off chunks of what looked like mica, the bendable, peel-able rock he'd played with as a child. It wasn't common in southern California, but on a trip to Canada, he'd been able to mine some at a tourist mine and returned to So Cal with pounds of the stuff. Seeing it in such quantities made him nervous. It wasn't exactly the strongest, most stable mineral. Their prison could collapse at any moment.

"Here," al-Aziz said loudly. He crouched by the floor of the cave, peering into a long fissure. Cruz bent down next to al-Aziz and aimed his flashlight inside. The flat tunnel moved forward at a slight downward slope further than Cruz's flashlight could penetrate.

It would be a hell of a squeeze, but the pulsing air told him that there was an opening somewhere. It was their only chance. They might not suffocate to death where they were, but they'd eventually starve and dehydrate. The risk had to be taken.

Cruz slid off his backpack. "We're going to have to follow this tunnel and see where it leads. If we can get to an exterior wall, thinner than the one we're in now . . ." Cruz tapped his backpack. "I'll blow us a way out."

Al-Aziz nodded. "I will go first. I am smaller."

Cruz nodded. He wasn't looking forward to this one bit. He felt like he was about to go on a deep-sea dive, but without the gear. He felt the weight of the mountain pushing in all around them like water. A sensation of drowning filled his body with dread for a moment, but his next breath reassured him that drowning was the least of his worries. He looked back down. Al-Aziz was already in the tunnel and shuffling forward.

Al-Aziz stopped suddenly. "Tie your pack around my foot. You will have access to it if you need it."

Yeah, and you'll be able to leave me in the dust if I get stuck, Cruz thought. But he was beyond distrusting the man. Al-Aziz, with his quick thinking, had saved their lives and risked his own by revealing the bomb around his waist was not trapped. Of course, al-Aziz had been lying about it being rigged in the first place..

Cruz looked around the small crevasse. What choice did he have but to trust al-Aziz? He quickly tied the backpack to al-Aziz's foot. "Good to go."

Al-Aziz shuffled forward on his elbows, military style.

Cruz knelt down and slipped forward on his belly. He was enveloped by cold stone a moment later. He picked his head up and felt the ceiling brush against his hair. Not a lot of space. He slid forward, pushing with his toes and pulling with his elbows. It wasn't the fastest way of moving, but both men were disciplined and they made good time. The downward slope helped, too, but Cruz knew if there was a need to go backward, it might be nearly imposs- ible.

Time seemed to move as slowly as they did. What felt like two hours was closer to twenty minutes, and after an actual hour, both men were exhausted. The tunnel slowly closed in on both sides. The space constricted so tightly around them now that Cruz pushed forward with his elbows stretched straight out, arms locked. He could only move a few inches at a time. His sides rubbed against the walls and where there was an outcrop, even if it was only an inch, he had to really push hard to continue. One protruding stone seemed as though it was cracking his ribs one at a time as he inched past it.

All he could hear was his own breath, ragged from breathing the dust kicked up by al-Aziz's movement ahead and the shuffle of his backpack being dragged. He had no vision of what lay ahead; he had kept his head down for the past ten minutes. Bringing it up, even a little, was impossible. The tunnel was closing in.

He felt the ceiling tickle his hair then rub against his back. All sides of his body were rubbed raw by the rough stone that felt more like a hundred tiny fingers clawing at him, trying to keep him still. With his arms stretched forward to shrink his body, Cruz began pushing with just his toes. Movement came an inch at a time. Then a centimeter. Then not at all.

With one last heave, Cruz moved an inch, squeezed tight, then stopped. He couldn't look forward. He couldn't move back. All he could feel was pressure all around his body, a constricting pressure that made breathing almost impossible. His lungs could not fill with air. Growing lightheaded and panicked, Cruz felt his mind give way to mania.

"Aziz!" The shout echoed loudly in the tight space. The effort pushed his ribs painfully against the surrounding walls. "I'm stuck!"

The response was muffled. He couldn't understand the man. The backpack would be blocking the tunnel completely by now.

The man's voice was faint: "I'll come back for you."

Al-Aziz was moving on, leaving Cruz to rot beneath the mountain. The sound of scraping grew faint as al-Aziz pushed on. But the sound wasn't fading with distance, it faded with consciousness. Panic and pressure had taken the air from Cruz's lungs. He fell unconscious, trapped beneath a mountain of stone.

 CHAPTER 58

Dreaming of Portsmouth and Sam, Whitney was displeased to wake up and find herself in the same gargantuan prison cell. Darkness loomed on the other side of the high window and a crescent moon glowed in the night sky. The cell was lit by reflected light from the hallway, the origin of which was hidden from view. What caught Whitney's attention was that the illumination did not flicker like firelight but was solid, like modern lighting. Whitney glanced out of the cell and cringed. The light also illuminated the bodies in the opposite cell. The smell of decomposition permeated the air. She winced and turned away.

A twitch of movement from the opposite corner caught Whitney's eye. "Dad . . ." Whitney stretched. "Has anything changed?"

"I'm afraid your father is still sleeping," a feminine voice said from the corner.

Whitney gasped and jumped to her feet. He heart pounded wildly in her chest. "Dad," Whitney called. "Wake up!"

"He was having nightmares," the woman said. "I gave him something to help him sleep."

Whitney's face contorted with fear. Was her father hurt? Knocked unconscious?

"Don't worry," the woman said. "You have nothing to fear from me." She stepped out of the darkness, shrouded in a hooded cloak. Her face was hidden in shadow.

Whitney was glad to see that the woman was human size. "We heard you talking earlier. To Enki."

The hooded woman nodded. "Yes. He has been in a rage since one of their soldiers was killed in battle. He was going to kill you both."

Whitney's attempt to hide her shock was useless. Her eyes gleamed wide. "They can be killed?"

"I have never seen it happen," the woman said, "but apparently so. When they brought in several bodies, all Chinese men, I saw them carrying one of their own. His name was Loki."

"Then you are not . . . with them? This is not your home?" Whitney asked.

The woman shook her head. "I was taken here years ago." The woman paused and seemed to inspect Whitney's face. "You would have been a teenager at the time. I knew who they were, the Nephilim, and they kept me alive to teach them."

"About what?"

"Our languages. Our cultures. The state of the world." The woman looked at the floor. "They wanted to know how best to conquer us, and I have told them everything they wanted to know."

Whitney heard the sadness in the woman's voice. "You did what needed to be done to survive. I would have done the same."

The woman looked up suddenly. "And you will, if you plan to survive the night. Enki will interrogate you shortly. Answer his questions as best you can and he might let you live."

"Why are you helping us?" Whitney asked.

The woman turned away and walked to the bars. She gripped them with her hands and Whitney saw the woman's skin. She was black. "When I was taken here, I believed my life was over. I gave up hope. I believed God had turned his back on me and left me for dead in this hell on earth. I turned my back on God. I . . . for a time . . . I hated Him for what my life had become. I am only now learning that God's plans are more complicated than I could have imagined."

Whitney couldn't make heads or tails of what the woman was saying. How could her and Merrill's presence here change her view of God's plans so dramatically? Was the woman plotting something?

The woman turned to Whitney. "How was I to know that the continent would thaw? How could I have foreseen the conflict between human and Nephilim? And how could I have known you would be in my care again? That I would bathe you as I had before. That—"

Whitney was horrified and confused. "You *bathed* me?" She looked at her father, sound asleep on one of the tall beds, not even stirred by the conversation. "Him? What gives you the right to bathe him?"

The woman's hands came up slowly. Whitney noticed they shook as she grasped the hood. One of her fingers had a gold wedding band. The hood fell back, revealing the woman's face in the pale yellow light.

Whitney found herself looking into a mirror. The woman's skin was darker than Whitney's and her hair was black instead of blond, but her eyes, her cheeks . . .

". . . *Mom?*"

A geyser of emotion plumed from inside Whitney's stomach and shot into her head. It was a sickening twist of euphoria and tragic sadness. She felt she would throw up, but instead fell to her shaking knees. Aimee was there in an instant, hugging her close, weeping. They remained so for several minutes, holding each other, making sure the other was real.

When they separated, Whitney's eyes were red with tears and her nose ran. Her mother produced a rag and handed it to Whitney. "Tell me about your father," she said.

Whitney could see the nervousness in her mother's eyes and understood her concern. Even after all this time, she was still worried that he'd remarried.

"He still wears your wedding band," Whitney said. "But he hasn't been the same since. He left Antarctica and didn't return to finish his work until last year."

Aimee nodded and her forehead became noticeably less wrinkled. It was good news, probably the first her mother had had in years. "When the ice melted and the Nephilim went out, they kept returning with bodies of scientists from Vostok, McMurdo, and the other bases. Some of them had been colleagues; I kept expecting to see your father arrive."

"He was the only Antarctic survivor," Whitney said then smiled. "Before now."

"Thank the Lord," Aimee said. "Thank the Lord. And the rest of the world?"

Whitney turned her eyes away. She hadn't thought about the state of the world in some time. It brought tears to her eyes.

"Is it that bad?" her mother asked.

Whitney nodded.

Her mother placed a comforting hand on Whitney's head. It was something she had done throughout Whitney's childhood. "I love you, baby."

Whitney sniffled and nodded. Any emotional walls she had built up about her mother's death and the global disaster were being torn down.

"And what about you?" Aimee said. "Did you marry? Have children?"

Whitney's last wall crumbled. She began sobbing uncontrollably. Her mind retreated, and for ten minutes she wailed like a child in her mother's embrace. She remembered that her mother was an insightful woman. She would know without having to be told that Whitney had lost loved ones. She didn't need to know the details. Not now. As the embrace of her mother's arms and body wrapped around her, Whitney realized just how much she missed her mother and how badly she needed her.

A slight vibration in the floor that Whitney would not have noticed if it weren't for Aimee's sudden reaction ended their embrace. "Wipe your tears. Feign sleep," her mother said. "They're coming."

Whitney leapt into one of the beds, her back to the cell doors. Aimee spoke in rapid-fire whispers. "Remember what I said. When they question you, tell them everything. But do not tell your father about me. He doesn't think well when overcome with emotion."

Whitney nodded. She knew her father wouldn't think straight if given the news. "Will I see you again?"

"If you survive the night. Prove your worth to them." Aimee moved to the cell door. "I will return at dawn. We will talk further then."

Whitney heard the cell door creak open then slam shut. Footsteps faded into the distance and were met by a deep questioning voice. After a quick verbal exchange, the vibrations faded, and Whitney was alone with her father.

Tears welled up again. She was torn between hope and hopelessness. As Whitney stared at the solid stone walls with blurry eyes, she wondered if she'd ever see her mother again. The thought of not seeing the joy of her reunited parents was too much to bear.

 # CHAPTER 59

Guilt crept up slowly with the morning sun and took firm root in Wright's consciousness. Never before in his military career had he left a man behind. He'd suffered injuries and even a fatality here and there, but no man was ever physically deserted. He'd lost five in the past few hours. Regardless of whether or not all of them were officially on the team, they'd become his responsibility as soon as he let them join the group. Now it was just the three of them, if he counted the dog.

For what it was worth, they were making good progress now. Between the heightened senses of Vesuvius and the keen eyes of Ferrell, they had managed to avoid further contact with the Nephilim. But it was a challenge. The Nephilim were everywhere. If not for their comparatively small size, they'd already have been spotted.

The ground shook as three more of the giants walked past. Hidden inside a group of boulders at the river's edge as they were, the Nephilim walked past them without a glance. It'd be like noticing the ants as you walked over your lawn, Wright thought. Then he remembered the Bible verse Jacobson had quoted: "We were like grasshoppers in their sight." That was the truth.

When they had arrived at the area, several Nephilim were knocking trees over into the river. Within minutes they had toppled fifty trees, some of which created a temporary bridge across the water. When the giants left, they each carried three trees on top of each shoulder—entire trees. Wright was sure they'd be back for the rest.

He couldn't help but wonder what they were doing with the trees. He felt sure the wood wasn't for burning. It was too warm. They must be building something. But what?

Wright pushed the question from his mind. It would have to wait. Right now, they needed to cross the river. Wright peeked up over the rocks. He didn't see any Nephilim remaining; the area was free of spying eyes. "All clear," he said.

He and Ferrell leapt from their hiding spot and Vesuvius followed quickly. They ran for the river, ducking and weaving past trees and shrubs. The roar of the water drowned out the crunch of earth beneath their feet. As they approached the river, Wright noticed the air cooling and could taste the sweetness of the water. He'd never drunk water so clean.

Wright jumped up onto the largest log that crossed the river, and Vesuvius vaulted onto the log in front of him. The dog seemed to always be one step ahead. Wright helped Ferrell up, not because she needed it but because any physical contact with his wife was a treat after hiding their affection for so long. And she didn't balk at the hand; she just smiled and said, "Thanks."

When they started across, Vesuvius was already halfway to the other side and still moving. The long, red-berried pine tree was over one hundred feet long and barely reached the other side of the river. With every step the tree bent and rolled under their weight, making each footfall unsure. Wright was surprised by the tree's flexibility and thought the wood must be a dream to work with. As they approached the far side, Vesuvius stood waiting. The tree line was thick with long branches that stretched out low over the water, slowing their progress, but with only twenty feet to go—

Wright glanced at Vesuvius and noticed the hair on the back of his neck rise. "Get off the log," Wright whispered fiercely.

Ferrell turned her last steps into a sprint and dove to the shore. She rolled behind a bush and disappeared.

Wright began to follow but a deep voice cutting through the thunderous water caused Wright to look back. And it was a good thing he did. Five Nephilim stepped out from the trees talking amongst themselves, and headed toward the felled tree. If he made a run for it now, they'd surely spot him.

Wright made like a frightened squirrel and slid around to the underside, gripping the bark with all his strength. He had no idea how long he would have to hang there, but he hoped it wouldn't be long. His fingernails felt like they were going to peel away from his fingers.

When it shook, he realized they were taking his tree. As the tree lurched up in the air, hoisted by one of the mighty giants, Wright let go and splashed into the water. Still holding his XM-29 and a backpack full of gear, he sank like a stone. Which, for the time being, was fine; they might see him surface.

The water was frigid and threatened to suck the air from his lungs. It wasn't cold enough to cause hypothermia, but it was at least twenty degrees cooler than the air temperature. Wright's feet hit the stone-covered bottom ten feet from shore. He discovered the water to be crystal clear and grappled for a root to grab to avoid being dragged away by the swift current. He locked himself down, holding his body rigid against the raging torrent.

Through the undulating waters, Wright saw tree after tree yanked up and away from the river. These titans were even stronger than Dr. Clark believed. They weren't just able to carry six timbered logs; they carried entire hundred-foot trees like they were made of packing peanuts.

Wright counted in his mind. He knew he could hold his breath for two minutes, but the counting helped distract him from the ache in his already-exhausted lungs. After two minutes, he'd have to kick up to the surface and hope that his momentum would carry him with the gear. In training, he'd been able to hold his breath for a minute thirty, tops. It had always been his limit, even when he was pushing himself to gain a second more. He never did. But now, if he rose and the men were still there . . . well, he'd be dead either way.

At a minute twenty, Wright could see that there were still two logs in the water. Still the Nephilim worked. Ten seconds passed and one log was still in the water.

He'd passed his level of endurance. Every sinew of his being told him to push up. But doing so would mean breaching the water at a high speed, pulling in a loud breath and splashing around to stay afloat. He would certainly attract attention.

White and purple spots began to dance in his vision as his mind called for oxygen. His jaw muscles battled, some instinctively trying to open and take a breath, others willed by him to stay closed. His chest ached like it would burst.

With failing vision, he saw the last tree slip out of the water and fade from view. Push! But there was nothing left in his body. His fingers slipped from their purchase and he was swept away by the cold waters.

 CHAPTER 60

They came with the dawn. The cell door slammed open, rousing Mirabelle and Merrill from sleep; before either could understand what was happening, their heads were covered and they were lifted bodily from their oversized beds.

Merrill felt a thick, heavy hand clutching his leg and a bulk of flesh, the Nephilim's shoulder, beneath his gut. He'd been slung over the giant's shoulder like a sack of potatoes. Every step brought a jolt of pain to Merrill's stomach. The Nephilim who carried him was either a rough walker or was doing it on purpose. Either way, Merrill was getting the wind knocked out of him.

But his concern was not on his physical being. He knew he shouldn't talk but chanced it anyway. "Mira, are you with me?"

"I'm here," came a quick reply.

"No talking," a deep, booming voice said.

The journey lasted five agonizing minutes more. At the end, Merrill felt his stomach rise sickeningly as he was dropped from the towering shoulder to the floor. It felt like one of those awful amusement park rides.

"You may remove your hoods," a voice said.

Merrill did so and found himself sitting on the floor next to his daughter. The room seemed gargantuan to him; to their captors it was probably of average size. It was decorated with carvings depicting ancient battles between man and Nephilim. Some showed men worshiping the giants. Others showed the giants eating men. One carving depicted a deluge . . . but there wasn't just one boat; there were two. One held a man, and the other was covered in Nephilim symbols. They had survived the flood.

The room had no furnishings except for four large thrones at the front of the room, each occupied by a Nephilim. The giants were not dressed in battle regalia but wore long flowing robes and masks over their heads. Merrill recognized them immediately.

Moving left to right, Merrill took the giants in. The first wore a jackal mask, black and sinister. Fitting for Anubis, the Egyptian god of the underworld. Next to Anubis was a taller Nephilim wearing a mask that resembled a pointy-beaked bird, an Ibis. This was Thoth, the Egyptian god of writing and knowledge, known as Hermes in the west; Merrill knew his real name was Ningizzida, son of the Sumerian god, Enki, who was next in line. Enki, the largest of the group, wore a tall crown that covered much of his face, though his yellow eyes could be seen through a pair of eyeholes. Running up the center of the crown were two snakes intertwined, the modern symbol for medicine. And next to him . . . Merrill was not sure who it was at first, but the details slowly became clear. The giant's red hair was twisted in braids and hung over his shoulders. On his head was a helmet from which rose two long twisting horns. Like Enki's crown, the helmet also covered his face, but its symbol resembled a lightning bolt. It wasn't until Merrill saw the large sledgehammer with an engraved head clutched in the giant's hand that he identified him: Thor, Norse god of Thunder. Even the hammer held a name: Mjölnir. Merrill was staring at some of the world's first and most powerful pagan gods.

Merrill stood to his feet and helped up Mira. The four giants just watched, apparently judging how the little humans would react to their presence. Merrill was terrified, to be sure, but the monsters represented an evil so great that he felt God was undoubtedly on his side and, even now, watched out for them.

Mirabelle looked at them then at Merrill. "Tell them everything they want to know."

Merrill's forehead crinkled. "Why?"

"Just trust me, Dad." She shot him a look that said he'd better trust her. She knew something he didn't.

"I'll do better than that," Merrill said in a whisper. "I'll tell them everything they believe I don't know." Merrill pointed to each giant, one at a time and called them by name. "Anubis. Ningizzida. Enki. Thor."

For the first time the giants moved, exchanging glances. Merrill had thrown them. Slowly, they removed their helmets, revealing their ancient faces and amber eyes. Though their masks were removed, each still wore a thick metal band around his forehead. It seemed a customary headdress.

"Very good, son of Noah," Enki said, his voice reverberating like a waterfall. "But we do not yet know your names."

"I am Dr. Merrill Clark," he said, stepping forward. He opened his mouth to introduce Mira, but she stepped forward next to him and quickly spoke.

"Mirabelle Whitney."

"Tell us, what do you know of the Nephilim?"

"Everything," Merrill said.

Enki seemed miffed. "Perhaps you would like to summarize your knowledge."

Merrill described the Nephilim's dual parentage, their attempt at sabotaging the future savior of the human race, and their motivation for doing so: the Nephilim's soulless eternal lives. He continued to put pieces of a puzzle together that he was still just seeing for the first time. He told them about the flood, how Noah had escaped in the ark, and how the Nephilim had escaped to Antarktos. The new portion of the story he'd only now just put together was that the Nephilim had returned, much fewer in number, to the land of men, in Canaan, but elsewhere as well. They became the basis for the world's ancient myths and religions. As man advanced and shrugged off the old religions, many of the Nephilim, spread out around the world, returned to Antarktos and waited for the right moment to again reveal themselves and continue their corruption of humanity.

Not all the Nephilim had returned. Those who were smaller had remained and merged with humanity, disappearing into its growing population . . . and waiting. They became influential men, warriors of fame, and leaders of nations. Perhaps they still were. When the strike finally came, it would not only come from the pure-blooded Nephilim emerging from Antarktos, but also from those hidden within the human population and their half-breed children. How many there were he could only guess, but it would no doubt be an army. It was a conspiracy theory for the ages, but as Enki nodded in confirmation, Merrill bit his lip. If he was right, the human race was indeed in jeopardy.

Suddenly Merrill had a revelation. In an instant he knew just who he was dealing with . . . and what they were after. He spoke the verse aloud, slowly and concisely, as he recalled every word. "'The locusts looked like horses prepared for battle. On their heads they wore something like crowns of gold, and their faces resembled human faces. Their hair was like women's hair, and their teeth were like lions' teeth. They had breastplates like breastplates of iron, and the sound of their wings was like the thundering of many horses and chariots rushing into battle. They had tails and stings like scorpions, and in their tails they had power to torment people for five months. They had as king over them the angel of the Abyss, whose name in Hebrew is Abaddon, and in Greek, Apollyon.'"

Merrill turned his head, eyes wide to Whitney. "Revelation 9:7-11."

Whitney's eyes widened. The verse described the Nephilim uncannily well. It was further confirmed when Enki stood and stepped toward them. His toothy grin revealed sharp teeth, like a lion's. His long red hair flowed over his shoulders. The metal ring around his head reflected the light, gleaming yellow, like gold. "*Now* you know everything."

"You are Apollyon?" Merrill asked, stunned.

"No," Enki said. "Apollyon, is our father."

Of course! Merrill thought. The sons of demons were returning to wage war on humanity. It seemed so clear, so obvious. But Merrill couldn't accept it. It was all too strange. "But you have no wings! No tails with stingers to torment! You can't be—"

Enki laughed and the deep roar of his voice echoed off the walls. Merrill covered his ears. With a quick yank, Enki was out of his robes, standing before them dressed for battle with an iron breastplate strapped to his chest. Then from behind, two wings peeled from his body like tearing flesh and spread, black and fleshy like a bat's. A tail, tipped with a five-inch stinger, dropped down and twitched behind the giant, eager to strike, like a threatened scorpion.

Enki leaned in close. "Gifts"—His breath smelt of the rotting flesh stuck between his double rows of teeth—"from our father."

Merrill backed away, hiding Mirabelle behind him. Her fingers gripped into his back as she clung to him. She was as petrified as he was. The enemy prophesied in the Bible so long ago had emerged to wage their war. This was worse than anything he'd ever imagined. He had always been a bit of an end-times pessimist. He'd hear others say, "We're in the end times because things are so bad." He'd always disagreed, thinking things would get much worse before Armageddon. But even his dire predictions paled in comparison to reality.

This was worse. Much worse.

"Take them away," Enki said to the guards who had carried Mirabelle and Merrill into the room. Enki looked directly at Merrill, his eyes almost glowing like light bulbs, and said, "We will speak again, when the hopelessness of your situation has taken root in your feeble mind. Then you will tell us everything we want to know about your world, and how best to destroy it."

 CHAPTER 61

Waking slowly, Cruz felt a comfortable pressure hugging his body. It felt like a freezing sixty degree day in Pasadena when he'd wake up for school and stay wrapped tightly in his blankets. He tried rolling over, but his body was stuck. He moved the other direction. Still nothing.

Then he noticed a dull ache in his shoulders, which were raised above his head. He opened his eyes, but saw only pitch black. He craned his head up to get a different view and cracked it on something hard . . . rock hard.

His situation returned to the forefront of his mind. He was trapped, still, under a mountain of rock. As hopelessness reasserted itself in his mind and tears began to form as he reverted back to a child-like state, a voice cut through his despair.

"Cruz, can you hear me?" It was al-Aziz. He hadn't left him.

Though he could only look down at the floor, Cruz could see light. Al-Aziz had come back! "I'm here," Cruz said, doing his best impression of a fearless military man. "Now get me the hell out of here."

"I'm sorry I took so long," al-Aziz said. Cruz had no idea how long it had actually been. "But the backpack got stuck and I had to unpack it from my side to get it through."

That was all he'd done? Crawled through and unpacked the backpack? That couldn't have taken more than a few minutes. Wait, Cruz thought, how did he unpack the gear? He had the pack behind him; unless . . . "Al-Aziz, where are you?"

Cruz felt a tap on his fingers. "I am here," al-Aziz said. "In a cave." The man laughed. "Your fear is misguided, my friend. Your hands are only inches from the cave entrance."

Cruz wished he could look up and see it for himself. Freedom was only inches away, though he was still stuck.

"Any ideas?" Cruz asked.

He felt al-Aziz take his hands. "You need to lock wrists with me. I will brace my feet on the wall and try to pull you free."

Cruz knew how stuck he was. Al-Aziz wouldn't have the strength to pull him free, not without stripping some flesh off in the attempt.

"Take several deep breaths then push all the air from your lungs. It will make you smaller."

Or maybe it would work.

Cruz did as al-Aziz said, taking four deep breaths and then blowing out all the air. He felt a stab of pain in his wrists as al-Aziz put his whole body into pulling Cruz free. Then the pain was overshadowed by another sensation—movement. Cruz slid forward, slowly, but he was making progress.

Al-Aziz could be heard grunting with exertion, but the pulling never eased. For a man who once had vowed to kill as many Americans as possible, he was sure doing his damnedest to save one now.

As the inches passed, the tunnel shrank, squeezing Cruz tighter and tighter. He felt his ribs bending inward. If one were to break, a lung could be punctured. He opened his mouth to tell al-Aziz to stop as the pain grew intense, but there was no air to form words.

Then the tunnel gave birth to a man; Cruz's barrel chest slipped from the confined space and his body spilled out into the small cave. Al-Aziz fell backwards and slid across the floor. Sucking in breaths was hard for Cruz at first. His chest had been so compressed that every breath brought a fit of pain as his ribs flexed back to their natural position.

When his lungs were full again and the pain had subsided, Cruz began to laugh. "Man, I thought you left."

Al-Aziz sat up. "I do not leave friends behind." Then he motioned around the cave with his flashlight. "Besides, there is nowhere to go."

He was right. A few holes in the wall allowed the air to continue moving, but they weren't human-sized. Not that Cruz cared. He'd rather starve to death in this cave than crawl through another tunnel. As the light played off the wall and floor, Cruz noticed the floor was unusually reflective. He clicked on his own flashlight and shined it at the floor. It glistened like dirty glass. "More mica."

In fact the whole floor was mica.

Cruz took a whack at the floor with his flashlight and chipped off a slab of the clear mineral. But it wasn't the slab that caught his attention; it was the hollow clunk the floor made when Cruz struck it. He hit it again. *Clunk.* Definitely hollow.

Moving quickly, Cruz took out a detonator cap and a tiny ball of C4. The explosion would be enough to put a small hole in the floor without blowing them to bits. If there was a space below, they still might find a way out. He arranged the C4 on the far side of the cave so that the energy of the explosion would shoot straight down.

Al-Aziz must have quickly realized Cruz's plan, because he was crouched on the far side of the cave, hands over head. Cruz joined him and pushed the detonator button. There was a loud pop and a cloud of dust. Breathing through his arm, Cruz looked back and saw a five-inch hole in the floor. It had worked!

Cruz got to his feet and walked toward the hole.

"Wait!" al-Aziz shouted as Cruz reached the cave's center. "Listen!"

Cruz held his breath. Then he heard it. Like cracking ice, a sharp crunch came from the floor. Cruz shone his flashlight down and saw the floor crumble beneath his weight. He attempted to dive to the side, but before he could push off, the entire floor of the cave collapsed beneath him.

Both men fell, arms flailing, into open space.

 CHAPTER 62

Merrill paced furiously in the oversized jail cell. He'd been muttering thus since they had been brought back an hour ago. He was driving Whitney crazy. "Dad, you need to slow down. You're not going to think clearly all worked up like this."

Merrill jolted to a stop, eyes wide, and looked at her. "I've never thought so clearly in my life."

She couldn't tell if he was telling the truth or if he'd lost his mind when confronted by the Nephilim's true form. She could barely stomach thinking about them herself. They were monsters, straight out of folklore: tailed, winged monsters. But her confusion was twofold. Not only were the Nephilim real, but it seemed there might be some credence to her father's beliefs. This lent her some hope that maybe a higher power was looking out for them. The state of her father's mind, however, did not.

"They're real," Merrill said. "And they're being led by the Destroyer, Apollyon. And there is nothing we can do to stop them. They have come to prepare earth for the final battle, for Armageddon."

"Dad . . ."

"Some people thought there would be actual locusts. Some said Apache helicopters spraying nerve gas, but they were all wrong. It is going to be so much worse."

"Dad."

The man was on an unstoppable tirade. "I just can't believe—"

"*Dad!*" Whitney grabbed Merrill by the shoulders and shook him. She had tears in her eyes. "The world doesn't need you right now. I do! We need to find a way out of here. Nothing else matters. The demons. The angels. The end of the world. It can all wait!"

Merrill finally looked Whitney in the eyes.

"All that matters is you, me, and Mom. We have to escape. We—"

"What did you just say?" Merrill's face grew pale. His clenched jaw grew slack. His taut muscles fell loose.

Whitney's mind rewound her last sentence and replayed it internally. Damn. All attempts to come up with some reason for the slip would not be believed. She'd have to come clean . . .

"Merrill," a sweet voice from the cell door said.

Merrill spun around so fast that he tripped and fell. His lips quivered. He still recognized his wife's voice. "Aimee." He clambered to his feet and stepped forward on shaking legs. "Aimee . . ."

Aimee, standing by the now-open door, draped in shadow, stepped forward. Her eyes were already wet. Merrill's legs gave out again and he fell to his knees. Aimee ran to him. Their tear-coated faces were only inches apart. Merrill's hands were on her face, touching her cheeks, her ears, her hair. "It's really you." His face became a wash of horror. "Had I known . . . I would have searched . . . I would have—"

"Merrill, there was no way you could have known." Aimee pushed his scraggly gray hair away from his wrinkled forehead and kissed him gently. "You have nothing to feel guilty for. What matters is that we're together now."

Merrill embraced his wife and kissed her long and hard. She collapsed in his arms and wept as he kissed her face and forehead, sobbing lightly like he had the hiccups.

Whitney joined them on the floor and wrapped her arms around her parents. They were together again, a family! The closeness Whitney felt with her parents now far outweighed any experience she'd had as a child when they were together. They'd been given a merciful gift. Whitney had no other way to describe the events surrounding her family's reunion. The world was in chaos. Mankind's greatest enemy had just resurfaced. They were jailed in a giant fortress surrounded by enemies, and yet it was the happiest moment of all their lives.

Merrill was the first to leave the comfort of the embrace. His eyes seemed hard, resolved to some course of action at which Whitney could only guess. But the mania that had overtaken him before was gone. His mind was at work. He was a father and husband again. She could see that was something he'd fight for.

As though the embrace had supplied him with clarity, Merrill looked at them and said, "My two favorite girls . . . I think it is time to leave."

Aimee brushed her hand against his cheek. "I have freedom to move about here, but there is no escape. The exits are well guarded."

Merrill looked at the pile of rotting soldiers across the hall. "Their weapons. Where are they?"

Aimee let out a sob. "Merrill, you cannot kill them."

Merrill stood, his face a mask of determination. "A champion named Goliath, who was from Gath, came out of the Philistine camp. He was over nine feet tall. He had a bronze helmet on his head . . ."

Whitney watched her mother's eyes widen with recognition. This was truly a David and Goliath story if there ever had been one . . . The gears of Whitney's mind clicked forward and everything became clear. She could see the correlation. The helmet. The gold bands around the Nephilim heads. They weren't decorative. They were protection. Goliath had been a Nephilim!

Merrill added a second verse. "'Reaching into his bag and taking out a stone, he slung it and struck the Philistine on the forehead. The stone sank into his forehead, and he fell facedown on the ground.'" He took Aimee's hands again and kissed her hard on the lips. "We've got better slingshots," he said. "And I will not let this family be separated. Not again."

Aimee nodded. "Follow me." She headed for the open cell door.

"We're just going to walk out of here?" Whitney asked.

Aimee gave a slight smile. "As a girl, you caught some beetles and kept them in a jar. One day you left the jar open and they escaped. Do you remember?"

Whitney nodded.

"Were we worried about the beetles? Was it hard to catch them again? And the ones we never found, did we give them a second thought? We are nothing more than grasshoppers in their sight. We are as insignificant to them as your beetles were to us. When they discover us missing, they will have little trouble hunting us down."

With that, Aimee stepped into the hallway and motioned for them to follow.

# CHAPTER 63

Images flashed across Wright's vision. Katherine on their wedding night, a quick affair in Vegas. His father behind the steering wheel of the family boat, cruising along the Florida coast. Harris, an old drill sergeant, cussing him out. Jaws, biting and snapping at his face.

He couldn't place the memory. Sharp canines and a black snout, pushing through water, bubbles rising. A bark. Then the jaws returned with pressure on Wright's shoulder. The visions seemed to be taking physical form.

Then, nothing.

The world grew black for untold hours.

Wright sat up with a gasp and promptly coughed up several cups of water. He heard nothing but his own retching and felt nothing but his lungs begging for more air. The sound created by his desperate breathing was like a deranged animal call, sure to attract attention.

"Stephen," a voice said gently. "Stephen, you're all right. Try to slow your breathing. We'll be heard."

Wright looked up. Ferrell was above him. Vesuvius, looking like a wet rat, panted next to her with a look of concern on his playful face. Wright quickly remembered where they were, what was happening, and who might be alerted by his ragged breaths. He coughed into his sleeve and finally caught his breath.

He tried to sit up but a lance of pain, like a hot iron stuck between his ribs, sent him back down. "What the hell did you do to me?"

"CPR, dear," Ferrell said. She smiled. "Broke your ribs. Sorry."

Wright sat up again, more slowly this time and with Ferrell's help. He grunted.

"Don't be such a wimp. I've done worse to you in bed."

Wright laughed then grimaced with pain. Ferrell knew he dealt with pain better if things were kept humorous. Otherwise he could get downright snippy. Vesuvius wagged his tail quickly, spraying water with every swoosh. "And what happened to him?"

Ferrell pet the dog's head. "He pulled you out. Jumped right in after seeing you floating away."

Wright couldn't help but smile. Vesuvius had proven to be one of the team's most valuable members. A pang of guilt struck. The dog would never see its family again. "Bandage me up quick. We need to keep moving."

Ferrell raised an eyebrow, offered a mock salute, and said, "Yes, sir."

An hour later, nearly noon, Wright was patched up and they were hiking uphill, straight for the Nephilim fortress. Every step brought a fresh jolt of pain to Wright, but the morphine Ferrell had given him, though it slowed his reaction time, took the edge off.

"Get down," Ferrell whispered, her tone unmistakably serious.

Wright looked back to see Ferrell and Vesuvius pinned to the forest floor behind a tree. Wright turned forward again and saw two sets of lumbering legs pass by, just on the other side of the tree line. He looked up. Two Nephilim strode past, clothed in armor and carrying swords. Neither looked down. Wright was unseen.

After they were out of view, Ferrell appeared at his side. "From now on, I take point."

They moved past the tree line and found themselves on a stone road that led up the mountainside, weaving back and forth in a lazy switchback pattern. It crested at the top of the mountain, just above the carved skull. Wright switched on his GPS unit. The device had been programmed to work only within three miles of the goal, to pinpoint the end location. This was in part to make sure that enough battery life was left in the unit to fulfill its ultimate purpose: sending its beacon and claiming Antarktos for America.

But there also wasn't much choice. Since the globe had been reduced to chaos, GPS satellite coverage was almost non-existent over Antarktos, and without satellite coverage, standard GPS devices were now useless on Antarktos. The modified unit Wright carried communicated with a single satellite locked in stationary orbit directly above their final location. The GPS screen showed their position and the point that marked the race's finish—at the top of the mountain, just above the skull. Wright pointed up the road. "Thata-way."

The hike up, while exhausting, was made easier by the road. Walking on any other open road would have been a bad idea, but any Nephilim would be easy to spot above the now-short treetops, while they would be safely concealed. It was a tactical risk.

They reached the peak within two hours without any interference from Nephilim patrols. Wright sat on a rock and took in the view. It was a panoramic sight that stretched out for hundreds of miles. They'd been steadily walking upward since the very beginning of the journey and were now at the highest point for hundreds of miles, the geographic center of Antarktos. And it was a sight Wright would never forget. The azure sky, speckled with white clouds, stretched on beyond the capabilities of human vision. The landscape was extravagantly decorated with sharp mountains, rolling hills, and lush plains. Rivers were etched across the landscape, intertwining and merging at various lakes before continuing their long journey to the shining sea.

Ferrell sat next to Wright and put her arm around his waist. She took a deep breath and smelled the fresh air. "Like the honeymoon we never had."

"I'll tell you," Wright said, "If we make it back, we're both getting some R&R. Where do you want to go?"

"I don't think tropical islands exist anymore, so scratch that."

Wright pictured some of his old vacation spots. The Florida Keys. Jamaica. Even Japan. All gone. He sighed. "Any place in the world worth visiting that wasn't wiped out?"

"You're looking at it."

Wright smiled. "Well, screw that. Let's get the hell off this continent. I'll spend a month in the frozen U.S. north before coming back here." Wright stood up slowly, reached into his backpack, and switched on the GPS unit. Quickly working the on-screen touchpad, he set the beacon to send its signal in two-second bursts every five minutes. It would run for a month. A green light blinked on. The GPS beacon was activated. Antarktos, at least one third of it, had been claimed by the United States.

With no other forces to fight or hold the area from, Wright was content to leave. He doubted any other team would make it to the finish. After hiding the beacon in some brush, he took one last look at the view. "You know, I feel like I should say something to commemorate the moment. We've just claimed a new continent for the United States. They might even talk about us in history books some day. But I can't think of anything worthwhile."

Ferrell ran her fingers through his hair and said, "How about this?" She extended the middle finger of her other hand toward the view.

Wright chuckled. The woman had a sailor's sense of humor, but he loved it. "That'll do," he said.

Vesuvius broke the cheerful mood, growling deeply yet quietly. Wright felt the ground shake.

They had company.

Without speaking, Wright and Ferrell secured their backpacks and slipped into the forest, heading back down the mountain, keeping a good distance from the road. Wright knew that their current route forced them even closer to the walls of the Nephilim fortress, closer to the evil that lurked within. He was confident that he and Ferrell could make it through undetected, and after that begin the long trek back to the coast where they would rendezvous with U.S. forces. As long as they could avoid open conflict, they'd be fine.

# CHAPTER 64

The tunnels of the Nephilim fortress were utilitarian, lacking any kind of decoration save the occasional crop circle-like symbol, which Aimee had explained were both magical symbols and simple words such as "armory," or "storage." The more complicated the symbol, the more likely it was to be a word or even a full sentence. The simpler ones were magic—symbols used to communicate with their fathers.

Merrill found it difficult to concentrate. He wanted nothing more than to hug his wife over and over, to express his love for her and to relish in the reunion of his family, but it was not an option at the moment. Focusing on anything other than escape would prove deadly. All it would take was one mistake. He could lose everything he'd gained.

As they headed to the weapon-filled storeroom, Merrill briefly observed the amazing light fixtures—glass tubes three feet in length that extended from the walls and glowed dully like forty-watt bulbs. They looked like images he'd seen in Egyptian tombs. He could only wonder how deeply the Nephilim had influenced early human religions . . . and how much they still did.

Again, Merrill forced himself from his mental tangents. He needed to focus on plotting a course out of the fortress and back to the coast. Now was not a time for Nephilim theories.

Now was a time for war.

They reached the armory, a short distance from their cells. In five minutes, they only had to pause once as a guard bumbled past. Merrill recognized the symbol on the man's belt—a crescent moon with three stars—as Metztli, the Aztec moon god.

The armory was a room much like their jail cell, but lacking the beds and window. Merrill looked through the bars and saw piles of weapons, some five feet high. His instinct was to let out a whistle, but he restrained himself.

Aimee opened the door.

"No lock?" Merrill asked.

"They have nothing to fear," Aimee said.

"They will," Merrill said.

Mirabelle was the first through the door and the first to face the danger that lurked within.

A thin man of Asian descent rose from behind a pile of weapons. He wore the rags of an olive-green uniform and twisted glasses. His dirty, wide-eyed face bore the expression of a man who had seen things that would haunt him forever. He brandished an AK-47 and Merrill could have sworn he was a fraction of a second away from unloading the entire clip, but he paused. They weren't who he had been expecting.

"Whoa," Whitney said, raising her hands.

Nothing more needed to be said. The man lowered his weapon and sagged back against the wall. He wept. "I'm sorry," he said.

Mirabelle placed a hand on the man's shoulder. He looked up through his glasses and met her gaze. "It's okay," she said. "We're getting out of here. You can come."

The man sniffled and nodded.

Merrill noticed the red badge with the gold moon and four stars. It reminded him of Metztli's symbol, but he'd seen it before. In the field, on the Chinese soldiers. "You're Chinese?"

The man nodded. "Lei Zhou. My father was General Kuan-Yin Zhou."

"Is he here too?" Mira asked.

Lei shook his head. "No. They are all dead." The man was overcome by emotion for a minute. When he spoke again, his voice was like that of a child's, weary and broken. "They dragged away groups of men at a time. When they returned, they deposited the men's half-eaten bodies in the next cell. The other survivors and I knew our fate was to be eaten too. I . . . I was able to squeeze through the bars." Lei revealed his arms and chest, showing lesions where he'd forced his body through. "I was to get help, to find weapons, to help my countrymen. But I hid here instead . . . waiting to be found out.

"I failed them."

"You couldn't have saved them, Lei." Mira said. "But you can help us."

That seemed to lift the man's spirit. He had a chance to redeem his mistakes. He nodded, stood tall, and wiped his tears. "Tell me what to do."

Lei and Mirabelle began sorting and equipping weapons while Merrill and Aimee stood guard. It was the first chance they'd had to really talk. Merrill felt nervous, like a kid at the drive-in on a first date. She was his wife, but here she looked so different, so tired, that he wondered if he still knew her at all.

"Did they . . . treat you well?"

Aimee met his eyes and smiled slightly. "Better than most. They brought in scientists from other regions around Antarctica and questioned them, tried to learn their language, but ultimately none proved as good a teacher as I. My knowledge of the Bible gave me an understanding that the others lacked. The more I taught them, the better I was treated. I now have freedom to move around the fortress. Before the thaw, I never went outside. It was too cold. After a few years, I got used to the dull light and enclosed spaces. Until two months ago, I hadn't seen the sun in years."

Tears formed in Aimee's eyes. "I missed the world. And you." She looked at the floor, allowing the tears to drip down. "But I have betrayed humanity by helping them."

Merrill took her hand. "I think the world will forgive you," he said, taking her by the chin and tilting up her face. He smiled. "Given the circumstances."

Aimee chuckled and wiped her nose. "And what about you, dear husband? What have you been up to for the past ten years?"

"I left Antarctica. I taught at Harvard. Paleontology and anthropology, mostly. Nothing exciting. Vesuvius and I lived in Cambridge and—"

"Who's Vesuvius?"

Merrill smiled. "A dog. A Newfoundland."

"You got a dog?"

"Someone had to fill the empty space on the bed. Would you have preferred a woman friend?"

"Merrill, in all these years . . . you never . . .?"

Merrill knew what she was asking. "Never crossed my mind. Marriage is a one-time deal for me." Merrill felt a twinge of anger. Had she forgotten the kind of man he was? After all they'd been through together before she disappeared, he thought his character to be indelible in her mind. Yet she doubted him. "Maybe you forgot."

Aimee looked down. "Sorry. You're right." She met his eyes again and gave a small smile. "Well, then, Vesuvius better be willing to give up his spot in bed."

Merrill couldn't help but grin. "He will." His anger was replaced by guilt. She'd been through so much. What right did he have to feel angry over something so trivial? It was a miracle she wasn't a raving lunatic after all this time spent with the Nephilim.

Aimee watched Mirabelle. She had found her 9mm among the weapons and was checking it over with acute proficiency.

Merrill didn't notice. "You remember what your name means, right?"

"Love," Aimee said, but she wasn't really listening.

"And you remember who shares your name's meaning?"

"Freya . . . but she isn't that nice." Aimee's eyes were still on her daughter. She was thinking about something else but had caught Merrill off guard with her statement.

Then it dawned on Merrill. He hadn't seen any female Nephilim, but that didn't mean there weren't any. Why had he assumed the offspring of demons would only be male? There were as many female goddesses as male.

"Where are the females?"

"Underground. With the children."

Merrill's eyes were wide. He hadn't considered the abomination of Nephilim children! It was a frightening concept: half-demon, winged children that were probably larger than a grown human male. "Chi—children? There must be millions of them by now!"

Aimee shook her head slowly. "No," she said without emotion. This was all new to Merrill, but Aimee had spent a good portion of her life here. Merrill felt a deep sadness as he realized the horrors of the Nephilim world had become normal for his wife. "Food was scarce during the freeze; their children are born quickly."

Merrill felt bile stewing in his stomach. "They eat them?"

Aimee nodded. "What happened to her?" Aimee said, nodding toward Mirabelle. "Who did she lose?"

The abrupt subject change threw Merrill for a moment, but he was happy to consider something other than Nephilim women and children. "She was married. His name was Samuel Whitney. A good guy. Mira's name is now Mirabelle Whitney. He . . . he was murdered."

A pained expression crossed Aimee's face. "Poor baby. At least one of us was there for her."

Now it was Merrill's turn to look pained, as though he'd been stabbed. Aimee quickly realized her mistake. "You weren't there?"

"I was here," Merrill said. "Truth be told, I fled here. She reminded me so much . . . of you. It hurt to see her, to hear her voice. I didn't contact her for a year. When I saw her again, I didn't know Sam was gone." Merrill sniffled and wiped his nose. "She's changed a lot in the last year."

"I don't understand, Merrill," Aimee said with a furrowed brow. "After losing me, you wanted to run away from the only family you had left? She's a part of me, a part of both of us. You were willing to let her go?"

"No! I just—"

"I was held here against my will, but I would have done anything to be with my family again." Aimee shook her head. "And you ran away from yours."

"Don't you think I know that?" Merrill said, keeping his angry voice to a growl. "I should have been there for her. I should've . . ." A sob escaped Merrill's mouth. "I lost myself without you. I lost sight of what was important. And now, now she's changed so much in the last year. I don't know . . ."

Aimee took Merrill's hand, the angry expression gone from her face. "You should see her from my perspective," Aimee said, a slight grin on her lips. "She's a beautiful young woman now. Smart and resourceful, too. You did a good job with her."

"I could have done better. She doesn't . . ."

Aimee placed a gentle hand on his shoulders. "We can't change the ways things have happened, but we can affect the way things turn out."

Merrill took her hand. "Maybe you're right."

Aimee looked back at Mira, who was slinging what Merrill recognized as an XM-29 over her shoulder. "She's young. There's still time."

# CHAPTER 65

The darkness of the place quickly overwhelmed the sense of falling. Without visual cues, it was hard to sense the downward motion, like weightlessness in space. It felt, for a moment, like death. Then cold enveloped Cruz's body, and he knew he was still alive. And underwater.

How long he would remain so was still up for debate.

In the total darkness, Cruz could not discern up from down, left from right. He held his breath, and slowly his body began to rise. The weight of his waterlogged backpack made swimming almost impossible, but Cruz would not be separated from his explosives. They were his stock in trade. Without them he felt naked, useless.

Kicking his feet and pounding his arms brought him higher and higher, but the effort seemed futile. He could be a hundred feet down and not even realize it. For a moment he considered losing the gear, but the water changed. It was still cold but less fluid, and his arms weren't pushing; they were flailing. Cruz realized he had broken the surface and was still holding his breath.

After sucking in several gulps of air, he heard al-Aziz calling to him. "Over here! There is land on which to put your feet."

Cruz spun in the water. He couldn't see al-Aziz anywhere, and the sound of his voice echoed, booming all around them. "I'll tap the water with my hand," al-Aziz said quietly. "Follow the sound."

Cruz used a sidestroke he'd learned at summer camp at Bear Lake to slowly make his way toward the sound of al-Aziz's hand tapping the water. The stroke didn't consume much energy and allowed him a free hand to drag his backpack behind. After a few minutes of swimming, he heard tapping just feet away from his head. He put his feet down and felt solid stone beneath his feet.

Al-Aziz reached out and found him in the dark, pulling Cruz up out of the water onto a pile of rocks, cold and wet. "Where are we?"

"No idea," Cruz said. He found his flashlight, and pushed the button. It clicked on, bright as ever. "Thank God for waterproof flashlights, eh?"

"I do not speak to God anymore," al-Aziz said.

"Whatever floats your boat," Cruz said.

"We do not have a boat."

Cruz laughed and directed the light in a broad circle around them. Water stretched out before them, ending well out of range of the powerful flashlight's beam. The underground lake could stretch for miles. There was no way to know for sure. Behind them was a wall that also disappeared into darkness. Cruz aimed the light up. Above them was a stone ceiling pocked with reflective sheets of mica. A dark hole thirty feet above them gave evidence of their fall.

Al-Aziz took hold of Cruz's shoulder. "Do you hear that?"

Cruz listened. He heard the gentle lap of water on stone, but there was something else: gulping. Cruz followed the sound, aiming the light in that direction. On the near wall was a hole. The water rose and fell near the hole, flowing through. "I bet this underground lake feeds the river."

In the reflected light, Cruz saw al-Aziz nod. "Then that is where we need to go."

Ten minutes later they had swum out along the edge of the wall, making a slow approach to the hole. Up close, they felt the water being sucked through. The current was not fast, but it would pull them through. Cruz went first, ducking under the water and into the hole. He was pulled through a five-foot passage and spat out the other side.

Upon reaching the surface he gasped, though not for need of air. He was in shock. Al-Aziz rose up behind him and had a similar reaction. Before them was a second underground lake, lit by rows of what looked like massive light bulbs. The other light source was from daylight pouring in through a cavernous opening to the world beyond. But most surprising were the towering docks along one wall, perhaps a half-mile long, each holding a massive ship.

Some looked old, out of service, and out of use for thousands of years, but others appeared to be recently built and incredibly seaworthy. They were constructed using entire tree limbs bent into position. They were like ancient, heavily armored battle cruisers. The gigantic ships could only be crewed by one race on earth—the Nephilim.

Cruz smiled. He knew he'd saved the backpack for a reason.

Al-Aziz noticed his smile. "What are you thinking?"

"I have an idea."

 CHAPTER 66

Whitney knew that sneaking out of a guarded fortress during the afternoon wasn't a good idea, but with Enki planning a second interrogation for that evening it was unclear if father and daughter would survive the night. Were it not for Aimee's intimate knowledge of the citadel's layout, they would be hopelessly lost.

As Whitney watched Aimee move, blending with shadows and deftly avoiding detection, she wondered how often her mother had to become invisible to survive in such a place. It was a miracle that one of the giants hadn't simply picked her up at some point and made a snack of her.

Whitney found herself worrying that her mother was somehow in league with the Nephilim, having been corrupted after all her time there. Perhaps even now she led them into a snare. But then she saw the clutch, the desperate squeeze Aimee had on Merrill's hand, and she saw that their love for each other had not wavered. Whatever favor Aimee had earned while being held prisoner she seemed willing to give up just for the chance of being with Merrill again. Even if the attempt ended in death.

But what about me? Whitney thought. After being separated for so long, why didn't she cling just as tightly to her daughter? Then again, Whitney wasn't exactly going out of her way to bond with her mother, either. It seemed they had grown apart. Her father had been with her through college and forged an adult relationship with her over the years. As strained as it had been over the past year, they had the previous nine years upon which to draw. To her mother, Whitney was a different person. Older. Mature. Independent. Whitney realized her mother probably had no idea where to start with her, so she clung to what she knew best: Merrill. Though Whitney understood her reasons, she wished her mom showed greater interest in getting to know her again. Of course, there would only be time for that if they survived.

Whitney pushed the thoughts away and refocused on the task of escaping.

Aimee led them down a long hallway. Rather, long for humans, but perhaps a few steps for the Nephilim . . . or none at all if they decided to fly. At the tunnel's end, Whitney saw sunlight streaming in and beyond that, a long walkway across an exposed wall. They were close to freedom, but once outside they would be easily detected. There would be no nooks and crannies in which to hide.

Aimee had explained that there wasn't much in the way of exterior guards. They felt secure here, untouchable. But there were two guards at all the exits, and the only way to kill them was to first remove the gold bands protecting their foreheads. They'd have to do this twice then escape through the gates before more Nephilim arrived. Whitney had her doubts. A lot of them.

They reached the end of the arched hallway and paused at the exit. A long, walled bridge extended for four hundred feet, spanning a courtyard. Beyond that was a gargantuan staircase, after which they would enter a long hallway that exited into a smaller courtyard at the rear of the fortress, where they would make their escape.

Whitney held her XM-29 at the ready and felt the weight of the 9mm on her hip. She was as ready for action as the day she'd set out for Antarktos. Lei was armed with several grenades, two semiautomatic handguns, and his weapon of choice, an AK-47. Whitney's parents had opted not to carry weapons, citing that they were more likely to shoot each other by accident than do any real good. "Besides," Aimee had said, "if God can create the cosmos, if God can bring this family back together . . . then he can save us here."

Whitney hoped her mother was right. Didn't God sometimes let people die, too? Whitney pushed the thought from her mind and crouched near the hallway's exit. She quickly scanned the area. She couldn't see any Nephilim on the levels above, but she became aware of a strange noise, like mumbling or chanting. She stood and poked her head up over the wall. Below were four Nephilim, dressed in robes and wearing masks. They stood around a symbol burnt into the courtyard floor. The symbol was a simple circle with two intersecting Vs. At the center was a dark hole, which was stained dark brown around the edges.

Whitney watched with morbid fascination as all four Nephilim held out their left wrists and slit them deeply with daggers. After the blades were sheathed, the giants held their injured wrists and pulled back on their hands, opening the wounds and allowing gouts of blood to flow into the hole below.

Whitney stepped away from the wall and looked at her mother. "What are they doing?"

"Fertilizer . . . for the continent," Aimee replied. "The land is drenched in their blood. Antarctica heals like they do. It's the source of the continent's rapid growth and the survival of its ancient creatures."

As ridiculous as it sounded, Whitney believed her mother. Merrill's anhydrobiosis theory might be at the root of Antarctica's fertile comeback, but the explosive growth and reemergence of ancient species seemed more . . . supernatural. "And the chanting?"

"Talking to their fathers." Aimee said, a wash of fear spreading over her face. "The demons that frequent this place are more evil a force than the worst of the Nephilim."

"And they're out there now?" Whitney couldn't believe what she was hearing. "I don't see anything."

"You can't see them unless they want to be seen," Aimee said.

"Can they see us?" Whitney asked.

Aimee thought for a moment. "I don't think so. The communication seems intense. If we stay low and quiet, we should be fine."

Merrill squinted at Whitney. "Why are you worried at all? I thought you didn't believe demons existed!" he said.

"I've seen enough to know that there are things beyond my understanding. So the Bible is accurate in places. That doesn't make it infallible from cover to cover." Whitney shook her head. "Let's just go."

Crouching low, Whitney started out across the bridge, staying close to the wall, deep in shadow. The others followed closely. They reached the opposite side quickly and without incident. Whitney paused at the wall's end.

A slight vibration in the floor made her glance around the corner. Coming up the staircase was a behemoth wielding an axe that could slice a man in two with its weight alone. She fell back against the wall and her facial expression told the group everything they needed to know: their position was about to be exposed and they would all soon die.

Before Whitney could understand what was happening, Aimee was on her feet and walking toward the staircase. Whitney opened her mouth but Merrill's hand quickly covered it. After all these years, he apparently still believed her mother knew what she was doing.

Even if it was insane.

# CHAPTER 67

Ferrell sensed Wright's pain as they moved down the mountain. The pace they had set was grueling and would remain so until they were clear of the Nephilim fortress. But with the exertion came rapid breathing, which for Wright meant the rapid flexing of his cracked ribs. The pain he endured in silence was intense.

She leaned by a tree, feigning exhaustion. "We should rest," she said.

Wright stopped and caught his breath. His face was beaded with sweat and his eyes were weary. Still he smiled. "Nice try."

"At least let me carry your weapon," she said. His XM-29 had been slung over his shoulder. The weapon weighed a good fourteen pounds, and his backpack added another thirty. The least she could do was lighten his load.

He nodded without argument and handed her the weapon. She slung her own over her shoulder and held his at the ready.

"At the first sign of trouble . . ." he said.

She smiled. "Of course." She looked around. "Where's Vesuvius?"

They searched the area quickly. The dog was nowhere to be seen. Wright bent down and found a paw print. "Here."

They followed the prints' direction and found more. Soon they were following the tracks at near full speed. Without discussion they were chasing after the dog like he was a full-fledged teammate.

They found him ten minutes later, standing atop a crest that overlooked the Nephilim fortress. He was lying low and whining. Wright and Ferrell lay down to either side of him. He noted their arrival with quick glances then returned to his vigil.

"What do you see?" Ferrell felt a rising embarrassment, like she had entered a lost, very twisted episode of *Lassie*, but Vesuvius did not seem to act without just cause. Something had drawn him there.

He whined and stared intently at the fortress. Ferrell cursed herself for losing her sniper rifle. The scope would have been useful at a time like this. Still, she had her mini-binoculars. She opened the tiny lenses and put them to her eyes. She aimed in the direction upon which Vesuvius was so intent and quickly found what held his interest.

On a bridge crossing an open court she saw Whitney and Merrill, along with two others she did not recognize, crouching low to avoid detection. Beneath them in a courtyard were four Nephilim, performing some kind of ritual, tracing lines in the air. The four moved as one. She focused on their faces and could see their eyes were closed. They appeared to be in a trance-like state. She lowered the binoculars and handed them to Wright. "On the bridge. Merrill and Whitney."

Speaking the names affected the dog profoundly. His tail thumped and he whined loudly. Ferrell shushed the dog and said, "Quiet."

Vesuvius stopped whining, though his tail wagged ever faster. Wright scanned to the left. "I think I see where they're heading," he said, "but they're going to need some help."

Wright handed the binoculars back to Ferrell. She found the spot at which Wright had been looking. A large gate not far from the group's position was guarded by two Nephilim. They'd never make it. She looked at Wright. "We better hurry."

They leaped to their feet and pushed toward a fight neither believed they could win. Vesuvius ran ahead, leading the charge.

 CHAPTER 68

Merrill kept his hand firmly planted over Whitney's mouth until he felt she had also understood her mother's plot. They and Lei leaned against the wall as tightly as possible and hid in the shadows.

Merrill heard what was being said, though he did not see it.

"Teacher," the towering image of a man said in greeting.

"Azag," Aimee said.

Merrill fought the urge to look up and see the man. Azag was a minor god, a savage brute who was often depicted carrying a double-edged axe.

"Early for your walk, isn't it, teacher?"

"Enki has called me for council this evening," Aimee said. "I was restless and needed the fresh air."

"Very well," Azag said. "Peace be with our fathers."

"Peace be with them."

A moment later, Aimee's gentle hand was on Merrill's shoulder. He opened his eyes to find her crouched beside him. "I've always hated saying that," she said.

"Does Azag carry an axe?" Merrill asked, unable to contain his interest.

Whitney nodded. Merrill had forgotten she was the first to see him coming. "A big one. But how did he not see us?" Whitney asked.

"I stayed on the opposite side of him," Aimee replied. "When they speak to me, they rarely take their eyes off of me. Though I can do nothing to them, they inherently do not trust me."

Merrill knew that was because it was on behalf of the human race that the globe was nearly wiped clean of Nephilim. They have every reason not to trust us, Merrill thought, especially those who believe in the very God who had drowned so many of the ancient Nephilim. It was only the lucky ones who, like Noah, had survived on a ship, perhaps on a vessel even larger than the biblical ark. A thought struck Merrill. The Nephilim could drown! They were becoming less and less immortal and impervious in Merrill's mind. They could be killed; it was just difficult to accomplish.

Before Merrill could share his discovery, Lei leaned forward. "Do you mind if we keep moving?" he said nervously.

Aimee led them down the staircase, which was like climbing down a mountain, but they quickly reached the bottom. There was a ten-foot expanse from the base of the stairs to the darkened tunnel that led to the fortress exit. Crossing it would mean being exposed to the four Nephilim chanting in the courtyard.

But Aimee did not slow. She walked out into the open and into the darkness beyond. "What are you doing?" Merrill whispered.

Aimee's voice shot back from the darkness. "They do not perceive our reality. When speaking to their fathers, they see only the spirit world. They will not see you."

Merrill found the explanation nearly impossible to believe, but the impossible was becoming reality on a daily basis now, and his wife had an intimate knowledge of their abilities. It seemed she had been busy learning all she could while she was teaching them. And she hadn't been wrong yet.

Merrill stepped out first and crossed the courtyard, ducking into the shadowy tunnel. Whitney and Lei were close behind. Concealed in darkness, they broke into a run, moving toward the exit at the far end. From their distance, the tunnel's exit into the rear courtyard looked tiny, but Merrill could still see the four trunk-size legs that belonged to the two Nephilim guards. The fight would soon begin.

 CHAPTER 69

Whitney found herself breathing more heavily than usual. She'd been a runner for a long time and had completed the marathon trek inland through Antarktos. But the strain she felt as they ran through the gloomy tunnel was almost more than she could bear. Her legs felt unnaturally weak. Her arms were like wiry tubes that strained to hold onto the XM-29, which felt like a hundred pounds of dead weight in her hands. But it wasn't from physical exhaustion.

It was fear.

As they slowed near the tunnel's exit and stayed out of the guard's line of sight, Whitney found her chest pounding, her throat constricting. She was terrified. Knowing that her parents and the timid Lei would look to her for leadership in a fight, Whitney tried to pull herself together. A game plan had to be formulated.

She was delighted when Lei spoke first. "Whitney and I will face the guards," he said. He didn't sound exactly confident, but his father was a general and he was well-trained. Lei's plan would be their best option. He pointed to Merrill and Aimee. "You two, unarmed, will stay in the tunnel." He looked at Whitney and held her attention. His steady gaze put her at ease, and he held his AK-47 at the ready. "I will aim for the metal rings on their foreheads. If I am able to knock them off, you aim here." Lei tapped his forehead.

Whitney doubted the plan would work, but it was the best they had. "I'll fire a few exploding rounds to confuse them."

Lei nodded his approval. "Strike fast and without mercy."

Whitney and Lei stood and turned toward the exit. Whitney was grabbed from behind and spun around. Her parents were there, staring at her through tear-filled eyes. "Be careful," her father said.

She hugged them both. "I love you guys."

"And we you," Aimee replied. "Godspeed."

Whitney followed Lei to the very edge of the tunnel's shadow. They saw the towering giants beyond. One was covered in intricate tattoos. The other had an array of piercing—eyebrows, lips, cheeks, and ears. Nothing on his face had been missed. On his head, above his metal circlet, was a crylo skull, worn like a helmet. Both carried long swords in sheaths and were clad in armor like a combination of Roman soldier and Norse Viking. Neither carried shields; they had no need for them.

Whitney aimed to lay a spread of exploding rounds at their feet in hopes that plumes of dust would block the guards' vision. And if a few rounds exploded in their feet, so much the better. Whitney fingered the trigger.

A series of distant explosions shook the ground and caught everyone off guard. The guards exchanged a few words in a language Whitney could not comprehend. Then the pierced one with the crylo helmet left, heading toward the source of the distant concussions.

Lei and Whitney exchanged a glance. Now was the time to strike.

Whitney fired three quick shots. The first two struck the stone floor and burst, sending up clouds of dust. The third struck the tattooed giant's foot and exploded. The giant howled in pain and pleasure. Whitney feared their attack would bring in more guards, but the din of explosions in the distance, far greater than their own feeble attack, would garner more interest from Nephilim forces. She hoped.

As Whitney switched from explosive to conventional rounds, Lei opened up with his AK-47, each bullet aimed for the giant's head. More howling erupted from the giant as a stream of bullets, like killer bees, rained down on his face, shredding the flesh. But as each bullet entered and was enveloped, new flesh grew to fill the hole.

Two shots pinged off the metal band protecting the giant's forehead, but if it moved it was an infinitesimal amount. Lei continued his barrage, moving in closer. Whitney took aim and waited for the right moment.

The Nephilim opened his wings and leapt into the air, sending up a sudden wind. Lei screamed and fell back. He apparently had not seen the Nephilim in their true form, that of demons. As Lei staggered back, he tripped and fell, dropping his AK-47.

The Nephilim descended like a hawk. The ground shook as it landed before Lei and snatched up the small man. "Shoot him!" Lei shouted, but Whitney didn't trust her aim, not with the recoil created by the XM-29. She dropped the modern weapon and drew her 9mm. She quickly took aim and fired several rounds.

The first missed completely, but the next six pegged the metal circlet dead-on, at an extreme angle. As Lei began to scream, Whitney took careful aim and pulled the trigger again. The shot rang true. Sparks flew from the metal ring, which was knocked clean off the Nephilim's forehead.

As the circlet hit the stone floor with a clang and warbled around in circles, the Nephilim showed true surprise. He looked at the ring, then at Whitney, who had taken aim again. She fired.

But the Nephilim was fast. He guarded his head with his hand and took the bullet in his thick palm, which healed over quickly. The giant dropped Lei and charged Whitney blindly. He barreled toward her, howling and gnashing his double rows of teeth.

Whitney fired three shots before the 9mm ran empty. A moment later, a massive arm smashed into her like a battering ram. The air in her lungs escaped as she was sent soaring into a stone wall. It was only the wide distribution of force delivered from the Nephilim's broad arm that kept her ribs from shattering. She sat up, gasping for air. As desperation set in, she froze like a cornered mouse. There was nowhere to run. She picked up her XM-29 and tried to take aim, but her head spun and the beast already loomed above her. Two more steps and he'd be on top of her.

Eyes clenched shut, Whitney braced for what would be a painful but quick death. Then a single shot rang out, followed by a ghastly howl that caused a chill to run through every sinew of Whitney's body. She looked up.

The giant staggered, as a fist-sized hole oozed blood from the center of his forehead, which ran down his body and mingled with the lines of his tattoos. Whitney could see that the injury had come from behind. She looked at Lei. He was on the ground, unconscious. Merrill and Aimee were emerging from the tunnel, but they were unarmed. Then she heard a bark and a voice yell, "Move your ass, Whitney! He's coming down."

Wright!

The shadow of the giant fell over Whitney just before his body fell forward. She dove to the side as he crashed down. The ground shook. Wright, Ferrell, and Vesuvius entered the fortress through the rear gate. Ferrell glanced at the back of the man's head, where her single shot had taken him down.

"How did you know where to shoot him?" Whitney asked.

"Saw what you were doing. How you removed the headpiece. Nice shot, by the way. Figured you wouldn't have done that without a reason and thought a shot coming out of the forehead would be as good as one going in."

Whitney smiled. The woman's adeptness at killing had become a blessing.

"Would have taken him down sooner, but this"—Ferrell motioned to the XM-29 in her hands—"doesn't have the best long-range sight."

The group merged around Lei's body. Wright felt for the man's pulse. "Still alive," Wright said. Whitney, now weaponless, said, "I'll take him." She bent down and hoisted the small man over her shoulder. Though he was a head shorter and perhaps fifteen pounds lighter than Whitney, his weight made her muscles protest. But Wright and Ferrell needed their weapons, and she'd be damned before leaving him behind.

The group exited through the rear gate and hurried around the outer wall toward the river. As explosions continued to shake in the distance, they moved with more ease. No one would be looking for them while all hell was breaking loose.

"Do you think," Merrill asked, "that the military found out about this place?"

Wright shook his head. "The explosions aren't mortars or missiles. This is something else."

"Sounds like timed charges." Ferrell said.

The group listened. Every fifteen seconds a new explosion filled the air. Wright laughed. "I'll be damned. Cruz is still alive!"

The group picked up the pace and cut through the forest. They found the river flooded with shards of wood and chunks of what must have been larger boats.

"Definitely Cruz," Wright said.

The river flowed swiftly, and a way across was nowhere in sight. But a voice gave them hope. "Hey, *gringos*, need a lift?"

Cruz floated downriver in a twenty-five-foot boat that would have been a dinghy to the Nephilim, but was near yacht-size for people. It had no mast but appeared solidly built and could be steered by rudder, as Cruz did, bringing the boat in toward a sandy portion of shore.

Thick ropes were thrown overboard. Al-Aziz's head popped up over the edge. "Quickly, friends. Time is short!"

Lei was tied on and hauled up first while Aimee and Merrill climbed the other rope. Wright turned to Whitney. "You next."

Whitney started climbing. Al-Aziz tossed down the rope that had hoisted Lei back over the side. Ferrell and Wright tied the rope to Vesuvius, who was hauled up by Aimee and Merrill. His tail continued wagging, even with the uncomfortable rope around his waist.

Whitney reached the top then turned to assist Wright and Ferrell, but she caught something in her peripheral vision. Something above her. She looked up.

High in the sky was a large bird-like creature, which Whitney almost took to be a pterodactyl, wings outstretched. It blocked out the sun then came around, straight for them. "Incoming!" Whitney shouted, pointing.

She heard Ferrell shout," Aim for the wings!" then a barrage of bullets and tracers rocketed skyward. The descending wraith spun and wove, dodging some bullets and taking others dead-on. But Wright's and Ferrell's aim was too accurate and the bullets came too fast. The beast's wings were shredded faster than they could heal, and it plummeted toward the earth. It landed in the river, sending up a geyser of water and casting out waves that shook the boat from its position.

They were floating away, leaving Wright and Ferrell behind. Cruz took the rudder and began steering back toward shore. Wright waved them on. "We'll catch up downstream! Go!" Cruz nodded and aimed the boat for the center of the river where the current was strongest. They were off.

As they floated away, Whitney saw the Nephilim that had fallen from the sky emerge from the water like the mighty kraken, rising from its ocean lair. It howled and leapt from the water, landing on the shore near Wright and Ferrell, who had already begun their attack. Whitney recognized the attacker: Enki.

Enki pounded toward Wright and Ferrell as the boat rounded a bend in the river. Whitney saw sparks flying from Enki's circlet. They were aiming at the right place. But soon the battle was blocked by a stand of trees. Gunfire and shouts echoed from upstream then stopped. The group waited in silence for some sign of what had happened.

Then it came. Enki rose up into the sky and flew toward the fortress. In his hands he held two bodies.

"Damn it!" Cruz shouted, the expression on his face pained.

Whitney was surprised to see Cruz express any kind of loss for Wright and Ferrell. But as the reality that they were gone set in, Whitney missed them both. The Boy Scout and the assassin. They had become her friends. Cruz's, too.

"Time to go," al-Aziz said.

"How?" Merrill asked. "We can only go as fast as the river flows."

"Then we'll speed up the river," Cruz said, revealing a detonator in his hand. "Better hold on to something."

A shriek cut through the air. It was Lei. He was looking up and pointing. Enki was back already and he had two friends. They floated through the air like bombers approaching a target.

Merrill herded the group to the center of the boat and clutched his arms around them. "Do it!"

Cruz thumbed the detonator and pushed the button. In the distance a massive explosion shook, followed by a roar that sounded as though the earth itself were shouting.

The water was coming.

 CHAPTER 70

As the roaring water grew closer, Merrill saw Enki balk. He either believed that the water would take care of them, which from the sound of it was entirely possible, or he had a healthy fear of deluges. Given his past history with God's flood, Merrill wouldn't be surprised if it was true. How fitting that humans were once again being saved from the Nephilim via a flood.

But Enki and the two other Nephilim suddenly dove straight toward them. The boat was a sitting duck and the rushing waters were still too far away to save them. Three shadows swept over the boat and a rushing wind blew past as the three winged giants flew just above them. Merrill looked downstream. They were waiting for them in the river ahead.

"Anyone happen to have a gun?" Cruz asked. No one did. Wright and Ferrell had fallen. Lei and Mirabelle's weapons had been left behind. Apparently Cruz had lost his as well.

"I have these," Lei said, motioning to the grenades still dangling from his vest.

Cruz smiled. "Good enough." Cruz moved to pluck the grenades from Lei's chest and lob them at the Nephilim in a final act of defiance.

"Wait," Merrill said. "Listen."

Sounds like wood being scratched rang out from the surrounding forest. "Get down and don't say a word." Merrill said.

Mirabelle, Merrill, Aimee, Lei, Cruz, and al-Aziz congregated at the bow of the boat and lay down behind its two-foot rise. Merrill peeked over the top. The three Nephilim stood in the river, waiting coolly for their prey to be delivered to them.

The roar of the river grew louder as water rushed in from behind the boat. Perhaps they simply waited to make sure that no one jumped ship before the deluge swept them to oblivion.

Merrill prayed that the rushing waters would drown out the cacophony of rabid turkey calls now emanating from the forest. He looked over the bow of the boat, watching the Nephilim. They seemed none the wiser.

Enki stood at the river's center, his wings slowly flapping as though he were prepared to take to the sky at a moment's notice. Merrill then noticed his head. The giant's circlet was no longer there. Wright and Ferrell must have managed to remove it before being killed.

Merrill recognized the other two Nephilim as well. Thor, brandishing his mighty hammer, Mjölnir, stood to the left, ready to bash the boat to splinters. To Enki's right stood Anubis. He wielded a scythe like a true lord of the underworld. The three represented so much ancient power on earth, it was inconceivable to fight them and win.

Merrill smiled as the brush around the edge of the river began to shake. It would take an equally ancient predator to accomplish that.

Shrieks filled the air that drowned out even the raging waters, which rounded the river bend and crashed toward them. A group of twenty-two crylos sprang from the shore on both sides of the river. They bounded out toward the Nephilim, claws extended.

The three Nephilim were startled by the attack but quickly regrouped as their wounds healed. Thor swung his hammer out in wide circles. Merrill was shocked to see the hammer actually throw sparks as it connected with one of the crylos, which shook from shock and fell smoldering to the ground. Anubis brought his scythe around with a whoosh, decapitating two crylos at once. Enki howled and drew his sword, plunging it into the nearest dinosaur.

The trees split open and the same large thirty-foot crylo pounded out into the river. With a flash of teeth, the monster crylo had Anubis's head in its jaws. A sickening crack and howl filled the air before Anubis's headless torso fell back into the water.

The sight of one of their own lying dead made the other two Nephilim pause for a moment, giving three crylos time to leap onto Thor's chest and push him back into the water. The boat was almost upon the battle scene now, and Merrill doubted that, between the frenzied crylos and the enraged Nephilim, they would make it through.

But as Enki saw the deadly torrent of water approaching behind the boat, his eyes opened wide and he sprang up into the air. The next moment Merrill felt the boat lurch up and bound forward. He looked back. A wall of water, fifty feet high, had picked them up and carried them forward. They careened over the drowned crylos and Thor. The boat held up to the punishment and cruised onward, surfing on the torrent's crest.

Merrill lost sight of Enki, who had flown high into the sky, but at the speed they traveled, he hoped the fight and their time with the Nephilim was over.

No one spoke as the boat careened down the river. Everyone simply held on for dear life, clutching onto each other. Merrill managed to look into the eyes of his wife and daughter. They had escaped together. They were a family again.

 CHAPTER 71

No one was sure how much time had passed, only that an amazing amount of distance had been covered. When Whitney saw the familiar blue inflatable boat resting on the shore of the large lake, she knew they had made good time. The water's flow slowed as they spilled out into the lake. The boat eased to a crawl but continued on its path across the lake, drawn to where the river re-formed and ran out to sea.

Whitney stood and stretched. Vesuvius was at her side, asking for attention. She petted him briefly before he moved on to the next person.

Glancing around the boat, Whitney took in the motley group. The missing members of their team, Wright, Ferrell, and Jacobson, had been replaced by al-Aziz, Lei, and her mother. They were leaving with the same number of souls with which they'd first landed on Antarktos, but the others would be sorely missed.

Whitney looked out over the cold, blue waters and remembered their kindness, and their sacrifice. It seemed fitting that Ferrell and Wright faced their end together. She sensed they wouldn't have had it any other way. And Jacobson, her guardian angel, had been the first to fall to the Nephilim. She missed him the most.

Whitney watched her parents stand arm in arm at the edge of the boat. She'd lost several friends, but she'd gained so much. She had never entertained the idea of seeing her mother again. But here she was. Whitney smiled at her parent's appearance. Outwardly they were remarkably different, but inwardly they were united.

Whitney ran her fingers through her nappy, blond hair and looked at her light-brown skin. She was the obvious product of her parents, with a look as unique as their love. After all they had been through, they had survived, only to find each other again. In hindsight, Whitney could see a design, a road map for their lives that had brought them all to this point. For a moment she entertained the idea that her father's belief in God might not be totally misplaced. But a moment was all she had.

"We got company," Cruz said.

Whitney followed his gaze to the last place she wanted to look: the sky.

Descending from above was the huge figure of Enki. He was alone and he still had no circlet on his head. As he dove toward them, Whitney saw that he had no weapon in his hand. She wondered if he was going to use his body as a bomb and simply shatter the boat beneath it. When he folded his wings to his back and began free-falling toward them, she was sure of it.

Enki fell like a missile. He was a thousand feet up, then a hundred. Everyone screamed and ducked, covering their heads and cowering. As Enki's shadow blocked out the sun, there was a sudden rush of wind and a loud snap as Enki opened his wings. He flew down only feet from their heads. He skirted the water's surface then pounded back into the air.

The group was stunned to be alive.

"He toys with us," al-Aziz said.

Whitney was the first to see the purple haze filtering down to them, sprayed as though from a crop duster. Lei coughed and passed out. Only Whitney and Merrill, who had firsthand knowledge of the purple dust, held their breath then breathed through their shirts. Even with the protection, Whitney felt the dust taking effect. She'd be unconscious within a minute, and Enki would have his way with them.

Whitney looked around for some option, anything that would help. All she saw were the unconscious bodies of her friends. Only her father still moved. They both reached for Lei's grenades at the same time. Merrill met her eyes.

"You can't," he said, taking her hand.

Whitney glanced up. Enki was coming back around. "I won't let mom lose you," Whitney said. "Not after you've just found her."

"I'm your father, Mira. It's my job."

Whitney pointed to Aimee's unconscious form. "She needs you more than I do, Dad. Don't you see the gift you've been given? After all this time!"

Merrill looked at Aimee for a moment then his resolve solidified. "No, you can't. You're not ready."

Whitney understood. She knew he was worried about her eternal soul. She smiled behind her sleeve. "If God exists. If He's as merciful as you think. Maybe there is hope for me yet."

Merrill's eyes went wide and quickly grew wet.

Whitney kissed her father's forehead. "Let me go."

"No." Merrill's fingers stayed tight and Whitney had to pry her hand free.

Tears slipped from his eyes and slid down his cheeks. It was the last time he'd see his daughter. They both knew it. He seemed weakened by the thought, but Whitney realized the purple dust was beginning to take hold of him.

All the better, Whitney thought. She didn't want him to see how it would end.

Whitney took two grenades and ran to the stern. Enki was over the water again, headed straight for the boat. Whitney pulled one of the pins and lobbed the grenade toward Enki. It splashed into the water ten feet short and exploded. A plume of water shot skyward but was shattered by Enki's body as he continued his forward motion.

With her sleeve away from her face, Whitney began to feel the effects of the purple powder. Her limbs grew heavy and her mind swam with random thoughts. She urged herself to stay focused but was snatched up, held between two massive hands, wind rushing by her ears, pulling at her hair. She became aware enough to remember what she planned to do.

"Did you really think you would escape us, daughter of Noah? Or that your feeble weapons would have any effect on me?"

"Who said I was trying to hit you?"

Enki snarled at her. He seemed confused and enraged.

"God gave me a message for you," Whitney said.

Enki flapped his mighty wings to stop his forward momentum and beat at the air, fifty feet from the water's surface and nearly a mile from the boat. He looked down at her. "And what might that be?"

Whitney tapped Enki's breastplate. "I put it in here."

Enki looked as though he might laugh until it was clear he felt the odd, hard shape against his skin, just beneath his chin, wedged between his chest and iron breastplate. "What did you do?"

Whitney smiled as consciousness began to fade. "Should've worn your helmet."

Enki let go of Whitney with one hand and raised it to his head. It was the first time she'd seen a completely horrified look on a Nephilim face. The soulless beast was about to disappear forever.

Whitney free-fell as Enki attempted to rip his breastplate from his body. It didn't budge. Whitney felt her body grow cold, partly from the drug, partly from the wind whipping by her body. Her stomach lurched as she fell, and the wave of heat and pressure mixed with a resounding boom to send her plummeting even faster.

She hit a wall and felt a frigid blanket wrap around her body. Her barely-conscious mind put the pieces together as her world turned black. She had fallen into the lake and was sinking to the bottom. She had no sensation of needing air. She couldn't feel her lungs burning or the water pressure pushing on her ears. She faded peacefully into the abyss. Her last thought was of how soft the bottom felt when she finally reached it.

Merrill saw the whole event through hazy eyes. He'd watched as Whitney was snatched up and carried away. He wondered what was happening when Enki stopped in mid-flight. Perhaps he was eating her alive? Then he saw her body fall and seconds later, Enki explode into bits. The charred husk of his headless body fell from the sky like the Nephilim's fathers had fallen from Heaven. He was swallowed up by the water and consumed by the deep. Merrill clawed his way to the edge of the boat, searching the water for some sign of his little girl. But she never surfaced.

Whitney was dead.

Merrill hadn't the strength to sob. He fell back and descended into unconsciousness with the others while the boat floated, secure in the water's current, toward the second river that would eventually deposit them in the ocean.

# CHAPTER 72

The journey downriver lasted two weeks.

The group survived on what was left of Cruz's military rations, which wasn't much. But thirst was easily quenched, as the river ran cleaner than most public waterworks in America. Since leaving the lake, not a crylo nor a shadow in the sky had been seen. It seemed they were clear.

Though the group had survived, they were far from cheerful. Lei had lost his father and two hundred men. Al-Aziz had lost his religion and his direction in life. Cruz had lost his teammates and friends. But Merrill and Aimee suffered the worst—Mirabelle was gone.

Merrill had wept for days, refusing water and sleeping often. Aimee had only just regained a daughter and was perhaps hardened by her time with the Nephilim. She experienced a deep sorrow, but her determination to continue on was undeterred. For that, Merrill was thankful. The woman tended to him gently as he experienced a separation that was akin to losing a limb, or all his limbs. While hiding on Antarctica, he'd always known in the back of his mind that he would see Whitney again, that their separation was temporary. But now she was dead.

One night, under the stars, Merrill had expressed these feelings to Aimee, though in the silence of the dark hours, everyone on board could hear what he said.

Aimee had no response.

No one did.

But as Merrill sat on the wooden floor of the boat with Vesuvius in his lap, he stared up at the twinkling array of stars and remembered some of

Whitney's last words to him: "Maybe there is hope for me yet." Merrill sniffed and began crying again, his shoulders bouncing with each lamentation. In the dark, he felt the comforting hands of his new friends and allies on his back and shoulders, lending their support. Such an odd group with such diverse beliefs had been brought together, united, in the face of mankind's greatest enemy. Perhaps there was hope yet.

As Merrill's tears faded and the group fell one by one to sleep, the gentle river brought them through the last miles of the journey to the sea. No one awoke as the boat was swirled back and forth in the briny waters where the river met the ocean. Not a soul stirred as the sturdy craft carried them through the choppy waves of the open ocean.

Not until a loud thud and jarring stop shook the boat did one of them wake. Merrill stood, confused, and scanned the area. Everything was dark, but he noticed a large portion of the sky was blocked out. It was as though the stars had ceased to exist over a quarter of the sky.

The others stirred from their slumber and took in the blackness.

"The stars are gone," Lei said.

Merrill felt Aimee's hands grasping his. "What is it, Merrill?"

At first Merrill feared that the Nephilim had returned to finish the job, but the shape was too large, too solid. Then he felt the waves beneath the boat and heard the rubbing of wood on metal. His suspicions were confirmed when Cruz clicked on his flashlight.

Before them was a cold gray slab of metal rising out of the water. Cruz slowly aimed the flashlight higher until it illuminated the finest words Merrill had read in months: USS *Preble*.

Cruz began laughing. "It's an AEGIS destroyer. Thank God for the Navy." Cruz opened his near-empty backpack and pulled out a flare gun, which he'd apparently been saving for this moment. He aimed it high and pulled the trigger.

Old fears came back quickly and Merrill imagined the Nephilim descending from above, preying on the unprepared and terrified crew. There would be no telling when their final attack would come, if it hadn't already.

Merrill's fears were put at ease when several floodlights burnt through the night sky and descended on them.

"Ahoy down there," a sailor shouted from high above. But his friendly voice masked his deadly intent. Merrill heard an array of weapons being pointed at them. "Name and rank."

"First Lieutenant Victor Cruz of the United States Marine Corps."

"And the others?"

"Two civies, Dr. Merrill Clark, and Dr. Aimee Clark." Cruz turned to al-Aziz and Lei. "You two can introduce yourselves."

Lei stepped forward. "Captain Zhou Lei of the People's Liberation Army of China. Your team rescued me."

Al-Aziz spoke while shading his eyes from the bright spotlights. "And I am Ahmed al-Aziz, previously of the Arab Alliance Army. But I would ask for asylum in America. I too was saved by your team."

"With all due respect," Cruz said, "we just put our asses on the line for the United States, and we haven't eaten in days. Haul us in before I climb up your anchor line."

A laugh descended from above. "We'll get right on it, Lieutenant. By the way, congratulations. Your team was the only one to activate a beacon and not one of the other teams has been heard from. Nicely done."

Merrill couldn't help but smile. Through all the chaos and confusion, Wright and Ferrell had completed their mission. It was a testament to their dedication and sacrifice. Merrill hoped the armies of the world would learn from their bravery and sacrifice. As the forces of Antarktos grew stronger, the world would have to sacrifice more than lives; they'd have to put aside grudges as ancient as the Nephilim.

If they didn't . . . Merrill pushed the thought from his mind. They would. He'd seen men and women, including his daughter, fight and die together, regardless of their beliefs. The world would fight the Nephilim.

 CHAPTER 73

Life aboard the USS *Preble* was a dramatic change from that of roughing it on Antarktos. Meals came promptly three times a day. Activities, even for the U.S. team who were viewed as heroes, were strictly regulated. The rooms were clean. The beds were made perfectly every morning. The group managed to have breakfast together and made time at night to share stories, play cards, and forge what would be lifelong friendships. Merrill was happy to see Lei and al-Aziz being treated well. Cruz made sure of it. The men had proven their worth in battle and Cruz had adopted them as his new teammates.

The five survivors of the U.S. team had been interviewed individually three times, twice on the first day and once on the second. Each time the same questions were asked in varying orders and worded differently. Merrill could only imagine the level of disbelief among their interviewers. He feared it would go on forever.

A knock sounded on the door of his and Aimee's temporary quarters, and Merrill knew he was in for a fourth round. Vesuvius jumped off his bunk and hopped up on Aimee's, where he snuggled with his new master. They'd become fast friends. Merrill kissed Aimee on the cheek. "Be back soon."

Aimee smiled. "I love you."

"Love you too."

Vesuvius licked Merrill's hand. He petted the dog. "You too."

Ten minutes later, Merrill was sitting in a stark, odorless room, seated on a folding chair across from Dr. Cole Gorski, the same man who had interviewed him two out of the previous three times. Merrill knew the man had not only been scrutinizing the story but was evaluating their psychology, making sure they hadn't all gone mad.

From the look on Cole's face, Merrill could tell the man was frustrated. The story each had told, in perfect harmony, involved giants with wings, half-demons from the Bible, not to mention resurrected dinosaurs, crop circles, and a global conspiracy mixed with a possible onslaught of Nephilim determined to undermine God's plans. By all rights, they should be insane; but Merrill knew the doctor had found them all to be completely, disturbingly sane.

And it scared him. Merrill could see it in the man's eyes as he sat down, keeping a metal table between them. "So, Dr. Clark—"

"Found anything wrong with me yet?" Merrill couldn't help rubbing it in. The man was getting on his nerves.

Cole scratched his head. "Not a thing. In fact, you are perfectly healthy, but that isn't the reason for this meeting."

Merrill furrowed his brow. "Then what is?"

"You see, I, well, after interviewing you and the other . . . survivors, I have become convinced that your story, while unquestionably outrageous, is nonetheless true."

Merrill's furrowed brows reversed direction and rose high on his forehead. "Oh."

"Yes, in fact, I was wondering . . . I went to church as a child. What I'm wondering is, if these Nephilim characters are real, from what you know of them in the Bible, can we win? Do we stand a chance?"

Merrill repeated Whitney's final words. "There is always hope."

"Yes. Yes, I suppose there is." Cole stood, even though he seemed as though he could ask questions all day. "We've been ordered back to Texas," Cole said. "The president and the joint chiefs want a direct debrief from you."

"About what?"

"What to expect when we take Antarktos. The Nephilim fortifications. Their weapons. How to kill them. Things like that."

Merrill was dumbstruck. "They're going to . . . invade Antarktos?"

Cole nodded. "What did you expect?"

"I don't know, I just don't see how . . . It's not . . . ."

"As you know, our radar doesn't work in close proximity to Antarctica."

"Antarktos," Merrill corrected.

"Right. And satellites are failing when they cross over the continent. The president believes a pre-emptive strike would be most effective."

Merrill nodded. The president was probably right. But before Merrill could expound on the matter, an alarm sounded throughout the ship. For a brief, fearful moment Merrill thought the Nephilim were attacking. It was a fear that emerged every time something unusual occurred. He was beginning to think he'd never shake the knee-jerk reaction. But voices outside the metal door revealed the true nature of the alarm. "Man overboard!"

Merrill rushed out with Cole close behind. They were on the deck, bracing themselves against a strong wind that had been buffeting the destroyer for the past day. Merrill's Navy-issue windbreaker flapped loudly in the wind as he approached the railing, where sailors were working to retrieve the poor soul who'd fallen overboard.

With his view of the action obscured, he looked over the railing instead. Far below, bobbing in the water, was a light-blue inflatable boat that seemed somehow familiar. His eyes grew wide and his voice cracked as he screamed, "*Mira!*"

Shoving sailors aside like they were twigs, Merrill forced his way past the men at the railing. "Mira! I'm coming!"

The rescue team saw him coming and quickly stepped aside. There on the deck of the destroyer lay Whitney, her body limp and bruised. But her eyes, her glorious brown eyes, stared up at him, full of life. "Dad . . ."

Merrill collapsed over Whitney's body and held her tight. He kissed her several times then looked at a paramedic. "How is she?"

"We need to get her on an IV and get her eating again," the paramedic said. "But other than a few cuts and bruises, I can't find anything wrong with her. She should be back on her feet in a week."

"Mira, how is this possible? I saw you disappear beneath the water."

"I had some help."

Merrill was confused.

"Some old friends," Whitney said, glancing toward the side of the ship.

One of the sailors picked up on her cue. "Sir, I think she's talking about them," he said, pointing to the water at the ship's bow.

Merrill stood on shaky legs and looked over the edge. There in the water, rising and falling with the waves, were twenty-odd Weddell seals, their long bodies swirling in the water.

Cole stood next to Merrill and said, "I suppose if God can use a whale, He can use a seal."

Merrill laughed, but through his joy, he was struck by one thing. The Bible had been accurate. Its history had proven true, but so had the prophecy in Revelation, the one he now knew referred to the Nephilim. He quoted the portion that came to mind. "'During those days men will seek death, but will not find it; they will long to die, but death will elude them.'"

Merrill turned to meet Cole's eyes. "Tell the president to call our forces back. Defend the homeland."

Cole looked confused. "But what about Antarctica—er, Antarktos?"

"Tell him Antarktos has already been claimed . . . twelve thousand years ago. This is no place for man to tread. Not yet."

Turning back to Whitney, Merrill felt his apprehension about the future dissolve. His family was whole again. It was more than he could have asked for, and it was accomplished by a grand design laid out eons ago, beyond the comprehension of mankind.

As a warning klaxon sounded and sailors began running, Merrill did what he always did: he looked to the sky. This time he saw his fears realized. High in the sky, winged shapes were flying in formation away from Antarktos's shores, headed for the world. But the fear had dulled, for the God who had been at work so adeptly in his life was still at work in the world, and ultimately, it was his will that would be done.

Not the will of man.

Nor the will of the angels, demons, or their half-breed children.

But God's.

"Your will be done," Merrill said. He looked into Whitney's eyes again and scooped her up, carrying her inside the destroyer, where he hoped they would be safe.

Your will be done.

ABOUT THE AUTHOR

Photograph by Aaron Brodeur

JEREMY ROBINSON is the author of ten thrillers including Pulse, Instinct, and Threshold the first three books in his exciting Jack Sigler series. His novels have been translated into nine languages. He is the director of New Hampshire AuthorFest, a non-profit organization promoting literacy in New Hampshire, where he lives with his wife and three children.

Connect with Robinson online: www.jeremyrobinsononline.com

Don't miss this exclusive look at THE LAST HUNTER – DE-SCENT, a five book series that begins 20 years before Antarktos Rising, and ends with the conclusions to both stories!

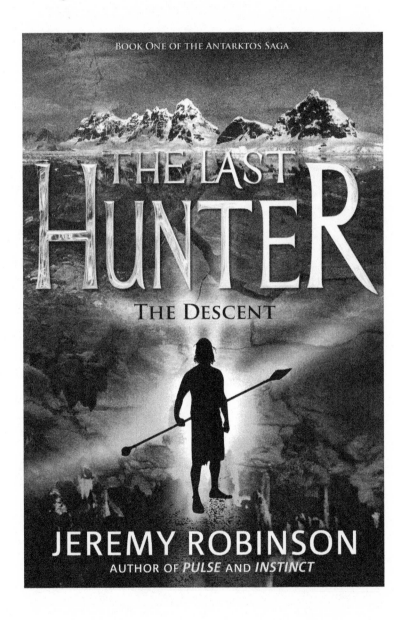

BOOK ONE OF THE ANTARKTOS SAGA

THE LAST HUNTER

THE DESCENT

JEREMY ROBINSON

AUTHOR OF *PULSE* AND *INSTINCT*

PROLOGUE
1911

Douglas Mawson tasted blood. The chapped skin of his lower lip peeled up like flakes of shaved coconut. The cold had started the injury, and then it worsened thanks to his habit of chewing the skin from his lip. But he was careful about it, nibbling at the still dying flesh like a preening bird. It was the sneeze that split the lip, tearing it down the middle. The sting cleared his mind, but the blood made him hungry. He looked around, hoping to see something that might take his mind off food, but he saw only white ice and blue sky.

Three hundred fifteen miles separated Mawson and his two men from camp; three thousand more from civilization. No man had ever ventured further from home, and only one of them would make it back.

Mawson, commander of the expedition, stood before a white glacial expanse. His angular face, typically clean-shaven but now covered by an inch-thick beard, hid behind a dirty tan scarf. The scarf did little to protect him against the Antarctic cold, which grated his lungs. The rest of him, bundled in a thick, beige snowsuit, felt warmer when moving. Not so much when standing still.

Dr. Xavier Mertz had stopped. He was the point man, riding on skis while Mawson followed with a dog sledge team and Lieutenant Ninnis brought up the rear with a second team and the majority of their indispensable supplies. That Mertz had stopped meant he'd seen something. Most likely something dangerous, like a snow-covered crevasse. They looked solid enough until you put weight on them. Then they could fall through like a trap door.

"What's the problem, Mertz?" Mawson shouted.

But the man didn't reply.

Mawson removed his hood in case the man's words were being muffled. He asked again, "What is it, Mertz?"

The only sign that Mertz had not frozen solid on the spot was his head, craning slowly from side to side.

Mawson signaled for Ninnis to remain behind and stepped off his sledge. He petted the nearest dog as he passed, then headed for Mertz. His feet crunched over the snow and ice, signaling his approach. Still, the man did not move.

Five feet away, Mertz finally responded, his hand snapping up with an open palm. The sudden movement sent Mawson's heart pounding. But the message was clear: *Don't. Move.* And he didn't. Not for three minutes. Then he spoke again. "Bloody hell, Mertz, what is it?"

Mertz turned his head slightly. "Saw someone."

"Saw something?"

"Some-*one*."

Ridiculous, Mawson thought. They were the first human beings to set foot in this part of the world. So sure was he of that fact that he spoke his mind aloud. "Ridiculous."

He stepped up to Mertz's side. "The land is frozen. Not only is there no way a man could live here, there's nowhere to hide."

Mertz turned to Mawson. "He wasn't wearing clothes."

Mawson frowned. Mertz had a reputation for being a humorous fellow. "My lip is split. My knees are sore. My stomach is rumbling. I'm not in the mood for jokes, so let's go. I want to be off this glacier before dark."

"His hair was red. As red as the blood staining your beard. But his body was pale." Mertz returned his eyes to the snow. "Wouldn't have seen him if not for the hair."

Mawson's patience wore thin. "Mertz," he growled more than said.

The man turned to him and Mawson saw wide-eyed fear. "I'm *not* joking."

With his eyes shut, Mawson took a deep breath. The energy he'd exert losing his temper would drain him later on. He'd need that strength to survive. Calming his voice, he said, "Mertz, look around. What do you see?"

He glanced at Mertz, who was indeed looking. "White. From horizon to horizon. White! There is no one there. Not now. Not before. And if we stand here one more minute, we will—"

A sound like a howl rolled across the frozen plain. Mawson's voice caught in his throat. It sounded...human. But it wasn't. "The wind," he said quickly, noticing the deepening wrinkles on Mertz's sunburned forehead.

Why hadn't the man covered his skin? Mawson thought. Before he could ask, a second, louder howl echoed around them.

Before Mawson could once again dismiss the sound, Mertz spoke. "There's not a breeze to speak of."

Mawson held his breath. Mertz was right.

Mertz looked at him again. *I told you so*, his expression said. But as he turned away, his head spun back around, past Mawson, toward Ninnis. His eyes popped wide. His arm reached out. A high pitched, "No!" shot from his mouth.

Mawson turned around in time to see the last of the sledge dogs pulled toward a hole in the ice. It whimpered, digging its claws into the ice. Then it was gone. Ninnis, six dogs and the sledge had disappeared. The glacier had come to life and swallowed them whole.

The two men ran for the spot where Ninnis had been. They stopped short, sliding on their feet as the ice opened up before them. Ninnis had parked the sledge atop a crevasse. Had they but continued moving, he would have made it across.

Mawson lay on his stomach, dispersing his weight, and slid to the mouth of the gaping hole. One hundred and fifty feet below, on a ledge, lay a lone dog. It twitched between whimpers, its spine broken. Ninnis and the other five dogs were gone, disappeared into the darkness beyond.

"Ninnis!" Mawson shouted. "Ninnis! Lieutenant! Can you hear me? Are you alive, man?"

There was no reply. He suspected there never would be. But they couldn't just leave him. For three hours the two men shouted until their voices grew hoarse. They tied all their ropes together, but the line wasn't even long enough to reach the now dead sledge dog.

Distraught over the loss of their colleague and friend, Mawson and Mertz didn't want to give up hope. But they had no choice. Ninnis had fallen with most of their food, their tents and warm weather gear. To survive the three hundred fifteen mile journey back to base camp, they couldn't spend one more minute mourning the man.

Mawson peeled a frozen tear from his cheek and returned to his sledge. They needed to move.

As they maneuvered the remaining sledge, and dogs, which would later become their food, around the crevasse, neither man heard the muffled cries coming from below. They left without pause, on a journey that would claim the lives of all six dogs and Mertz. Mawson alone would survive the journey and eventually return home to England.

But Ninnis would outlive them both.

Had either man thought to descend the rope they'd fashioned, they would have found their man tucked inside a hollow hidden by an overhang only fifty feet from the surface. After regaining consciousness, he'd tried to call out to them, to reach for the rope, but some unseen force pinned him down. An hour after Mawson and Mertz gave up the search, a hand so white it was nearly translucent, came away from his mouth.

"Welcome home, Ninnis," a voice whispered in his ear, the breath smelling like rotten, jellied eel.

Ninnis filled his lungs and let out a scream, but the sound was cut short as he was taken by his collar and dragged deeper into the ice.

1

I scream.

I'm too terrified to do anything else. My hands are on my head. I'm pitched forward. My eyes are clenched shut. Every muscle in my body has gone tight, as though clutched in rigor.

The monster knocks me back and I spill into a pile of bones and old skin. But I feel no weight on top of me. No gnashing of teeth on my body. The thing has missed its tackle, striking a glancing blow as it passed, but nothing more. Perhaps because I bent down. Perhaps because it can't see well in the dark. I don't know. I don't care.

I'm alive. For now.

And I don't want to die.

But I'm certain I'm going to and the events of the past few months replay in my mind. I can't stop it. I can't control it. And in a flash, I'm back at the beginning.

I've been told that the entire continent of Antarctica groaned at the moment of my birth. The howl tore across glaciers, over mountains and deep into the ice. Everyone says so. Except for my father; all he heard was Mother's sobs. Not of pain, but of joy, so he says. Other than that, the only verifiable fact about the day I was born is that an iceberg the size of Los Angeles broke free from the ice shelf a few miles off the coast. Again, some would have me believe the fracture took place as I entered the world. But all that really matters, according to my parents, is that I, Solomon Ull Vincent, the first child born on Antarctica—the first and only Antarctican—was born on September 2ⁿᵈ, 1974, thirteen years ago, today.

Of course, I don't buy my parents' seeming lack of memory when it comes to my birth. When I broach the topic they start ducking and weaving like spastic boxers. What I'm sure of is that something strange occurred when I was born; something that frightened them enough to bury all record of it. And they've done a good job. I've searched in and behind every drawer in this house. I've scoured the attic and the basement. I've even flipped through every one of the thousands of books they have on shelves around the house in search of a hollowed-out core. I've found nothing. But occasionally, at a Christmas party or get together, someone who heard the story slips up and reveals a tidbit before covering their mouth and offering an, "Oops."

They think they're protecting me, but all they're really doing is making me feel like a freak. More of a freak, I should say. Every

one else I come into contact with thinks I'm weird, too. My parents just feign ignorance.

In celebration of my uncommon birth, my family is celebrating in the most common way imaginable: a quiet dinner at home. In attendance are my parents, Mark and Beth, and my only real friend, Justin McCarthy. We eat in silence, first enjoying the hot orange grease of Maria's Pizza, and then the fudgy, chunky center of a Dairy Queen ice-cream cake, all polished off by tall glasses of Cherry Coke.

Nothing like massive amounts of fat and sugar to make you feel older.

Though the party, if you can call it that, is a subdued affair, I look at the gifts with great anticipation, the way a lion does a zebra before pouncing—hunter's eyes. I don't want toys. Didn't ask for any. Not interested, despite grandfather's continuous donations of G.I. Joes. My parents always know what to get me. Because despite their constant lies about my past, they're like me.

Smart. Uncommonly so.

Nerds. Geeks. Bookworms. I'd heard all the names at school. Being smarter than everyone in my class exacerbated the issue. No senior in high school likes to be upstaged or outsmarted by a thirteen-year-old with a cracking voice. Though I sometimes wonder if their real problem with me was my resistance to 1980's pop-culture; I don't feather my hair, wear friendship bracelets, or watch Music Television. It doesn't matter now. All that went away when my parents decided to home-school me. My nervousness, tension and boredom has been replaced by excitement,

learning and stimulation. Not to mention a name-calling cease fire.

Well, almost. My parents call me Schwartz. The name evolved from my mother's first nickname for me: first and only, which was short for the "first and only baby born on Antarctica." They quickly shortened it to FAO and then, thanks to the FAO Schwartz department store, I became Schwartz. After the movie *Spaceballs* came out a few months ago, my parents stopped using the name in front of Justin because, almost as a Pavlovian response, Justin would say, "I see your Schwartz is as big as mine."

The first gifts I open are books—fiction and non-fiction, popular and obscure—I like them all. Next come three boxes of Robotix kits. I'll put the dinosaur-looking robot on the cover to shame with the creature I'll create. The biggest box comes last. I tear into the bright blue wrapping paper as Justin slurps grease from a leftover pizza slice.

The loud slurp stops short and grease drips on to Justin's plate. "Whoa," he says.

To Justin, this is a "whoa" moment. He likes to blow things up. To me it's a big letdown. My parents see my down-turned lips even as I fight to reverse them.

"You have to build it yourself," mom says.

"The box says it mimics the pattern of a real lava flow," dad adds.

I let out a grunt, wondering if my parents IQs have dropped. Or maybe they've finally given up caring? The gift is nothing more than a cardboard cone, some quick drying clay, a pouch of red-colored baking soda and a small bottle of vinegar. This is the *big present*? They had gone on about how surprised I would be. About how incredible the gift was. This is...simple.

Boring.

Justin punches my shoulder. It hurts. I know he didn't mean it to, but I seem to feel pain more than other people. Justin's dark brown eyes are impossible to see behind the tinted sports glasses he always wears, but I know they're wide with excitement. I focus on that to avoid thinking about the pain in my arm.

"Are there any G.I. Joes we haven't melted?" he asks.

"A few."

"Let's go!" Justin dashes from the dining room and takes the stairs two at a time. "C'mon!" he shouts from the top.

"Go ahead," mom says. "He has to go home in an hour. Mass starts at six in the morning."

Saturday morning mass is something I never understood. It's a sacred time. Not mass, mind you. Saturday mornings. A bowl of Cocoa Pebbles starts the morning. *Starvengers*, *Gaiking*, *Robotech* and more, followed by Creature Double Feature, which promises at least one *Godzilla* movie, fills my day until noon. It is a TV line-up so good that I am sure God skips mass for it too.

"May I be excused?" I ask with a sigh.

Dad chuckles. It's the kind of chuckle that's a substitute for calling someone stupid. I've heard the laugh enough to recognize the sound. "You don't need to ask after we told you to go."

I brush some of my long blond hair, which has garnered more than a few Einstein taunts, out of my face. Mom and Dad wear unreadable smiles. Like they know something I don't. I hate that feeling—I've felt it every day of my life—so I slide off the chair, pick up the large, but light, volcano box and march it upstairs. When I hear mother giggle—just like the kids at school used to—a tear forms in my eye.

I'm such a wimp. No, wimp isn't the word. That's like calling someone a chicken. Means they're afraid to fight—which also describes me—but that isn't what I mean. *Crybaby*. That's the word. One laugh from my mother and I'm all weepy. Of course, the laugh combined with the silly present confirms that they don't take me seriously. And if they don't take me seriously, they'll never notice I'm not a kid anymore—if you ignore the fact that I'm about to bury a bunch of action figures in a miniature volcano—and that means they'll never reveal the mysteries surrounding my birth. I'm not sure why the day I was born interests me so much. You don't hear other kids asking about when they were born. But there is something in me, something raw, which longs to know more.

As I near the top of the stairs I wipe my eyes dry and focus on the soft rug lining the stairs. It feels squishy beneath my socks. I find it comforting. Through the banister rungs I see Justin hunkering over a fishing lure case filled with odd toys. I scuff my feet, sliding sock against rug. I walk like that all the way to the bedroom doorway.

"Put out your hand," I say.

Justin does.

I reach out a single finger and touch it to Justin's palm. A tiny blue arch of electricity zaps between us with a sharp crack. Justin yelps and flinches away, knocking over the box of toys. "Hey!" he shouts and then moves to retaliate with a finger flick.

I put the volcano box between us and raise an eyebrow.

Justin pauses. "Ugh, fine. Oh! I almost forgot." He fishes into his pants pocket and pulls out a clear blue cassette tape. Then he closes the door. "My cousin made this for me. Said my mom wouldn't let me listen to it."

He puts the cassette into the shoebox sized tape-deck and hits play. Loud music, unlike anything I've heard before, fills the room.

I place the volcano box on the floor and let Justin tear into it. I sit down on the bed hearing the music, but not really listening. My eyes turn to the wall, where a five foot by five foot poster of Antarctica is tacked up. I've marked all the active United States bases—McMurdo, Amundsen-Scott, Palmer, Siple, Willard—as well as some of the larger foreign stations. A bright green circle marks one of the few bases that no longer functions: Clark. Snow and ice buried the site within a year of my birth. How does something like that happen? Even on Antarctica. Just another one of the mysteries no one seems to know anything about.

Though I haven't been there since shortly after my birth, I miss the place. I've become an expert on the continent and hope to return when I'm old enough. There are so many interesting aspects of Antarctica I long to explore. The founder of Clark Station, Dr. Merrill Clark, is my personal hero. His search for evidence of a human Antarctican civilization—my geographic ancestors—captivates me. And I want to follow in his footsteps.

But it will be a long time before that can happen. I doubt my parents will let me go until I'm eighteen and they can't stop me. Of course, I do understand some of the reasons I'm not yet able to go. I might be smarter than most adults, but I'm also smart enough to know I have the emotional fortitude of an eight year old. Happens with smart kids, I've read. Understanding how awful the world can be is hard for someone without emotional defenses. I should be more concerned with the outcome of the daily ant battles waged on our sidewalk than the starving children in Ethiopia. I stopped watching the news a year ago. The images tended to fuel my imagination, which was not a good thing.

I'm painfully shy, especially around girls. I'm quick to cry, especially if someone is angry with me. And, though no one knows it, I'm afraid of the dark. Not just afraid, I'm *terrified* of the dark. It's not a fear of what might lurk in the shadows, closets or under the bed. I'm afraid of my own thoughts. When my imagination is freed from the coils of intentional thought, it drifts to places far darker than deepest black. The horrors of school, of starving kids on TV, and of my parents' mortality are passing thoughts by comparison.

I sometimes wonder if the dark thoughts are a true reflection of what lies within. Of my soul.

The words of the music finally sink in. "What's a brick house?" I ask.

Justin shrugs as he places a volcano-shaped cardboard cone onto a sheet of plastic.

"Thirty six, twenty four, thirty six. Are those measurements? Is this a song about construction? Why wouldn't your moth—"

"They're measurements all right," my friend says with a fiendish grin, then holds his hands in front of his chest like he's gripping two baseballs. "For boobs."

My immediate embarrassment is multiplied tenfold when I hear mother clear her throat. I spin toward the door, mortified.

"Forty-five minutes," she says with a grimace. She closes the door behind her as she leaves.

"Thanks a lot," putting as much anger into my whisper as I can manage.

Justin, who is unfazed by these events, tugs open the pre-moistened bag of quick drying clay. "Just for the record, your mom is a brick house."

I rub my socks on the rug.

"Ok, ok!" Justin says. "Just help me put this together. We have forty-five minutes to blow it up."

I sit down next to him and look at the materials. There's enough here to make three mediocre eruptions. All for—I look at the box—thirty bucks. There has to be a way to make sure my parents get their money's worth out of this thing. I smile as the idea comes to me.

* * *

We finish forty minutes later. The quick dry clay is solid and authentic look-ing if you ignore the embedded action figures. *Nice knowing you, Snake Eyes.* But there are a few invisible modifications. First we expanded the internal cyl-inder that holds the red-dyed baking soda. Instead of three small eruptions, we will now have one large one. And to make things really exciting, we sealed the top of the volcano. This eruption will be as genuine as I can make it.

We both hold syringes pilfered from a chemistry set. Each contains six ounces of vinegar. "On the count of three," I say. "One."

"Is this going to explode?" Justin asks.

"Two."

"Should we wear safety goggles?" He grins before touching his sports glasses. "Oh wait."

"Three!"

We plunge the needles into the volcano and inject the vinegar.

The bedroom door opens. "Ok, boys. Time to—"

"Mom, get back!" I shout. But a loud hiss behind me signifies it's too late. I turn around in time to see the entire volcano, which neither I nor Justin had thought to attach to something solid, erupt—from beneath. The entire cone launches off the floor, spraying red-dyed lava as it spins in the air like one of DaVinci's airships. The cone tilts, shoots forward, slams into the poster of Antarctica, and explodes. Red gore splashes against the poster and the wall. It reminds me of the *Greatest American Hero* episode where the voodoo loving villain splatters chicken blood on the walls.

I turn to my mother. Her white blouse is covered in red streaks. There is no humor in her eyes as she looks at Justin and says, "Your mother is on her way," and then leaves.

"What happened to you?" I hear my father ask. He pokes his head in a moment later, eyes wide behind his glasses. "Oh...geez."

"Sorry," I say, eyes on the floor.

When he doesn't reply, I look up.

He's trying to mask a smile, but failing miserably. "You're lucky it's your birthday, Sol."

"How angry do you think she is?"

"Chernobyl, at least."

Chernobyl is bad, but nowhere near as bad as super nova. If dad is right, she'll be over it by morning. I smile back at my father. "It flew."

My father snickers, looking at the red stained wall. He rubs a hand through his curly black hair. "I can see that."

The doorbell rings. "That'd be your mom," Dad says to Justin before leading him from the room. He stops at the top of the stairs and turns back to me. "Clean yourself up and brush your teeth."

"What about the room?" I ask.

"No amount of scrubbing is going to get that dye out of things. We'll worry about it in the morning." He takes one step down and pauses. "Sorry about the poster, Schwartz."

I hear Justin say a quick, "I see your Schwartz is as big as mine," from the foyer before opening the front door for his mother.

I look up at the poster. The circle around my birthplace is smudged, the ink running. "Yeah..."

As my mother changes and my father explains the red dye on Justin's clothes to his mother, I enter the bathroom. Head lowered, I wash my hands and face. With water dripping from both, I reach out and take hold of a hand towel and dry myself. With the towel still over my face, I sigh. I think about my gifts. My birthday. My age. My life in general.

I sigh again. *At least tomorrow is Saturday.*

I pull the towel from my face and look in the mirror. My skin is white, like snow. My eyes are bright blue. My hair is so blond it only contains a hint of yellow. But I've seen all this before and it doesn't hold my attention. That's when I see it. Something taped to the shower door behind me. An envelope. On it, the words, "Happy Birthday", have been written backwards so I can read them in the mirror.

The envelope is in my hand a moment later. I tear into it. My eyes catch sight of what's inside. I stumble back, sitting on the toilet. As I take out the contents of the envelope, my eyes blur over. I can't read the words, but I know what I hold. Plane tickets. An itinerary. A map that looks just like the ruined poster on my wall.

"Happy birthday," the voice of my mother says. I blink my eyes. She's crouching in front of me, dressed in jeans and a gray Phil Collins T-shirt. She's smiling.

I wrap my arms around her in a burst of emotion and say, "Thank you."

My father is standing in the bathroom door. I launch at him, hugging him around the neck, feet dangling above the floor.

When he puts me down, I sniff and wipe my eyes, feeling no embarrassment over the tears. "When are we going?"

"Summer in Antarctica begins in about seven weeks."

The tears well again, as a single thought repeats in my head.

I'm going home.

CPSIA information can be obtained at www.ICGtesting.com
Printed in the USA
BVOW08s2205250216

437896BV00002B/66/P

9 780983 601715